GIRL SOLDIER

T.R. HORNE

Copyright © 2016 by T.R. Horne

Printed in the United States of America
First Printing, 2016
ISBN-13: 978-0-9911063-4-9
ISBN-10: 0–9911063–4-2

Ordering Information:
Quantity sales. Special discounts are available on quantity purchases by corporations, associations, and others. For details, inquire at the website below.

Yoshima Books
www.yoshimabooks.com

YOSHIMA BOOKS

Book Design by Pink Ink Designs
Cover Design by Humberto Glaffo

For Mom and Dad

PROLOGUE

2001

THE DUSTY ORANGE SKY pierced through the sequoia trees, spreading light along the mossy green edges of the grass, highlighting the shiny beetles that scattered away from her footsteps and hid inside hollowed logs. Rain Wilson took in the scent of the greenery, smelled the lake in the distance, the faint metallic scent of blood in the air. Her boots crunched atop the moist earth, littered with rotten leaves and jagged rocks. Too loud, she thought as she tiptoed through the muck, leaving imprints of her ridged soles in the dirt. She stalked slowly, dipping her head below low-hanging branches laced with silvery webs, watching closely the tracks in front of her. At sixteen, she was dexterous and agile. She gripped the rifle in the well of her armpit to kick her leg over a moss-covered log, half protruding from the dirt, petrified. She heard the sound only faintly at first as she stopped moving to home in on the source. The sound was quiet and low, then more irritated as she heard steps echoing through the forest, birds fluttering above at the distraction. Their flapping allowed appropriate cover to quickly dart behind a large oak tree unheard and unseen. Rain crouched down, readied her rifle, stock against her shoulder, cheek pressed tight to its shaft. She spotted the wounded deer trying to squeeze the pain out by thrashing its body against the cool ground. The wound was not fatal. She'd missed his heart, hitting only the fleshy parts as the bullet entered and tore through the other side. She'd tracked it for two miles, trying to end its misery and not scare the other deer into hiding. Now, under the shadow of dusk, she saw the trickle of blood that seeped from the wound and traveled to its underbelly. It would suffer for three days before dying of infection or blood loss. Rain hated missing her shot, but more than that, she hated leaving an animal in pain unnecessarily. Her finger itched on the trigger as she steadied her breathing, forcing the air from her lungs even though she wanted to hold it and wait for the powerful recoil to awaken her senses. The deer, as if sensing its demise and welcoming its fate, shuttered and dipped its head low to the ground, giving a spectacular shot just below the base of the skull. It'd be dead in two seconds. Rain focused on the spot, exhaled calmly, and pinched the trigger as a round exploded from the rifle. The birds frenzied at the sound as the deer dropped to the ground in a heap, blood streaming from a perfect shot. Rain dropped her head and completed the same ritual after each successful hunt.

"I'm sorry," she whispered to the silent forest as a tear fell down her cheek.

ONE

WILSON RANCH, COLORADO, 2003

"RAIN!" HIS HUSKY VOICE rang out through the cabin, startling her awake.

She glanced at the clock—to her dismay it read four thirty. She pressed her pillow to her ears, aching for a few more minutes of sleep. Unfortunately, Tolley felt differently as he hollered her name a second, third, and fourth time until his anger seeped through the pillow, poking at Rain's sleep. She slammed the pillow to the floor, kicked the covers back insolently, and sat on the edge of her bed with a pout.

"Coming, Dad!" She rolled her eyes with a groan.

Work never ended on the ranch, at least not for her. She'd stayed up late last night checking the fences, making sure the cattle hadn't damaged the posts again. Last week she'd discovered an ugly dent in the post that threatened to take down the whole fence along the north side, steel wiring included. She'd repaired it before any cattle escaped but she'd kept an eye on it before bed, just in case.

She pulled on a T-shirt and jeans from yesterday's dirty laundry, pushed her ratty dark hair into a ponytail, and pounded down the steps rubbing the sleep from her eyes.

"Glad you could make it up this morning. I was beginning to think you were dead up there," her father said without turning his large body from the stove.

"Then who's gonna take care of this place?" she mumbled under her breath.

The smell of roasted ham and buttered biscuits wafted through the room as she flung herself onto the wooden chair waiting for Tolley to finish breakfast. Rain spotted a cherry pie settling in the center of the table, oozing with red filling onto its perfectly toasted crust. It was homemade and smelled fresh as she picked at the crust and poked her finger into her mouth for a taste.

"Who made the pie?" She already knew who'd made it but asking seemed like the polite thing to do.

"Rebecca from next door," he said and smirked at her over his shoulder.

Rebecca Billingsley lived next door to the Wilson Ranch. Using the term *next door* was a stretch since it meant that she lived roughly ten miles east across the bridge. Even with the distance, she'd found a way to drop off pies, cookies, meat loaf, and other vittles to Tolley on a daily basis. If he ate everything she brought by the house, he'd be overweight and in need of a diabetic shot, Rain thought to herself.

"What does she think she's doing? Cooking her way into your heart?"

It was no secret that Rebecca had a crush on Tolley even before her much older husband died a year ago. He'd left her his ranch down the dirt road and childless as the day they'd met. Since his death, she'd been overly eager to travel down the path with goodies in tow with a dream of children flittering in her eyes like coal-covered diamonds.

"Be nice, Rain. She's just trying to help out around here any way she can."

Tolley slid the sizzling ham onto the plate straight from the skillet, radiating heat from the pan against Rain's face. She leaned back. Tolley pushed his slice onto the plate across the table.

"Well next time you see her, tell her I need help with the fence," Rain retorted, grabbing a warm biscuit.

Tolley chuckled. "She's a lady, Rain. She's not gonna fix any fences around here."

Before he caught his words, Rain felt the sting of his blind eyes toward her own femininity. She sat with her fork gripped tightly in her hand. Was she not a lady? At eighteen, she wanted to wear dresses and go on dates, maybe bake a pie for a boy *she* liked, but did she ever have time for that? No. She was stuck fixing fences, shucking hay, and driving the tractor while Rebecca was busying herself in tight pencil skirts and pumps, all while completing the laborious task of being a *lady*. Tolley glanced across the table at Rain—who hadn't taken a bite of food—and realized what he'd implied to his only daughter.

"You're a lady, too. Don't go taking it the wrong way," he said coolly before shoving food into his mouth and washing it down with milk.

"Right. Why would I take it the wrong way?" Rain said sarcastically.

"Don't fret."

Tolley was a strong man, built like a workhorse with strong limbs and a barrel chest. He was above average in height, usually dwarfing most people in tight spaces. His dark hair was brushed back against his scalp then flared in curls at his neck with spots of gray dotting his temples. His hands were thick and roughened by a lifetime of repairing heavy machinery and lugging bales of hay onto the back of a rickety pickup truck, but Rain still thought he had too much charm with the ladies in town. His green eyes always made them swoon in the shops as they fanned themselves like he was Brad Pitt or Matthew McConaughey. Her father was *no* Matthew McConaughey, she thought to herself on those occasions.

"Can we go shooting today?" Rain asked, happy to change the subject to her favorite thing to do with her father. He'd taught her to hunt from the time she was old enough to carry a rifle and survive in the woods.

"After the chores are complete, we may have a few hours of daylight left. Then maybe so . . ." Tolley nodded, filleting his biscuit to pack a spoonful of honey inside.

Rain loved skeet shooting with her father. Tolley was the best sharpshooter in Colorado, infamous for one-shot kills while hunting wild game. He'd taught her his tricks over the years, helped her find her comfort behind a weapon that could mean life or death—for those in front of or behind the barrel.

"Well then let's get to it, old man," Rain said, newly motivated to show her father that she could shoot better than him with her eyes closed. He'd won last time by three clean shots but she'd been practicing on rodents ever since, determined to steal his title.

Tolley gobbled the last of his food as Rain picked up the plates and rinsed them in the porcelain farmhouse sink. It was dark outside but the whine of the animals let her know they were awake and ready to graze. Rain pushed through the screen door as it slammed against the hinge behind her. The morning air was thick with the repugnant smell of horse and cow feces. It didn't matter much to her since it was like waking up and smelling home; after a while it was just a normal scent, something to remind her where she was in life. Among the shit and piss but more content than being anywhere else. Rain pulled open the barn door to the horses' stable and began shoveling the dark, prickly mess at the bottom of the stalls out into the wheelbarrow, patting the mares as she moved along.

Once the cattle had been fed, Rain checked the fence post again to find that it was still sturdy from her handy work. She began tightening the wire coils on the post as a precautionary measure when she caught sight of Rebecca Billingsley driving down the dirt path toward the house, a blizzard of dirt clouds fanning behind her vehicle. The sun had started to shine brightly across the ranch and Rain hated that Rebecca Billingsley was en route to distract her father when they already had plans together. She sucked her teeth as Rebecca killed the engine. Rebecca looked ridiculous to Rain in her heels, wobbling against the gravel driveway, struggling to gain her footing as she stepped from her luxury SUV. Rain tossed her ponytail back and forth in amusement. Rebecca always arrived in high heels and struggled with the gravel but she never gave up on the heels. Rain eyed the shiny black SUV. Maybe marrying was a good business to be in, she thought.

Rebecca was winded. When she'd made it the fifteen feet from her truck to where Rain stood, she dabbed at the sweat on her brow. Rain smirked at her flailing arms trying to maintain her balance in floral-print heels and a tight skirt. One hand held tight to a Tupperware dish that was surely destined for her father.

"Afternoon, Rain. Is Tolley here today? I brought him a li'l somethin' to eat." Mrs. Billingsley smiled through fuchsia lipstick, her gap-toothed grin shining white in the sunlight.

"Afternoon, Mrs. Billingsley. Yep, he's around here somewhere. I think he's by the coop if you want to go see him. I bet he'd like it very much to see you alone over there." Rain leaned on the fence post and smiled sweetly through her lie. The chicken coop was clear across the ranch and hadn't been cleaned yet, so the smell was sure to sting her nostrils if she made it through the manure.

"Oh, really?"

Mrs. Billingsley looked off in the distance toward the coop, squinting her green eyes and assessing whether she wanted to walk that far for the man she was trying to impress. "Well alright, then. I guess I'll see you a li'l later. I'm gonna meet your pa down by the coop," she said with a smile, shifting her hips toward the grassy pasture. She tucked her Tupperware dish under her arm like a celebrity poodle and wobbled off toward the coop.

Rain sifted through all the things Mrs. Billingsley probably thought would happen in the chicken coop with Tolley. Maybe a kiss from him would suffice, or she'd try to run her hands over his body, Rain thought with a sickening shutter. Her stomach turned at the idea of her dad with fuchsia lipstick on his face and neck. She glanced at Mrs. Billingsley walking through the fence line and into the grass. Rain almost fell off the post in laughter as Mrs. Billingsley wobbled on the soft grass only to get her heel stuck and trip out of her shoe. She flailed her arms, Tupperware shooting into the air like a cannon, before she landed chest first on the newly fertilized lawn.

"Gosh darn it!" Mrs. Billingsley screamed to no one in particular as she rolled over with embarrassment. She gathered herself from the putrid ground and flicked off dark dots of manure that sprinkled her outfit and clung to the bottom of her fiery red hair. Her face pulled down into a frown as she dug her heel out of the soft earth with a groan.

Rain laughed hard enough that her side ached. She clamped a hand to her mouth behind the fence post praying Mrs. Billingsley hadn't heard her. Before Rain could catch her breath, the screen door slammed closed and Tolley was halfway across the driveway to assist Mrs. Billingsley.

"What the heck are you doing in the grass? Can't you see it's been fertilized?"

"I thought you were in the coop and wanted . . ." Mrs. Billingsley's eyes darted around the front yard, realizing she'd been duped. She stared at the post where Rain had once stood but was now out of view.

"Why would I be in the coop? Ahh, never mind . . . let's get you cleaned up."

Rain raised her head over the post an inch and caught Mrs. Billingsley's angry stare. She hadn't taken her eyes off the post for a second. Rain smirked at the sight of her covered in funky manure, hair disheveled. Mrs. Billingsley, realizing she'd been tricked, scanned the ground in thought before feigning a limp in her right leg.

"Oh Lord, I don't think I can make it, Tolley." She favored her ankle but still juggled her high heel and Tupperware dish.

Tolley grabbed the Tupperware and shoe from her hand and spied Rain behind the post as she tried to duck.

"Rain, get over here. You're just gonna let Rebecca fall and not offer any help? Taught you better than that. Take these . . ." He shoved Rebecca's dirty shoe and Tupperware bowl into Rain's arms then effortlessly picked up Mrs. Billingsley.

"Oh my . . ." Mrs. Billingsley purred in his arms. He walked her to the door, her hands wrapped around his muscular shoulders and head resting with her mouth to his neck. She stared at Rain as she sulked behind them while carrying her Cinderella slipper. Rebecca smiled in triumph as she bobbed in his arms toward the house.

After setting her down in the kitchen and offering her some of Rain's clothes, which wouldn't fit at all and luckily she declined, Tolley fixed her tea.

"You are too kind, Tolley Wilson. And strong, too . . . to just pick me up like that." She paused, almost as if reliving the moment he'd hoisted her into his arms. "I just wanted to bring you some of my famous chicken parmesan." She flipped the Tupperware over in her hand and frowned. "But it's ruined on account of my clumsiness."

Tolley chuckled. "It's alright, Rebecca. The pie last night was more than enough."

She smiled with pride at the half-eaten pie on the table and smoothed her skirt down over her thighs, secretly wishing she'd lost a few more pounds so it wouldn't fit as tight.

"I wanted to ask you something. Since it's such a long trek from my house to yours—and I know you gotta eat and all—I was wondering if maybe going out to dinner sometime might be a good enough compromise." She played with the hem of her skirt. "I hope I'm not being too forward."

Tolley was leaning on the edge of the stove, legs crossed, smirking at her passive flirtation. She'd waited a full six months of hauling meals once or twice daily to ask him that. Her round cheeks looked fair under the kitchen's weak bulb. Rain was waiting in the doorway, out of Rebecca's sight, but he could feel her there, listening to their conversation. He'd always wondered what it'd feel like to date again after Rain's mom had split over ten years ago to chase a dream. Her mother was all set on fleeing the ranch for good, but was never strong enough to admit it. She coaxed him with words like *temporary* and *soon* far too often. He'd busied himself on the farm after she'd left, only having a few one-night stands with some small-town girls. Rebecca Billingsley was kindhearted and sincere. She'd married young to a much older man until he suddenly passed away. He figured she'd be a nice start back into the murky world of dating.

"Dinner would be nice," Tolley answered after a pause. Rebecca smiled hugely.

"Okay. Uh, well, I'm going to go get cleaned up. Can't go out smelling like a cow's hind parts, now can I?" They chuckled together as he helped her from the chair and she walked barefoot to her truck without assistance. Tolley found himself watching her walk away, her rotund body jiggling with its womanly shape as she tiptoed across the smooth gravel light as a feather and backed her truck from the base of the driveway.

Rain's voice sliced through his ogling. "So you're gonna stand me up for her? You said we'd go shooting today."

"And we will," Tolley said as he stalked away.

"What's eating you?"

"I know what you did today to Rebecca and I don't like it. She's a nice lady. You'd rather me be alone forever, don'tcha?" He spun on her, towering over her and waiting for a response. She hadn't noticed how tall he was until then.

"Of course I don't want you to be alone, but what about Mom?" Rain said, raising her chin. She wanted her mother back, not Rebecca Billingsley. Rebecca's floral pumps could never fill her mother's shoes.

"Rain, you better get this and get it good. She ain't coming back. Not *ever*." Tolley slapped his leg with his hand, frustrated at Rain for bringing her up again. "You're gonna have to forget about her, Rain. Because she's forgotten all about us."

Tolley left her on the front walkway to lament over her mother as the sun threatened to set in a few hours. Rain had given up on her father understanding that some things take time. Her mom would be back. She just needed some time away like she'd told Rain years ago. She'd come to her bedside back then with her dark doe eyes watering at the corners and explained that she'd be back soon, that she needed to leave her behind this time. She kissed Rain's tiny shoulder through her purple pajama top. It was a habit they'd developed since she was born of kissing their birthmarks instead of their faces. In response, Rain kissed her mother's wrist, her light-brown birthmark like an ink blot on her smooth skin. Then her mother blew a kiss from the doorway and vanished from her bedroom for the last time, ten years ago.

Rain heard the big truck engines roar at the rear of the house and tucked her memories aside to investigate it. She jogged around the side of the house, dodging a dog and chicken on her way to see Tolley gunning the truck outside the car port. The truck was shaking slightly in its old age, sputtering and kicking out exhaust as it grumbled. Rain hopped in the passenger seat next to Tolley and smiled. He smiled back. They could never stay mad at each other for too long. It was a strange and comforting bond they shared.

Rain looked out the open window as the green pastures, wired fences, and herds of cattle passed by in a familiar blur. She'd grown up in the country and saw things differently than most. She noticed the apple tree, not yet ripe with its sweet fruit as she passed McAllister Farm. She remembered sitting under the shade of the large tree at the center of his farm, knocking down apples to quiet her appetite on days when Tolley would sell a few cattle to Mr. McAllister for the winter season.

Tolley hummed a popular country tune with his arm hanging out the window. The autumn wind felt nice as it swirled through the truck's cabin and whipped Rain's dark hair around her face as though she was in an audible vortex of country music and engine sounds.

"Where are we going?" Confused, Rain looked at him. Skeet shooting was a left at Baker Road, but he'd taken a right turn.

"I'm going to take you somewhere to learn a few things from your ole man. That alright with you?" He smiled.

"I guess so, but I just think you got scared of going against me today in skeet." Rain settled back in her seat and prepared to wallow triumphantly. Tolley chuckled at her and patted her head like she was a golden retriever that'd brought back a stick.

"Don't worry. I'll still whoop you in skeet next time," he added before making a bumpy left turn into a gravel driveway after twenty more minutes of driving. Rain settled her gaze on the dilapidated shack of a building with a white hand-painted sign that read Shooting Range above its screen door in what looked like dripping black tar. Cars littered the parking lot outside the range as if the little shack was the one stop every rancher made before running home to their wives and hot dinner. Tolley jammed the truck in Park as it whined and quit in its spot.

"You ready for this?" Tolley turned in his seat, face more serious now than before.

"Ready for what exactly? It's just a range, Dad. What's the big deal?"

"It's not *just* a range. It's the only place you can go to see how good you really are. You're used to your rifle. Hell, you been hunting with it since you're eight and you've tested out the shotgun a bit, too." Tolley looked to the ceiling of the dusty truck, trying to count all the weapons Rain had used. He gave up. "I'm going to teach you some of my ole tricks."

"Where did you learn all these old tricks anyway?" Rain wondered aloud, grabbing the door handle to exit the truck.

It caught Tolley off guard and he sat back with a sigh. Rain tensed, not sure whether her question was rude or if she'd hit a particularly sensitive button in him.

"There's a lot you don't know, Rain. But I'll share with you one day." He smirked. "If you can beat me."

Rain snorted sarcastically. "You better start preparing your story now, old man."

The shooting range was nothing but a one-room open gallery of weapons with the sound of muffled gunshots permeating the walls. Guns of all types stacked high from the roof to the floor and ordered by deadliness, most likely. Rain took in the curve of each stock, the length of each barrel with amazement and giddiness. A man with graying whiskers chewed tobacco and spit it in his paper cup as Tolley and Rain stood at the counter perusing the weapons.

"What can I do ya for?" he said through yellow, crooked teeth, spit dribbling down his chin and snaking its way through the white of his goatee. He brushed it away with the back of his wrist. Rain grimaced.

"We wanna shoot a handgun and a sniper rifle," Tolley answered quickly. Sniper rifle? Rain's eyes trained on Tolley's face, tight with concentration on the weapons lining the wall. He seemed different in this range. More focused, less playful.

"Take your pick." The man raised his hand lazily toward the wall without turning.

"What happened to the SR-25 with the twenty-inch barrel?" Tolley asked the man who had just finished spitting in his cup and catching the front of his shirt with brown saliva.

"Goddammit." The man looked down at his shirt. "That rifle's in the back. Wasn't gettin' too much use out of it. These damn hicks don't know the difference between their assholes and a jelly doughnut. Let alone a good sniper rifle when they see one."

"Well, I think we'll try our hand at it." Tolley rested his hands on his belt loops as the man struggled from the stool and limped to the back closet, emerging with the rifle moments later.

"The rounds are expensive, ya know." The man squinted at Tolley and stopped in his tracks. "Do I know you?"

Tolley shook his head. "No, sir. Guess I got one of those faces."

The man was satisfied with Tolley's answer and plopped the oversized rifle onto the glass, almost shattering it with his carelessness. He reached under the glass counter, grabbed the bullets, and slid them next to it.

"And a handgun for the girl?" The man's bottom lip jutted out, threatening to spill brown spit on his chin again.

Tolley smirked. "The handgun's for me."

The man almost lost his footing—due to either his bad leg or the surprise that Rain was going to fire the most powerful rifle in his shop.

Rain was just as stunned as she grabbed Tolley's elbow and said, "You sure about that?" The rifle looked bigger than she was.

Tolley chuckled. "Don't go trying to back out now. You were all brawn in the truck. Let's go."

The range opened up behind the wooden door of the main gallery as Tolley and Rain ambled through. Her lugging the large rifle by the stock, and him easily handling his Glock. The scent of gunpowder made the air cling with a unique thickness as they glanced down the corridor, trying to make room for each other in the slim space. Inside, a long, narrow hallway with numbered doors and rectangular windows showcased the lackluster skills of the marksmen inside and made Rain think of her own skills. Would she be able to rise to her father's expectation with this new, powerful weapon? Or would his face fold in disappointment at her lack of talent? The thought made her shudder as the rifle clanked against her thigh and she struggled to keep it steady. Tolley opened the door to room five and held it open as Rain propped the rifle against the wall.

"We're gonna work on your skills with the Glock. Come on, step up here." Tolley pointed to the white line on the floor. She could faintly hear him through the earmuffs he handed her when they'd stepped into the hall.

Downrange, a silhouette of a bald man with six ovals and a red dot on his chest hung from a metal clamp about fifty feet away. Tolley placed the Glock in Rain's hand and stood near the door of the tiny room. Rain snapped off the safety and pointed the gun at the silhouette.

"Breathe, Rain."

Rain let out a gush of air and fired the first round. The recoil on the weapon was fierce, pushing her arm upward and straying her shot. The bullet landed in the silhouette but near the underarm. Definitely not a kill, Rain thought to herself with annoyance. She turned to look at Tolley who waved her to keep going. She steadied her hand, reassessed her stance, and fired again, this time hitting the neck. She lowered the weapon, defeated.

"What's the problem?" Tolley asked calmly.

"It has too much recoil. I can't contain it."

"Change your stance. Look at the red dot down there. Nothing else. You know the feel of the recoil now, right?" Rain nodded. "Well, use that to your advantage. Think of it like dancing. Keep the rhythm."

Rain remembered that she wasn't a very good dancer. She knew what he meant, but could she do it? She fired three more rounds into the sheet, each getting closer to the red dot—but no bull's-eye. She was discouraged.

She wanted her rifle, needed to feel it on her shoulder and against her cheek. It was the only thing that could boost her spirits. Failure was not something she'd grown accustomed to.

"Give it here." Tolley took the gun from her and shooed her to the rear of the box. He pressed the red button on the wall which dragged her dismal sheet to the box and released the next silhouette, clear and unmarked, within minutes. Tolley stood on the white line. Rain saw his legs relax, his shoulder blades pinch beneath his shirt and then a barrage of shots rang through the small box, startling her even though she knew it was coming.

Once he was finished, he pushed the red button. The silhouette whirred to the box and stopped in front of Tolley. The red dot had disappeared from the sheer number of shots that had ripped through the page. He'd hit the spot almost fifteen times in a row. Rain was amazed but rejuvenated. She wanted to hit the red dot more than ever now that Tolley had shown her it could be done so easily.

"I want to go again," Rain said with vigor. Tolley chuckled and shook his head at her newfound motivation. If he ever needed her to do anything right, all he had to do was make it a competition.

"Once more then we gotta move on." Tolley handed her the Glock with a wink. She smiled at the silhouette at the end of the lane.

Rain steadied herself behind the white line and mimicked Tolley's legs and back before firing the weapon until the clip was empty. She pushed the red button to see her results up close. She was giddy with pride as her silhouette revealed that she had hit the mark six of fifteen times while the others were close inside the first white oval of the chest.

"Hmm," Tolley said and grabbed the gun from Rain. "Not bad."

Rain felt her insides jump with excitement as Tolley pointed to the rifle leaning against the wall like a bored visitor. He walked out of the booth without a word, traveling down the corridor and out the far door into the waning sunlight as Rain ran behind carrying the SR-25 like a child in her arms, its long barrel almost touching the mottled concrete outside.

The air was refreshing and light compared to the indoor range. Rain could still smell the remnants of gun smoke but it mingled with the fresh air. Her head was starting to pound from the constant sound of gunfire. Tolley set up the tripod legs for the sniper rifle when they appeared on the bench outside the door marked Main Office. The old geezer from the gallery must've brought it out, Rain thought. She instinctively looked toward the Main Office window and spotted the old man, bottom lip jutting out, staring at Tolley and her. She felt an uneasy chill down her spine as he spit in his cup and watched them carefully under bushy gray eyebrows.

"What's up with the old man? He gives me the creeps." Rain pushed her chin toward the office window. Tolley looked over his shoulder, saluted, and continued setting the rifle on the stand and locking it in place as if the man was nothing more than a bystander.

"He's probably interested in seeing what you can do with this rifle. Not many people can handle the power of it and still hit the mark," Tolley said, looking down at the rifle and adjusting the scope.

"It doesn't seem much different than my hunting rifle. Just a longer barrel, I guess . . . and *fancier*." She eyed the smooth, matte blackness of the rifle. It definitely was nicer than her rifle's wooden stock and scratched bodice.

"Well, take your time with it. It's like a woman . . . she'll make a fool of you if you don't respect her." He grinned.

Rain could tell by the looks of the rifle that it was heavy duty and not to be played with. She felt the excitement of firing it boiling deep in her belly, making her feel nauseous. She knew she wouldn't throw up— she'd had that feeling before when she first started hunting, but it stopped when she felt the coolness of her rifle against her cheek and shoulder. On instinct, she glanced back over her shoulder and found the old man had vanished, leaving the window bare and dark. She breathed a sigh of relief. He made her feel like he knew something that she didn't with his dark eyes and hard glare.

"Let's go." Tolley's commanding voice ripped through her thoughts of the man.

"Sure thing," Rain answered, readying herself at the rifle, fighting to contain her enthusiasm.

"Listen closely, Rain. It's just like your hunting rifle but a little more powerful. Don't balance it on the tripod; keep it steady on your shoulder as you would in the forest. Got it?" Tolley instructed.

"Sure thing."

Tolley stepped back to the bench, sat, and crossed his ankle over his knee, ready for the first round to burst from the weapon. He was nervous and anxious, too, but wouldn't show it to Rain. She was excited, of course, but she had no idea how far back her roots with this weapon ran. If Rain was anything like him, she'd have a knack for that particular weapon, *his* weapon, and hit almost anything at any distance. He'd sold it to the shop owner over eight years ago, not wanting to look at it anymore.

The first shot rang out as Tolley uncrossed his leg and leaned forward to peer down the lane at the closest target. It was unmarked. What the hell? Tolley slumped back on the bench trying to hide his disappointment.

"Did you see that, Dad? Whoa!" Rain stood erect by the rifle, looking down the lane, then ran over, her face flush.

"You missed it, Rain. Try again. You'll get it," Tolley said sadly.

"No, I didn't." Rain pointed down the lane. "I shot the farthest one first . . . it was dead on!"

Tolley grabbed the binoculars from the bench and peered down the lane, up the hill almost to the tree line at the thousand-yard mark. He blinked twice before realizing his gaze had not lied, and neither had Rain, for that matter. She'd slugged it right above the center on her first try. She was definitely his daughter to have the skill to see that far and adjust for the wind, odd angle of the hill, and the power of the rifle, but he mulled over an even scarier thought—maybe she was even better than *him*.

After letting Rain have free rein of the rifle for a few hours, the evening haze had fallen on the range, making it harder to see the targets, so Tolley called it quits.

"Can you believe I hit that thousand-yard mark . . . on the first try?" Rain was still excited about her shot, and frankly, Tolley was still in shock. He knew she'd been skilled with rifles since he began training her as a teen and hadn't doubted her ability to shoot any weapon after a bit of practice. She'd shot well for the rest of the evening, splitting her red dots frequently enough that she'd gotten less excited and started trying different prone and kneeling positions to challenge herself.

Tolley turned in the rifle and handgun at the counter and handed over the cash for their session.

"She's a good shot on that rifle," the old man said, his eyes roaming Rain's body in confusion.

"Yeah, she's good at most things thrown at her." Tolley patted her head with pride but Rain winced at the action. She'd just shot a thousand yards and he was treating her like a baby again.

"Where'd ya learn to shoot like that, li'l girl?" the man asked, handing Tolley his change.

Rain smoothed back the hair that had fallen in her face and said, "I'm not a little girl, old man."

"Don't mean no harm . . . just tryin' a' make conversation with ya." He turned to Tolley. "Good lawd, you showl got a feisty one on ya hands, huh?"

He never tore his eyes from Rain's cold stare. They were battling with their stares as Tolley interrupted, "Thanks for the rounds. We'll be back again."

The old man nodded, the staring game now broken between the two, and he settled back on his stool behind the counter. Tolley and Rain walked out the front door as the screen creaked closed behind them. The parking lot had emptied in the four hours that they'd been at the range except for a black SUV with its lights illuminating the front of the building. Tolley covered his eyes against the glare, trying to peer past the light and into the vehicle's window.

"Get in the car," he said abruptly. Too abruptly.

"Huh? What's wrong?" Rain asked as she rounded the front of the truck and pulled open the door. She heard the car doors slam on the SUV and couldn't pull herself to get in the truck without looking. She saw two men in black suits walking toward them and noticed the flash of their weapons on their hips. What the hell? Rain thought to herself, fear bubbling in her chest and convincing her to run back to her father's side. Tolley felt her presence and sighed as he looked at her face trained on the men walking toward them.

"Special Agent Wilson, my name is Special Agent Brack and this is Special Agent Krueg." The tall, dark man speaking motioned toward the shorter, blond man with the crooked nose.

"I'm not an agent anymore," Tolley answered gruffly. Rain looked up at him, confused as to why they were calling her father, a well-known rancher and game hunter, a *special agent*.

"We're aware of that, sir. But there have been some dire circumstances that have led us to look for you." The dark-skinned man rubbed his chin and looked at the shorter man as if to ask for help in explaining the *dire* situation. He settled with, "We need you to come with us, sir."

"Like hell I will. I don't work for the agency anymore. Thought I told you that already." Tolley turned around and pushed Rain to get in the trucks driver's-side door, which was still open and swaying.

"Agent Wilson . . ."

Tolley burst into anger. "Don't call me that, you fuckers. I'm not in the agency and I'm not going anywhere with you. Whatever the dire situation is . . . it can fix itself without my help." Tolley pushed Rain to the passenger side a little too roughly and slid into the driver's seat, slamming the door hard enough to make the truck wobble. The dark man rested his hand in the open window as Tolley gunned the engine.

"It's about Dahlia," the man said quickly, hoping his hand wouldn't be snatched off by the truck as it revved.

"Mom?" Rain said across her father to the man in the window. "Dad, something's happened to Mom?" she asked with a hint of fear in her voice, her eyes begging for answers, tearing holes into Tolley.

"Shit." Tolley turned the key out of the ignition and gripped the steering wheel with white knuckles. "What's happened to her?"

TWO

LANGLEY, VIRGINIA, 2003

Riding in the SUV with Special Agents Brack and Krueg was not bad. It was the flight that shook Rain's core since she'd never been higher than the farmhouse's rooftop, let alone on a jet thousands of feet above the ground. She'd made it the five-hour flight with lots of prayers and a sickeningly tight seat belt that forced her legs to feel like jelly as soon as she got off the plane. Tolley had been stoic from the time he'd left his truck at the shooting range and piled into the backseat of the SUV with Rain. She'd had a million questions in her eyes but he didn't know how to tell her all the things she yearned to know without changing her view of him. He'd wrestled with telling her about his past when she'd turned sixteen but felt she wasn't ready. At that time, she was still emotional over killing wild animals. He knew she wouldn't understand all the things he'd had to do before she was born.

He'd promised himself that at eighteen she needed to know but hadn't gotten around to it. In his own way, he'd prepared her for the truth. He'd taught her how to hunt, how to shoot, and how to care for herself. Those were all lessons she needed to survive. Now he wasn't so sure that he'd taught her enough about himself, enough to warn her of life's real dangers.

To Rain, the CIA headquarters building looked like a glass statue with its arced entrance and spotless windows. The two agents guided Tolley and Rain through a series of checkpoints that included emptying pockets and standing in a futuristic scanning booth similar to the one Rain had seen at the airport. After they'd been emptied of everything and stood weightless except for the clothes on their backs, Agent Brack spoke lowly to Agent Krueg and moments later he walked in the opposite direction than they were heading.

"I'm going to take you to the briefing room." Agent Krueg motioned down the hall and kept a brisk pace ahead of them.

"Don't you mean interrogation room?" Tolley said smartly, falling in step with Agent Krueg.

Rain noticed that each corner they turned, Tolley led the way like he was visiting an old friend's house. Agent Krueg was now slightly behind him, in front of Rain. Rain assessed Tolley's mannerisms as he walked— chest jutted forward, his jeans and boots dirty from the day's work. Rain looked at her reflection as she passed thick glass windows revealing orderly office spaces. The people inside looked out at them like animals in the zoo. She'd silently wished she could have freshened up a bit; she hadn't showered that morning and spreading manure at the ranch wasn't exactly her idea of applying perfume. No one seemed to notice her anyway, she thought to herself. They were too wrapped up in Tolley with their eyes following him through the glass. How could Tolley help them? She thought to herself, still in shock over the ambush at the gun range then the flight and now the oddly sterile building. She was startled to hear her mom's name from the agent's mouth back at the range. Maybe she could see her again or help her get out of whatever trouble she was in?

Agent Krueg opened a white door to a white room with a long mirror attached to the far wall. It looked like an asylum room, built to make the crazy even crazier. Four uncomfortable-looking chairs surrounded the stainless-steel table, the leather seat cushions dented by too many years of people waiting, she guessed. The hum from the overhead fluorescent light was the only sound after Agent Krueg shut the door behind him and closed them in alone. Rain tried the handle.

"It's locked," Tolley grimly said what he already knew to be true.

"Why's it locked? Are we under arrest or something?" Rain sounded confused and a little alarmed. She didn't like being out of control.

"Something like that."

"We didn't do anything. Why'd they lock us up in here?" Rain tried the handle again as if it would magically open by her asking more questions.

"Sit down, Rain." Tolley was already seated and was rubbing his temples. His dirty, ragged nails reminded her that they didn't belong in a place this sterile.

"Dad, what's going on?"

Before Tolley could answer, a stubby middle-aged man with glasses entered and closed the door behind him. His suit looked expensive, as did his brown leather shoes. He sat down in the seat across from Tolley without acknowledging Rain from the corner where she stood. Rain finally took her seat next to Tolley, assessing the man that reminded her of Stuart Little with a bad diet.

"Agent Wilson, my name is Christopher Dalton. I'm the chief of staff for the CIA. I recall seeing your file earlier this month." He propped open a file that must've been hidden in his jacket pocket because Rain hadn't seen him come in with it. And she was watching him ever so carefully.

"The name is Tolley and don't act like you don't remember me. We know each other quite well. I'm only here to find out what's happened to Dahlia. That's it." Tolley clasped his hands on the steel table tightly, restraining from punching the next person that addressed him as *agent*. Christopher Dalton stirred in his seat before speaking again. Rain noticed he looked very uncomfortable sitting this close to Tolley and she didn't know why.

"Oh, we're going to tell you more than you care to know about Dahlia, but first I need to ensure you are willing to help and not hinder this investigation. You know how these things go, right? You've been on my side a couple times." He pulled the rim of his glasses down and scanned the documents, trying to break eye contact with Tolley. Rain strained her eyes to read upside down the file marked Top Secret.

"Where's Dahlia?" Tolley leaned back in his chair and Rain mimicked his motion.

"Dahlia is in Russia, *Tolley*. Or that's the last place she was when we lost contact with her." The man wrinkled his nose to inch his glasses back into place. "She's been off the grid now for two months. We can't locate her and she hasn't tried communicating with the special agent in charge. We've tracked her cell, which has been destroyed, and looked for her in all the cameras we have access to."

"And?" Tolley said easily.

"And we have reason to believe she's gone rogue." Dalton stared at Tolley with beady eyes, trying to gather intelligence through his body language.

"And you seem to think she reached out to me all the way in Colorado? That doesn't make any sense. You've probably had my phone tapped since she started the mission. You'd have intercepted the call. So why am I here, Chief?" Tolley said with a hint of emotion.

"You're here because we need your help locating Special Agent Wilson. You're the only one with enough intel on her to bring her in. You know her moves, where she's been, what she's prone to do."

"So you want me to catch my wife and hand her over to you? And for what? What will you do with her when you have her? What do you want from her?" Tolley leaned forward to glare at Dalton through his thick glasses. The heat was on. Dalton stiffened under Tolley's questioning. His brow was wet with perspiration, Rain noticed.

"Tolley, we won't hurt her, of course. We just need to gather valuable intel and ensure she is properly debriefed."

"Of course, my ass. I know how you operate. Loose links get pulled and replaced," Tolley said, glancing at Rain whose jaw had dropped open as her head swiveled between the two.

"This isn't some game, I assure you. She is in grave danger . . . if she's not rogue as we suspect. She won't have any backup should something go awry. She's totally off the grid, Tolley." Dalton glanced at Rain before looking back at the documents on the steel table.

Tolley thought about the possibility of Dahlia, his first love and mother to his beautiful daughter, being killed while undercover and he had the chance to stop it. He'd never forgive himself for her death.

"What do you need me to do?"

"We want you to get back on the team."

"Hell no. Absolutely not." He'd do anything except that.

Dalton braced himself to persuade Tolley while Rain looked on at his futile attempt. If it was one thing she knew about her father, it was that he never did anything he didn't want to do. Stubbornness ran in their family.

"Tolley, look . . . it's not going to be the same as it was before. We just want you back as a sniper and informant. That's it. You'll search with the team and make sure Dahlia makes it back safe and sound to CIA headquarters."

"That's it, huh? Just a sniper. I'm done with that life. I'm not killing anymore." Tolley looked at Rain who had trained her sights on every word coming out of his lips. The shock on her face was like a shot to Tolley's heart. He didn't want her to find out like this.

"Tolley, we need you on this team. You're the best sniper . . . hell, the best weapons guru we have at the agency. You still hold the record for the longest kill shot at eighteen hundred yards; no one's beat you yet." Dalton tried to grease the wheels but found it didn't budge Tolley one little bit, so he added, "The boys want you back."

"Dalton, I'm done with this conversation. You can find Dahlia on your own. I'm not getting behind a rifle again." Tolley stood up, signaling that he was ready to leave.

"What about me? Can I do it?" Rain asked the weasel-faced man as his eyes opened wide at the question. His face looked as if he'd just realized there was another person in the room with them.

"What are you talking about, Rain? Have you lost your mind?" Tolley grabbed her shoulder and turned her face to him. "This ain't hunting in the damn woods he's talking about. He's talking about hunting people, Rain. *People.*"

"Not hunting, per se," Dalton mumbled.

"Shut up," Tolley said without looking away from Rain. Dalton bit the inside of his cheek dramatically as if waiting for the family spat to conclude was taking longer than expected.

Rain swallowed hard at the thought of hunting a living human being, shooting them down without care. The thought of her mother being harmed made her puff her chest out.

"I understand what he's saying just fine. I want to help bring her home."

"Goddammit, Rain." Tolley sat back down in the chair, shaking his head in disbelief.

"Your daughter has guts, Agent . . . I mean, Tolley," Dalton said with a smirk. "It's too bad she's just a kid. I can't risk my guy's lives by taking her out in the field anyway. But that's really cute."

"I'm not a kid," Rain said defiantly. "Just today I shot one thousand yards on my first try with an SR-25. You got someone that can do better?"

Dalton looked at Tolley in disbelief. Tolley nodded his head as confirmation that Rain had hit the shot she claimed. Dalton swallowed, thinking about the possibilities, and shook his head.

"Well, even with your lucky shot behind the rifle, it doesn't mean you know how to handle yourself when the going gets tough. You're too much of a risk." Dalton slid the folder off the table in preparation to leave.

Tolley knew that the nail in the coffin had been placed and pounded with those words. Dalton had challenged Rain by doubting her and there would be nothing that would stop her from proving that she could do it.

"Let me try. I promise you I can do it." Rain pleaded with her brown eyes.

Christopher Dalton looked at Tolley who had settled on staring at the steel table with his arms crossed, disengaged from her pleas. What would it hurt to add the girl to a training roster? She wouldn't make it out of agency training anyway and that'd possibly buy more time to convince Tolley to join the team again, Dalton thought to himself.

"What the hell . . . you can start sniper training next week but if there's one mistake, one mishap, or even a semblance of a tear . . . you're out." Dalton's voice was strong and assertive, very different than the one he'd used with Tolley.

"Yes, sir," Rain replied and settled back in her seat with a grin as Dalton closed the door behind him.

The room was silent for what felt like hours. After basking in her momentary victory, she remembered Tolley was still seated next to her and was not happy about what she'd just done.

"Dad, I want to bring Mom back."

Tolley shook his head slowly. "No you don't, Rain. You just want to see if you can do it, see if you can be better than us. What you don't understand is that it's a life-or-death game. If you lose, you die. You're in over your head on this one."

Rain rolled over his words in her mind. Normally she listened to Tolley's advice. But since she'd heard the agent speak her mother's name, she felt like she had a new lease on life, a new understanding of her purpose after learning that her parents were agents. Important agents at that. Maybe she was motivated by seeing if she could accomplish the same thing they had but in the pit of her heart, she wanted to see her mother again. Feel her kiss her shoulder and wish her good-night. She'd missed ten years of that and wouldn't miss any more if she could help it.

"I'm going to do this, Dad. I hope you're behind me. I have a feeling I'm going to need your help along the way," Rain said, gripping her father's hand, which was tightened around his bicep. She was trying to butter him up but he remained at a distance.

"I'm behind you, you know that. But I think you're making a mistake going after her. She's not the person you remember."

"I don't care who she is. She's still my mom."

Rain laid her head on Tolley's muscular shoulder and listened to his heavy breathing. The constant intake of breath relaxed her.

"Just remember to follow your instincts. If it feels wrong, it probably is. Trust yourself."

"Okay, Dad."

"So do you still feel going after your mother is right?" he asked, his green eyes hopeful.

Rain thought about it for a moment. "Feels right to me."

Tolley sighed. "Well then, let's get to it, li'l girl."

"Let's get to it."

The door opened and Agent Brack stood in the light of the hall, ready to escort them out of the sprawling CIA headquarters and into an awaiting car.

THREE

BAGHDAD, IRAQ, 2004

T HE UNYIELDING SUN MADE the hood of the grimy cars look like sparkling gems as they inched toward the gate. Rain inspected the line, watched closely through her scope for anything out of the ordinary. The line was especially long as the checkpoint was lightly manned today due to heightened security at the headquarters building, which meant only twenty soldiers were prowling the line with dogs pulling on their leashes, sniffing out the scent of bomb material. Rain was in the tower with Sergeant Willow, her battle buddy and second shot. As second shot, Willow was to remain steady, peering through binoculars until she spied something worth calling in. Willow was an army-trained sniper but she'd only needed to call him if she'd missed, and that would never happen.

She'd trained at Langley to be in the CIA like her mother, passed every task—in line with the best of the recruits—but in the end, Dalton had abandoned her. He'd placed her in the army instead of the CIA, touting an undercover mission for her in the works and to be patient. She knew that Dalton was a weasel and not to be trusted but she had nowhere else to go. Going back to the ranch with Tolley wasn't an option. Not after all she'd worked for. She still needed to find her mother and being in the field, off the ranch, felt like she was getting closer to that goal.

"Sergeant Wilson, you got any more Oreos left?" Sergeant Willow asked with the binoculars still pressed to his sunburned face. He'd been on special assignment before being tasked to the tower with her. He'd earned his stripes on that mission to get this high up, Rain thought to herself when she'd first met Willow.

"Nope. I ate them," Rain said, still peering through her scope, watching a red car pull up to the line.

"I'm tired of drinking water and eating MREs up here. I mean, you're good company and all but you don't share. What if I get weak in the knees from hunger? You gonna give me one of your snacks?"

"If you get weak in the knees I'm going to prop you up on this tripod so you could still do your job. Mission first, remember?" Rain snickered, still eyeing the red car that had a large man sitting in the front seat. He was digging for something under the steering wheel.

"You're cold, Sergeant Wilson . . . so cold," Willow said, chuckling as he raked his hand through his sandy-brown crew cut.

"Can you get an angle on the red car, rear of the line, large male, and driver side? I don't see any others in the car. He's reaching for something . . . see if you can see it on your side," Rain announced quickly.

"I'm on it."

"What do you see?"

"Uhhh, he's got a book. Looks like a magazine or something, not a weapon," Willow reported within seconds.

"Good." Rain scanned the other cars in line, searching for the extraordinary, the out of place.

"How'd you get in this job? You know, in the birds' nest?" Willow asked after a few minutes had passed. He'd only been working with Rain for four weeks. She'd been alone in the tower until then. She was beginning to miss the silence already.

"I was placed here," Rain said with a twitch in her eyelid. She didn't want to think of the raw deal Dalton had given her by placing her in the army, in a hot box of a tower until God knows when.

"You must be wicked with that thing to be placed in the tower, especially in Baghdad," Willow said. "Only the best get to go to the main tower." Willow was amazed. He'd never seen a girl in a tower in his five years in the army.

"I'm alright." Rain smiled and scanned the line of cars again.

It was two minutes before the loudspeakers would blare its ghostly hymns of Arabic prayer across the country. The sound gave Rain a creepy feeling and to see the effects on the Iraqi people were astonishing at first. It was a hypnotic volley of words that forced the men to leave their cars running, lay out their rugs, kick off their shoes, and kneel down to Allah. They'd hum along to the loudspeaker in a meditative state, praying to their God like someone had flipped a switch in the back of their neck. It was eerie to see from the tower so many people kneeling in unison and bobbing their heads to the dusty mats. Rain had seen it many times over the past year and only now it was beginning to dull her senses. Iraq was mostly Muslim and for those few Iraqis that didn't follow the Muslim doctrine, they did so quietly as a tactic of self-preservation. Christianity was a taboo that could cost an Iraqi their life and the life of their children in this country. Rain sighed against the rifle, her back soaked with sweat from the hundred-and-fifteen-degree heat that beat the top of the stone tower. The shade and a battery-operated fan struggling in the center of the tower didn't do much in the way of cooling Sergeant Willow and Rain. They suffered silently with bags of snacks and a case of water in the treacherous heat.

"What is it, a hundred twenty degrees today?" Willow said, leaning against the concrete curve of the tower, unbuttoning the top of his uniform.

"One fifteen," Rain said, blinking her eyes in the scope, clearing her vision.

"You need to rest, Sergeant Wilson. You haven't come up from that thing in over two hours."

"I'm alright; I've stayed longer than this. It's just the damn sun glaring on the roofs of the cars that's got my eyes watering." She wiped the tear that etched down her tanned cheek.

"The speakers gonna come on in a minute. You can rest then. You know for sure they won't desecrate their holy time trying something stupid," Willow reasoned, shaking the sand from his binoculars before raising them to his face.

He's acting as if he cares about me, Rain thought to herself. She allowed herself to glance at Willow for a short second before looking back through the scope. He wasn't bad looking. Sergeant Willow had to be in his early to mid-twenties with deep blue eyes and no wrinkles in sight. Rain scanned his body through his brown T-shirt—he'd taken off his desert uniform top while she was spying the line. He was well built, mostly biceps and chest, and the sweaty shirt clung to the silhouette of his slim yet muscular frame. Rain swallowed hard. She hadn't been this close to a guy since training, and the last thing on her mind was getting laid by any of those pompous, middle-aged men. They'd badgered her constantly, tried to break her for being the only female . . . and young. She wasn't supposed to make it to the top of her class but she had despite their dismay. Then, within days of graduation, Dalton pulled her from training barracks and put her on a flight to the goddamn desert, dropped her off with an army uniform and a new military-issued sniper rifle. She'd cursed him for three months as she roamed the tower alone, thinking of why he'd put her in the middle of war when all she wanted was to find her mother.

Willow grabbed his M4A1 carbine, hoisted it on the ledge of the tower, and readied for the loudspeaker to start its eerie hymnal. Seconds ticked by as Rain still kept her sights on the men who were digging rugs and mats from their trunks and backseats. She scanned them all—around fifty in total—zooming in on their items, searching trunks and car seats for anything suspicious. The man in the red car hadn't moved; he sat with his hands on the steering wheel, staring straight ahead.

"Look at the red car again. Something seems strange there." Willow was already looking through his scope and spotting the man.

"Yeah, I was thinking the same thing. Want to call it in?"

"Yep. Better safe than sorry, right?"

"Echo Mike niner, this is Birdie Two. We have sights on a red car, last in line, Iraqi male. Suspicious activity."

"Roger that, Birdie Two. We are sending two there now. Sights up, copy."

"Copy that," Willow said into the two-way radio.

Rain noticed his chest heaving deeply, the adrenaline rushing through his veins. She smiled at the thought that someone other than her father could share her excitement behind a rifle. Her heart was racing, too, but she knew how to contain it now. She breathed deeply and focused on the red car as she trailed the two guards that stalked toward the vehicle, weapons drawn. They were more than two hundred yards away from the car when the prayer started over the loudspeakers and a group of men ambled about, crossing the path of the two guards, heading for the sand beyond the cement road to engage in prayer. The passersby moved away as they saw the guards' weapons drawn, pointing toward the end of the line. The goose bumps on Rain's arms and the chill down her spine let her know that something was awfully wrong. Another car, this one black, pulled up behind the red car, attempting to inch its way past.

"Birdie Two, eyes on the black prize. Birdie One, eyes on the worm."

The command team instructed Wilson to keep his eyes on the black car, probably an important guest of the base that needed protecting. The black car was snaking its way past the red car into a VIP lane which was still blocked by a steel barrier, all within Rain's sight. The guards were closer now, almost one hundred yards from the red car, the black car at their left, stuck at the barrier.

"Why aren't they opening the goddamn barrier?" Willow spat angrily.

"I don't know." Rain was wondering the same thing. Under regular operations, the barrier would have been open before their arrival. It was safety protocol for all VIP guests. Why weren't they letting them in?

"Want to call it in to command? Maybe they didn't know they were coming."

Willow eased his hand from the stock of his rifle, propping it on the tower's concrete for leverage, then called it in.

"Birdie Two to Command, come in."

"Command here, go ahead, Birdie Two," the nasal voice answered.

"We have the black prize at the entrance, barrier unopened. High risk."

"Copy that, Birdie Two. We have a situation. Keep your eyes on the black prize. Copy."

"Copy that, Command. Eyes on the prize. Birdie Two out."

Willow looked at Rain confused and fearful by the use of the word *situation*. Whenever there was a *situation*, it was never a good sign. Rain could see the guards yelling at the man in the red car. The music blared too loud to hear from this distance but Rain could imagine them telling the man to exit the vehicle with his hands raised high. By the looks of things, he wasn't complying or even remotely responding to their advances on his vehicle. He sat, hands on the steering wheel, lips moving slowly.

"Oh shit," Rain whispered to herself. "Call it in, it's a suicide—" Rain couldn't finish her sentence against the harsh boom of the car bomb that exploded below. She stared through her scope as the two guards went flying in pieces to the sandy street. Helmets, weapons, severed legs, and unidentifiable pieces were lying on the bloodstained concrete.

"*Oh God,*" Willow yelled beside her. He was already firing rounds from his rifle into the throngs of men who had left their rugs and were advancing on the soldiers below. It was an ambush. They were trying to overtake the barricades. Rain swept her scope to the black car. It still sat at the barricade, untouched by the masses of people fighting below. Her gut felt uneasy. Something was off about the vehicle but she didn't know what.

"Wilson, hostile at your one o'clock!" Willow screamed through Rain's trance on the black vehicle.

Rain swept her rifle to the area Willow marked and found a hostile violently attempting to behead a fallen soldier with a machete. He gripped the soldier's head by the hair, pulling his body high to make a clean cut. Raising his machete to the soldier's neck, Rain saw the hostile's head explode like a ripe watermelon, red matter flying from the point of the bullet's entry. His body dropped, headless, on top of the soldier.

"Damn good shot!" Willow said in excitement. He turned smooth in the heat of battle, his voice pitched low and laced with confidence. "Eyes are on the black prize. Shit, we got action here."

"I'm on it." Rain was staring at the vehicle's opened door as a leg slid out. The boot landed on the yellow line marking the VIP lane and a tall man of Iraqi descent escaped the interior of the car, tugging on something from within. Rain gasped at what the man pulled out after him.

"Dalton?" Rain said, loud enough for Willow to pause.

"You know him?" Willow asked in shock, still watching the dumpy man with the pistol held to his temple.

Christopher Dalton, chief of staff for the CIA, did not fight against the assailant. In fact, he looked eerily calm as the attacker pushed and pulled him, the gun rubbing against his temple with each movement. He'd been struck against the head, Rain noticed, as she spotted the line of blood trickling from his hairline above his right eye. He was probably beaten into submission, forced to come here and get them into the gate. At least he was smart enough to warn the command.

"What do you want me to do?" Willow asked.

He wanted to take the shot but Rain knew his rifle would never make a clean enough entry. Even if he had a clean shot, which he didn't, the chief would be dead if Willow was off by even an inch—and from eight hundred yards, with all the jerking and pushing, it was far from easy.

"No. Don't take it. Call it in," Rain said, following protocol, her eyes never leaving Dalton's face.

Willow moaned in response. He'd wanted the go-ahead but it was Rain's tower and she called the shots.

"Command, Birdie Two. Come in."

"Command here. Go ahead, Birdie Two."

"We have a shot on the black prize."

"Do not take the shot. I repeat, do not take the shot, Birdie Two. Copy."

"Copy that command." Willow sighed heavily as he leaned back from his scope, blinked twice, and reset his vision on Dalton.

The assailant was yelling to the gate guards to open the gate or he'd shoot Dalton in the head. His voice was nothing but a whisper on the stale Iraqi air but Rain could hear it from the distance. The other attackers had been neutralized and soldiers hid behind the line of cars, waiting for the word to engage. Everyone was in a holding pattern, waiting for the signal, for some sign. Rain still glared through the scope at Dalton who looked sleepy and limp as he bumped against the attacker after each pull of his collar. The attacker was getting more upset as the minutes ticked by, the realization setting in that he was the only man standing from his team of vagrants. Dalton didn't have much time left. The assailant knew there was no going back—they wouldn't let him leave the area alive with Dalton in tow. The only other option was to kill Dalton in revenge for his men's deaths and surrender willingly to the head shot waiting for him so hell could swallow him up.

"We don't have much time left," Rain said to Willow, who was now standing right next to her, his weapon at the ready.

"I know. He's becoming unhinged. I think he's got a bomb on him," Willow said.

"Spotted that earlier. He's gonna shoot Dalton or blow them both to smithereens," Rain said with growing anticipation. She tightened her grip on her rifle.

"Want me to call it in?"

"Nah. We already know the answer."

"Look, he's backing up to the car," Willow said. They both knew if he made it to the car, the only thing coming out would be a barrage of flames and shrapnel.

"Shit," Rain said under her breath. She couldn't lose Dalton. He was the only lifeline to her mother.

She looked at Dalton's face though the scope. Fear trickled down his cheeks in the form of sweat. The terrorist, now draped in sweat that leaked through his gray shirt, continued to pull him roughly toward the open car door. Just then, in a second's glance, Dalton's eyes caught hers. Rain blinked. It was too far for him to see her in the tower, but somehow he'd spotted her. It was as if he knew she was there watching the whole thing transpire, counting the seconds before his life ended in a blaze of fire. In that second, Dalton nodded his head, staring directly into Rain's scope. She knew what she had to do. She breathed deeply and squeezed the trigger, her sight pointed at the black mole right above the attacker's upper lip. The sound from her rifle echoed on the air as the bullet whizzed to its resting place. It took only a split second to pass through the man's skull, jumbling his memories, erasing images of his family, as it bore a shallow hole through his hateful brown eye and out through his black hair now wet with blood and traces of hot lead. Dalton fell to the ground as the attacker's grip was still tight on his collar. His body hadn't realized he was dead; his grip had not gotten the memo that the mission was over. Before Dalton could roll his chunky body into a sitting position, soldiers raced to him, covered his head with a Kevlar helmet, and half ran, half carried him from the scene behind the barricade and out of Rain's view. Rain's heart was beating from her chest; she heard its quick rhythm in her ears, bumping like a tune to the rifle's echo, which still vibrated in her body.

"Whoa! Holy fuckin' smokes . . ." Willow wiped his forehead in awe as he looked down at the chaotic scene below.

"You can say that again," Rain said, and slid her back down the concrete wall until she was sitting. "I think I'll take my break now."

Willow chuckled, still looking out across the gate at the red car, gutted and mangled, its debris lodged into other cars in the blast radius. The explosion had turned cars into one another, moved the sand into a ripple effect like dropping a stone into still water. The cleanup crew, dressed in all black with steel bulletproof shields, snaked through the lanes, looking for any other hazards or devices left behind in the ambush. Their dogs barked and snarled at the scent of explosives in the air. The man Rain shot was carefully handled by the bomb squad. His vest was released, dismantled, and taken in a large black bag for investigation while his body lay on the ground like a piece of discarded trash, waiting for pickup.

FOUR

COMMAND TACTICAL OPERATION CENTER, BAGHDAD, IRAQ

RAIN PULLED HER SHOULDER-LENGTH hair into a tight, neat ponytail and stared at her reflection in the mirror. Her round brown eyes and straight nose made her look tough, but her insides were like jelly after she fired her rifle into the face of the attacker holding Christopher Dalton. Tolley was right—it was different than hunting. Very different. She let the cool water run through her fingertips before splashing her face, letting the coolness calm the retching in her stomach. She was drenched from the neck down beneath her DCU top, unsure if it was from the humidity outside or the fear of sitting before the panel. She'd been called to the command TOC after the ambush for debriefing by the base commander and to write an incident report for the investigation team. Anytime a round was fired, it was looked into by the investigation team for proper protocol. Needless to say, in Baghdad they were a very busy team. Rain exited the restroom and stood next to Willow who'd waited outside the door for her to collect herself.

"You alright? You're not looking too hot," Willow said, reaching to her forehead and touching it with the back of his hand. "I guess that was the wrong choice of words because you're burning up."

Rain wanted to lean into his hand, fall into his body for a hug, but she knew it was not appropriate and could get her reprimanded. She wanted her father more than ever right now, but she was alone. She'd made her choice. The image of the man's body going limp from her bullet kept replaying behind her eyes like a skipping CD. Over and over she tried to think of something else, and over and over she kept envisioning his body on the dirt. She feigned a weak smile at Willow, trying to remain composed under his scrutiny.

"Don't worry. You did the right thing, Sergeant Wilson. That man would've been dead if you didn't take the shot." He tried to convince her, calm her.

Her heart still hadn't slowed, even after her climb down from the tower and Humvee ride to command central. Her stomach was aching something terrible, lurching around as if she'd eaten bad meat and it was threatening to come back up. The thought of the attacker's head whipping back, his eyes stunned as the bullet entered his skull, made Rain run back into the bathroom and empty the morning's Oreo cookies and water into the porcelain toilet. She felt better now—at least her stomach did, anyway. Her mind and heart was a different story entirely. After rinsing her mouth, she met Willow outside again.

"Better now?" Willow looked worried, his broad forehead etched with lines.

"If I was doing any better, I'd have to be twins to take it." Rain offered the expression Tolley used on occasion. Willow smirked at the joke and wrapped his arm around her shoulder, putting his head to hers. "Let's do this."

Rain couldn't escape the feelings bubbling in her chest with her face so close to Willow's. She tracked behind him, watching the rhythm in his gait, until he stopped outside the briefing room and looked back at her. He winked at her before pulling open the door and disappearing inside. Rain felt a surge of energy from him and caught the door before it could swing shut.

The command's briefing room was an intimidating chamber with a long podium in front of six seats, accompanied by a panel that resembled gods instead of base officials. The name of each interviewer was accompanied by their position titles on white placards with black letters, nailed to the cherrywood facing. The post commander was a hard-as-nails General Mansfield. He was a man rumored to have earned a purple heart as an officer in Bosnia and earned a star when he was asked by the President to fill a gap in leadership during the start of the second Iraqi war. Rain swallowed her fear as General Mansfield stood front and center, his blue army uniform looking as if it hadn't ever been wrinkled or out of place, his buttons shining under the pot lights. The folds of his cheeks indicated he had dimples when he smiled, but Rain doubted anyone had ever seen them as he stared through rigid eyes. As Rain and Willow sat in the two seats next to each other behind a desk swallowed up in the vast room, the commander cleared his throat loudly.

"Sergeant Wilson and Sergeant Willow, we want to commend you on neutralizing the subject that held Mr. Christopher Dalton this morning. Your heroism will not be forgotten at this base or any other in the region. Do either of you know who Mr. Christopher Dalton is?" His hazel eyes looked through their sagging lids for an answer.

"No, sir," Willow said, and looked at Rain for the same answer.

"Yes, sir. I know Mr. Dalton," Rain answered, avoiding Willow's surprised blue eyes.

"So you do know Mr. Dalton, Sergeant Wilson? He was pretty happy to hear that you were the one who'd made that shot today."

The commander smoothed back his eyebrows and clicked his tongue in his cheek, leaning far back in his chair. "That shot today brings me to another line of questioning. Who gave you the authority to make that shot?"

The room was silent. The five other members, mute, moved uncomfortably in their seats awaiting an answer. The gray-haired woman on the far right was the only one to keep her gaze fixed directly on Rain's face.

"I did," Willow blurted through the silence. "I told her to take the shot."

Willow grabbed Rain's leg under the table as she tried to refuse his answer and tell the truth. The tight grip made her lips seal shut. The truth was that she'd done it on her own. She'd told him not to call it in, which was direct insubordination. She hadn't followed protocol, taken the law into her own hands to save Dalton. She'd selfishly made the choice knowing Dalton was the only link to her mother. Rain couldn't allow Willow to take the fall for her. She wouldn't be able to live with herself.

"He didn't . . ." Rain sputtered. Her words weren't coming out the way she wanted them to.

"Sir, can I have a moment? I think Sergeant Wilson may still be in shock from the day's events. She's not been well since," Willow pleaded to the panel. The commander glanced at all the members before nodding his head.

Willow dragged Rain into the empty hall, looking over his shoulder for anyone listening, but no one was there. "Sergeant Wilson, listen to me. Don't tell them what really happened up there. They'll be looking for a scapegoat if Dalton wants to sing to the higher-ups about his near-death experience or about how the army put him in danger. This goes deeper than you or I could ever know." His eyes bore through her, begging her to heed his warning.

"I'm not going to let you take the fall for this. Trust me, I know how it works, Sergeant Willow." Rain looked over her shoulder, paranoid. "I was placed here by Christopher Dalton."

Willow leaned back, pushing his hands through his cropped cut and wiping his forehead in disbelief. Rain knew he would never understand why she was so confused and in shock after the shooting. What was Dalton doing on the base she was watching? Was it a coincidence that he needed to be saved by a sniper? The one sniper he knew could save his life? There were too many loose ends and Rain was digging through every possible angle, coming up empty each time.

"Why...what...I don't understand," Willow muttered. His normally strong features softened as he looked at her, searching for an answer she couldn't give.

"I don't know what's going on, either, but my gut tells me it's something deeper than what happened here today. And I always trust my gut," Rain said with conviction. "We need to talk to Dalton. I need some answers."

"Roger that," Willow said, his eyes still searching the hall, trying to figure out his next move. "They probably have him in the command clinic. He looked pretty banged up."

"True, but how're we going to get to him? They'll have Dalton sewn up tight after the threat on his life."

"Let's just get through this briefing and we'll figure something out. Since you know Dalton, he'll be able to scrub my record if I get crucified for calling the shot, right?" Willow looked scared but focused. The wheels were turning. He was coming up with a plan.

"Sure. He'd do it, I guess. He's not the most reliable, but if we have something he wants, he'll work with us."

"What does he want?"

Rain frowned at the question. "Dahlia."

Willow looked confused but Rain wasn't ready to tell him about her shoddy family history. She needed to get through the briefing without being court martialed so she could find Dalton and ask him about her mother and why he was in Iraq in the first place.

"I'll tell you more after we get out of here. After, let's find Dalton and talk to him. He has answers I need," Rain said, her spirit rejuvenated now that she had a semblance of a plan. She opened the door to the briefing room and Willow filed in behind her, taking his seat before the panel.

"Commander, I fired the rifle without permission because there was an imminent threat. If the attacker had made it back to the vehicle, you and I both know we'd be scraping Mr. Dalton from the roofs of those cars, instead of treating his injuries in our hospital." The commander's eyes bucked open wide at her curt. "As for Sergeant Willow, he was doing a fine job of taking out insurgents on the sandy area, covering Mr. Dalton's safety from the secondary attackers. My apologies if we did not handle the job appropriately or to standard, but under the conditions we made a choice that saved the lives of countless soldiers, maintained the security of the base, and saved a high-ranking official that'll get to see his family again . . . sir." Rain said in a rush of air, her head held high. She felt good getting it out, ending the commander's inquiry. She could feel Willow's eyes on her but she stared straight into the commander's eyes, unwavering.

The commander, at a loss for words, looked down the panel at the softened faces staring back at him. They'd understood the logic behind the shooting, maybe even saw themselves in Dalton's position. All of them would have wanted Rain to take the shot, save their lives.

"Sergeant Wilson, even though that was a statement full of conviction, your actions of insubordination cannot go unnoticed by the command." General Mansfield leaned into his microphone as if there was an audience listening instead of two soldiers in a sea of empty seats. "We are taking you from the tower until further notice. You will be on desk duty until the investigation has been reviewed and voted on by the panel."

"Yes, sir," Rain said, looking at the faces on the panel and seeing allies.

"Sir, what about me?" Willow asked under veiled eyes.

"You are to remain in the tower until further notice," the commander said definitively. Rain felt her heart split at the thought of being away from Willow for any length of time. Her punishment was not desk duty; it was separation from Willow.

"Sir, I'd like to volunteer for desk duty, as I didn't call the shot in like I should have. I can't let Sergeant Wilson take the entire blame for today's events knowing I did not do my duty as well." Willow glanced at Rain quickly as she hid a smirk.

"Well I can say that that's the first time I've ever had a soldier insist on being reviewed." The commander looked at Sergeant Willow through squinted eyes, searching his face for his purpose. "Your honesty is refreshing, Sergeant Willow, but as you stated, the day's events have cast doubt on both your abilities to hold the safety of this base at its highest regard. Both of you are to check in at 354th Replacement Battalion by zero eight hundred tomorrow with your full incident reports. Meeting adjourned."

The commander stood from behind the polished desk, his broad chest and shoulders squaring to the soldiers below. He studied them as he walked out the rear door behind the other panel members. He wasn't sure whether to congratulate the two for a job well done or investigate their odd behavior in the briefing. Either way, he'd have more than enough time to learn about Sergeant Willow and Sergeant Wilson in the investigation he'd sprung on them. He wasn't going to leave any stone unturned with those two. The part he'd hated most was that Sergeant Wilson had made the fatal shot that killed the attacker and saved Mr. Dalton. He'd have felt much better if Sergeant Willow would have finished him. It could've saved the army the threat of an external investigation and stopped the CIA from digging a new cavity in his ass. Now he had to face the media swirl about the shooting. He'd heard the headlines, despised their interest in the girl soldier that saved the CIA's chief of staff. What was the world coming to? This was a man's job, he thought to himself. The media loved a hero and he wanted to give them a real, true hero to sink their teeth into.

FINDING CHRISTOPHER DALTON WAS like entering a labyrinth. With the help of Willow's friends, a few marines he'd traveled with on his last assignment, they'd found the command clinic and made it inside two empty rooms that Dalton had occupied. Unfortunately, the command had moved him to another location, fleeing from hospital beds to medical buildings around the base.

Willow asked the corpsman behind the receptionist desk once more for his whereabouts, hoping the computer would access his latest location. The kid pounded on the keyboard, glancing up at Rain every five seconds.

"You know, I can get in big trouble for doing this, Prescott." Rain smiled at Willow's first name; she didn't realize she'd never asked.

"Don't worry about it. No one will know. It's our little secret." Willow warmed the young boy up, kept his fingers typing across the keys in a steady *clickity clack.*

"Ah, here we go," the boy said, looking at Rain as she leaned over the receptionist-style desk to see the computer. "Hey, who is she?" He turned his screen from her view with a look of distrust, finally brave enough to ask.

"She's my battle buddy. She has some important information for Mr. Dalton about the shooting today. We need to see him, bud." Willow smiled at the young kid, his cheeks reddening under Willow's gaze.

Rain saw a flicker of jealousy in his eyes when he looked at her again, unsure of whether to proceed in the search. She scooted down the desk, away from Willow, and smiled at the boy. They needed his access.

Her spacing must've satisfied his urge because the printer shot out a sheet of paper within seconds. The boy quickly grabbed it, looked around the edge of the desk, stuffed the paper in an envelope, and stamped CONFIDENTIAL in red on the front.

He handed the letter to Willow, then said, "Oh, almost forgot . . . it's gotta be sealed." He curled his fingers signaling Willow to give the letter back. Once he had it in his hands, he licked the envelope's flap, never taking his eyes from Willow's. Once he'd finished his seduction and full-on paper rape, he handed it back to Willow with a shy smile.

"There you go," he said, happy that he could give Willow something he wanted.

Rain looked on with displeasure. The nagging urge to snatch the envelope from Willow and rip it to shreds crept up the back of her neck but she discarded the feeling and stayed focused on the plan. She didn't have time for foolish possessiveness over a man who had no interest in her.

"Thanks, Lance." Willow popped the envelope against his palm.

"Remember, you need to show the guards that envelope to get in. I'll call ahead and tell them you're on the way with an important message from Dalton's medical doctor. Don't let anyone open it, okay?"

"No problem. You're a lifesaver," Willow said to the beaming boy behind the counter before escorting Rain from the medical building out into the breezeway.

Once they were alone in the breezeway, Rain blurted, "You're gay?"

She hoped and prayed for the right answer. Her heart fluttered waiting for Willow as he laughed loudly in the corridor and said "No" between breaths.

"Of course not, Sergeant Wilson." He chuckled. "I can't be gay if I'm interested in you, now can I?" He winked slyly.

Rain felt the heat rise from her neck and into her cheeks. She looked at the ground, away from his eyes that were delighted by her shyness.

"How can you shoot a guy in the head so easily but can't even take a simple compliment? I don't think I'll ever understand women." Willow shook his head with a smile and started down the corridor, leaving Rain looking at her boots. "You don't have to worry about me coming on to you. I know we have a job to do. I won't complicate things," he said, turning at the end of the breezeway.

Rain felt silly for being so vulnerable and naive. He was right—there was too much riding on them making it to Dalton and cracking the mystery of his arrival to get sidetracked with a schoolgirl crush, even if he was handsome and irresistible.

"Okay. Cool." Rain couldn't say much else as she picked up the pace to meet Willow. It was the first time a guy had ever said he was interested in her. It felt foreign to her to be wanted but it comforted her to know someone finally saw her as a woman, not a girl.

FIVE

ETTING TO DALTON PROVED easier than Rain expected. The confidential letter seemed to light the path to his bedside. His room was large and his bed hid behind a white curtain, the sound of his cell phone keys clicking rapidly as a television droned on in the distance about a shooting on the base. "No additional information yet on the attempted assassination of CIA chief of staff Christopher Dalton . . ." a reporter said, her voice irritatingly perfect. Willow looked to Rain and nodded, making sure she wanted to do this. Rain nodded back and advanced on the curtain. The guards waiting outside the room would be more than happy to move them out at Dalton's command. Rain knew there wasn't much time—Dalton was a slippery snake who could wiggle out of her intense questions.

Dalton's voice cut through the silence, scaring Rain as it rang out, "Gretta, is that you? Bring me some water, will you?"

Rain scanned the room, spotted a water bottle by the entry, seized it, and snatched the curtain back.

"Your water, sir?" She handed the bottle to him. He took it from her without looking up from his cell phone. After a few seconds, feeling the nurse was still standing nearby, he looked up with eyes that filled with mixed emotion.

"Rain Wilson . . . have a seat. Please." His hand flicked to the chair at his bedside. Rain was caught off guard; he actually seemed pleased to see her there. He looked over his shoulder, finding Willow there. "Who's he?"

"He's my battle buddy. Can't go anywhere without him," Rain said.

"What's up?" Willow said confidently, leaning on the arm of Dalton's bed, inching the call button from his reach inconspicuously.

"Nice to meet you . . ." Dalton searched for his name.

"The name's Sergeant Prescott Willow." He smiled.

"What is this, some type of secondary ambush?" Dalton chuckled to himself, typing on his cell phone keyboard with his thumbs at a rapid pace.

"No, sir. We're just coming for answers," Rain said easily.

Dalton stopped typing, rested the cell phone on the thin cover over his protruding belly. "Answers, huh? Everyone wants answers, yet no one can handle the truth. So which do you want, Rain? You want answers or you want the truth?"

"I'd like the truth . . . if you could remember what that is."

"Still feisty, I see. Is she like this with you, too?" Dalton turned to Willow who had just managed to unhook the call button from his armrest as it landed on his boot quietly.

"Oh yes . . . all the time. But I like 'em feisty, sir." Willow winked at Rain, acknowledging that his part of the plan had been completed.

"Stop fooling around, Dalton. I want to know why you came here and, more importantly, why you sent *me* here," Rain said, leaning forward to retrieve Dalton's cell phone. He grabbed for it but Rain was too quick, slipping it into her cargo pants pocket.

"That's top secret information you're trying to extract from a high-ranking official with nothing but the safety of the American people on his mind. You sure you want to go down this road, little girl?"

Rain couldn't resist the urge to slap his face. Her hand darted out and smacked the chubby skin of Dalton's cheek. It rippled from her power.

"What the . . ." Dalton held his face. "Do you even know what you've just done? You could get court martialed . . . no, *jailed* for putting your hands on me . . . and, and . . . stealing my phone! Are you trying to go to jail . . . is that it?"

Willow's blue eyes scanned Rain's face as her chest heaved beneath her top. She hadn't expected to actually strike him, but he was so unnerving. As he kept talking, keeping her fist out of his face was proving more difficult.

"Look, Mr. Dalton, we just want answers. My friend here is a little fed up with your . . . how do you guys say it back in Washington . . ." Willow snapped his finger. "Your *bullshit*. Yeh, that's the proper term. Give her the answers she needs or I'm going to accidentally put you in a whole lotta pain. Understood?"

"You can't touch me," Dalton spat between gritted teeth. Rain could see that his eyes didn't quite believe what his mouth was saying.

Willow found the soft, mushy spot where Dalton had been bludgeoned in the attack and pressed his thumb roughly against his skull as Dalton retched in pain. The curses spewed from Dalton as he held Willow's wrist, trying his best to pull Willow's thumb off his pounding wound. Rain looked toward the door, fearing the guards would overhear his wails.

"It's a good thing they moved you to a quiet room, huh?" Willow said, acknowledging Rain's concern and erasing it with his own bit of knowledge.

"You are dead . . . dead for this." Dalton winced, his glasses crushed on the bed under his weight.

"You first," Rain said, with more anger than sarcasm. "Tell me why you sent me here."

Dalton squirmed in his bed, his legs bending and unbending under the pink covers publicizing his pain. Willow's thumb circled on the freshly sewn, now-dripping wound.

"Shit, you're just like your damn mother," Dalton spat, eyes red from the tears that threatened to spill on his cheek. "You're here because we can't have you seen at the agency. We've found your mother and there's intel that she still keeps tabs on you and your father."

Rain nodded to Willow who released his thumb from the wound. Dalton breathed heavily before snatching the napkin offered between Willow's index finger and thumb. Rain stood near his bed. The thought that her mother still cared about her . . . and Tolley, made her heart skip a beat. She needed to find her, let her know she was okay and that she wanted her to come home.

"Well, when can I go see her?"

Dalton chuckled. "You're not going to see her, Rain. She's too far gone." He winced at the soggy red napkin he blotted against his hairline. "Like we speculated, she's rogue, completely embedded in the Russian Mafia."

"That's not true," Rain said, feeling the anger rise again at the lies he was telling.

"Told you. You don't want the truth." Dalton rolled his eyes. "Are we done here? I need a nurse."

Willow looked at Rain. "He's right, Sergeant Wilson. That cut is gushing pretty badly."

Rain leaned against the bed. "What were you doing here today? It's no coincidence that I saved your life."

Dalton smirked. "You're smarter than I gave you credit for."

"You still want to thumb wrestle with Sergeant Willow?" Rain said smartly.

Dalton swiveled to Willow, assuring him with his eyes that he didn't want to wrestle.

"I came here with the hope of setting your mother up. She needs to know you're in the army, in Baghdad at war. We were hoping she'd reach out to you. You know, have some ounce of a heart for her child. Sadly, we were wrong. She hadn't tried to make contact in a year and I can't wait much longer. We checked your mail, email, your calls, and even your house in Colorado. It all turned up nothing. I had to do something, something to make sure she *noticed* you."

"So all of it was fake? The shooters, the ambush? The deaths were a *game* to you?" Willow interrupted, stunned.

"No, not all of it was fake. For one, I wasn't planning on getting taken by a couple of damn jihad extremists and getting knocked over the head." He rubbed the tender part around his wound. "The ambush was not planned, just the car bomb. You were supposed to call it in. Be the hero. Unfortunately, things got out of hand."

Rain wobbled against the bed and steadied herself. All those lives lost under her perch in the tower were in vain, some sick joke to get her mother's attention. Why would they do this? What kind of information did they need from her mother so badly?

"Wilson, we're out of time," Willow said as the door to the room opened and a portly black nurse pulled back the curtain, shocked to find two strangers huddled around Mr. Dalton's bed.

"Do you guys have clearance to be back here? Mr. Dalton, are you okay?" she asked, eyeing the two soldiers suspiciously.

The silence was deafening as Dalton looked from Willow to Rain and back to the nurse who stood even more cautious at Dalton's prolonged stare between the two.

"It's okay, Gretta." Dalton smiled. "These were the two that saved me today."

"Oh . . . well, thank you for your service." Gretta smiled and began searching for Dalton's call button. "Mr. Dalton, you've dropped your button clean under the bed," she said as she gripped the metal rail and peered underneath. She reached down without a second thought, her rear end waving in the air as she fished for the plastic wand that Willow had kicked far from reach. When she finally managed to grab the button and slide it back onto Mr. Dalton's bedside table, she realized the two soldiers had vanished.

"Gretta, be a doll and get General Mansfield on the line," Dalton said as his face twisted into a wicked smile.

"Sure thing, sir." Gretta smiled kindly and set the portable phone from the wall in Dalton's hand as it rang.

"This is General Mansfield." His voice was harsh on the line even though it was meant to be a greeting.

"General, this is Christopher Dalton."

General Mansfield coughed. "Oh, yes, sir. How are they treating you in the hospital? Better quarters than the last one I hope."

"Oh, I'm fine. Even better now that I was paid a visit by your darling of a soldier, Rain Wilson, and her sidekick. What was his name again? Willow, I believe."

General Mansfield was taken off guard but wouldn't give Christopher Dalton the satisfaction of knowing it. How'd they manage to get close to the chief without his knowledge? He had 100 percent security around the clock, or so he thought.

"I'm sorry if they've disturbed you, sir. I'll make sure to have a word with them about interrupting you while recovering."

"Oh no, there's no issue of a disturbance, per se. But there is an important request that I need you to carry out," Dalton said easily.

"Sure. If I can't do it or get it, then it can't be done." The general sounded assured of himself.

"I want them both relieved of their duty."

"Sir?" Mansfield wasn't sure he'd heard the request properly. Was

Dalton requesting he fire the two people that had saved his life?

"You heard me, General. I want them released by the end of the day. Call me when it's done."

"But sir, they saved . . ."

"Oh, and another thing . . . make sure you get my cellular phone from Rain Wilson immediately and return it to me straight away. There is some important information awaiting my reply. I'm sure you understand the severity of the situation, General?"

"Yes, sir, but how did she get your phone?" General Mansfield was hoping he could find something to smear Sergeant Wilson's name after all. Instead, he heard the click of the line in response. He leaned back in his chair in disbelief listening to the empty toll of the dial tone. The day was getting stranger by the hour. First, a terrorist cell brings the fight to the front gate, and he was still trying to figure out how they happened to nab the chief of staff of the goddamn CIA in the process. He was the most guarded and highly sought after potential prisoner of war. The secrets he held inched him to the top of most terrorists' hit list. General Mansfield had checked and double-checked the status reports and he could find no schedule or report of Dalton's visit to the base that day, or any day in the near future. Mansfield spun around in his seat and faced the carved wooden plaques lining his office wall. Something wasn't fitting right with Christopher Dalton and now Rain Wilson. He needed to talk to Sergeant Rain Wilson. She seemed to have some business with Dalton that frazzled him enough to call a favor from the base commander. Plus, he thought it'd be a good idea to get his tech guys on that cell phone before they returned it to Dalton. There might be information he could use on that phone to at least catapult him into a new starched coat with a second gold star. He smiled at the thought of blackmailing his way into leadership as he fingered the number to the base police from memory. Hadn't all leaders forged their way by dragging through the piss and shit of the military life?

When a voice answered with its customary dry greeting, he gave strict instructions to bring Sergeant Wilson to him quickly and quietly. He explained that he had no use for Sergeant Willow and that the sergeant should be detained in the brig until further investigation of his crimes. Mansfield chuckled to himself after he'd smashed the speakerphone button to end the call. He thought the shooting this morning was going to wreck his image but with Rain Wilson, things were starting to look a little brighter.

SIX

RAIN PLOPPED DOWN ON the air mattress that doubled as her couch and dining room table depending on the time of day. Her space was a perfect square covering an eight-by-eight-foot space near the middle of the tent. Her makeshift shelves were cluttered with random items like cereal boxes, washing powder, and a dusty television with a DVD attached to its underbelly. She shared the space with eight other soldiers that had quarantined their areas for privacy. She was fighting the overwhelming feeling in her chest that she had crossed a line with Dalton. She hadn't gotten the answers from him that she wanted, and that left her completely vulnerable. And for a guy like Christopher Dalton who loved to prey upon others' vulnerabilities, she knew the incident today wouldn't go unnoticed or unpunished. She wanted to know where her mother was and how she could get her back, but Dalton wasn't releasing any information. He played mind games with her, confused her with his half-truths. That's why she'd snatched his phone—it seemed like the most important thing to him at the time.

Rain pulled the elastic band from her hair and let her dark strands fall against the pillow as she lay down across the bed fully dressed. She'd just returned from the hospital and Willow said he needed to check on a couple things before they reported to check-in. She heard the footsteps echoing in the empty tent before she saw her flimsy sheet dividing her space from the hallway rip back and reveal her bushy-haired roommate, Private Brianna Gills. Private Gills was like a little sister to Rain, always bringing her snacks from her mother's care packages. But Rain couldn't get over the fact that she had just bombarded her space without so much as a couple stomps on the plywood floor.

"They're coming for you." Gills panted, trying to catch her breath.

Rain sat up quickly, grabbing her rucksack and snatching the zipper open. "Who exactly?"

Gills looked back at the entrance to the tent with fear in her eyes. "The MPs."

"Shit," Rain said, sliding food into her bag with the sweep of her arm, snatching matches, bottled water, and a small wooden box from beneath her bed. "How long I got?"

"Five minutes. Maybe less." Gills was starting to catch her breath, the fear evident on her face. *She must've run to warn me,* Rain thought with a sense of friendship she'd never felt before. Gills stepped inside the curtain and let it fall closed behind her.

"I don't know if I should do this but I will," Gill said slowly.

Rain looked at the note in her outstretched hand. "What's this?"

"A message someone told me to give you. I didn't know who it was but they stopped me on my way here. Said it was important to give it to you. I wasn't going to. But now . . ." Gills trailed off.

Rain grabbed the message, put it in her pocket, and felt the cell phone that caused all this mess. She didn't have time to read it right now or dwell on the fact that she might be plastered on the news as a national security risk. She could sense that her five minutes were quickly dwindling down to two minutes.

Rain continued rushing around the small space, packing for a trip she had no idea she'd be taking. She had to get off the base, and fast. She knew if the military police found her, she'd be in the brig then shipped straight to Leavenworth with real hardened criminals, not the kind that stole cell phones.

"Sergeant Wilson, you better go now. I think I hear them."

Sure enough, Rain heard them, too. Well, not the voices of the actual police but the voices of the bystanders that questioned them as they passed. *Who are you after? What happened? Is this about the shooting?* The questions were loud enough to hear, which meant they were close enough to find her. Rain looked around the boxy, makeshift bedroom once more before snatching back the curtain and eyeing the front door. It cracked open softly as she ducked back into her room, bumping into Gills.

Rain slid a finger over her lips and nodded to Gills, who nodded back instinctively. Silence would be the key and a good ole stalling by Gills might get her out of there. The fear in Gills's eyes made Rain jolt. Her brown eyes matched the color of her dark skin and they looked like pools of chocolate against the sweetness of her round face. Rain hated to put her in this position but she had no one else. Rain surveyed the space and tried to think of an escape plan that didn't involve walking out the front door.

With that realization she grabbed Gills's hand quickly, mouthed the words *Thank you*, and escaped under the side curtain dividing her and her neighbor's living space. Rain remembered the housing tent had a hole by the floor near the back bedroom. They'd asked for it to be glued shut but no one had come to do it yet. *Maybe I could fit underneath the tent*, she thought quickly. Her neighbor's space was identical to hers except the bed was without a mattress and only blankets draped a green cot with steel legs. She shuffled past the bed and picked up the next curtain and inched into the next space. She slid around a makeshift dresser that was only four pieces of wood nailed together like a large box. She saw the boxes of cereal and canned goods lined up inside the box and lifted the curtain behind it. The next bedroom was at the rear of the tent where she remembered the hole being. She could wedge herself under the heavy tent material and come out in the sliver of space between the next tents. There wasn't another option since she heard the sound of the door creaking completely open as a voice yelled, "Military police!" into the quiet. The gruffness of the voice reminded Rain that she was up against the same type of men she had trained with at Langley. Men who only cared about following their orders even at the risk of their own lives or by ending someone else's. She remembered her training clearly. *One shot. One kill.* She pushed her bag through the hole quietly as she heard Gills talking to the police.

"Where's Sergeant Wilson?" the man with the voice like sandpaper demanded.

"Uhhh, she's not here, Master Sergeant," Gills said softly.

"No shit, Sherlock. I asked *where* she is, Private. Not where she's not," he said with attitude that felt like he'd slapped Gills across the face.

"I—I—I don't know. I just came here to see if she wanted to walk to the mess hall. We were supposed to meet at the mess hall," Gills offered, sounding more assured.

"The mess hall, huh?" The man sounded like he was peering around the tent, around her space as he spoke. Rain had pushed her legs under the tent and was still working on getting her upper body to squeeze through. "You wouldn't be lying to us, would you? That could get you in the brig."

"No. Why would I be lying? Why are you looking for Sergeant Wilson anyway? Didn't she just earn a medal for saving someone's life?" Gill quizzed the officer.

"I wouldn't go putting medals on her just yet. She might be wearing silver chains instead." He chuckled. Rain heard the laughter of the other men with him. Maybe two or three, she guessed. "Check the tent, fellas."

Rain squeezed her body under the tent but the flap wouldn't give enough for her shoulders. She felt the beads of sweat on her forehead dripping down her nose as she dug the toe of her boots into the sand outside the tent and pulled hard while trying to make herself as slim as possible. She heard the boots on the plywood and the soft *whoosh* of the curtains being pulled back. They were nearing the last bedroom and they definitely wouldn't miss an upper body sitting in the corner of the room. Rain struggled harder, jerking herself now as she felt the tent shaking with her movements.

"What's that?" the man said, his boots slapping on the wood loud enough to thunder in Rain's ears so close to the floor.

"What, Sarge?" one of the men in the adjoining room asked. He sounded close enough to touch through the curtain divider. Rain felt a hand grip her ankles hard enough to make her eyes buck in surprise. She felt the tug of someone pulling roughly, jerking her against the tent walls. She scanned the room, scared that the military police had found her and were pulling her out of the tent by her feet. Her shoulder released first and she caught a glimpse of the thick hand pulling back the curtain, the barrel of a pistol entering the room as she pulled her head from beneath the tent and sucked in the dry, humid air. She closed her eyes, reveling in how close she was to being caught or worse. Her eyes popped open instantly in alarm, remembering someone had pulled her out of the tent and she wasn't sure who. Standing at her feet gathering her rucksack and the water bottles was Willow, his sack already on his back like he had prepared for a camping trip months ago.

"Get to the mess hall!" The muffled voice came from inside the tent as the sound of boots on wood echoed through the thick vinyl-like material of the tent. Willow's face looked more worried than happy to see her, so

Rain rolled to her feet and trotted after him.

"Did you know this would happen?" Rain asked, eyeing Willow's sack, almost two times the size of hers.

"I had a feeling Dalton couldn't be trusted," Willow said, pushing her behind a tent as soldiers ran by in a hurry.

"I guess everyone on this base is looking for me." She looked behind the soldiers as they turned onto her row of tents and out of sight.

"Not only you. I had visitors when I got back to my tent, too." Willow's brow curled in agitation.

"How'd you get away? If it wasn't for Gills . . ." Rain trailed off. The thought of Gills getting in trouble stabbed at her. She groaned, "Gills . . ."

"She'll be fine. They'll interrogate her but if she sticks to her story, she'll be fine." Willow peered around the tent and started walking quickly toward the back gate. Rain had no idea how they were going to get off the base without being checked, rechecked, and cavity searched. Baghdad wasn't the type of place you toured around in your free time. They'd look suspicious going off base without military orders or a vehicle.

"What about getting off base?" Rain questioned. Willow heaved his pack to the ground and pulled out two sheets of paper. Orders?

"How the hell did you manage that without knowing we'd need them less than ten minutes ago?" Rain said in shock.

"Remember my friend at the hospital? He heard the order to capture us before we did. He knew what we'd need."

"Talk about friends in high places . . ." Rain said under her breath.

"Says the person who knows Christopher Dalton," Willow retorted. Rain winced at the sound of Dalton's name. He'd been a thorn in her side since the first day she'd seen him at Quantico.

"How'd you get the pack?" Rain questioned, eyeing his bulging rucksack.

"Why are you interrogating *me*? Didn't I just save your life?" Willow spun on her quickly. She almost bumped into him as she marched behind him in the sand just off the edge of the makeshift road that ran throughout the camp.

"It wasn't my *life* you saved. Just maybe a few years in jail," Rain said defiantly.

Willow rubbed a hand down his face and kept walking. "Do you always have to be a hard-ass, Rain?"

The sound of her name in his mouth made her trip over a sandy dip in the ground. She felt silly for doubting him.

"I'm sorry," Rain said to his back, keeping in step.

Willow shook his head. "Look, I thought I had time to get a few things but they were already at my tent when I got there. I keep an emergency pack in the tower. That's what took me so long to get to you. Okay?"

Rain remembered that it was protocol to have a pack in the tower in case they had to flee on foot. Her emergency pack was there as it should have been, tucked beneath the table waiting under a thick layer of dust. She kicked herself for not thinking of that when she was in the tent. She didn't have to put Gills at risk if she would've remembered. Rain felt silly for being high strung and taking it out on Willow. He had indeed helped her escape prison and kept his head cool enough to even secure walking papers.

Willow glanced around under his desert cap. "Do you want to try and get your pack in the tower? I'm pretty sure that's going to be under watch, though." His blue eyes pierced her with worry. It was the first time Rain had seen Willow without a smile or a joke. *Fear is not a good look on his handsome face*, Rain thought.

"No. I think I've got enough to last me a few weeks in my bag." She shifted the ruck strap on her shoulder. "Where are we going? We need to get off the road."

"I've got keys to a vehicle. We're getting the hell out of here," Willow said with new vigor.

"And then?"

"And then . . . I don't know."

She pushed her cap low over her eyes and tucked her dark hair into the back until she looked more like a boy than a woman. She felt the weight of the cell phone in her pants pocket and remembered the note Gills had given her from the stranger. She fished it out and read it quickly before balling it up and tossing it to the ground in confusion. *Trust no one,* Rain recited the note in her head. She wondered who had given it to Gills and how they knew she would be in trouble. Rain had more problems to think about. They had to find a place to hide and figure out what all this was about. She wanted to get into Dalton's phone and see if there were any clues on her mother's whereabouts. And most of all, she needed to call Tolley.

SEVEN

"**D**ad?"

"Rain?" Tolley edged the phone deeper into his shoulder to hear the voice clearly.

"It's gone bad. It's gone . . ."

"Stop talking. I'll call you back on this number in twenty."

He hung up the phone quickly and put on his trousers. Rebecca Billingsley was strewn across his massive king-size bed, her bare leg creamy and smooth, pale in contrast to his dark-gray comforter. He yearned to get back into the sack with the wild woman who had made him feel like a man again. She'd done things with her body only a contortionist could attempt. He shook away the thought as he slipped on his shoes and walked bare-chested to the front room. He opened his gun cabinet in an office that looked more like a storage room with boxes layering the desktop and papers hanging out of four-foot steel filing cabinets in colorful folders. His desk was barely visible under the chaos. He'd given up trying to keep accounting files for the ranch years ago. It had been Dahlia's job when she was there. He'd told himself he'd clean it out last summer and the summer before but couldn't find the time. But he knew exactly where everything was in his chaos, which made it better for the snooping eyes he figured would eventually come. He thumbed the key hanging behind his Smith & Wesson .357 Magnum with the wooden grip. He'd loved shooting that gun years ago, made him feel like a real badass back in the day. He swept it aside now, looking for the small key with the circular top hanging on a nail behind it.

He rushed back into the bedroom and slid the wooden box from under the bed as Rebecca stirred. Her lips were pink from the forceful kisses she'd planted all over his body like she would die without him inside her.

"What's wrong, sweetie?" she said, propping her head on her hand sleepily.

"Something's wrong with Rain and I need to talk to her. Go back to bed." Tolley planted a kiss on her forehead and swept the hair from her temple. She looked as if she wanted to say more but couldn't get it out.

"You sure you don't need anything?" she said, finally laying her head back on the goose-down pillows. Her milky breasts were illuminated in the dim room, the nipples taut and pink. Tolley looked her over a second longer as her head slid into the dent she'd left in the pillow, and within minutes she was sound asleep.

Tolley shut the door gently behind him and tiptoed to the stale-smelling basement. The stairs creaked under his weight as he padded to the bottom. He pulled the hanging bulb and light splayed across the chilly space illuminating his old tools. His equipment was stored along the cinder-block wall, hanging neatly on drilled-in pegs all the way up to the ceiling. It reminded him of the shooting range and how vast the wall looked as it displayed large and small handguns. Instead of guns hanging, he had tools. He eyed the tools he'd used in the past and to the untrained eye looked like a construction worker's wet dream but he knew better. He and Dahlia had received many answers from the use of those tools and he couldn't find it in himself to part with them after leaving the CIA so many years ago, or with the memory of his partnership, his marriage to Dahlia. Tolley jammed the key into the wooden box and opened the lid until it rested on the worktable. He fished through the passports and stacks of money from all areas of the world. He dug to the corner of the box until he found what he was looking for. A black universal phone, untraceable and always available. He turned it on and the screen came to life with the words *TacticalEdge* jumping across the face in digital jitters. He was grateful his battery was still good after all these years. The phone was older than Rain but he'd managed to invest in a fine piece of technology that he'd hoped would last long enough for a day like today. Within minutes, he'd dialed the number and it rang twice before Rain answered.

"Is everything okay, Dad?" she said without a hello.

"Yes, but more importantly, how're you doing? I'm on a secure line now."

"How'd you . . . never mind. I need your help. Things have gone very, very wrong here. Christopher Dalton showed up on the base this morning. I ended up saving his life," Rain said without a hint of pride or enthusiasm.

"Hmmm . . ." Tolley breathed to himself. Rain could hear the wheels turning in his head the same way hers had when she'd spotted Dalton in her scope. "What's he doing in Baghdad?" Tolley said, more to himself than to Rain.

"I don't know. I had the same question but didn't get answers when I talked to him in his hospital room. He's a real asshole."

"Rain, watch your damn mouth. He's in the hospital? Is he hurt badly?" Tolley asked eagerly. A little too eagerly, Rain noticed.

"He's bruised up but he'll live."

"Alright, then what do you need help with? Sounds like you'll be a bona fide hero in a few days once the story gets out." Tolley let himself ease against the worktable that groaned with his weight. He saw the shadows dance around the basement as the naked bulb still swayed gently from the low ceiling.

"Dalton tried to have me detained."

"What the hell? Detained for what?" Tolley said, tensing.

"Well, we kind of threatened him and stole his cell phone," Rain said like a smile child awaiting punishment.

"Who's *we*?" Tolley said, picking apart the story in an instant.

"Sergeant Prescott Willow is on the run with me. He was my enforcer, so to speak. Unfortunately, we didn't get any answers from the fat man," Rain said, looking over her shoulder at Willow who was listening intently, his blue eyes scanning her face as he slumped against a dried-out drainage pipe protruding from the sand.

"Rain, you do realize the shit storm you're in, I hope," Tolley said under his breath. Rain could envision him shaking his head at her like the time she was eight and let all the chickens out of the coop with the idea that they should be free like other birds. He'd shook his head at her that night as she gobbled the remaining bits of meat off the bones of the same chicken she'd tried to free. The circle of life. Now she was playing a dangerous game of hide-and-seek with Christopher Dalton, the last person Tolley wanted to tango with again. Once again, the circle of life. He'd known he'd meet up with Dalton again, just not this soon and under these circumstances.

"Yes, I realize it. *We* realize that he's not going to stop until he gets us," she said sadly.

"Well, you said you got Dalton's phone, right? People are gonna be hunting y'all down like rabid dogs for that thing. Find a place to hole up. You'll need to catch a flight out of Baghdad, like, yesterday," Tolley instructed.

"How're we going to get a flight? They'd snatch us at the airport if we step two feet in the front door."

"That's why you're not stepping in the front door. You're leaving out the back," Tolley said without a hint of doubt. "Meet you at your location in twenty-four to forty-eight hours."

"Wait, how will you know where we are?" Rain said quickly.

"Tracking device. Turn the phone off when we end the call and take the battery out. I'll see you in a few days."

"Okay, I will. Dad?"

"Yeah, Rain?"

"Thank you," she said softly.

"Keep your head low. You know how to survive in the field. Call this line if you get into any trouble," Tolley said with a sigh.

Rain could tell he was worried about her alone in a hostile country. Well, not exactly alone, she thought to herself, glancing behind her at Willow, his blue eyes piercing hers. He tore his gaze away, hoisting their packs into the drain pipe.

Rain ended the call and looked around the sandy dunes of Iraq before dismantling the phone as Tolley instructed. She slipped the memory chip into her bra and stuck the phone parts into her cargo pocket. Rolling hills of loose, quicksand-like grains fanned into the air with a strong wind and scratched at her eyelids. Rain lifted the scarf from her neck and covered her nose. She'd found the scarf in her rucksack during the long trek into the desert. She felt so tiny in the middle of the vast desert, its wind kicking up in the distance making the horizon look foggy and gray despite the sweltering sun. She glanced back at Willow, now sitting in the sand finding shade from the large roundness of the drain that smelled of rust and mildew. Rain followed the drainage opening and saw that the drain extended fifteen feet then sank beneath the sand, disappearing into the brown unknown. Rain realized there could be a town close by if they followed the drain pipe.

"We should hole up in the drain. It's good cover and we'd be safe from being spotted," Willow said grimly, dusting sand off his thighs and standing with a wince. The hike into the desert had been nearly fifteen miles of stumbling around in the one-hundred-ten-degree heat on loose sand, traveling away from a road that held their abandoned, gasless vehicle. They only held the hope that no one could track them. Willow's brown T-shirt clung to his body like a second skin, dark patches of soaked cloth ran down his spine, and a ring had formed around his neck and armpits. Despite the treacherous walk into the desert, Rain was surprised how easily they'd slipped off of the base. Willow had handed the orders to the gate guards and they eyed them through pitch-black lenses for only a few seconds then waved them on as if they had better things to do in Baghdad. Rain had let a rush of air escape her as they'd peeled out onto the pavement that looked like it was drowning in golden sand. The ground waved as the wind had carried the sand across the road in ripples and the tires of the SUV ground into the cement at high speed. They weren't only escaping the base but rushing into hostile territory. Rain didn't know what was worse: sitting in jail or the possibility of running into al-Qaeda.

"Think we'll be safe in there overnight?" Rain gestured to the pipe.

Willow nodded. "Yeah, as safe as we can be in Iraq."

The sound of whirring floated on the dusty winds that blew warm against Rain's face, scratching against her eyes as she closed them briefly. The sound broke through her thoughts and she stared up at the sky, searching for the source.

"Get in here!" she heard Willow yell to her before she felt his firm grip on her forearm. She half ran, half slid as he pulled her into the drainage pipe before she could fully squint through the haze. The whirring grew louder as the sand kicked up violently and swirled in tornado-like cylindrical shapes. The loud hum of the helicopter engine and constant *whoop whoop whoop* of the propellers were thunderous in Rain's ears. She felt the helicopter hover over the drain pipe for a second too long, long enough to make Rain's finger tense against her Glock. Protocol was that every military personnel leaving the base would have their weapon, and she was thankful for it. The sand settled as the sound faded into the distance at high speed. The pipe was not tall enough to stand in, so Rain stooped on one knee, quieted the fast pace of her heart. *That was too close*, she thought to herself. Willow was sitting in the traces of sand and debris on the floor of the pipe, staring out at the horizon, at the butt of the helicopter getting smaller and smaller until all was quiet.

"Goddammit." Willow slapped his knee in frustration. His eyes were deep blue, almost dark enough to look like the blackest part of the ocean. He knew they were in a bad situation and he was also aware that they may not last the few days until Rain's dad found a way to get them out.

"How did they get so close?" Rain questioned.

"Close? Rain, they are looking in every crack and crevice for us. You think Christopher Dalton or General Mansfield are going to let up? They've been trained to do this. You know, *find* people who don't want to be found." Willow tried to squelch his irritation but the corner of his eye winced involuntarily.

Rain could sense that he knew both men did more than find people but he was sheltering her from what could inevitably happen to them both for going up against Christopher Dalton and General Mansfield. Rain shuddered at the thought.

"We can't leave this area. My father is coming. We just need to hole up for another day. He'll get us out." Rain sounded assured as Prescott Willow turned to stare into her brown eyes brimming with quiet fear.

"Don't be scared, Rain. I didn't mean to scare you." Prescott pulled her head to his shoulder, fingers laced in her hair. She fell into his body, his musky scent mixed with sweat. She closed her eyes and felt his tight embrace cover her shoulders as she finally rounded him with her arms. His palms touched her back, rubbing in a circular motion that made her feel the safest she had felt since she'd landed in Baghdad a year ago.

"I'm sorry to bring you into this, Sergeant Willow," Rain said with her head on his chest, looking into the dark abyss of the drain pipe.

"Stop calling me 'Sergeant.' I think we can be on a first-name basis now, seeing as we're fugitives . . . and I'm pretty sure we've been stripped of our rank." Willow leaned his head against the rusty insides of the pipe, his neck revealing sweat and caked-on dirt as he swallowed. His voice was lighthearted but his eyes were filled with worry, stuck on what he'd lost, on what was to come. "Call me Prescott."

"Okay, *Prescott*," Rain said with a smirk. His name felt odd on her lips but she liked feeling close enough to use it.

"You know, in times like these, it makes me wonder why things happen the way they do. Who would have known that I'd end up in the tower with you and be where you needed me at the right moment at your tent? It's starting to feel a little bit like fate to me." He turned his head to look at Rain closely.

He brushed a sweaty patch of dirt from her forehead and Rain felt his eyes on her lips. She licked them involuntarily, feeling the grit of sand in her mouth. She could feel his breath on her face, sweet and warm.

"Fate, huh?" Rain whispered.

She felt Prescott's moist lips on hers as he lowered his head and pressed into her with a hunger she'd never felt before. Her body vibrated under his touch, his hand gripping the back of her head, pressing her deeper into the kiss until she felt his tongue travel into her mouth. A moan escaped her, startling her.

"I'm sorry . . . I shouldn't have . . ." Prescott pulled away. Rain felt his sensuality swirl around her and wondered why he'd stopped so abruptly. She yearned for more. She couldn't help but see the pain and confusion in his eyes. What was so painful about her kiss?

"Don't be sorry. I wanted you to . . . for a while now," Rain confessed, lowering her eyes with the shame she felt by his reaction.

Prescott seemed to pull himself together, his face brightening enough to smirk at her, but his eyes still hiding something behind them. He gently moved her off his chest until she sat next to him, breaking the hug and distancing their momentary bond.

"I wanted to as well but we have a lot going on. We should stay focused on our survival right now, okay?" Prescott said with finality, his eyebrows tightly knitted together.

"Mmm-hmm." Rain nodded but couldn't stop her heart from falling into the pit of her stomach. Was her first kiss *that* bad?

"You ready to tell me what exactly I got myself into?" He turned his eyes toward Rain, changing the subject.

She saw the exhaustion in the depths of his blue eyes. She didn't know if it was from her or from being on the run. Either way, she knew the root would always be her, a product of her decisions with Dalton. "I'm not even completely sure what's going on but I think Dalton has something to do with my mother's disappearance."

"Your mother's disappearance? What's so special about your mother anyway? Don't tell me all this is over you trying to get your parents back together or something crazy like that." He turned toward her, fully engaged and less brooding than two seconds ago. It didn't escape Rain that he had fully engaged only when emotions were not on the table. There was more to Prescott Willow than met the eye, Rain surmised in that split second.

"No. It's nothing that simple. I wish it was." Rain leaned back against the pipe next to Prescott, searching for the answers to his questions, or at least a good starting point. "My mother is . . . or *was* a CIA agent. She's been missing for over a year and Dalton is trying really hard to find her. A little too hard, if you ask me." Rain looked down at her fingernails, chipped and dirt-laden. She'd never cared much about her appearance on the farm, but sitting next to Prescott made her take notice of her femininity. Maybe it was his masculine edge that made her feel small, but with his body so close to hers, she found herself feeling more comfort in a dank, rusted pipe than she'd had since leaving the farm.

"Why would he want to find your mother so bad?" Prescott asked the same question Rain had asked herself since she'd spotted Dalton's face pressed against a pistol outside the gate.

"That's what I want to know, what I *need* to find out. He put himself in danger coming to Baghdad and I know it has something to do with me, with my mom."

"I'm not buying his story about your mother. It must be something big if he's risking his own life to find her. When's the last time you spoke to her or seen her?" Prescott said.

"Years," Rain said softly, pulling the scarf from around her neck.

"How can a mother leave her child for years? It's hard to believe she's never reached out to you." Prescott sighed to himself then glanced at Rain apologetically.

Rain shrugged. "Exactly. There's a lot of questions that need answering and that's why I'm trying to find her. I just want my mom back."

"What if she's not the mom you remember? What if she's as bad as Dalton thinks she is?" Prescott offered.

"Then I'll get my answers and leave her where she is."

"Just like that?"

"Just like that."

Prescott shook his head and looked out the pipe again at the horizon. The sun was slowly making its journey toward the waving sands, turning everything a reddish hue until it faded below the vista. Still, the heat didn't let up.

"I guess this is home sweet home for the night." Prescott waved a finger in circles. The darkness of the pipe's inner core looked like a cave that went on for miles until it faded into a tiny, black dot too far to see. Rain wondered where it led and if others used this pipe regularly. What if someone found them during the night? Prescott followed her eyes to the blackness.

"Don't worry, I'll stand watch while you get a little shut-eye." He pushed a stray strand of hair behind her ear, then took his hand away quickly. "Get some rest. You'll need it."

The feel of his hand and the twinkle in his eyes made Rain feel like maybe he was right about staying focused. It didn't mean he wasn't interested. She couldn't fault him if he just wanted to live long enough to have another kiss. Rain settled into a fetal ball against the curve of the pipe as Prescott climbed out and stretched outside the entrance. He raised his hands high and groaned in satisfaction, like a cat that had just woken from a long slumber. It had indeed been a very long day. Rain couldn't even imagine that only a few hours ago she had blown the head off an insurgent, saved Dalton's life, threatened and stole from him, and almost gotten captured, twice. Prescott peered around at the sandy dunes and didn't see anything moving in the dusk.

Rain said to Prescott's back, "Hey, I know I never said thanks for getting me off the base and all," she lowered her eyes, "but I'm glad you're here with me."

He pivoted in the sand to face her. His eyes looked sad, lips pursed tightly.

"Don't mention it." He turned around slowly, scanning the darkening horizon.Rain fumbled around in her pack before cracking open the lid on a bottled water and guzzling it down hungrily. The wetness stung against her dry throat, pushing the sand deeper into her belly. She'd have a desert cough for a week. Rain continued to watch Prescott as she settled her head against her pack and thought of being back on the farm. She saw her mother's big brown eyes, wet with emotion as she tucked back her hair and stared down her small frame. Rain felt the soft warmth of the kiss again as her mother laid her in her bed and waved from the doorway. There was no way that same woman, soft and gentle, was a murderer or rogue agent, as Dalton accused. Rain knew she had to help her. Help her clear her name and come back home.

RAIN HADN'T NOTICED THAT she'd fallen asleep until she felt the hands on her ankles, sliding her roughly from the pipe and onto the firm sand. Her head bounced against the sand with a muted *thud* before she could fully open her eyes into the pitch-black night.

"Get up!" The voice boomed in her ear, sending shooting pain down her neck. She felt the sleep fading away and her eyes catching the sight of two men dressed in tan cargo pants and brown T-shirts, both built like linebackers with their shirts stretched tight against their muscular bodies. They looked inhuman in size and stature. One man led the way to a black SUV, its lights casting a yellow glow in the darkness, highlighting the pipe's entrance. Rain could only see the black head of hair almost to his shoulders as he stormed toward the vehicle. The other man, a monstrous double for Quasimodo with his crooked nose and thin lips, obviously had the task of getting Rain into the vehicle. She noted the pistols on their waists and noticed that they weren't government issued. *Oh shit*, Rain thought. If the Iraqis had captured her and Prescott, there was only a slim amount of time before it was too late to save her own head and his. They were known for beheading their victims on national television when captured. They didn't look like Iraqis—military-style clothing, English speaking—but that was the least of her worries. She was captured and she needed to get away before she was put into the vehicle. She wrestled to stand but the ominous, bald man was dragging her, kicking sand in her face as he pulled her toward the vehicle. She saw the man with the long hair pull a black bag from the passenger-side door. Her adrenaline raced and her mind flared with so many ideas of escape. Once the black bag was on, she knew it was not going to be an easy escape. Nearly impossible. This was her only chance.

"Let go of me!" Rain scratched at the man's hand, which was in a vise grip around the collar of her shirt, choking her as he tugged.

"Stop fighting me or else I'll make you regret it. You hear me?" he yelled in the same booming voice that vibrated Rain's chest. She quieted but continued to fight, trying her best to get his grasp loose on her shirt while she wiggled out of it.

"Where's Presc—" she started but couldn't finish. She felt the punch to her face like a bolt of lightning that struck her to her core. She remained lucid but the darkness was slipping in. Her head bobbed rhythmically with the man's gait as he dragged her across the sand, closing in on the awaiting SUV. Rain tried to hold on to her consciousness—she needed to know where they were taking her, keep track of the turns, the minutes. She felt her fingers tightening around the man's hand for leverage as she groped for her weapon, which she left on her waist belt. Rain whimpered at the realization that it was gone as the man turned back and caught her watery gaze, her eye threatening to close, swelling instantly. The man released a sinister laugh at the resignation in her eyes; she knew she was captured but that hadn't diminished the fight left in her. Or so she thought. The second blow to her face made her limp. The pain settled into blackness and she heard and felt nothing.

EIGHT

"**D**ID THEY PICK HER UP YET?"

"Yeah. I saw them pull up."

"She didn't see you, did she?"

"No."

"Good. I may need you again. She seems to trust you," Dalton said into the phone easily.

"That's my job, right?"

"And a good job you are doing. Well done, Prescott. I was beginning to worry you were taking too much pleasure in hurting me at the hospital." He paused briefly. "Did she tell you anything about her mother? Any contact?"

"She doesn't know anything. She knows even less than you thought. She couldn't decrypt the phone messages."

"Good . . ." He chuckled. "Good. Just to make sure there's been no contact with Dahlia, I'm going to take her to the Basin. Then we'll know for sure if Dahlia has reached out to her and maybe get some helpful information out of her before she becomes completely useless to me."

Prescott feigned nonchalance as he said, "Do you think the Basin is necessary? I'm positive she doesn't know anything. She hasn't seen or heard from her mother in over ten years."

"Have you gotten off your mark, Prescott? Don't let the opportunity for a young piece of ass deter you from your mission. You do still want that immunity deal, don't you?" Dalton said with little amusement.

"Of course I want the deal, sir. You promised this was the last mission and I know your word is good, but I think she could lead me to her mother if she still trusts me. We could do this *clean*. She doesn't know anything but she's determined to find her. I think I've gotten further than any other plan you've had thus far."

"Hmm . . ." Dalton filled the air with a silence that made Prescott wonder if he'd hung up. "You can clean her wounds. Be the savior. How's that for a real love story? She'll be eating out of your hand if you save her from the big, bad wolf . . . *me*." Dalton chuckled deeply, amused with his impromptu plan.

"Her wounds? I don't want . . . need her wounded. I need her able to lead me to her mother."

"It's motivation, Prescott. She'll be more motivated to find mommy dearest with a little incentive. I'll tell the guys to save her arms and legs. Does that make you feel better? Hmmm?" Dalton said rhetorically. "Her hating me will compel her to find her mother much faster or draw out her mother into the open where I can get to her. And when she does, there will be no need for either of them anymore. The less she knows the better it is for her. I'm getting restless with this bitch and her puppy, Prescott. I need answers *now*, not yesterday, not next week or another year from now. Dahlia's getting closer to . . ." Dalton coughed with the realization that he was going off on a tangent and revealing much more than he intended to Prescott. "Just remember, while you're nursing your little puppy, you better watch out for her bite. Young teeth are sharp. If she has any part of Dahlia and Tolley in her . . . she'll kill you before you have a chance to kiss her good-night." Dalton's words reminded Prescott of the kiss they shared and how different it felt from any other kiss he'd ever had. It felt so real, so honest. He didn't know what to think when his nerves jolted as their lips touched. He was never nervous around girls. Dalton had explained to him that Rain Wilson was a black widow, very high kill ability and a fierce compassion for her family. Prescott couldn't see a black widow in Rain's sad eyes when she talked about her mother. All he saw was fear, confusion, and sheer determination. After the taste of her lips had taken him off his guard, he had to remind himself that he had a mission to complete and should not get close to the mark, no matter how many times he'd second-guessed it.

"She wouldn't hurt me. I'm a friend, remember? She's loyal to a fault. She's chasing down a mother who left her ten years ago, for Christ sakes." Prescott used Dalton's words against him. He needed Dalton to believe that the Basin would hurt the plan, not help it.

"It's settled then. Give me a few days with her then you can have your puppy back," Dalton said quickly. Prescott dropped his head in defeat. Rain was in for the worst days of her natural-born life, only she didn't even know how deep she was about to go into the depths of hell.

"Oh, and another thing . . ." Prescott saved the best news for last. "Tolley is on the way to Baghdad."

The silence on the phone swelled around Prescott like an air balloon as he waited for the loud pop that signaled Dalton's deflated ego. The mention of Tolley had hushed Dalton's bravado, put him in a trance.

"How long ago?" Dalton said coldly.

"Eight and a half hours at best."

"I take it he knows your location. If she talked to him, he's already found her," Dalton said matter-of-factly.

"I'd say so. She said he'd find us at the drainage pipe."

"Clean up around the pipe. Don't leave a speck of evidence. I want him to think you both disappeared into thin air. You understand?" Dalton had an edge to his voice that Prescott could only describe as fear. "When the job is done, go with Jordan and Tony to the airstrip. There's been a change in plans."

"We aren't going to the Basin then?" Prescott asked with a hint of a smile.

Dalton said with a menacing growl, "At least try to hide your excitement. You won't like this plan any more than the first plan."

The Basin was not a place that people visited and lived to speak about its horrors. Those that lived to tell the tale were undoubtedly in hiding somewhere and winced at the name if heard in even a whisper. Prescott felt the small airplane bounce over turbulence and heard the groan of the engine spring to life as it carried them higher a few more feet into smooth air. Rain was in the rear of the cabin, the steel-encased cargo hold, her body splayed out across the metal floor, no harness to stop her from bouncing with the plane. Prescott glanced over his shoulder, worried that she'd go sliding into the butt of the aircraft and suffer a concussion. Tony and Jordan, Dalton's personal cronies who had taken Rain from the pipe, were seated behind Prescott, their bodies like overinflated dummies, overtaking the thin seats on the aircraft. They sat in front of Rain's metal cage, locked tight with a thick chain snaked through the handle.

It reminded Prescott of the fence surrounding his grandfather's house, cheap yet strong. It kept constrained his grandfather's large Doberman from the outside world, the only thing keeping innocent people from an undesirable fate should they wander through the gate to drop off the mail or solicit his business. The single sign that hung on the gate, smacking on the fence with each small gust of wind, was small in contrast to the amount of trouble you'd be in if you'd missed it and wandered in. It said simply Beware of Dog in red script on a white background. Grandpa hadn't liked visitors. Or family. Or anyone breathing the air he breathed unless it was Rex, his Doberman and only known companion. After ten years, he'd found a way to tolerate the young Prescott, whom was named after him. His mother had wandered into the streets as a teenager after graduating from the school of hard knocks, left him on the doorstep of Prescott Willow, Sr. a week before his seventh birthday. Prescott had actually learned to love the old man who didn't speak much to him. He found solace in the messages he'd tape to walls and tables written in shaky script. *Take out the garbage* or *Do your homework*, he'd write, never speaking to Prescott and staying hidden behind the double doors to his bedroom as Prescott got older. He had written messages for years until he noticed Prescott no longer needed the notes as a reminder. It was just as well— Prescott had guessed that he was probably not well enough to write them anymore anyway. Prescott Willow, Sr. had aged quickly with early signs of dementia. By the time Prescott was eighteen and contemplating what he'd do with his life, Prescott Willow, Sr. was admitted to hospice for some rare form of cancer that Prescott knew nothing about, only that it was fatal without being diagnosed early on. And, well, Senior was not a people person and surely hadn't made it to the doctor in the twelve years since Prescott had arrived on his front porch. This left Prescott to call a nurse to the home when his grandfather wouldn't leave his room for days, not even to eat. Prescott appreciated his grandfather for taking him in but was saddened by the fact that he hadn't really known much about the old man throughout all his years living under his roof, one floor below him. His old Victorian house with the aged white lattice and wraparound porch was willed to Prescott's mother whom he discovered had died two years earlier from a drug overdose. Therefore, the house was his and even though he'd grown up there, it felt like he was trespassing on the old man's safe house so he enlisted in the army and never looked back.

Prescott glanced again at Rain, who was still in the same position as before, arm stretched out over her head, feet shaped into a V as her boots bounced with the turbulence. She'd been drugged in the vehicle on Dalton's orders. He winced at the sight of her eye. It had swollen into a bluish-purple hue and looked like someone had stuck a Ping-Pong ball under her cheekbone. She was still beautiful, he surmised. He couldn't figure out why she was going to such lengths to find her mother. He didn't feel any loss of his mother or grandfather, so the thought was incredibly confusing and foreign.

"Hey, what do you know about the boss's plan?" Prescott maneuvered in his seat toward Jordan, who was sitting diagonal to him. Jordan acted as if he didn't hear him, pushing his greasy black hair backward on his scalp and staring out the window at the endless sand dunes. His face reminded Prescott of a cartoon character with doe eyes big enough to cover his whole face. He'd have looked kind, had it not been for the menacing thick eyebrows that stayed hooded over his eyes. Prescott could tell he was the type to trust no one.

"Come on, guys. We are on the same team, right?" Prescott offered.

"Turn around, Willow." That came from Tony, the smaller of the two men but definitely the more dangerous. He kicked his long leg out past Prescott's seat and snuggled deeper into the seat like he was ready for a nap, but he didn't close his dark eyes. They stayed trained on Prescott.

"Tony, you guys act like I'm the enemy or something. I'm trying to help," Prescott said.

"Do we look like we need your help?" Tony said, smacking Jordan's arm as they both laughed together. Tony's smile was a chipped tangle of teeth, his goatee like a visual landing strip for his bad dental work.

"You may not need my help in the muscle department *apparently*, but who knows? We all have valuable skills. Dalton wouldn't have me on his team if I didn't have a skill he needed. You never know when *you* might need me." Prescott smiled genuinely.

"Us? Need you?" Tony laughed again. "I guess the boss put you on the plane to be the comedy act so we don't get bored. Do you hear this guy?" Tony said to Jordan again who was trying his best not to be a part of the conversation. Tony chuckled and shook his dark, bald head in amusement.

"I wish you'd both shut the hell up," Jordan finally interjected.

"You don't have to be a pussy about it," Tony said, frowning. "I'm just having a little fun."

"Jordan is probably getting all worked up about having to do the dirty work on the girl." Prescott went out on a limb with his accusation but he needed to know what was in store for Rain. He didn't want her hurt too badly. "You're not fond of roughing up women, are you, Jordan? I saw how you looked when Tony punched her out back at the pickup spot."

Jordan folded his arms across his chest and stared at Prescott with menacing eyes. Prescott knew he wanted to thrash him around the airplane until it landed in Mosul, before they went deep into the Basin. Tony turned up his thick lips and cut a quick glance in Jordan's direction. Prescott waited patiently.

"You think you know me?" Jordan pressed, his anger peeking through his nonchalant facade. "You don't know a damn thing about me."

"So you *do* like roughing up little girls then?" Prescott asked quickly.

"What the fuck did you say?" Jordan leaned up in his seat as his nostrils flared with each breath. "I don't hurt young girls."

Prescott leaned back, raising his hands in defeat. "Okay. Okay. Don't get all up in arms about it. Jeez."

Now Prescott knew that Tony would be the one handling Rain at the

Basin and his stomach felt queasy at the thought. He'd have felt better with Jordan handling Rain. Tony was a two-bit hustler turned hard-nosed killer since Dalton employed him after seeing his story on the news about beating the hell out of a crime boss on the east side of the Bronx. There had been a flurry of media on whether Tony should have been hailed a hero or a murderer since he'd bashed the boss up so badly that he'd died in a coma three weeks later. With the media efforts, he was deemed a street cleaner and catapulted to a hometown hero worthy of saving dozens of kids from drugs and a life of crime. What the media didn't know was that Tony had been a killer before that day, doing jobs for the highest bidder, and along the way dabbled in the dirty underworld of underage prostitutes and runaways. The mob boss was a hired hit and he unfortunately was caught by a few witnesses passing by. He hadn't been able to finish the job, at least not that night.

"Nothing to worry about, Jordie. I got the little teen dream tonight." Tony smiled like a dirty Santa Claus, his front teeth prominent and turning Prescott's stomach even more. "She's a looker, too."

"Boss said don't spoil the goods," Prescott said, hating the jealousy that flared up over Tony's insinuation.

"What the boss don't know, the boss don't know." He snickered to himself and glanced back over his shoulder. "Wonder if she's a virgin. That'd be my lucky day, huh?"

Jordan reacted quickly and Prescott heard the smack to the back of Tony's head before he even knew it happened, before he could even organize his own attempt to hurt Tony. Tony yelped in surprise and held the back of his skull tightly.

"Damn, man, what you do that for?" he said, wincing at the pain and looking at Jordan, confused.

"You better not touch that girl, Tony. Not on my watch you ain't," Jordan said with a finger to his face. "I've got a daughter, you lowlife bastard, and I'm not letting you prey on a young girl while I'm in charge. You got me?" Jordan was breathing hard. Tony looked through eyes like black slits, assessing whether he should attack Jordan or let his actions slide. His answer clear as he leaned back in his seat with a huff and stared out the window with a look of sheer disgust painted on his dark skin. Prescott knew he was plotting some recourse but on the cramped airplane, he knew the outcome wouldn't be in his favor.

Jordan's gaze never left Tony's face but his breathing had at least decreased back to its normal calm rhythm. Prescott eyed both men with amusement. Clearly, Jordan had the vision of his teenage daughter etched in his mind with a grotesque Tony's hands groping her pubescent body. The thought alone was enough incentive for Jordan to protect Rain, and Prescott smiled at the thought of the turmoil he'd created between the two men. Tony touching his daughter was probably an image that Jordan would never be able to scrape from his mind. Prescott eased back into his seat, satisfied. He'd gathered enough intelligence for now. He knew who would be taking Rain into the Basin but he still didn't know what Christopher Dalton had in store for both him and Rain. He had the aching feeling that whatever it was, he wasn't going to like it. Better yet, he could only hope that Rain would survive it. He felt the plane jerk against the turbulence and his hands involuntarily gripped the armrest until the jarring had subsided. He saw the ground getting nearer through the small plane window, which meant they were descending into Mosul and before long they'd be at the Basin, the pit of hell. Prescott racked his brain with ways to escape whatever plan Dalton had in store for Rain and he knew he'd have to get Jordan and Tony to help with his plan, unknowingly, of course. Too bad the two cinder-block guards didn't know Prescott's real skill that Dalton had hired him for or else they would've never spoken to him. He was the man who could get anything from anyone. Anyone.

NINE

THE NEXT DAY, BAGHDAD, 1743 HOURS

TOLLEY DISMOUNTED THE small aircraft and stepped into the loose desert sand. His lungs filled with the dry heat of the desert, the sand settling in the places he remembered as if it were yesterday. He coughed up a few grains but settled his eyes on the drainage pipe a few hundred yards away. He'd tracked Rain's call to this location. He could feel the uneasiness flood his chest when he'd not seen movement from the sky. He knew Rain would not leave unless absolutely necessary, and if it was absolutely necessary the odds of escape were not good in an open desert. He tried to wrap his mind around the idea that Rain wasn't here and could have been captured but he stared deeper into the desert, watching the sun slowly fading below the orange horizon in the distance.

Shanty, a shaggy-bearded fellow with watery green eyes, sidled up behind Tolley after he'd cut the engine and sent the propellers winding down to a slow rhythmic whir behind them. Shanty was a drunkard, a self-proclaimed lush, and a procurer of all things technological. Tolley liked him because he could hack anything with a code—with a little assistance by Jim Beam, of course—and could shoot more accurately than any sober person he could think of.

"You see them?" Mogli said in a husky tone, fighting back a cough from the thick desert air. Mogli was the youngest member of Tolley's team and definitely the muscle at just over six feet, long, wavy brown hair pulled into a low ponytail, and shotgun arms that easily hoisted his pack onto his back. He looked more like an Italian model than a trained-to-kill martial artist but Tolley glanced around the group and realized that they all looked pretty much the same. Like average law-abiding citizens, not the controlled killers they once were. Mogli had been placed with the group at the age of twenty and now looked like his days in the field had aged him; thin lines crept across his forehead now.

"Nope. No sign of movement from this distance," Tolley said, pushing his binoculars to his eyes and surveying the exterior of the pipe and the surrounding area. His heart was starting to race the longer he didn't see Rain running from the pipe.

"Where's Black?" Shanty said, spinning in the sand, unstable. Tolley shook his head. The man had just flown them hundreds of miles from the coast of Kuwait but couldn't walk without tripping.

"He's unloading his gear, I think," Mogli said, turning to visually locate Black as well.

"There he is," Tolley said, his eyes still glued to the binoculars, watching as Black slithered across the sand in a low crouch toward the pipe. "Here we go, guys." Tolley started in the direction of the pipe.

Black was an accomplished navy SEAL who was secretly honored for the tactical takedown of bin Laden and shortly after was handpicked for the CIA. He was drafted into the team after he'd asked for a more challenging assignment or he threatened to bail on the agency. Dalton knew he couldn't let someone of his talents get away; his spoken and written knowledge of Arabic, Farsi, Spanish, French, Russian, and Japanese meant he was a valuable commodity at the agency and thus, he'd landed himself in Tolley's small group of highly trained, elite, and unknown killers more than twenty years ago. Black had the intelligence to run his own unit but his lack of preparation and gut reactions led to an unpredictability that wasn't safe for a team. Tolley crouched low as he waved Shanty and Mogli toward the left and right. Black had already made a *u* shape in the sand as he investigated the area on his knees. Shanty seemed to come alive as he ran in a crouched position with feet that looked lighter than bird wings and landed on top of the pipe where the sand was still thick. Mogli edged along the side of the pipe opening and held Tolley's gaze as he pulled his weapon from the holster and peeked around the edge of the pipe wall into the empty darkness inside. Mogli was the first to thrust his head in and look.

"Looks cleaned," he said, scanning the floor and noticing the sand had been wiped in the same direction and looked like a neatly laid blanket.

"It's cleaned?" Shanty said, jumping down from the pipe and tottering on his left leg while wincing. "I'm getting too old for this shit," he said under his breath, shaking his leg out.

"The only reason it would be cleaned is if they didn't want us to follow them. Rain knew we were coming so she wouldn't have left unless it was involuntary or dangerous," Tolley said to Mogli, who was now inside the pipe and feeling along the walls.

"Clearly it's involuntary since it's been cleaned. But the fact that whoever took her knew to clean it, that's the kicker. How could they know we were coming?" Black said behind Tolley. His pale skin was an oxymoron for his name because there was nothing dark or black about his blond hair and blue eyes. Tolley always wondered how he'd managed to get that name but there was never enough time to inquire.

"Don't know," Tolley said, wiping the trickle of sweat that tickled his brow.

"They got it out of her," Mogli said from deep inside the pipe. Tolley grimaced at the thought.

"No, I doubt it. They wouldn't even know to ask the right questions. Maybe the boy she's with spilled it," Shanty said in a throaty voice, patting Tolley on the shoulder like an older brother. Tolley could tell they were all thinking the same thing he was but didn't want to say it yet. Her traveling buddy may not be who he says he is.

Tolley had looked up every bit of information on Prescott Willow and called in a few last-minute favors to dig a little deeper than the house in Vermont left to him by his grandfather, the druggy mother, and the stupid high school trophies for wrestling and football. He'd grabbed hold of his military personnel file and knew that he'd been a decorated marine before being stationed in Baghdad. Prescott Willow had a sealed portion of his file that Tolley couldn't get access to and it bore into his curiosity like a rabbit hole. He could feel something was amiss with Sergeant Willow. He'd only need to meet the boy to know if he was friend or foe. That's what he was hoping to do when they'd landed in the middle of the desert looking for his only daughter. Instead she was gone, and for the first time Tolley felt like a piece of him was missing.

He'd felt the same way when Dahlia had first left them both to save the world one bad guy at a time. The nights were the hardest without Dahlia in the beginning. The lonely, cold bed that still smelled like her shampoo. The empty chair at the dinner table. The answerless phone number when Tolley wanted to tell her something Rain had done spectacularly as a child. He'd learned to live without Dahlia, stop loving her so hard, and allowed her to live in the world in which she felt she made a bigger difference. She'd never returned to him from that world, lost to his calls, his pleas to see Rain. She'd at least write from their safe house, an island off the coast of North Carolina, to let him know she was alive. She'd use his grandmother's signature, shaky and written lightly as a cover. Tolley knew she feared bringing hell to their doorstep but she wasn't able to stop them now since she had turned from the hunter to the hunted. He hadn't received a postcard in months before her drop from contact with the CIA. He knew deep down they'd come to visit him one day about Dahlia. He knew they'd either hand him a folded American flag and a letter from her superior officer stating how sad he was for his loss and how good of an agent Dahlia had been—or they'd simply come to tell him that Dahlia was missing in action. He was almost right; Dahlia was missing but she wasn't dead. He knew where she was but he'd never go after her. She was too far into that world, and coming back to the farm wasn't going to be an option for her, ever. So extracting Rain from Dalton was a round-trip ticket for two back to the farm. He would be damned if he let the same world that took his wife take his daughter, his little girl.

"Boss?" Shanty said for what must've been the fifth time because he was leaning into Tolley's field of vision with a look of confusion etched across his face.

"Yeah?" Tolley answered, trying to hide his annoyance at Shanty interrupting his thoughts.

"Mogli's found something you might want to see." Shanty pointed to the pipe with Black standing outside it, looking into the distance as if he'd catch sight of Rain running toward them in the desert. If only it were that easy, Tolley thought to himself. It was supposed to be that easy. Tolley kicked the sand, his boots now filled with the annoying grains chafing against his ankle. When he made it to the pipe, Mogli was still hunched over inside looking at the ground like it was a road map. Mogli was one of the best trackers and had proven himself to be an asset in piecing together the where and how of an event.

"Looks like there was a struggle in the pipe . . . well, not really a *struggle*,"

Mogli said, pushing loose strands of hair behind his ear.

Tolley looked at the divots in the sand and trailed his eyes along the path until it ran to the edge of the pipe.

"You see? It looks like she was dragged out clawing and scratching." Mogli pointed his flashlight toward four barely visible lines in the sand that wavered until they reached the edge of the smooth sand that had been wiped. Tolley felt like Rain had disappeared into thin air along with the marks.

"Which means she didn't know it was coming and didn't know who. So it's safe to say it wasn't the boy that took her," Shanty said from outside the pipe, his beard bobbing as he spoke.

"I wouldn't be too quick to let him off the hook. There's only one set of handprints and I don't see anywhere outside the pipe where he's helped her." He looked around the area as if he hadn't gone over it with a fine-tooth comb before anyone else. "I only see one set of boots leading to tire tracks. So the place has been swept," Black said slowly, his voice low and ominous.

"If it's swept then we are getting farther and farther behind. Black, how long ago since the vehicle left?"

Black took off in a trot to the vehicle tracks, yards away from the pipe.

"Let me take a look, too," Mogli said, brushing past Tolley, jumping from the pipe and meeting Black by the tire tracks that were beginning to cover with sand. Black kneeled down and stuck his finger into the imprint of the tread. Mogli stood over him, looking into the sky and into the distance as if in thought.

"It's been about eight to ten hours, I'd say."

"I'd say you're right, closer to eight," Black said easily, standing up to rest his hand on his holster.

"Then we don't have much time to figure out where they were going before the trail gets cold."

"I've been thinking about that. *We've* been thinking about that," Shanty said, his eyes darting from Black to Mogli as if to ask their permission to share what was on his mind.

"So what have y'all come up with? Any idea is a good idea compared to what we got," Tolley said without hiding his agitation at the length of the conversation. He needed to get moving. Needed to *do something.*

"Well, we was thinkin' maybe, you know, since it's Dalton and all, that he'd use his old stomping grounds . . ." Shanty said, moving his feet in the sand like a child ready to receive punishment.

Tolley felt his heart rate quicken as his memory brought up images of a place they'd all been before. His stomach felt queasy at the thought of the name, the place where all sin, fear, and lies are snatched from the body and watched clean.

The Basin.

Before he knew it he'd sprinted off toward the airplane, his foot caught a sand mound on the wrong edge, and he rolled his ankle slightly before stumbling to the ground. Sand flew everywhere as Black, Mogli, and Shanty scrambled after Tolley, all hoping that their brother would make it through. They knew his fall was not a result of his loss of balance in the thick sand but his emotional state at the thought of his daughter being tortured at the Basin.

As they approached, they found Tolley punching the sand with seemingly endless bursts of power. His hands moved at such quick speeds that it looked as if a small tornado had formed as sand swirled around him, spiking toward the darkening sky. Night had begun to fall but in the haze they saw their brother struggling with thoughts of his young daughter, taken by men who were much like they were. Men who followed orders, inflicted pain until a person could no longer recognize who they were and what they'd done to cross Dalton. The irony only served as a gut punch to Tolley and he was fighting back, giving his pain and fear to the earth and serving it up with the same hatred he had for Dalton for so many years. All he could see was Dalton's face in the sand through the warm wetness that seeped from his eyes, made brown trails down his dirty cheeks, and sank into the collar of his T-shirt. Shanty was the first to try to hold Tolley, grabbing his elbow only to have it wrenched from his grasp. A guttural growl filled the silence like that of a beast, not a man. Tolley continued his fury, punching away at the sand until a ditch had begun to form and his arm would disappear to the elbow; only then did his punches slow. The steam was running out of the old man but they knew he needed to vent.

"Come on Tolley. We're going to get your daughter back," Black said without judgment, his blue eyes never settling on Tolley, who had both fists planted in the sand as he heaved. "And we're going to get Dalton . . ."

Black walked off, leaving his words hanging over the trio like the last line of a symphony, the moment before the bravo, the clap, the uproar. Shanty reached for Tolley again once the sound of Tolley's wretched breathing had become too much to bear but Mogli intercepted his hand and nodded toward the plane. Shanty gave a sad smirk under his ratty beard, his green eyes wise enough to know when a man needed a moment to cry in the dark. Mogli placed his hand on Tolley's shoulder, which still rose and fell as if he'd run a marathon, then sauntered off after Black and Shanty. Within minutes the sound of the plane's engine vibrated in the air.

Tolley brushed the wetness from his face with the back of his arm; sand grains rolled against his face, scratching at his eyelids. He was going to kill Dalton. He'd resigned himself to that fact right then, right there, in the desert, under the failing daylight.

TEN

THE SMELL OF DIESEL, OIL, AND hot stickiness wafted around the aircraft as the plane's engine slowed to a soft whir. Prescott squinted into the empty blackness in front of him. There were no lights shining on a stone-faced building, no menacing gargoyles or statues to foretell the eerie feeling that swept through Prescott at the entrance to the Basin. The Basin was only noticeable by two overgrown cacti with nearly invisible spikes surrounding a six-feet-by-three-feet door in the ground with reflector lights strung tightly around the base of the plant. How the pilot had been able to land so near, he wasn't sure. The darkness of the desert was enough to make a person feel like they were alone in the world, with nothing existing outside the length of their arms.

He'd only heard stories about terrorists being taken to the Basin for interrogation. Interrogation and torture was a very fine line, he realized, looking at the nondescript steel door covered with rust sunk deep into the sand. Fifty feet away, Jordan pulled Rain from the side hatch of the plane by her armpits, her head dangling like a tetherball toward the ground. The plane's lights provided only a ten-foot glow around it, which Prescott knew meant they couldn't see him as he watched them. Tony ran to the side of the plane and caught Rain's legs with his forearms as they dropped from the hatch. Seeing them carry Rain like a dead body on the way to the morgue made Prescott's stomach churn. He pushed the feeling as deep as it would go. He didn't need Tony or Jordan thinking they had leverage over him. He'd only wished he'd thought of that when Christopher Dalton had come to his rescue, or to bid on his soul, as Prescott thought of it.

Dalton had come to him after he'd been sitting in a cell waiting for a court martial for killing fifteen insurgents that had turned out to be innocent citizens, mostly mothers, harboring their children from al-Qaeda. He'd been a gunny that day, sitting atop the Humvee with the relentless sun beating his back like he was being punished for a crime he had only yet to commit. He remembered the sizzle of his skin, the drip of sweat down his spine, tingling his senses as his comrades exited the vehicle to assess the small, crude town sunk into a sand dune miles from any man-made roads. He hadn't let up on the .50 caliber machine gun; his hand still rested on the side of the weapon, finger pointed down the nose of the barrel, ready for the action he'd been dreading would come one day. His eyes darted from each house—five houses alone in the middle of the desert, closely stacked upon one another with only a sliver of space between them. In America, all five houses would have equaled the size of a duplex, yet this was the entire town. Shabby clothes, mostly blankets and shirts, were hanging alongside the houses swaying in a breeze that Prescott couldn't feel. A deflated ball was in front of the mud-stacked houses, left forgotten and unwanted by the looks of its thick layer of dirt covering the original material. Weathered wood protruded from the corners of the houses as if the framing was running from the thick, clumpy siding.

These houses are definitely not up to code, Prescott thought to himself as he scanned the area. He noted the makeshift windows: no glass, just dark holes like dead eyes to the sad houses. He saw a figure move in the house to the left and steadied his grip. The other soldiers had already knocked on all the doors and in Arabic announced that everyone should come out with their hands up. The hard-edged faces looked back at him, hidden behind black material that stretched from their eyebrows across their mouths and seemed to drop to the floor, covering their entire bodies. The brown hands waved toward the sky reminding Prescott that these women were not black ghosts, they were alive. He blinked the sweat from his eyes. A twitch in his shoulder had developed from leaning on the .50 caliber for too long. He ignored it and watched as women filed from the houses one by one, each with their rough hands waving in submission. Little girls covered in shaggy garments from head to toe inched toward their mothers and looked back and forth between the large weapon pointed at them and the stone faces of their caregivers.

"Where are the men?" a soldier with *Branson* stitched on his chest asked in Arabic, pointing toward the cluster of homes.

An elderly woman spoke in a raspy voice and explained to the soldier that the men had gone to get food. Her eyes were round and gray, larger than Prescott thought imaginable. He saw them darting about, betraying the lie she was trying to hide. Before he could warn the soldier below about his suspicion, a boy, possibly twelve years old, darted from one of the homes with a machete held tight in his unwavering hand. The woman screamed at the boy, pointing toward the house, motioning him to go back inside. The soldier, understanding her pleas, lowered his rifle slightly but Prescott had not removed the crosshair of his powerful weapon from the center of the boy's chest. Branson tried to talk to the boy as he stood with his weapon high as if ready to slash at the air. He was only a few feet from the soldier, looking back and forth in confusion and defiance from the elderly woman who spoke softly now and the soldier whose finger rested beside his trigger.

Prescott could sense the boy only wanted to protect his family but Prescott would protect *his* family—his platoon—at all costs as well. As eyes were trained on the young boy who was slowly realizing he wasn't going to win a gunfight with a machete, the whisper of an engine floated on the air until it became loud enough for his squad to crane their necks in the direction of the open desert. Prescott swiveled the .50 cal in the direction of the approaching silver SUV that bounced along the loose sand, kicking up feathery brown clouds as it sped recklessly.

"We've got company!" Prescott yelled to his squad as he saw them scramble for cover behind the vehicle and along the edge of the homes.

From his peripheral vision, he saw the elderly woman move quickly to hook the young boy to her bosom and kneel down toward the ground. The first shot that sailed past Prescott's head was too high but close enough to make his eye flinch in shock. The SUV continued to violently bounce over the sand dunes closer to the squad as a barrage of bullets *tink tinked* against the armored vehicle. Within minutes, Prescott released the boom of the .50 caliber weapon as it jerked against his shoulder, reminding him that he was the swing shooter to the fight. With his firepower, he could keep off an entire army. Yet the SUV absorbed his bullets and continued to dart and shift dangerously on its wheels toward the village. Prescott's squad was in a full-fledged battle with the SUV, whose occupants had managed to stick three rifles from the windows and spray across the town in a maddening thunder of hot lead.

Prescott settled his sight on the driver, who bobbed his head from the steering wheel only long enough to catch glimpses of the terrain before jutting his head out of sight. *No wonder the vehicle is swerving,* Prescott thought to himself. Through his scope he could see the tips of the fingers on the wheel gripped tight. Prescott waited. In minutes, the man would peek his head over the wheel, leaving himself open for a swift hole in the head. As Prescott tried to force his shortened breath, he heard the rasping groan behind him, which was faint enough to miss, but Prescott had found himself in a zone that heightened his focus. The sound broke his focus.

He looked quickly over his shoulder to find Branson reaching toward the top of the Humvee, his brown eyes etched in pain and helplessness. Prescott still heard the bullets whistling in the wind but he turned toward Branson and took in the scene of the twelve-year-old boy slashing his machete into Branson's back, blood flying from the blade as he whipped it back and continued relentlessly with his skinny arms. Branson fell to the sand, his eyes dead to the world, void behind the deep brown irises. The boy's chest heaved as he spat on Branson's body and yelled in Arabic, as if Branson could still hear his war cry. The boy's eyes seemed to snap from Branson's unmoving body and remember that his job was not done. His eyes crawled up the Humvee and settled on Prescott's disgusted face. *Branson had tried to save the boy. I guess some people just aren't worth saving*, he thought in the split second before swiveling his .50 cal toward the boy, undoubtedly leaving his back open to the real threat, the raging SUV of gunmen. To avenge Branson, Prescott wanted to turn the boy into a pool of red mush soaking into the unforgiving desert floor.

Before Prescott could fire his first round, the boy sprinted from the edge of the Humvee toward the houses and slid in between two of them for cover. "Smart fucker," Prescott said as he pointed his rifle toward the corner of the house. He knew the house would crumble under the force of the bullets. His finger pulled the trigger back as far as it would go and the constant kick of the rifle felt good bucking against him as he shrugged away the hot wetness of his tears. He sprayed the houses in anger, filling every inch of them with holes that crumbled the facade piece by piece. He could faintly hear the yells within the houses but he couldn't stop the rifle until it was empty and lifeless in his hands.

When the rifle had stopped its loud blasts, Prescott felt a rush of air break into his lungs. The silence was maddening. No bullets flying. No more yelling. Just the sound of the wind, flapping through the clothes on the line, washing away the sounds of death and carrying it off into the desert. He looked around as he sucked air into his lungs and saw his squad, incomplete without Branson, staring back at him with their weapons hanging down by the thighs. He spun around to see the SUV which should have been rushing at him but was instead flipped on its side twenty feet away, blood smeared against the windshield which was webbed with cracked glass and bullet holes.

The squad had won the fight against the insurgents in the silver SUV. Prescott had won against the twelve-year-old boy who was in bits, half-exposed from the sliver of the house. Prescott's eyes scanned the houses and a sob choked him as he saw the elderly woman lying in the doorway, her body twisted as if it had fallen at a strange angle and never righted itself. Small children, the same little girls he'd seen earlier in the tattered clothes and confused faces, were littered along the ground beneath the hanging clothes that snapped in the stifling breeze like an angry whip. The sob that wretched Prescott's body sent him into hysteria. He laughed at the irony of the boy that Branson wanted to save, killing him in the end. He cried for the elderly woman who had only tried to protect her children and whose efforts were futile. All the children were dead. Prescott had killed them.

Prescott felt the heavy hand on his shoulder that snapped him from his memory. He heard Tony's annoyingly deep voice in his ear.

"Are you gonna stand there staring at the damn door or help us out and open it?"

"Yeah, I've got it." Prescott shrugged off Tony's hand and pulled open the thick steel door as sand spilled from around its edges. He let the door fall open and peered into the hole in the ground. The cavernous entryway had raw, bumpy stone steps that led down into an even deeper darkness. Prescott could feel the cool air from below waft around him, beaconing him into its depths.

"Ladies first," Tony said, nudging past Prescott and starting down the steps, Rain's legs still in his hands. After three steps, Prescott couldn't see his face; soon after, Rain's bottom half looked severed by the darkness.

Jordan carried her shoulders easily, as if moving a paperweight across a desk. Prescott stared at Rain's face, bluish and swollen over the eye where Tony had hit her. She looked complacent, her pouty lips slightly open, dark eyebrows relaxed over her closed eyes. He ached to see her open her eyes again. She felt dead to him with her eyes closed. He needed to be able to see the energy and tenacity, to know she was still fighting alongside him.

Prescott followed closely behind Jordan taking the steps carefully, not fully aware of how far down they led, and he didn't want to think about the damage that could be done if he took a tumble. They finally reached a landing at the bottom of the stairs. It was as if a veil of blackness cloaked the inner areas of the cave. Prescott couldn't see the back of Jordan's head when he marched off the last step and disappeared into nothingness.

"Is it always this dark down here?" Prescott said into the cool air. The underground space carried a moistness in the air that couldn't be found in the stifling desert heat above. Prescott waited for the light, for either man to strike a match or click on a flashlight, but he felt an uneasiness wash over him almost as soon as he left the last step.

It was too quiet for him to feel comfortable. He felt the hairs on his neck stand on end. Something was off. Tony was way too loud and clumsy to be this quiet. Before Prescott could turn toward the stairs and head back, he felt the first punch rattle his teeth. He landed backward on the stairs, his neck falling dangerously near the edge of the stone step as he cupped his face in shock. He heard the sound of boots shuffle against the concrete and reflexively kicked his leg out to connect with whoever had served him a ringer. He tasted the metallic liquid in his mouth, felt his split lip, but he hadn't worried much after he felt his foot sink into a man's gut. He heard the *uumph* clear enough to figure where in the dark his assailant was. He jolted upward, reminded of the pain in his neck, and used every sense in his body to grab into the darkness near the sound of a menacing chuckle. His hand landed on the blazing warmth of a meaty shoulder, gripping it roughly before slamming it down into his knee with enough force to make him stumble into the darkness. The body curved warmly around his knee as he felt bone on bone and the soft squishiness of a nose explode against his flesh. The *crack* of the bone broke through the darkness and a sickening yell rent the air.

Prescott smiled through his own blood, which had stopped pooling in his mouth and now clung to his teeth. He was ready for the next blow, only relaxing when he heard the body fall in a lump to the ground. He reached into the darkness and felt for the body on the cold, damp stone floor of the cave. His fingers bumped along the dusty coolness of the dirt and gravel until they hit an object. His hand eased across the warm, slick surface . . . a bald head . . . *Tony*, he presumed. Prescott felt anger rising within him overcoming the jubilation of triumph. Was this the plan Dalton had conjured up? Was Tony supposed to kill him in this dank cave? Prescott started to feel his heart rumbling with the next question that bumped around in his brain as he struggled to see in the blackness. If this was Tony lying unconscious on the ground, then where was Jordan? In the split second it took for Prescott's focus to return from his confusion, he felt the steel butt of a weapon bear down on his spine in a striking blow that made his legs give out beneath him. The last thing Prescott remembered was resting his cheek against Tony's bald head, wondering why.

ELEVEN

S HANTY WHEELED THE SMALL aircraft into a flat speck of land nearly two miles from the Basin. It had taken them only a few hours to spot the reflective cactus that they all knew so well. Shanty circled wide and put them down far enough from the entrance that whoever had snatched Rain wouldn't hear them landing.

Black counted his ammunition belt for the second time, holstered his pistol, and patted each pocket of his vest and pant legs, mentally counting his supplies. He slid a black skull cap over his cropped hair and sank back into the seat. Tolley looked on, feeling faintly relaxed by Black's routine that had brought back so many memories of his former life.

Mogli opened the hatch once the aircraft settled and jumped out into the darkness. Shanty killed the lights and after taking a long sip from his metal flask, he swiveled his chair and bounded out behind Black. Tolley was the last to exit but once he had, he knew Rain was close. He could feel a buzzing in his chest.

"So what've we got, boss?" Shanty asked, shrugging into his holster, guns clapping against his rib cage.

"We know the Basin's layout. What we don't know is how many men we are up against and where they will be," Tolley explained.

Mogli interrupted, "My best guess is that there was a small group. Maybe two or three men. We only had one set of tire tracks back at the pipe. To hold two hostages . . . if there were actually two hostages and not just one . . ." He looked around at the men. " . . . the pickup team had to be small enough to fit comfortably in an SUV with two hostages."

"So we're looking at a two- or three-man job," Tolley surmised.

"Highly skilled. Armed, of course," Shanty said.

"Are we going to powwow here for the next hour or go get the girl?" Black said with annoyance.

"Black, you take lead. I'll take the rear. This is not a search and capture, gentlemen," Tolley said before clicking the safety off his weapon.

The group of men strutted low in the darkness toward the reflective cactus, the entrance to the Basin.

Black reached the door first, his blue eyes trained on the men before nodding and pulling it open slowly. Only a small squeak sounded as he softly laid it against the sand and disappeared down the dark hole. The men knew their way in the darkness and found themselves trailing along the inner tunnel walls, stopping outside each doorway before stepping in. Fire blazed in lanterns along the stone walls, making the shadows dance along the tunnel. The first three rooms of the fifteen rooms below the surface of the desert were empty. Tools lined the interior stone walls in various shapes and proclivities for pain-induced questioning. Tolley remembered his own basement back home and finally understood how his prior life still bled into his new life. The floors were slick with a mucus-like substance as they worked their way in and out of the rooms.

The team started down the tunnel again only stopping when Black held up his fist to halt the line. Tolley heard the sound of screams before he could smell the scent of burning flesh in the air. Black dipped low to the ground and pointed at Mogli who stood close behind him to flank across the tunnel. Shanty dropped down low behind Black while Tolley took his cue and settled behind Mogli along the far wall. Black motioned that he and Shanty would continue down the hall for cover. One door, closed and presumably locked, was in front of Mogli. His shoulder rested on the door frame. He nodded back at Tolley as he tried the knob and found it stiff and unmoving. Tolley held up a finger and stepped in front of the door. He knocked twice as was customary Basin rules when interrupting an interrogation.

"What the hell you want, Jordan? I'm just getting started."

Tolley heard the footsteps making their way across the grimy floor with a *schlop schlop*. The door creaked open and before Tony could register that Jordan was not the uninvited guest, his forehead was pounded with the butt of a weapon hard enough to send him reeling backward. Tolley didn't expect him to recover from the blow but Tony landed on his butt only long enough to gain his footing and storm toward Tolley with livid eyes. Tolley raised his pistol but heard a quick *twap twap* as Tony's head snapped back from Mogli's shot. Tolley looked over his shoulder at Mogli who nodded in response to the unspoken gratitude. Tony's body was dotted with a red blister above his chest and in the center of his forehead that slowly oozed blood, which mixed with the dark, stained floors. A muffled noise in the corner reminded Tolley that there was another person in the room. He swiveled his weapon to a naked boy strapped to a chair. He had been beaten almost beyond recognition; his body looked more purple than human. His right eye was swollen shut with a deep cut at the corner of his left. Tolley knew that cut well. He'd cut many men down here at the corners of their eyes, so that the blood, sweat, and tears were maddeningly painful. He'd made the blade scrape so close to their eyeballs that they'd scream in fear of what they thought would be impending blindness. That was always the first cut. The beginning of the process. The boy had survived it, although barely. His nipples had been set ablaze, which must have been the scent in the tunnel. Tolley said a silent prayer of thanks that they'd arrived in time, before the dead guy made it to his genitals. That was always next.

"Your name," Tolley said, training his weapon on the boy. He didn't put his guard down until he identified every threat.

"P-P-P . . ." the boy tried but his mouth was swollen, tongue thick.

"Spit it out, boy," Tolley demanded, although he knew already.

"P-P-Prescott Willow." The boy shivered as if stating his name had given him a fright.

"You want to let him loose, boss?" Mogli whispered.

"How'd they know where you were?" Tolley ignored him, focusing his attention on the mangled boy in front of him.

"D-D-D-Dalton, sir," he said, hanging his head down to his chest in exhaustion.

"You better hope they didn't hurt my daughter or you'll be on the floor next to him."

Tolley pointed the barrel of his gun toward Tony's body, which was gushing blood from various orifices. He motioning to Mogli to release the boy from his bindings. Prescott groaned in gratitude and pain as Mogli loosened the restraints.

Mogli moved fast, cutting the tape, ripping it from the boy's wrists and ankles unceremoniously and without regard for his comfort. Prescott stood slowly on shaky, Jell-O legs and fell back into the wooden chair. His arms hung by his sides, almost scraping the ground in exhaustion, and his chest heaved rhythmically. Finally his head rolled to its upright position and Prescott's eyes trained on Tolley with a strange smile.

"Took you long enough," he said in jest.

Tolley's brow arched menacingly. He did not have time for games until

Rain was found. He rounded back toward the door to peer into the tunnel. He hadn't heard any shots fired but he knew Black had the skill to work silently when necessary. Mogli found Prescott's pants and threw them in his direction. They landed on the edge of his knee. The pant legs swept the dirty, soiled cement.

"How many men brought you here?" Tolley said without turning from the hall, his voice even yet urgent.

"Two," Prescott said, swallowing as if it hurt. "The other one is Jordan. Not much worse than this one." He glanced toward the body in the corner, lazily thrown toward the wall and out of the way. He slowly slid his soiled pants back on, wincing at the undeniable pain in every inch of his body. He could feel the pent-up rage toward Tony slowly dying. If he'd had the strength he would have stomped another hole in his head to feel better.

"See any others?"

"Do I look like I had a chance to see someone else?" Prescott offered sarcastically.

"I see he got his bearings back," Mogli said under his breath.

"Good. Then it's time to move." Tolley rounded the corner and disappeared into the hall.

Tolley was surprised how quickly Prescott recovered and found the boy standing behind him in a crouch. His bare feet tiptoed on the dirt floor and Tolley knew he wouldn't last too much longer without blacking out, no matter how tough he thought he was.

Mogli sidled behind Prescott along the wall as Tolley traveled past rooms without bothering to go in. He knew he was looking for a sign. Some inconsistency that would tell him where Black and Shanty had been. The fire lanterns were sporadically lit along the path and the deeper into the tunnel he traveled, the less light crossed his path. He could hear Prescott's labored breathing now. The boy was trying to stay lucid even though his body was fighting to shut down and rest after the hours of torture and dehydration he had endured. Tolley saw movement ahead and raised his fist quickly. Prescott couldn't register the meaning in time and bumped into Tolley, making him grunt in annoyance. The person Tolley had spotted turned down the tunnel, looking into the intense blackness that hid the three men. Tolley knew he wouldn't be able to see into the darkness but he stopped breathing, just in case.

TWELVE

RAIN FELT THE WATER SLICE across her face in a cool rush, knocking the air from her lungs. She coughed and sputtered, attempting to catch her breath. She had blacked out again. The pain was becoming too much but she knew she had to hold on. She had to make sure Prescott was okay. She needed to get in contact with her father somehow. She would think of something. Some way to get out of this hellhole.

"Are you going to tell me where you hid the memory chip now?" The muscular man placed his hands on his knees and leaned his face toward her like she was a child. She could smell the peppery scent of his breath.

"I told you. I lost it while we were running. It's in the desert somewhere." Her throat ached against the words. She felt the small poke of the chip against the underside of her breast and was thankful he hadn't unclothed her yet.

"So you insist on lying to me, Rain? We tracked the phone to your location in the desert. We found the cell phone in your pants, but no chip." Jordan stood upright and stretched his back lazily. "You think I like this type of work, huh? You think I will like plucking off your fingernails one by one or burning your flesh piece by piece until you give me what I want from you?" He shook his head, not waiting for an answer as he sauntered to the stone wall and pulled down a tool with a hooked edge. A blade protruded from the wooden handle on the other end, making it look like an ancient device that a Viking might use to kill a wild beast.

"They never clean these things," Jordan said, eyeing the blade, which indeed looked grimy with black remnants of its last use.

He shook his head like a mother who'd found a dirty dish in her spotless kitchen as Rain tried to calm the butterflies in her stomach. She knew she was due even more pain than she'd already suffered. He'd gone easy on her, smashing her knuckles and striking her repeatedly with a wooden board and rubber ball attached to a long cord. The ball had hit a sensitive spot beneath her breastbone and sent her vomiting all over herself. But the paddle had made her pass out. She didn't want that again and she knew her attacker's patience was wearing thin. Her hand, now swollen into their grip around the ropes that bound her to a chair, worked against the knots. She knew it would be hours before she'd be able to loosen them, but her only hope was to free herself. That's all she had left. *Hope.* She hadn't seen Prescott when they'd taken her and she wasn't sure whether he was dead, alive, or captured. Her father wouldn't be able to find her. It was up to her to survive.

"Why is Dalton doing this? Is it about money? I can get you money," Rain lied.

"The phone, Rain. Where is the phone?" His voice sounded soothing, as if talking a baby to sleep. It unnerved Rain for him to be so passive, yet so tortuous.

"I don't have it!" Rain yelled as she struggled against the ropes. Jordan was behind her now, the blade touching the sensitive skin around her blackened eye. He then switched to her good eye.

"Don't struggle, Rain. You wouldn't want me to nick your beautiful brown eye now, would you?" Jordan cooed in her ear.

"You're sick," Rain spat, but went rigid as he traced the blade along her cheek. She indeed did not want to lose an eye, not her good one at least.

Jordan plunged the hook into Rain's shoulder and her howls of pain filled the room. She felt her head become light from the pain, almost vibrating her vision. She cried out, begged for help, for anyone to find her and save her. She could feel the cold steel of the hook in her skin, chilling her from the inside out. The warmth of her fresh blood covered her shoulder and dripped down her back and chest. The sensation of warmth calmed her to a whimper. She sucked in air trying to stay focused, meditate and breathe through the pain like she'd been taught at the agency.

"That's only the beginning, Rain. I still have to get my hook *out*. Where is the chip?" Jordan cooed again, unfazed by her whimpers.

Rain blew her breath in and out trying to calm her body before it leaped into full-fledged shock. She didn't want to become delirious and start talking about where she'd hidden the cellular chip. The hook bobbed every time she wheezed, still implanted in the meat of her shoulder.

"Fuck . . . you," she said through gritted teeth.

"I thought you were smarter. Maybe I gave you too much credit."

Jordan tore through her skin with the hook as it dislodged, spilling rivers of warm blood down her bare arm. Rain screamed until the sound of her own voice pounded against her skull. She hoped she could be heard by someone outside the room, anyone within earshot who could save her. After what felt like hours, Rain groaned, the pain overriding her will to exert any energy to scream. She just whimpered softly, head drawn back against the chair. She was shaking but it made her feel better. Made the pain subside a bit, if that was even possible. Jordan labored slowly to the wall, taking great care in cleaning the tool with a dark rag before placing it in its rightful spot. He then grabbed a blowtorch from the wall and set it alight with a flick of his finger. His eyes danced at the sight of the blue flame and the soft hum of its radiant heat.

"I really think now is the time to tell me whatever it is you want to tell me because unfortunately, burns never really heal quite right. And it'd be a shame since you're such a pretty girl." He tsked-tsked as he began walking to Rain. She shivered in her chair despite the intense heat of the room.

"P-please, we can work something out," Rain begged. A tear slid down her sweaty face. She never dreamed she'd be in a place like this a year ago. She missed the farm. She missed her father even more now that she wasn't sure she'd ever see him again.

"Oh, Rain. Don't take this personally. I actually really like you. I think you and my daughter would be best friends under different circumstances. She's a little younger than you. But I think you'd like her very much. But right now, you are my *job*. And I always do my job, Rain." Jordan was standing in front of her now, the torch low but still gripped tightly in his massive hands. Rain sensed something amiss at the same second Jordan looked toward the door. He'd heard something, too. A slight shuffling like the movement of paper on a desk. Maybe even footsteps, Rain thought to herself, hope like a distant memory finding its way back into her heart.

"Tony? That you?" Jordan asked as he walked to the door.

A loud blast of heat filled the room and blew Jordan back against the wall of torture tools. He hit hard enough to dislodge a large hacksaw from the wall and it landed on top of him, knocking him flat to the ground. Rain closed her eyes from the force of the blast. She felt the dirt materialize in the air and scrape against her skin. When she opened her eyes, she realized that the steel door had been blown off its hinges and now lay in the center of the room, warped and smoking. The cloud of dust in the room was thick but slowly being pulled into the hall outside, clearing the air around Rain.

Rain could hear voices through the ringing in her ears. Her head pounded but she was sure it was real and not imagined.

A voice stood out as she tried to register what was happening. She saw a group of men shuffle in. Two men grabbed Jordan while another man, tall and muscular, filtered through the haze. It was Tolley. It was her dad. His worried eyes found her in the smoke and he kissed her forehead. He looked at her shoulder, blood-soaked and shaking, then scanned her swollen black eye with a painful look. She tried to smile at him to let him know it was okay. She was okay because he was there. Tolley was cutting through the ropes when she caught sight of another figure. A figure limping toward her. It was Prescott, she realized once he'd gotten within arm's length, but his face was mangled and swollen as if he'd been on the other side of the blast. He came to her and put his hands on her face.

"I thought we were too late," he said through split, dry lips. She could see the sorrow in his blue eyes hidden behind the bruises.

"Get me the hell out of here," Rain said as her hands were cut free. She tried to reach up and hug Prescott but her shoulder was in too much pain. He kissed her on the cheek instead and waited for her legs to be released. Tolley looked up at Rain from where he worked to free her ankles and then over to Prescott. He could tell there was something between the two of them but he still didn't like the idea of Prescott being a part of this mess. The boy would owe him some answers.

"Thank you," Rain said to Tolley, though the words choked her and sent tears springing down her cheeks.

"Told you I'd come get you," Tolley said, wrapping her shoulder quickly with gauze from his vest.

"Boss, we gotta go. What's the call?" Black pointed to Jordan, who was being subdued, although barely conscious, by Shanty and Mogli.

"Rain, go on to the plane with them. You'll be safe. I'm going to clean up down here, okay?"

Rain knew that he was going to torture Jordan for what he'd done to her, maybe even kill him. She knew he needed it in order to right himself with not finding her in time to keep her from being tortured. She knew her father better than anyone in the world and he'd be back on track after settling the balance of right and wrong.

"Okay," Rain whispered to him, her eyes soft.

Prescott helped her from the chair and they leaned on each other as they exited to the hall. Black led them out of the tunnel, slowly up the stairs, and across the early light of the dawn to the aircraft. Black administered first aid and a sedative to both of them before the other three men entered the plane silently. Before long, the engine was purring happily away from the horrors of the Basin.

THIRTEEN

SAFE HOUSE, HOKKAIDO, JAPAN

RAIN AWOKE TO THE BRIGHTNESS of the sun shining through the lace curtains. She rubbed her eyes and listened to the sound of the television in the next room. She couldn't understand the Japanese language but the exaggerated tones kept her eager to listen. She rolled up her sleeping pallet and stored the mat in a nearby closet. The tatami room had a soft woven covering over the floors and she found it easier to sleep on than her military cot, so she hadn't complained. They'd flown here a week ago to recover from their ordeal at the Basin. Tolley told her it would be a while before things got straightened out and they'd be safe in America. She knew Dalton had reach and wasn't sure if any place in the world was safe for them anymore. She'd trusted her father and his gang of misfits, though, when they said Japan was the best place to lay low.

Rain could smell the breakfast cooking with a heavy scent of brewing coffee. She knew the team was already up and working on their strategy as they had been every day since they'd arrived. Rain used the quiet moments to stretch and meditate. She was working on rehabbing her shoulder after what Jordan had done to it through yoga and stem-cell therapy. Luckily, he'd only left a shallow wound and an annoying pain that ibuprofen could override. Her hand was still stiff but acupuncture from the local Japanese healer seemed to ease her discomfort and increase her range of motion. During her meditation, Rain thought of Dahlia. She knew Dalton was trying to draw her out by using her, but he was wrong. She wouldn't come out for her own daughter. She'd left her and that was exactly where she wanted Rain to be, away from her. Rain was tiring of the search for a woman who evidently didn't want to be found and cared very little for what was once her family.

After her meditation, Rain found the guys huddled around the coffee table with maps strewn about and photos spread in every direction.

"What's this?" Rain asked, grabbing cold bacon from a plate on the counter. She could see a map of Russia on the table. She noticed four red dots and two blue dots near Moscow. She cringed at a picture of Christopher Dalton on the edge of the table. He looked like an evil nerd even on camera, she thought to herself.

"We're tracking Dahlia," Prescott said over his shoulder. His eyes flitted to hers before he smiled. He still had a blue circle around his eyes but the swelling was down. She didn't realize how much she missed the way he used to look until then. She frowned at the thought of how she must've looked to him with her dark-rimmed eye and bandages.

"So you found her? I thought she was too hard to track? If Dalton can't find her . . ."

"Dalton doesn't really know her. Not like I do," Tolley said before flipping over Dalton's picture and sweeping it off the table.

"So what are our options? Where are we right now?" Rain asked, confused as to why they wouldn't reach out to her mother if they knew where she was.

"Your mother . . . Dahlia, she's not going to be found unless she wants to be found."

"And we think she wants to be found," Prescott said, looking at Tolley.

"Found by you," Black said as his sky-blue eyes dropped to the map again.

"Found by me? What for? She hasn't seen or talked to me since I was a kid. I doubt she even cares what happened in Iraq." The men stared at her as if she had a third leg.

"Dalton was trying to bait her and she's very smart. Smarter than any of us in this room." Shanty snorted disdainfully at the implication but Tolley continued. "She knew I would be there and she wouldn't risk being captured. But I'm pretty sure she knew what was going on and why," Tolley said.

"How can you be so sure, though?" Rain quizzed.

"Because she radioed us in the plane through Morse code. No one else would have done that," Shanty said, happy that his part of the conversation had finally arrived.

"What did it say?"

"It just said, very simply . . . thank you." Shanty smiled hard through his scraggly beard as if he'd finally hit the jackpot in the conversation.

Tolley wiped a hand down his face. Rain noticed he looked older now.

"Why don't we just quit looking? Let's just go home," Rain said. The group of men all shook their heads at the thought.

"We can't go home. Dalton ain't gonna stop hunting you 'til he puts a bullet in your head or your momma's head. He's not the forgivin' type. He don't like to lose and what happened at the Basin . . . well, that's as big a loss as any," Shanty said, pulling on his scraggly beard.

"That's a good point, Shanty," Tolley said as he rolled up the map slowly. "Have you even stopped to wonder how you guys got taken down in the Basin anyway? How'd they find you in the middle of the desert?"

"Jordan said they tracked the phone," Rain said, looking around at the skeptical faces.

Mogli leaned back in his chair silently, pushing his long hair behind his ears. Rain could tell Mogli was the observer on the team because he hadn't said much to her since they'd left the Basin. Black looked suspiciously at Prescott while Tolley piggybacked the sentiment. Shanty just took another sip from his flask and sighed audibly.

"Alright already. No need to hang in silence. I'll tell her," Prescott said, slapping his hand to the table before standing in front of Rain.

Rain sensed a shift in the men. They were all staring at Tolley now but Tolley wouldn't meet her eyes. So she looked in Prescott's instead. His eyes burned with worry and some other emotion she couldn't pinpoint. She knew he didn't want to say whatever it was he was about to say.

"Well then, spit it out," Rain said, her hand moving to her elbow instinctively to cradle her injury as her stomach told her his words were going to hurt.

"I called Dalton to tell him where we were," Prescott said.

Before Rain could hold back, she slapped Prescott hard across the cheek. He absorbed the hit and stared at the ground in shame.

"How could you do that?" Rain's lip quivered in anger. "*Why* would you do that?"

"I was working for Dalton against my will. He put me in place to watch you and report back."

"So you were *hired* to befriend me and learn my secrets?"

"Yes, but . . ."

"I *trusted* you, Prescott! The whole time they were torturing me I was hoping that you'd gotten away." Rain couldn't stop the tear from streaming down her face so she wiped it fiercely with her hand.

"I'm so sorry, Rain. I didn't know anything about your mother. He didn't tell me why I was watching you. Just to report back about anyone you speak with . . . and to get close to you."

"So I was a job, Prescott? *Everything* was a part of your job." Rain felt the bitterness rise within her. Her shoulder ached and reminded her of the words Jordan had said to her at the Basin. She was his *job*, too.

"No. Not everything," Prescott answered quickly. "I told Dalton I couldn't and wouldn't let you get hurt. That's why I was sent to the Basin, too."

"So because we got tortured together I'm supposed to forget that you betrayed me? You were the reason we were there in the first place!" Rain yelled. The silence in the room from the other men felt like she was in a cave hearing the echo of her own voice.

"I'm sorry, Rain. I can't apologize enough." Prescott's eyes watered but Rain felt no sympathy for him.

"You're right. No apology will ever be enough for what you put me through. What you put this team through." She looked at the guys huddled around the coffee table. None were looking in their direction but she knew they heard every word.

Prescott reached for Rain's hand and she snatched it away from him with a look of disgust. "Go back to your employer."

Rain pulled on her coat and boots, wincing as she shoved her arm in and felt the shooting pain in her shoulder. She stomped out into the deep snow and down the narrow path behind the house. She needed to clear her head. She wasn't prepared to hear that Prescott was the reason she had a hook in her arm, her face rearranged, or her knuckles smashed to hell. She remembered praying that he'd gotten away and wasn't going through what she was. Now to find out that he was playing her the entire time and could be playing them now, she didn't know how to react. She heard the footsteps behind her crunching heavily in the snow and turned to see Tolley catching up with her. He was still zipping his coat as he walked alongside her.

"I guess it'd be silly to ask if you're alright. That's some pretty heavy stuff to hear."

"Yeah, beyond heavy. Most girls are upset that their boyfriends cheated, but mine, well, Prescott sent me to get tortured."

"So he's your boyfriend?" Tolley tried to crack a smile but it came across too tight-lipped.

"Well, before . . . I don't know," Rain said, shaking the thought from her head. She could still feel something brewing deep inside for Prescott but how could she know it was real? She didn't even know who he really was.

"He seems like a good kid, minus the ties to the most deadly man in the world." Tolley chuckled, a mist of white smoke clouding from his mouth and vanishing.

"How could you say that? You, of all people, should be angry. He had your men risk their lives to save us," Rain said, rounding the street and seeing the 7-Eleven sign beaming along with the sun, which had no effect on the snow.

"He could've let you die there but he tried to fight back. The first guy at the Basin we ran across had been in a pretty good fight. Prescott helped us find you and let us know how many people were there. He helped out where he could. But there is one thing I saw that made sense in all that ruckus . . . when he saw you were safe, I hadn't seen a look like that in a man's eyes in a very long time."

"So you came out here to convince me to get over it?" Rain said with disdain.

"Nope. Not at all. I came here to see if my baby girl was alright." He laced his arm around her shoulder as she winced from the weight.

"Oh, sorry," he said, picking up his arm quickly.

"I'm okay, Dad. Just a little sore. How's this?" She laced her hand around his arm and he smiled. They walked in silence down the winding streets, passing small shop doors that hid the contents of their goods behind signs made of squiggly lines. Tolley helped her into a ramen shop and they laughed over the slurp of noodles and green tea. Before long, she felt like home wasn't as far away as it seemed.

FOURTEEN

"JUST HOLD ON A MINUTE!" Tolley heard Black say when he opened the door to let Rain in from their lunch.

Black held the world phone in his outstretched palm and Tolley took two large steps to grab it. Black withdrew it to his chest and looked past Tolley as his eyes landed on Rain's surprised face.

"It's for her," he said with a look of worry before dropping it in her hand and turning away.

Rain looked at the phone in her palm before placing it to her ear.

"Rain?" The voice was familiar and awakened something in Rain that had been dormant for years. It was her mother.

"Hello, Rain?" she repeated.

"I'm here," Rain croaked through her shock. She'd wanted to hear her voice for so long that hearing it now seemed ready to make her faint.

"I'm glad you're alright. I can't talk long but I want to give you a message."

"A message?"

"Watch the boy. He is not as clean as he seems."

"Trust me, I know." She eyed Prescott who was sitting alone in the corner of the room, his shame etched across his face.

"We will need to meet soon," she said matter-of-factly.

"Meet? When? Where?"

"I will send the information at a later date when I have worked out a few things. Keep your focus. Dalton is still looking for both of us. You are his greatest asset against me but he underestimated your father, apparently."

Rain could hear a sense of pride in her voice at the mention of her husband, Rain's father. She glanced at Tolley who was still standing beside her, his eyes squinted with worry, listening intently to one side of the conversation.

"Okay ... *Mother.*" The word felt foreign on her lips. She hadn't said it to anyone else but that was well over ten years ago.

The call went dead without a breath of good-bye. Rain stared at the phone in her palm, unsure of whether she had just spoken to her mother, the fugitive, the possible rogue agent, or the legend. Tolley was hugging her before she could crumple to the floor. She didn't realize how weak she was from the events of the past week, but suddenly the weight of her experiences crashed down on her and she went limp in Tolley's arms. She wanted to be strong like her father and as smart and daring as her mother, but it was harder than she thought. She sobbed into Tolley's shoulder until her body wretched with the anger, pain, and fear of what her life had become. She knew as she clung to her father that her life would never be as easy as it was on the farm ever again. She'd never trust again like she used to. She had fallen into a world that was destined to chew up her soul and spit out death and betrayal. A world where having a family was simply an asset against an adversary. Tolley brought Rain to the tatami room and unrolled her pallet of thick covers. He laid her across the mat, pulled the covers to her shoulder, and sat with her. He didn't say a word, just took in the pain and loneliness that radiated from Rain in hopes that she'd be renewed after her release. She rolled away from him and pulled her knees to her chest.

"She doesn't love us, does she?" Rain whispered.

"She does. Very much. It's very complicated but you'll understand over time," Tolley said as he smoothed her dark hair down her back. "If she wants to meet then that means something important is happening and she needs our help."

"But she never needs anyone, right?" Rain looked over her shoulder.

Tolley caught her eye and in a reassuring tone said, "Exactly."

THE INFORMATION CAME IN the form of a Japanese courier three days later. The bell chimed throughout the house and brought everyone from their resting places. Black eased his pistol from his holster, which seemed to never leave his side. He looked at the video on the wall streaming a live feed from the camera outside the front door. He saw a spiky-haired Japanese kid bobbing his head to the music in his headphones as he patted his leg to the beat. The kid rang the bell again and waited a few seconds before he pulled a clipboard from the back of his pants and began writing. Black opened the door a crack.

"*Kon-ba-wa,*" Black said to the boy as the boy smiled crookedly, lifted the headphones, and hung them around his neck.

"*Kon-ba-wa. Ame-san no pakkēji.*" He held the clipboard out to Black, who took it but kept his eyes on the kid while signing.

"*Domo arigato!*" The kid glanced at the signature quickly then held up a finger to show Black he'd be right back. He retrieved the package from the back of his motorbike and trotted up the walkway. Black held his weapon ready behind the door, its barrel pointed at the kid through the wood. The courier held a small brown package that he thrust in Black's awaiting palm and bowed deeply before turning to sprint back to his bike. Black watched him on the video screen put his headphones back on, jam the bike into gear, and speed off. He lifted the package to his ear and felt satisfied that he couldn't hear the tick of a bomb. He handed it to Mogli who also checked the package wrapping and noted that there was no return address or postage.

"The kid must've been locally procured and not through the regular Black Cat couriers."

Tolley knew who it was from. He was waiting on the package since Dahlia had called. He grabbed the package and saw kanji for the name Rain written in black marker across the front in Japanese.

"I'll open it for you," he said to Rain, who was still half-inside the tatami room shielding herself behind the wall.

"No. I'll do it," she said, coming to sit next to him on the couch. She wrapped her flannel shirt tighter around her chest and sunk into the couch next to Tolley. He nodded with a half smile and slid the package in front of her on the coffee table.

She unwrapped the package carefully, as if ripping the paper meant she was ripping a piece of her newfound bond with her mother. She folded back the edges to view the contents of the box: a pistol, a stack of Russian rubles totaling nearly three thousand dollars, a passport with Rain's picture, and the name Anastasia Volkov next to it. She dug deeper into the box and found a letter with a red wax closure. The closure reminded Rain of reading old classic stories like Shakespeare. She thought it was a sign of royalty and old-world charm as she ran her finger across the symbol of an origami bird imprinted in the wax. She carefully opened the letter.

It had a short inscription:

Tuesday at 9:00a

Krasnaya Presnya St., 13, Moscow 123242, Russia

Rain passed the letter to Tolley who stared at it quickly then set it down.

"Do you know the place?"

"Oh yes. Very well. It's where I asked your mother to marry me."

"What? In Russia?" Rain said, trying to hide a smile by looking surprised. "I guess you were right . . . she does love us . . . or should I say, she loves *you*."

Rain couldn't help but chuckle, but her father wasn't joining in. He strode to the kitchen, stone-faced, and called the men to huddle around. He unrolled the map again on the table and started pointing as they all nodded at his instructions. Rain wanted to listen but she couldn't tear herself away from the box. She ran her fingers along the pistol. It had been used before; she could tell by the scratches and nicks on the steel. She looked closely at the handle and saw the letters *DW* inscribed in swirly font along the ridge. She smiled at the gift, knowing this had been her mother's personal weapon. The weapon she'd done the most dirty work with and she'd wanted her to have it.

FIFTEEN

CAFÉ MICHEL, MOSCOW, RUSSIA

Café Michel was a quaint, French-styled building with a superb placement in the center of bustling Moscow. The red planter boxes flanked the highly detailed arching windows covered by burgundy awnings. Small mounds of old unmelted snow crawled up the side of the building, peppered with black speckles. Rain and Mogli rode around the café twice before they pulled into a parking spot two buildings down.

"I will be checking the perimeter by car. Prescott is on the roof and has a clear shot on the western window, so please sit there. Tolley is at the pub across the street and you should be able to hear him in your earbud. He will be able to hear everything you say. Black will be roaming around the building and alleyway. Shanty is checking on another lead. If you feel danger at any moment, just give the signal and you always have your weapon as a last resort," Mogli finished.

His brown eyes bore holes in Rain. His serious nature took away any thought of how handsome he was and made Rain focus on her mission. Mogli was only interested in making sure she knew the plan. She could feel her mother's gun resting on the small of her back. She felt closer to her already.

"Why do I need all this if I'm just meeting my mother?" Rain asked, pulling her long brown hair from the elastic and shaking it out.

"Better safe than dead," Mogli said without a smile and unlocked the doors. Rain knew the sound of the lock was her cue that he was done talking about it. Rain sat in the passenger seat and tried to quiet her mind. Her thoughts raced about what her mother would be like after so many years. She wondered why they were guarding her so heavily when her mother had offered to meet her to ask for her help. She remembered that they were all fugitives of Christopher Dalton and felt instantly safer to have them there with her, but she still couldn't squash the unease in her belly.

Mogli's voice tore through her thoughts. "You understand the plan, don't you? If you should run into trouble, pull at your necklace or say the code words *red snapper*. Prescott will be watching, Tolley will be listening. Sit on the western edge of the building."

Rain nodded faintly and exited the vehicle. Before she could take two steps on the pavement, Mogli pulled off into traffic and rounded the corner out of sight. Rain felt alone even though she spotted Tolley in the pub sipping on a beer in the window with a paperboy hat pulled low over his brow. She didn't dare glance up at Prescott but she could feel his eyes on her. She strutted to the café on shaky knees, her heart racing in anticipation. She was surprised to find the ambience welcoming in the café when she pulled open the wooden door. She envisioned her mother and father sitting at the window, sipping tea and laughing like inseparable lovers. Rain planted herself in a cloth chair near the western windows as instructed and surveyed the exposed-brick walls, the bookcase of classic novels, the burnished gold candelabras, and soft lighting. Under different circumstances, she would have loved to meet her mother at a place like this for brunch. She shrugged out of her coat and ordered hot tea while she waited.

A woman, tall and statuesque, wearing large black glasses and a long fur coat entered the café and scanned her surroundings. She was twenty minutes early but Rain was ready. She'd waited too long to meet her after so many years. The maître d' helped her from her coat as she held a small tan-colored handbag. Her dark hair cascaded in waves to her waist as she turned to thank the young man. She was dressed in a black turtleneck tucked into black leather pants but her red lips were bold. Rain swallowed. The possibility of the beautiful woman being her mother was likely. She was almost how Rain remembered her, except she couldn't see her eyes behind the oversized glasses. The woman smirked as she walked over, then showed perfectly white teeth as she sat across from Rain without a word.

"Are you . . ." Rain asked.

"Yes. I am," she said with a silky voice that held a note of privilege and snobbery. Rain was having trouble piecing together how Tolley and the woman across from her matched so well for so long. She seemed so out of his league. She wasn't exactly the farming type with her perfectly manicured nails.

"What's happened to your face, dear girl?" she said while reaching across the table to softly turn Rain's chin from left to right, assessing the damage.

"I'm okay." Rain smirked. It felt good to have her mother care so much for her already.

Her mother pulled her hand back and composed herself before saying, "I'm sure you have a lot of questions but I don't have much time. It is important that I establish a relationship with you but until I have finished my business here, we are both at risk from Christopher Dalton." She placed her napkin in her lap as the waiter brought her hot tea.

"What does he want?" Rain asked. She was hoping her mother had a simple answer but she feared it wasn't.

"I'm figuring it all out, Rain. The less you know, the better. I just need to get the chip from you to keep you safe. I don't want him coming after you. You don't deserve to be in the middle of all this," she said, clinking her spoon noisily against her teacup before taking a sip. Rain's gaze lingered on the imprint of her red lips against the white cup.

Rain remembered what Tolley had told her. There were specific things she was supposed to ask before she told her anything. It was a secret code that they had started when they were partners at the agency. It was a way to have a conversation without having a conversation, he'd told her.

"I've finished school, you know? I was studying the anthropological status of Viking warriors. It was a great class," Rain said, sipping from her tea and keeping her eyes on her mother.

"Really? Well, that's quite interesting, dear. But you should be studying things that have more significant value to our family, like espionage and torture tactics." She smiled tightly and rested her hands in her lap. "That was a joke," she said, chuckling softly to herself.

Rain felt an unease cross over her. She had a feeling that things were going all wrong. Her mother's answer was incorrect.

"You're probably right, Mother." Rain chuckled. "I've heard from Mr. Bundant that I should travel to China this year and learn how to speak Mandarin. That could be useful."

"Indeed. Now that's better." She smiled and swept her long hair over her shoulder.

"Can you excuse me? This tea has gone right through me," Rain offered, her fingers trailing up toward her neckline as she fought with uncertainty.

"Maybe I should go with you. It's never safe when you're alone," her mother said behind the glasses with a slight smile.

Rain was confused. Her mother had not answered any of the secret codes correctly. Had she forgotten after so long? She wasn't sure she wanted her mother away from the western window and in the bathroom with her, so she stalled.

"Of course. Wow. Your nails are really beautiful." Before she could pull her hand back, Rain grabbed her wrist and lifted the edge of her sleeve. The oval-shaped birthmark was not there as she had remembered. Instead there was a small tattoo. The woman sensed her discovery and within a second that seemed to drag on, she flipped the table with a sleight of hand, clattering the dishes onto the tiled floor with a loud crash. Rain scrambled back in her seat narrowly missing the saucers that shattered into shards and skidded across the floor. The woman pulled out a pistol from her lower back, a silencer extended from the nozzle, and pointed it at Rain's head. "Stand up! Time to go!" She jerked the pistol twice toward the hallway.

Rain knew the shot was coming before she heard it. A bullet smashed through the western glass window sending a large shard at her face. She felt the burn on her cheek as the glass cut into her flesh. The sound of shattering glass filled the café and Rain could hear the woman yelp in pain. Her hand had been blown into a bloody mess, dripping onto the tile in bright-red rivers. She held her mangled hand as she breathed in and out trying to tame her shock. Her weapon had slid across the ground near the bar in the chaos and it was closer to her than to Rain. The woman followed Rain's eyes, which rested on the pistol, and scrambled toward the gun. Bullets riddled the ground around her with each step and she detoured quickly to preserve what was left of her body. She jabbed passed the bar, gripping her bleeding hand like a football, and disappeared down the back hallway into the kitchen. Rain looked out the window and saw Tolley sprinting across the street and within minutes he was next to Rain, huffing with adrenaline.

"You okay?" he asked quickly, grabbing the pistol the woman had left behind.

Rain nodded, still in shock, as Tolley took off down the hallway in pursuit of the woman in black. Rain struggled to get her head wrapped around what had just happened. Everything was moving so quickly. The bloody floor looked like a murder had taken place in the café and she was still crouched beside her chair in the midst of broken dishes and large shards of window glass. She cursed herself for not stopping the woman and hated that she'd frozen at a time when it was critical to get answers. She wrestled herself to the front door of the café, her feet heavy like she was wearing lead shoes. Mogli was in a car in front of the building when Rain stepped out, dazed by the daylight that hid the tragedies of the café. People who had seen the debacle were crowded across the street, phones in hand, attempting to capture the excitement for their friends who'd missed it. Rain sucked her teeth in disdain as she lowered her head to protect her face from the cameras. She slid into the vehicle as the tires spun wildly before catching and shooting them forward into the street. The smell of burned rubber filled the car as Rain stared at Mogli's serious glare.

"You didn't use the signal," Mogli said, staring straight ahead and maneuvering the vehicle easily through traffic.

"I'm sorry," Rain said in shame. She had only one job to do and she had failed them, again.

Mogli ignored her response, his eyesight trained on the road. Rain sat back in the vehicle as it grazed over potholed streets without care for its durability. She wanted to crumble under the weight of her mistake. It could have cost her life or the life of one of the team members, and it had definitely shattered their anonymity in Russia. She didn't want to even think about whether video would be leaked and if they were spotted. It could turn into an international political debacle.

Mogli revved the engine and swerved behind a car as he spotted the woman running across traffic with Black on her heels and Tolley, pumping his arms in full stride, not far behind. Cars swerved to avoid hitting the woman while loud honks and yelled curses rang out in the busy intersection. A car screeched to a halt in front of her, moments from sending her flying like a discus across the pavement. Like a ninja she slid across the top of the Mercedes, landed on her feet, and kept running without pause. Rain's eyes widened in surprise at the agility of the woman. Mogli was a block over, watching the woman intently as he whipped through traffic and turned his head quickly to see her route and to modify his own. He turned the wheel hard to the left to intercept her from the front, and Rain grabbed the door handle in the vehicle, gritting her teeth as she was carried by the momentary inertia.

TOLLEY COULD FEEL HIS GUT burning. He hadn't run this far or this hard in a long time, but he wanted this woman. He *needed* this woman. She was a direct link to Dalton and he knew he could get her to talk and finally find out what Dalton really wanted from Dahlia. The woman was stealthily dodging traffic when a black BMW SUV swerved next to her. The rear door shot open and the woman grabbed the door handle with her good hand and swung her body into the vehicle. Her feet disappeared quickly as the SUV rounded a stopped car and sped away.

"No!" Black said, pulling out his pistol and aiming at the speeding SUV.

"Don't do it, Black!" Tolley said breathlessly. "We don't need police on our tail. Time to go."

"Dammit!" Black said, trotting next to Tolley as if the high-speed chase hadn't fazed him. Tolley felt as if he was going to spill the contents of his breakfast on the pavement but he swallowed hard to keep it down.

Within minutes, Prescott pulled up in a small gray car and honked the horn.

"Yes!" Black said, jumping into the small sedan quickly. Before Tolley could shut the door, the car shot off after the black SUV. Tolley could see Mogli's car dart into view, trailing the SUV closely.

THE SUV WAS STILL TRAVELING at a high rate of speed when Mogli and Rain finally caught up with it. Tolley radioed that they were still in pursuit about a mile back and still had a visual. Mogli pressed the gas down further as the car lurched toward the back bumper of the BMW. He bumped it lightly, still trying to work the engine hard to stay close. The SUV shot off again, leaving a foot of space between the cars. Mogli pushed the car to its limit, gaining on the bumper again. He heard the engine rev with a growl and he bumped the rear end of the vehicle enough to make it fishtail slightly and right itself within seconds.

"Shit!"

Rain saw the brake lights before she felt the car plunge into the back of the SUV. The impact jarred her forward. Mogli's head hit the steering wheel roughly and bounced back like a Ping-Pong ball on a wooden paddle. His head rolled back against the headrest and he moaned in pain. Rain had only been slammed against the seat belt but she felt as if her chest would cave in. She coughed in response, trying to loosen the leather strap from across her bosom. The BMW, although wrecked in the rear, pulled off again, the back bumper dipping slightly toward the ground as it picked up speed. Mogli tried to push the pedal to the floor even though his eyesight was blurry and his head ached like he'd been hit with a hammer.

Within a few yards, he found that the car wouldn't go any faster. In fact, it was gradually slowing as smoke billowed from the crumpled hood, gray fog misting out the side. Prescott's car shot past them in a gray blur. Rain's head whipped around to see him but all she saw was the back of the vehicle darting around cars attempting to make up ground.

Mogli looked at Rain, his eyes bloodshot but more coherent now. "Got to ditch the car."

He climbed out of the car on wobbly legs. He held his chest upright as onlookers and other drivers questioned if he was okay in Russian. He nodded curtly to the caring strangers who stared in disbelief. Rain trailed him from the vehicle, her head aching and her cheek bleeding again. She was sure they looked like they'd been through a meat grinder. Mogli took a baseball cap out of his jacket pocket and placed it on his head. Blood trickled from his temple and down his cheek as he pulled his long hair carefully toward the front of his face. Rain followed him into a taxi that waited in the traffic caused by their wreck. The driver twisted his wheel and sent the car down a side street to head in the opposite direction. She looked back over her shoulder hoping to catch a glimpse of Prescott but there was only slow-moving traffic. Signs of a high-speed chase were nonexistent as if life had kept on moving regardless of a shooting at a nearby café or gruesome accident on the roadway. The onlookers had moved on and the drivers had continued on their way, avoiding the mangled vehicle in the middle of the road as if it was a simple orange cone to protect them from a pothole.

TOLLEY AND BLACK SAW THE collision with Mogli and Rain. Tolley glanced at Rain as they sped by to make sure she was safe. He soon realized that the woman in the SUV was no longer chasing Rain but instead wanted nothing more than to evade capture. He knew that meant he needed whatever information the woman had. She was the priority.

"Careful, Prescott. Try to spin them," Tolley said.

Black strapped on his seat belt in the rear of the vehicle as Prescott gunned the little engine until it was near the left corner of the truck. Prescott tapped it lightly, which fishtailed the vehicle, but it still darted through traffic, gaining more space. It took a hard left down an alleyway and Prescott skidded to a halt, almost missing the street as he struggled with the lack of power steering in the small car. He reversed quickly amid the agitated honks of cars around him, then he sped down the alleyway, avoiding baskets of trash and boxes littered along the sides. Ahead, the SUV screeched to a halt at the edge of the alleyway and the woman escaped into a doorway attached to a building on the corner.

"Come on," Black urged in the backseat, willing Prescott to make it to the building before they lost the woman.

Before Prescott could stop the vehicle, Tolley was out of the car running into the door the woman had entered. Tolley heard her footsteps on the stairwell moving fast and rhythmic as she climbed up the industrial building.

"Follow the truck," Black yelled back to Prescott as he trailed Tolley into the building.

Prescott gunned the engine and leaped out into traffic. A couple walking jumped back from the edge of the alleyway and yelled curses as he turned in the direction of the SUV. He spotted the black truck ahead, only about five hundred feet away, no longer speeding recklessly but keeping a pace that blended with traffic. Prescott hung back, elated that they thought they'd lost him. He followed the vehicle as it turned on the highway keeping three or four cars between them.

TOLLEY COULD HEAR THE CLAP OF her heels against the linoleum landing and then silence. He stopped at the same level and entered the sixth floor slowly, his weapon drawn. The way the woman had bounded through traffic, he knew she was trained very well and could probably kick his ass in a street fight. He didn't let that thought discourage him because he knew behind a gun, he was just as fierce. The level was an unfinished office space with white walls and low-hanging electrical lines from the ceiling. The smell of fresh paint was strong. Tolley could hear her running through the plastic barriers between rooms and took off after her. He heard Black enter the door behind him and looked back long enough to motion him to follow. Tolley entered the first set of hanging plastic barriers, straining to see behind its blurry translucence. Black rounded the same room to close in from an opposite angle in hopes of cornering the imposter.

"You think you're so smart, Agent Wilson? You don't know a damn thing about what you are into," the woman said loudly, her voice gruff and breathy from overexertion. Tolley rounded the corner and saw that she was riddled with sweat, chest heaving, standing in the center of the room. Tolley scanned the area. He felt uneasy with her running into a closed-off space seemingly on purpose. It felt wrong to him.

"How did you know about the meeting? Who do you work for?" Tolley questioned. His gun was still trained on her but his eyes darted around the space, searching for an avenue of escape or subterfuge.

"You don't get to ask the questions. It would be good of you to listen," she said with a wicked laugh. "You think you're on the right side of this, don't you? Your wife is going to bring down the entire agency. You understand the severity of that, don't you? You know what that could do to the infrastructure of our country, the American people's faith?" she said through gritted teeth. Her face shined with sweat and her chest heaved as if ready to explode.

Tolley swallowed. He indeed did not realize how deep the well of deception ran or why the CIA seemed hell-bent on keeping Rain and Dahlia apart. He eyed the woman in front of him. She only slightly resembled Dahlia but her eyes were wide and wild, darting from him to the floor and to the large windows surrounding the space. She looked as if she were on drugs.

"There's only one thing that can fix the infrastructure and the American people's faith . . . and that's the truth," Tolley said with a squint. The woman wobbled on her heels. Tolley could see her thin thigh jiggling with adrenaline and possibly shock from her hand wound. She gripped the mangled flesh and fingers in a tight fist, likely trying to control the bleeding, which dripped onto the dust-covered floor.

"You don't even know the truth you seek," she spat with a sinister grin before popping a pill into her mouth with her good hand. Blood from her wounded hand smeared across her face and made her look deranged.

Her pretty face shifted into an ugly scowl as she grabbed her stomach and fell to the floor like a rag doll. Within seconds, a seizure racked her body. Her arms and legs thrashed about wildly as foam frothed from her red lips. It was only a few minutes before she was completely still on the linoleum, a red streak of blood pushing the last of the foam from her mouth and down the side of her cheek. Tolley noticed she'd made a dust angel on the floor and shook his head at her unnecessary demise. He wouldn't have killed her, not unless he needed to, so why would she take her own life? Black stepped from his hiding spot and attempted to examine her as he knelt beside her. She was dead. It wouldn't take an autopsy to realize what Tolley and Black already knew, that she had taken Vaxitram, the same pill terrorists used in Iraq to quietly kill leaders across the world. The symptoms of the pill made death hard to identify since there were never any traces of a foreign substance in the body.

"I'm betting she was an agent. They're the only ones that run this type of operation," Black said, running a hand through his close cropped blond hair. "Why would she have Vaxitram?"

Black pulled her pockets inside out, searching for any information, but there was none. She was clean. He raised her sleeves to the elbow and found a small birdlike symbol on her inner wrist. He showed it to Tolley but neither could figure out the symbol. Black committed it to memory and vowed to look into it later.

Tolley looked around the room, stunned that she'd been a patriot and an agent but had succumbed to some sick belief that Dalton was helping the world instead of using it, and her, for monetary advantage and power. He knew better. His history with Dalton was scarred. Old wounds that had healed but hadn't been forgotten.

"Vaxitram . . . you remember the supplier?" Tolley said.

He knew Black had many talents, one of which was a great memory. If he'd learned it, read it, or seen it then Black could pull up the memory without hesitation. That's part of what made him a great fighter and tracker. He never forgot a detail about the person he was after.

Black dropped his head, still holding the woman's wrist and answered, "The Sallad Musad Pharmaceuticals Group. They manufactured it and sold it to the agency. This symbol, I've seen it before." He ran a finger across the tattoo and struggled to remember. He dropped the woman's wrist and stepped to the window, its white-painted wood cracked and peeling. The streets were moving freely, shoppers crossing the sidewalk with bags, oblivious to the death and despair a few floors up.

"I can't remember where I've seen it before. Must have been in passing," Black said, searching his memory and growing agitated that it was just out of reach.

"Looks like we're in some deep shit, indeed," Tolley answered under his breath. "If Sallad Musad is involved, that's a big problem. If Catwoman here—" Tolley gestured to the dead woman, "—would kill herself to keep a secret even when she could have gotten away, that means that there's no going back for her. She gave her message as a last-ditch effort to get us off the trail."

"What was she talking about when she said your wife is going to bring down the entire agency?" Black said, his blue eyes intensely trained on Tolley.

"I don't know. That's what we need to find out." Tolley remembered that Prescott was still following the only lead they had left. He pressed his earpiece hoping it was still in range. "Prescott, do you read me?"

"Loud and clear, sir." Ironically, Prescott's voice came through with loud static.

"What's the vehicle's location?"

"Still traveling northbound on the M10. They've slowed down but I'm trailing," Prescott responded, his voice getting louder and softer on the line from the bad reception.

"They've slowed down? How fast are they going now?" Tolley said, pinching the earpiece until his eardrum ached.

"Only fifty miles per hour. Why?"

"Get out of there now!" Tolley yelled.

PRESCOTT DIDN'T WASTE A MOMENT. He gunned the engine and swerved lanes without a second thought. His body was on autopilot as his hands gripped the steering wheel tightly. He looked in his rearview mirror and noticed two black SUVs speeding toward him. *Shit*, he thought. He was two seconds from becoming minced meat. He knew the SUVs were going to try and sandwich him until they had a clear shot.

The two SUVs quickly ran alongside him and he saw the windows roll down to reveal gun barrels. He swerved hard into oncoming traffic, clipping the front light of one of the SUVs and narrowly missing a head-on collision with a sedan that swerved in the opposite direction. Cars jerked left and right as he pushed the pedal to the floor and jolted in unison to avoid oncoming cars. The jerking movement made his stomach jump along with his racing heartbeat. He couldn't hear Tolley in his earpiece, just a buzzing sound that let him know the line was dead on Tolley's end.

Prescott banked left when traffic opened up for what seemed like a minute sliver of time and ran off the opposite side of the road. He hit the grassy valley that opened up on the other side of the highway harder than he imagined he would. The car lurched forward and went airborne as he jumped a small ditch that threatened to dislodge the wheels from the axle. He chanced a look in the rearview and saw one of the SUVs bounding across the lanes, avoiding the cars as he had and taking the first bump off the highway with a spit of gravel flying. The second SUV was still dodging the swerving cars and couldn't make it across the lane completely. Prescott hit the accelerator and the car felt as if the bottom would break into two as the uneven grassy terrain punished the car's shocks at a high rate of speed. He spied a dirt road a hundred yards away and turned hard in its direction, feeling the car almost drift on the high grass. He raced past cows that had not even looked up as he sped by with the SUV lagging a little further behind.

"And they say German cars have the best handling," Prescott said to himself as he finally reached the dirt road and kicked up pellets of black gravel as he righted himself in the lane. The SUV was bounding through the cows, trying hard to maneuver around the sedentary beasts. Prescott saw a small town emerging and slowed his engine a bit to see whether he could find a good place to ditch the car. He passed rows of thin storefronts that looked squished next to one another, almost too close to be separate entities. He passed by Olga's Hair Menagerie, a small grocer, and slowed even more until he spotted what looked like an auto body shop. He wheeled the sedan into the open-door hangar, wedged the car into a dark space of the garage, and killed the engine. The car rattled to a quiet wheeze until it settled with a huff. Prescott let his forehead rest on the steering wheel. He couldn't believe how wrong everything had went from the time he saw the dark-haired lady arrive at the café.

"You got an appointment?" a man with a long salt-and-pepper beard said outside the window in Russian. He must've seen Prescott pull in and thought he'd had a new customer.

"No, sir. But I could use a little help." Prescott tried his best Russian and realized he should have studied more.

The man cocked his head to the side like a loyal old dog and scrunched his brow in confusion. Prescott dislodged the keys and handed them to the man with a smile. An awkward silence fell on the two in the small garage as the man put a cigarette to his lips and lit it without response. Prescott kept the dangling keys out the window and held his smile until it started to make his cheeks twitch with muscle failure.

"Alright then," the man finally said in English, blowing smoke in Prescott's face.

"Okay," Prescott said, straightening his shirt and kicking open the door with a creak.

Prescott ditched the car with the old man after assuring him he'd pay when he picked it up the next day and headed to the café across the street. He used the pay phone near the bathroom and called Tolley to arrange his pickup. He just needed to lay low until the cavalry came. After telling Tolley his location, he slumped at the makeshift bar and ordered a café latte from a thickly built woman with a face that looked like it'd seen a few more bad days than she wished to admit. The server didn't meet his eyes as she slid the latte across the slick glossy top of the bar. Prescott sipped it slowly and relished the warmth as he felt it slide down his chest and into his stomach.

He savored his drink and glanced around the empty café. It was midday and he looked more like a stranger than a local in black cargo pants and black crewneck. He hoped the goons that were chasing him had passed through the town but he had a feeling he wouldn't be too lucky if he didn't start moving soon. *After I finish this drink,* he thought as he took another sip. His mind was racing over the day's events, trying to figure out what went wrong and how the lady knew exactly where they were meeting if she wasn't sent by Rain's mother. Had the message from the courier been intercepted? Had it been a setup all along by Dalton to capture or kill Rain and possibly himself? Prescott knew that Dalton would not let their escape from the Basin go unavenged. But one thing he was infinitely sure of was that he couldn't bear the thought of losing Rain. His heart sped up thinking about the possibility of her being stripped away from him. He swallowed another gulp of coffee to suppress his desire to vomit at the thought.

His last vision of Rain's face broke into his thoughts. He saw her eyes when the imposter mother across from her had made the fatal mistake of not answering her correctly. Her eyes were the windows to everything she felt and he was sure the woman noticed that she'd made a grave mistake. Prescott remembered how he'd hesitated shooting at the woman because he couldn't take his eyes from Rain and she hadn't given the signal. He'd felt a drop in his stomach when everything had gone wrong so quickly at Café Michel. He couldn't lose Rain, not ever. He saw her through the scope, her dark hair pulled behind her ears as she spoke with her mother, the look of desperation in her body language. She really wanted to be loved by her mother. To be wanted by a woman who seemingly wanted nothing more than justice.

He knew the feeling well enough with his own mother, a junky who gave her child to the only person that would take him. Just like her, he'd been abandoned, too. He felt the same void in his own life without a relationship with his mother but he realized Rain still had a chance. She could find her mother and uncover the mysteries of their relationship. Where was Dahlia? Why didn't she show up at the café as she promised? He felt an ache in his soul for Rain that it was not her mother who showed up, and how foolish she must have felt at not recognizing the fact sooner. But Prescott couldn't figure out one reason why her mother would want to kill her.

SIXTEEN

RAIN TOUCHED THE WET RAG to Mogli's temple and softly sponged away the dried blood. He'd hit his head pretty hard on the steering wheel during the car chase. His long brown hair had streams of blood turning it to a reddish hue. She was surprised he'd made it into the taxi and back to the rendezvous point without blacking out. Now that they were in the third-floor walk-up in a lower-class Russian neighborhood, he settled back on the sunken brown cloth couch and let his head drop back. Rain saw his knees bow out in exhaustion as she sat in the chair across from him with the smell of mildew strong in the room.

"You should clean your wound." Mogli's voice was like sandpaper as he spoke without opening his eyes.

She placed the rag in the warm water and squeezed the excess out. She dabbed at her own cut across her cheek and winced from the stinging sensation. She'd gotten cut by the glass when the café window exploded but walked away from the car wreck without even a stiff neck. She wasn't sure if Mogli had intentionally taken the full force of the hit.

"Why are you doing this?" Rain asked, surprised to hear her own voice in the silent room.

"Doing what?" Mogli said, sighing heavily.

"Helping us . . . I mean, me."

"I'm one of your father's best friends. Isn't that what friends are for? To put our lives on the line for each other?" He tittered softly. Rain liked the sound of his voice.

"I guess that's the unwritten rule of friendship," she said with a smirk. "But I never even knew you guys existed. My father never talked about you guys . . . ever."

"Agents are normally good at keeping secrets, Rain. Even from the people we love," he answered quietly. Rain could sense there was something hidden behind his words, a sadness.

"Do you lie to your wife and family? Do they think you're on a fishing trip with the guys right now?" Rain joked.

"No. I don't have any family. After giving fifteen years to the CIA, I realized that I didn't have much to give anyone other than constant paranoia, shitty nightmares, and a bad case of wanting to kill shit every now and then."

Rain couldn't help but laugh. She covered her mouth to stifle it but Mogli peeked through his eyelids and joined her in laughter. Before long, she calmed down to a giggle and said to herself more than him, "I can't believe you're not married. Look at you."

Silence entered the space and she could feel the awkwardness. She wanted to pound her palm against her head for being stupid enough to compliment someone twice her age, albeit a gorgeous and funny man.

"And I'm surprised you are a soldier," Mogli said after a moment of silence.

"*Was* a soldier . . ." Rain corrected.

"Well, you're definitely too pretty to be a soldier or an agent. You need to be on that beautiful farm, making babies and making some man very happy," Mogli said, turning his head toward her from the couch, his hair falling into his face seductively.

"Well that's quite sexist of you," Rain said, flicking water on him. He turned his head but didn't move much from the wet sprinkles.

Rain eyed him as his barrel chest rose and fell under his button-down shirt. A few dots of blood had ruined the perfection of his body in the shirt. She glanced down his long, lean body before feeling utterly ashamed. She swirled the water to keep busy. He was the classiest of all the group, Rain decided. She could see him being a father or husband in his normal life. He probably knew how to blend in with regular society. She wasn't sure if she would ever be able to again after what she'd seen and done.

"Yeah, maybe." Rain smiled and looked down at the murky water in the bucket next to her. Being a wife and mother seemed much better than suffering with PTSD alone. She hid from his brown eyes that bore into her so deeply she felt a flutter in her belly.

"Yeah . . . maybe," Mogli said before placing his head back on the couch and closing his eyes. Rain eyed the strong curve of his jaw, riddled with light stubble, then sunk back in her own chair.

The interior of the apartment was similar to the exterior, shabby and run-down with its chipping, claylike cement walls and sunken windows which pooled rainwater around the seams. Rain scanned the worn carpet and traced the balding spots from the living room to the kitchen then another path which led to the front door. Tolley told the group it'd be safer in a neighborhood where they could blend in and where the police weren't going to be hanging out voluntarily. He'd been right. Rain hadn't seen any police since they'd returned back to the apartment, even after all the commotion in downtown Moscow that the car chase had created.

"Go ahead and rest. I'll wait for them to come back," Mogli said in a gruff voice, snapping Rain from her rumination. His eyes looked tired, lids closing and opening slower than usual.

"No, you sleep. You need it more than I do. I'll stay up and wait," Rain said and squeezed Mogli's firm shoulder to reassure him. "Unless you have a concussion, then you need to stay up," she added smartly.

He mumbled a response before stretching out on the length of the couch, kicking his boots up on the armrest. "It's just a scratch," he said sleepily. Within minutes, Rain heard his soft snore fill the room. Just touching Mogli made her feel like she wanted to sit at his feet and listen to him talk all night. He had made her smile even though she was worried about everyone else. He was *comforting*.

She grabbed the bucket near the chair and walked over to the kitchen to dump the tepid water down the drain. The slender window over the sink had a view of the parking lot. She checked the parking spot; it was still empty as she poured the water out and left the bucket in the sink. She rested her hands on both sides of the sink and let her head drop between her shoulders. They'd been in the apartment for nearly two hours without contact from the rest of the crew. Rain was starting to worry about their safety, the outcome of the mission. Had they caught the woman?

She'd never forgive herself if she'd been the cause of any of their deaths. It was her fault that they were involved with Dalton. She only wanted to bring her mother home, but unknowingly she'd only escalated things, put too many people in danger. *I should just quit this and go back to the farm*, she thought to herself. She heard a tinkering outside that made her raise her eyes back to the weather-beaten window. A black vehicle pulled into the parking spot quickly and she watched Black, Tolley, and Prescott exit, their necks craning to look down the street, up the building, then to the window. Tolley saw her and began his ascent up the exterior steps. She heard their footsteps outside the door as she stood in the living room, hand on hip, waiting to see them when they entered. Her heart was beating fast;

she hadn't realized how wound up she'd made herself while waiting to hear something from them.

Tolley swung open the door and it bounced softly against the doorjamb. He smiled with relief when he saw Rain standing there.

"Glad you made it back safely," he said, embracing her in a bear hug tight enough to be uncomfortable, but she didn't release him.

"We lost Prescott and had to go retrieve him," Black said, giving her a tight smile and walking past like he had something on his mind more important than a simple greeting. Rain knew he was all about business and didn't take it personally. Her eyes fell on Prescott following on Black's heels. Rain finally released Tolley from his warm hug.

"Hey, can I talk to you?" Rain said to Prescott as he attempted to walk by. Tolley looked at Prescott with a frown and nodded before walking into the living room and jostling Mogli awake.

"Yeah. Come on." Prescott opened the door to the spare room and Rain followed behind him.

The room hosted a bouncy bed, dressed in brown storm-shelter-style covers flanked by a scratched wooden nightstand, no lamp. The windows had faded sheers hanging loosely from a thin white bar. She sat on the edge of the bed and felt it sink down with his weight a few feet away.

"I want to apologize for how I reacted the other day." Rain swallowed hard. "But I also want to thank you for what you did today. I don't know what would have happened if you hadn't kept her from that gun. I froze. I forgot to make my move. It happened so fast." Rain tried to control her emotions. She didn't want to cry in front of him, show any weakness, but the feeling burned in her throat.

"You don't owe me anything, Rain. I owe you. All of you." Prescott scooted closer to her on the bed. "I'm sorry for lying to you, but it was before I knew anything about you. Once I spent time with you, I knew that Dalton had to be up to no good. He made me think that you were aiding a terrorist. So I thought I was doing something good, something worthwhile to make up for . . ." He pinched the bridge of his nose and continued. "It doesn't matter. The important thing to remember is that I know better now. And Dalton will pay for what he's done," Prescott said, turning toward her. Rain could see his eyes glaze over, felt the sincerity in the crack in his voice. He was swallowing the lump in his throat to keep from crying in front of her. She could see his remorse in his slumped shoulders and needy stare.

"I don't know what it is they want from my mother. Hell, I don't know what she wants from me, either. I can't tell you whether she's good or bad. I just have a feeling that she needs me now and I want to be there for her. We're family," Rain said. Prescott scooted closer to her on the bed and ran his fingers down her back. She felt her heart quicken a beat and hated that his touch still made her jittery, even after all the lies he'd told. She smiled at him demurely and stood up to get away from the warmth and comfort she felt beneath his touch.

"Do you still have the cell phone chip?" Prescott asked softly.

Rain looked at him with a suspicious glare. "Why?"

"Because I think I can get it decrypted. We need to know what's on it that is so important to Dalton." He looked into her guarded face. "I wouldn't hurt you, Rain. Not again."

"I don't know, Prescott. It's the most important thing I own right now. The only thing keeping us alive or getting us hunted . . . depends on how you look at it. The least amount of people who know where it is, the better. Nothing personal," Rain said, patting her hands on her thighs, anxious with the quick turn in the conversation.

He smiled gently, nodding. She knew he could sense that she didn't trust him completely. How could she after his betrayal? She wouldn't tell anyone other than Tolley where it was hidden. She knew she could trust him and that he was the only person in the world who would die before hurting her.

"So about this decryption, what do you need to get it done anyway?" Rain questioned. She knew absolutely nothing about technology—the gift of growing up on a farm, where you checked out the local news in a newspaper, not a television.

"There's a special type of technology that breaks codes. It could take a few hours with the guy I know but I'm pretty sure he could do it. Aren't you just the least bit curious what's on the damn thing that's making Dalton go to these lengths?" He searched Rain's face, pleadingly.

"Of course I'm curious. It could answer a lot of questions, but . . ." Rain was confused as to what to do. She massaged her temples that throbbed from anxiety. She didn't know whether she should trust Prescott again.

"Come on, Rain. Let's figure this thing out together," Prescott said. He stood and put his hands on hers, pulling them gently from her temples. "Just relax and tell me where it is. We can fly out tonight, meet with my guy, and have all the answers by the morning. I just want you to be safe."

Rain looked into Prescott's eyes. She saw the yearning to keep her safe but she also felt her instincts nagging at her. "Don't try to manipulate me, Prescott. I know why Dalton sent you to me. He's a genius at finding the right people for every job. I've seen you play people like pawns as part of a great big chess game. Me included. You think I didn't notice how you handled the guy at the hospital or Dalton or *me*?" Rain said, her breath quickening. "I'm not telling you where it is and if I want to decrypt the chip, then I'll find my own *guy*."

Prescott sat back on the bed as if he'd been slapped with the full force of her power. "I wasn't trying to manipulate you." He looked wounded. Rain gave one last cursory glance before exiting the room and closing the door firmly behind her.

Tolley looked up when she shut the door. He saw the pained look on her face and immediately went to her side.

"Good talk?"

"For the most part," Rain said, walking into the kitchen and grabbing a bottled water from the fridge. She uncapped it and swallowed it all before speaking again. "He knows a guy who can decrypt the chip," she said with a look of sarcasm.

"You don't believe him, I take it," Tolley said, leaning against the counter across from her.

"I don't know what to believe. I believed that was my mother today and her twin tried to put a bullet in my head. I don't think I'm the best judge of character right now." She frowned at the memory of the day's events. "Part of me wants to just give it to Prescott and then it could all be over. We could either see what's on the chip or he could stiff us and give it back to Dalton. Either way, it'll be done. Then the other part of me wants to finish what I started. I want to see my mother, help her if I can." Rain closed her eyes and fought back the urge to punch something in her frustration. The pressure of her decisions weighed her down. Whatever she'd decided before had gotten them in a deadly game with Dalton. She felt like a stupid child trying to play a very serious life-or-death game.

"Dalton wants more than the chip, Rain. He wants to win at all costs. He won't let our escape from the Basin go unpunished, nor will he stop hunting your mother for whatever she has done to gain his attention. He doesn't like the idea of witnesses, so unless you work for him, you're an enemy. The first thing we need to do is talk to Dahlia. Ask her why he's following her and then that information, along with the chip, will possibly lead us to the truth. Think of it as a puzzle. There's lots of pieces but we only see the two or three pieces we've put together, not the whole picture."

Rain felt like she was sixteen again, learning how to hunt alone. She remembered Tolley telling her something similar about how she needed to view the woods as a big picture and the animal she was after as just a small figure on the picture. She didn't know what he was talking about then but she finally gathered his meaning now.

"How do we get in touch with her? I'm ready to end this," Rain said with renewed strength.

"That's my girl." Tolley said with a smirk.

"Dad?" Tolley turned to her, waiting for her to continue. "I'm sorry about getting us in this mess. I should have listened to you when we were at the CIA headquarters."

"Don't worry, Rain. You're not a girl anymore. You're a woman. You can handle it," Tolley said before heading over to the group of men huddled in the living room, Prescott included. Rain took a deep breath and followed closely behind him. She knew she was no longer a child, but she hadn't realized that being a soldier for justice would be a life-threatening mission.

They walked in on Black talking aggressively with the group. He leaned over a large map of Russia with three large orange circles over a site in Moscow, the café, and an industrial site.

"If you look here—" he pointed at the café, "—this is where we met our imposter. We followed her to this industrial site. Shanty found a bit of information while we were on the mission. The industrial building was purchased by Greenbreadth International."

"Okay, so?" Tolley said impatiently, leaning against Black's chair.

Shanty swallowed brown liquid from his equally brown glass and pounded his chest a few times before speaking. "Well, the good news is that we found out where your mother is . . . excuse me, *was*. Took me almost the whole damn day tracking all the surveillance cameras around the café to see if she really was coming to meet you or not." He swung a finger in Rain's direction. "She was a block over, on foot, when the imposter came into the café. She woulda made it just in time had she not seen that there was another woman sitting with you. Here's the footage we have."

Shanty opened his black heavy-duty laptop and pressed play. The image was grainy and repeatedly switched angles but Rain could see a slender woman with dark hair, very similar to the imposter, in the corner of the first camera. She wore glasses as well, although not as big as the woman's she'd met in the café. Her hair was long and in a low ponytail. She carried a tan handbag and crossed the street with a quick, dainty gait after looking both ways. When she got closer to the café, she paused briefly then turned her head twice, spotting a park bench across the street. She sat on the bench and crossed her legs as if she had not a care in the world, only a leisurely rest in the park after a long stroll. Rain could see her hand pull a black item from her coat pocket and rest it on her knee as if she was clasping her hands as any woman would. Rain stared hard at the video as her mother didn't move for many minutes.

"That's her taking pictures. So I'd reckon that she wasn't in cahoots with the imposter," Shanty said lazily, interrupting her focus.

"So why didn't she come help?" Rain said in a whisper, almost to herself, still watching the woman, her mother, sitting with her hands across her knees.

Black answered her with a sigh. "Your mother has much more to lose than you."

Tolley cleared his throat and gave Black a look of resignation. "He means your mother doesn't want to get caught. She knew I would be there watching and wouldn't let anything happen to you," Tolley finished. Black pursed his lips together in response.

The events on the screen caught everyone's attention. Mogli leaned forward as he saw his car pick up Rain in front of the building. Rain stumbled out in shock, her hair swirling around her face in the wind as she struggled to put on her coat in the brisk cold. She didn't even remember grabbing her coat. She remembered feeling dazed and as if she was out of her body. Rain scanned the video of the park bench and spotted her mother still and watching the events unfold. Another camera captured Black running after the woman and within seconds he left the frame and appeared in another camera at the bottom of the screen. Moments later

Tolley followed behind, running out of the frame like a cartoon character, hands pumping wildly.

"Those were the only cameras I could get that captured the café. Luckily there was a camera at the bank at the end of the street I was able to hack. I caught a blurry license plate of the vehicle that picked up the imposter. I ran it back to a distribution company named Greenbreadth International which has a subsidiary named Sallad Musad Pharmaceuticals," Shanty said proudly. He grabbed his long beard and curled it around his fingers with a smirk on his face.

"Okay, I'm confused. What does pharmaceuticals have to do with anything?" Prescott said to Shanty.

Black looked at Tolley for confirmation before telling what he knew. Prescott dropped his head, knowing that he was not completely vetted by the group after they'd learned which side he'd started on.

Tolley nodded his approval and Black began to explain in his soothing deep voice. "Sallad Musad is an Arabic company that is a front for nuclear weapons. They ship, sell, and negotiate nuclear and biological weaponry to the highest bidder. We had a mission many years ago to gather intelligence on Sallad Musad Pharmaceuticals and identify the leader of the company. We found out early on that it was technically impossible to get to the head of the company. We'd spent almost a year on it before realizing that the trail led back to an American, not anyone in Saudi Arabia as we were led to believe. Once we reported our findings, we were taken off the mission and it was closed."

"Let me guess, Christopher Dalton closed the mission," Prescott said, looking from Mogli, who sat motionless, back to Black.

Rain felt sick. Dalton had been screwing Americans for twenty years without ever being caught. Her odds of going against him suddenly seemed dismal. If Tolley's team couldn't get him back then, what made her think they could now?

"Wait, I know that symbol." Rain saw the logo as Shanty clicked through Sallad Musad's website.

"I've seen it, too. Where have you seen it?" Black asked quickly, his square-shaped jaw serious and tense.

Rain rose from her seat and moved quickly to her bag in the front closet. She fished out her clothes until she felt the box her mother had sent to her in Japan. She popped open the lid and pulled out the envelope she was looking for.

"Here it is."

She held it up for them to see. She passed it to Tolley who looked at it and gave it to Black who said to no one in particular, "The same tattoo on the woman." It was passed around the group, each person looking at the broken wax on the back of the envelope and the red origami bird stamped into it. It was identical to Sallad Musad's symbol on the website.

"What?" Mogli said as he touched the wax. "Why would she use this stamp?"

Tolley put a hand over his eyes and walked away. Rain left the group and found him in the hall, pacing.

"What's going on? This is getting stranger and stranger," Rain said with a hint of fear in her voice.

"Your mother is in trouble. She's finished what we couldn't so many years ago. She's working for Sallad Musad, on the inside," he said, his face turning a shade of red. "That was her message to us on where she is and why she can't be seen with us. If Sallad Musad figured out what she's doing, she could disappear forever. The CIA agent was undercover for Sallad Musad. I'm sure Dalton reached out to her to come get the chip. Now that she's dead, it won't be long before they realize there's a link between her, Christopher Dalton, *and* the CIA."

"Breathe, Dad."

She could sense her father's fear welling up inside him, ready to overflow. She knew that he had insider knowledge on Sallad Musad and how deadly a mission like that could be. So she felt her own fear rise up.

"I've got to get a plan together. We've got to get her out before Dalton gets to her or figures out where she is."

"We need to decrypt the chip. We have to stop Dalton or at least slow him down. The chip can give us some bargaining power," Rain said, pulling his hand from his forehead and stepping in his line of sight. They both looked down the hall and simultaneously their eyes landed on Prescott, sitting on the couch quietly looking in their direction.

"Shanty can't do it?" Rain said, hoping she wouldn't have to ask Prescott for help.

"Not quickly. It's not his thing but it can be done," Tolley said.

"We don't have time to waste." She began walking toward Prescott.

When she entered the room with Tolley trailing not far behind, all the men stopped talking and looked at her. She felt uneasy with their eyes trained on her, waiting for her direction. They knew she had the chip.

"Prescott, call your guy to decrypt the chip. If you screw us on this . . . I'll put a bullet in you myself. Got that?" Rain said, her eyes cold and serious.

"Got it," Prescott said and launched from his seat to use the world phone. He went into the kitchen and spoke softly on the line. Mogli, although usually silent, spoke up first. "You think that's a good idea?"

"We need to get this chip decrypted before the end of the night. I'm sure the imposter was sent by Dalton and if she got that close to both me and my mother in the same location, he's getting closer as the days go by."

"And you don't think that's because we have our own imposter living with us?" Mogli jutted his chin in the direction of the kitchen.

"No. I don't feel that way and if anyone does, now's the time to get out, take a vacation, grab a beer, and call your family. Because where we are going isn't going to be pretty . . . but you already know that much," Rain said defiantly.

Mogli smiled for the first time since Rain had met him. He had a childlike smile that made her smile back involuntarily. He wrested himself from the couch, grabbing his neck with a groan. Before heading to the back room to prepare his bags, he put a hand on her good shoulder and whispered, "Don't worry, I'll watch him."

Rain felt good that they'd figured out another piece of the puzzle. She was still worried about Prescott's intentions but she knew that there wasn't any other choice if she wanted to help solve her mother's problem before Dalton found her. Mogli would travel with him and she knew that he would not let anything happen.

Rain went back to the front closet and found the box her mother had sent her. She searched through the items until she found the weapon. She'd placed it in its rightful spot when she'd returned from the café. The pain of not seeing her mother and her slipup at the café had caused her to put it away. She didn't feel worthy of carrying it. She ran her fingers across the initials and pulled out the clip. The chip popped out into her hand. She held on to it firmly, thinking of what could happen if she lost it. She hoped Prescott was telling the truth. She could see in his eyes that he cared for her, but was it enough?

SEVENTEEN

Shanty waved from the driver's-side window of the black sedan as it pulled out of the parking lot. Rain stared at the vehicle from the kitchen window as it traveled down the street. She felt naked without the chip in her possession but she knew Mogli would take good care of it. She'd given it to Mogli for safekeeping until it was time to hand it over to Prescott's contact. Mogli, Shanty, and Prescott packed quickly and were in the vehicle within ten minutes of her handing over the chip. Prescott had given her a small smile and reassured her that he would be back with all the answers. She wanted to believe him but couldn't fight the feeling that she was saying good-bye for a lifetime. Mogli had given her a small kiss on the cheek and filed out behind Prescott without a word.

She turned away from the window and listened to Tolley's mumbling in the next room. He had immediately gotten on the world phone and closed himself into the back bedroom. Black had started mapping out new locations on the coffee table, studying routes and locations of Sallad

Musad sites and subsidiaries. When Rain glanced over his shoulder, he had nearly a dozen red circles around the city.

"That many locations to investigate?" Rain said pessimistically.

"No. I've narrowed it down to two locations of where your mother would work," Black said without looking up from the map. He used the blue marker to circle another site on the map.

"What's that one?" Rain said.

"Blue is for the American embassy or other friendly locations," Black explained. "If we ever get in a jam, getting to one of these blue spots would increase your chances of survival." He turned to look over his shoulder. His blue eyes pierced her and she could sense he was agitated about not being in control. Tolley had explained to her that he was a loose cannon if he didn't buy in to the plan. Rain knew that she needed his buy in.

"So what do you think we should do?" she asked, sitting across from him on the couch. It squeaked beneath her weight. Black's eyes seemed to soften at the question and Rain felt herself ease a bit. She needed to bond with Black, gain his trust, for the sake of the team.

"We should talk with Dahlia. That's the most important thing we could do while we wait for the chip to explain the real mystery. At least by talking with Dahlia, we can assess why Dalton was after her in the first place. In order to figure out how this will end, we need to start at the beginning," Black said, rubbing his hand back and forth over his crew cut.

"How do we get in contact with Dahlia? Or do we wait for her to send a pigeon?" Rain said bitterly, leaning back on the sofa in despair.

"We meet her tonight," Tolley said as he walked into the room.

Rain sat up eagerly. "Tonight?"

"Yep. Just got off the phone with her. She's pretty sure we need to meet sooner rather than later since today's events at the café. She knows the window for escape is getting smaller."

"Then why won't she just catch a flight somewhere and we can meet her . . . act like none of this ever happened? We could disappear."

Tolley shook his head. "There is no disappearing, Rain. Once you're on the radar, Dalton's agents will never stop searching for you, for her . . . for us. You'll be in a grocery store, five years from now, maybe a kid or two . . . putting groceries into your trunk. Then you'll be a tragic story on the news, a woman mugged and killed for her groceries." Tolley's eyes looked sad, knowing.

"It could be different for us."

"No, Rain. You don't understand. We were those people! We were the people who they called to make problems disappear. It didn't matter how long we had to wait. We would wait for years to find a weakness, a simple moment in time to complete the mission. You can't outwait these people, Rain," Tolley said solemnly. Black rubbed at his scalp again and Rain could feel the tension as thick as smoke in the room.

"You were a hired killer?" Rain's voice sounded wounded. She tried to muster the courage to hear the answer to her question.

Tolley nodded slowly as Black stood abruptly.

"There's nothing to be ashamed of, Tolley. We did our jobs and we did it for the right reasons . . . to protect our goddamn country from all the scary monsters that go bump in the night. The most wicked and evil men and women you could ever dream up are *real*." Black turned to Rain. "You're either too young or too jaded to realize that the world is not a pretty place. There are evils and sick individuals that run the highest forms of government across the world, not only the United States. When you uncover one rat hole, millions flee to new places, make new alliances, and come back with a vengeance. We have to cut the head off the rat if we ever want to have peace . . . or he will align with more people, make more chaos, and ultimately, he will kill us or someone we love without a second thought. So you need to really think about if you are ready to go down this road with us." Black pointed a thick finger at Rain who sat erect in her seat. "So yes, we were hired killers, Rain. And because of that, you should be thanking your lucky stars that we are on your side right now." Black couldn't hide the fury that welled inside him. His cheeks were red and his thin lips were pinched tight. Tolley touched his shoulder to calm him. He scowled at Tolley before striding to the back bedroom and slamming the door behind him.

Rain felt the wetness on her cheeks before she realized a tear had fell. When she had found out that her father was an agent, she thought he was the strongest, most honorable man. Now she struggled with seeing him as a killer, a father, a patriot, and a man who easily tortured people. How could he still be the Tolley on the farm if he was so many other things, too?

"I'm sorry you had to find out about us this way . . . about me. I was going to tell you when the time was right," Tolley said, sitting in the chair Black had left vacant.

Rain sat in astonishment. She didn't know what to think anymore. Everything that she'd come to know about the people she loved was so convoluted.

"I was so stupid." Rain shook her head and rubbed the wetness from her cheek, wincing as she passed over the fresh cut.

"You aren't stupid, Rain. I raised you to know the good in people, to respect life. That's why I taught you to hunt, to respect animals and their lives. I didn't want you to end up like me or your mother. You lose a piece of yourself every time you do what we do. I want you to be whole," Tolley said, reaching for Rain's hand. She felt the slightest urge to pull away but gripped his warm hand anyway. She needed him more than anything right now.

"The only way I'll be whole is if I have my family . . . *all* of my family," Rain said, peering into Tolley's eyes. He nodded in response. "So when and where are we meeting Dahlia?"

"Don't you mean your mother?" Tolley questioned sternly.

"Until she proves that she's a mother I'll reserve the right to call her by her given name," Rain said defiantly. She'd had enough of looking at life through rose-colored lenses. It was time to toughen up, stop dreaming, and start confronting her issues. One of those issues being her selfish mother since she'd already confronted her lying boyfriend and murderous father.

"We meet at Rasputin. Are you ready for your first undercover mission?" Tolley said with a flicker of hope.

"Of course."

Rain could feel the jitters again as she took the black bag her father handed her into the bathroom. She flicked the light on and looked at herself in the mirror. The scratch on her face had started to lighten but the open wound still stung when she dabbed it with ointment. She looked worn, her dark eyes riddled with puffy bags from lack of sleep and too much adrenaline from car chases and gunfights. Luckily the swelling was gone. She took one last look in the mirror and gripped the scissors from the black bag. She wrapped her hand around her ponytail and cut her hair off above the elastic band. She let the hair drop in a heap behind her. Instantly she felt weightless, reinvigorated, like a new person. She shook her hair out and let the strands fall in her eye, covering her cut. Her hair, which fell in choppy layers just below her chin, gave her an edgy, mysterious look. She considered her new persona with a devilish grin and fingered the box of blond hair color on the sink.

Rain put the color in her hair and crawled into the hot shower. She let the water pelt her skin until it felt painful. She relished in the pain, felt it stretch over her body, coat her in warmth. She rinsed the color, shaved, and exited the shower with a renewed sense of being. She wiped the fog from the mirror and gaped at the blond bombshell looking back at her. The hair color made her lips look pinker, her eyes more mysterious. She felt like she was a new woman.

After blow-drying her hair and painting her face with makeup to hide all the cuts and bruises, she slid into a black sequined dress that hugged her curves. She hadn't ever worn a dress as beautiful or as tight as the one she had on. She turned in the mirror, investigating the plunging line of the dress that stopped above her lower back and exposed her flesh. Her nipples perked against the fabric and she felt self-conscious walking back into the living room.

Black glanced up from his maps and dropped his marker in amazement. His blue eyes were like deep pools as he took in Rain's new appearance. His mouth fell open. Rain pranced through the living room, circling the chair Black was seated in, and wrapped her arms around his neck.

"Cat got your tongue, sweetie?" Rain said with her best Russian accent, trying her best to get in character even though her nerves were raging.

"What in the . . ." Black said, gripping her wrists to release him. He stood to look at her closely, coincidently putting the chair between them.

Rain stood erect, hand on her hip as she smirked at Black. She could feel him trying to match Rain the girl with Rain the woman.

"Rain, you look . . . well, first, I want to apologize," he said, placing his hand to his forehead in amazement.

"Don't apologize. I needed to know," she said with a wave of her hand.

She heard Tolley snickering behind her. She pivoted on her heels to see Tolley dressed in a well-fitting blue suit with white shirt beneath. He'd kept his dark hair tamed and cascading to his neckline. The sprinkle of gray at the temples made him look distinguished.

"I think she's ready. What do you think, Black?" Tolley said, still chuckling.

"Well, yeah. I think she's ready," Black pushed out, shamelessly letting his eyes run over the length of Rain's toned body.

"We're taking the metro. Make sure to trail us, just in case."

"If anything happens, you remember the exits I showed you." Black closed his laptop and put it in his brown messenger bag. "I'll remain in the safe spot, keeping watch of the location. Meet me there once you've completed your meeting."

"See you soon, amigo," Tolley said, patting Black on the shoulder before ushering Rain out the apartment. Rain felt empowered by the way Black's eyes lingered on her as she left.

They arrived outside Rasputin within thirty minutes. Rain couldn't help but look over her shoulder for any sign of Black. She knew he was there but he was like a phantom, appearing and disappearing from her peripheral vision.

"Remember, you work here. Time to turn on the charm," Tolley whispered as he walked her to the front door of Rasputin Club, through the crowd of young men dressed in shiny suits. Some men whistled at Rain as he ushered her to the front of the line. She blew a kiss to them and smiled as she walked by, squelching her nerves with each step.

Rain knew to act as if she was intoxicated by leaning against Tolley and laughing loudly. Tolley had told her about the club and that most of the women who worked there were either drunk or high. So she needed to fit in.

An oversized man waited outside the door allowing patrons in with a skeptical eye after a barrage of pat downs, license checks, and questioning. Tolley stepped up behind a greasy, weasel-like man who had three gold chains around his neck and wore an oversized velour jacket. After the short greaseball entered the club, Tolley inched up to the guard with his arm around Rain's waist. The guard eyed him suspiciously before letting his eyes linger on Rain.

"I'm returning her from my date," Tolley announced with his best slimeball chuckle. He tapped the man's chest. "Do you get free action for working out here?"

The man flexed his oversized muscular chest and squared his large body to Tolley without a word. Rain could hear his heavy breathing like a bull ready to attack. His eyes pierced into Tolley's before scanning over Rain as she bent over to buckle her stacked heels. His eyes rolled over her short skirt, inching up her creamy thighs to just under her buttocks.

"Was she good? You satisfied?" the bouncer asked as if on cue. He didn't tear his eyes away from Rain as she straightened her skirt and jutted her chest forward.

"Very good. Very satisfied," Tolley answered, winking his eye at the man.

The guard smiled with crooked teeth and licked his lips. "I don't remember her. What her name?"

Rain inadvertently rolled her eyes at his broken English. She propped her hand on her hip and fiddled her fingertips, indicating she was growing tired of the conversation.

"She's new. I was told I was the first." Tolley leaned in close to the guard and patted his arm. "Ehh . . . you know, those are the best ones, right?"

"Ahh, yes. I did hear of new girl," the guard said in his thick Russian accent, still eyeing Rain's svelte figure. "Come here, sweetie." He reached for Rain's arm and Tolley tensed.

"No, you dirty boy!" Rain said with an accent, slapping her small purse against his chest. "You have to pay me to play," she replied seductively and walked into the door without looking back at Tolley. Before the guard could compose himself, Tolley entered the same door, turning only to shrug and say, "I told you she was good."

Rasputin Club was a purple-and-gold menagerie of nakedness and debauchery. Rain had entered the dark cloth inside the front door too quickly and hadn't prepared herself to see the jiggling breasts of topless women bouncing by with too-white teeth and perky struts. Women in colorful panties of all textures of shiny material strutted around with buttocks bouncing to the deep hypnotic techno bass that pumped through the club. Sex oozed from every crevice of the building as men sat with their legs spread as women gyrated on their laps, hair swinging in a variety of brunette and blond whirls. Rain stood in the center of the club, surprised by a place she'd only heard about in conversation. Now that she was here she couldn't figure out if she was disgusted or turned on by the scenery.

"Let's go to the VIP. She should be here shortly," Tolley whispered in her ear, grabbing her elbow firmly. He led her to a curved couch that reminded Rain of a centipede with its purple velour seats and yellow legs that looked as if it could get up and walk away. He placed his money, a sizable roll of Russian rubles, on the round table in the center of the space and sat on the other side of the couch. His eyes roamed the crowd. Rain wasn't sure if he was looking at the women or searching for Dahlia. She felt odd sitting in a place like this with her father. She smirked at the thought of young boys who settled into manhood in places like this with their fathers.

"You don't want her to dance on top of the table?" a guy with blond hair questioned with enthusiasm. Tolley knew he must've been the manager, with his gray button-down shirt and skinny black tie. He also realized how suspicious it looked to have a dancer sitting down in VIP without even so much as a drink, a grope, or a dance.

"We're ordering our drinks . . . then a private room." Tolley grinned broadly. He straightened his black V-neck sweater and coolly pulled off a piece of imaginary lint.

"Oh. Yes, sir. What drink? I get for you, sir," the manager said animatedly, his eyes large as silver dollars. He was aware that the private rooms meant a hefty payout for him as the manager.

"I'll take scotch on the rocks. And she'll have a shot of vodka," Tolley said, easing over to Rain and putting his hand across her nearly naked thigh. She purred under his touch and stared at the manager with overt seduction. Her sexy tone almost made bile rise in Tolley's mouth. The manager dutifully marched away as if getting the drinks would seal the deal on his commission.

"You are playing this role too well for me," Tolley said with a pained expression.

"Thanks," Rain said with a smirk. "I live to make you uncomfortable."

Tolley tried to contain the discomfort of waiting but soon he spotted Dahlia in the rear of the club, heading for the private room. He stood up before he realized it and Rain looked quizzically at him standing in the middle of the VIP section staring off into the dark space.

"She's here," he said in a trance.

"Your drinks, sir." The manager had arrived like a leprechaun, full of toothy smiles and fake happiness like the rest of the people who worked in the club. Rain knew the manager was selling the ultimate sexual experience to his patrons but his excitement in selling sex made her swallow the urge to vomit. She wondered how any self-respecting woman could work here.

"Yes, we'll take those with us," he said, giving Rain a hand to help her from the couch.

"I can take them to private room for you." The manager's eyes looked over Rain, assessing her. She could see he was trying to remember her name. Rain stirred under his appraisal.

"No, I can take them," Tolley said aggressively enough to make the manager startle and tear his eyes from Rain to Tolley. His hand gripped at his chest in surprise at Tolley's tone but he nodded silently in response.

Tolley smiled through tight lips and handed Rain her shot, which she tossed back quickly and slammed on the table. She coughed as the liquid burned going down and she felt it melt into her stomach with a buzzing warmth. Tolley nodded to the manager who still stood watching them walk to the rear of the club and enter the private room that Dahlia had escaped into.

The private room was elegantly designed, a stark contrast to the main dance hall, which had an overabundance of purple, gold and lace fabric. The private room was a dimly lit cave with scented candles flickering from alcoves in the wall. A dark-colored U-shaped couch flanked a low wooden table that had a platter of wine, scotch, and vodka waiting with selections of juice and soda. Multiple glasses upended on the glass serving dish shined in the candlelight. Rain could smell the aromatic lavender and vanilla from the candles as Tolley closed the door behind her.

"Rain?" She heard the voice in the dim light before she saw the face and it almost made her knees give out beneath her. She blinked in the dark, hoping for her eyes to adjust to the new level of darkness, when she felt the slender arms encircle her in an embrace. She felt her mother's bosom against her own, although she was slightly taller than Rain. She smelled her pungent perfume, which smelled of flowers with a hint of something spicy like cinnamon. She wrapped her arms around the lean, warm body in front of her and rested her head on her shoulder. Every feeling in Rain's body burst out of her as tears flooded her cheeks. She bit her lip to keep from sobbing. She'd been waiting more than a decade for a hug from her mother and to have it now made her feel like a missing piece of the puzzle had finally been pushed into place.

"Don't cry, my sweet girl," she cooed to Rain and rubbed her short blond hair.

Rain couldn't hold back the emotion. She could smell every essence of her mother from her fresh shampoo, refreshing as a summer's breeze, to the mint of her breath as she spoke so softly. She wanted to hold her mother for a lifetime, never let her walk out again.

Her mother pulled away to look deep into Rain's eyes, which now ran with dark makeup down her cheeks. Rain was shocked to see that her mother looked as if she were young enough to be her sister. Her face was smooth and creamy, with only a hint of lines at the corners of her almond-shaped eyes. She had a slim nose that led to full lips, dressed in deep red lipstick. Thick brows, perfectly shaped, looked scrunched in sadness at the sight of Rain's confusion and anxiety. Her mother's hair was curled in deep waves cascading down her shoulders to her elbow. Rain felt sad that she'd cut her own long locks, which looked just like hers only hours earlier. She was the most beautiful woman Rain had ever seen. She gripped her mother's wrist, saw the telltale birthmark, and planted a soft kiss on it. Dahlia's eyes looked like they would burst with tears if she blinked.

EIGHTEEN

"**Y**OU'RE BEAUTIFUL."

Dahlia tenderly held Rain's chin and turned it from left to right. Rain felt like a prize beneath her awestruck stare. Dahlia smiled as she assessed her daughter, feeling relieved that she'd grown into a beautiful young woman without her being around. She'd worried that Tolley would raise her as a hunting, fighting farmhand. But by the looks of her, she was feminine and sexy, although a bit too sexy in her flashy, clingy dress. She'd remembered the last picture she'd seen of Rain five years ago and she'd been holding a rabbit under her arm, smiling like she'd won a prize for the cutest daughter-and-pet duo. Dahlia had refused all other mail from Tolley because she realized then that the hurt and pain of being away from Rain was causing her to second-guess her mission. She couldn't turn back then—she was too close to getting answers. Now that she had most of the answers she sought, she wondered if being away from the girl in front of her—no, the *woman* who had lived the majority of her life without her—if it was worth it. She frowned at the answer.

"Tolley . . ." Dahlia opened her arms to him. He'd looked so conflicted standing behind Rain, waiting for his moment to embrace her. It'd been years since they'd shared a bed in the hotel room near their farm. She'd missed him then and come calling for his warmth and comfort. She needed someone to help her remember who she was. She'd been undercover for too long and the lines were blurring. That night, Tolley had made her remember. He'd given her back a piece of herself while unknowingly she had stolen another piece from him. He'd begged her to stay but she knew she couldn't go back to the farm . . . not yet. Not until she solved the case that made their team disband and leave the agency.

Tolley hugged her tightly, feeling the curve of her body fit his perfectly. His arms wrapped around her waist and she let her hands grip his scalp and comb through his dark waves. He felt her body shudder against his. The bond between the two was electric and Rain stared quietly in the recesses of the private room, wondering why she could ever leave a man she clearly still loved. Their embrace lasted for a few minutes before Tolley held her from his gaze and stared in her doe-like eyes. She smiled sweetly at him, pushing his dark hair from his forehead. A smile crept across his lips and within minutes, their lips touched softly.

"You're still beautiful, Dahlia."

"And you're getting gray." Dahlia chuckled, touching a finger to his graying temples. "But you haven't changed a bit more."

They separated but let their hands linger together for a moment before sitting down on the couch.

"Did you get my message?" Dahlia turned to Rain and then looked back to Tolley expectantly.

"Your message? The letter, you mean?"

"She means the stamp, Rain," Tolley answered. "Yes, I got it. I was a little late because I didn't see the envelope but when I did . . . I knew."

Dahlia pursed her lips and nodded. "So then you know that I work for Greenbreadth International under the subsidiary of Sallad Musad Pharmaceuticals. I've been undercover there, working in midlevel jobs trying to learn how the process works and where the supply is coming from in the United States. I started out working for Christopher Dalton to infiltrate a Russian Mafia that I found out wanted him dead. When I was looking into why, I stumbled upon Greenbreadth International ties and wanted to investigate it further. When I finally touched base with the agent in charge, he promptly told me to forget about Greenbreadth. It reminded me of how we were tossed off Sallad Musad's case and I couldn't let it happen again. I've learned more than I thought I would, actually. Most importantly, I think I finally found out who the head of Greenbreadth International is."

Tolley straightened. He had his assumptions but he always wanted to know who was behind the terrorist supporting organization.

"So what happened to you at our meeting in Café Michel? How did the agent know about our meeting?" Rain interrupted. She had been waiting to ask her about that day since she saw the video. She knew there were more pressing issues to discuss but she couldn't concentrate without an answer.

Dahlia's face went dark. "I was there moments before the gunshots. I saw her in the café window. I knew there must have been someone who'd intercepted my package, which meant they were either watching me or watching you. I'm not sure which one it is, though, even now."

"So if they are following us then they know we are here," Rain said with a hint of fear cracking her voice. Her eyes landed on the door. Only one exit.

"I've not been followed," Dahlia said with a hard stare. "I am worried that it may be someone on your team."

"I know what you're thinking. I don't think Prescott had anything to do with the café imposter. He was the one who shot the agent, remember?" Rain tried to hide the defensive tone. She didn't want her mother to know that she still had feelings for landed her a night in the Basin. "He saved my life."

"And we saved his life," Tolley said with a huff.

"He was chased down just like the rest of us," Rain argued.

"Or so we think. No one else was there," Tolley said with a raised brow. "And he only shot the imposter in the hand, not a kill shot, as he was instructed to do."

"I can't believe this." Rain breathed heavily and wiped the makeup from beneath her eyes to busy herself. She was done with defending the innocent. She'd seen Prescott's eyes and knew that he was hurt and mourning his mistakes. She wanted to move past it but no one else could.

"Don't worry, we're watching him."

Dahlia nodded her approval to Tolley and turned back to Rain with a soft look in her eyes. "It's important to stay grounded and follow your gut intuition with these types of things, Rain. You know him better than we do but what you think you know isn't always the truth. Sometimes there are just very good agents." She pointed at herself and Tolley. "Just remember, the dirt that doesn't come out in the wash will always come out in the rinse."

"I trust him." Rain raised her chin defiantly. Tolley sucked his teeth and shook his head but Dahlia only grinned through tight lips. She was done discussing Prescott. Her motherly advice had been denied so she settled for the business of why they were meeting.

Her eyes fell on Tolley who had sunk back into the couch, drained from the excitement of seeing Dahlia, then engaging in family banter.

"It's higher than we originally thought. Christopher Dalton is only the task manager. Defense Secretary Bolen is the top, a silent puppeteer."

"What? That's impossible. He'd be fighting the war on both sides."

Tolley's voice lowered in disbelief. "No wonder Dalton's reach is so far. He has every missile and bomb that the country owns at his disposal."

Dahlia nodded. Rain could feel herself swimming mentally with the depth of the news. The world as she knew it was not filled with horse stalls, milking cows or mending fences. She'd never known this amount of evil in the world. For a second she wished she hadn't ever known the sordid details of politics and terrorism. She wished for the days that she'd roll out of bed to frying bacon and scrambled eggs.

"I found that Sallad Musad has shipped nearly one hundred thousand firearms and ten missiles off the coast of Russia under the guise of pharmaceutical equipment. With ties to America, I'm pretty sure Dalton and Bolen are trading arms and missiles with terrorist organizations and pocketing the money."

"How can that much artillery be missing and no one notice?" Rain asked.

"That's what we were trying to figure out before we were snatched off the case twenty years ago. We couldn't understand how, but now I know. Dalton is in cahoots with Bolen, so he ships the items and uses the agents as transportation and security while Bolen makes sure the numbers are skewed from one destination to the next. If the American agencies don't know how much artillery left the site, they don't know how much is supposed to arrive. It's a brilliant plan." Dahlia shook her head as she poured a half glass of liquor and brought it to her lips.

"How did you find out all this information?" Tolley said, pouring himself a scotch.

"I dug deep into the files whenever Sallad Musad would schedule a shipment of large equipment from America to Russia. It took me years to get access to the sealed files, then searching for a pattern or inconsistency took even longer. Finally, a year ago, I found what I was looking for. When I realized who had to sign off on the shipments out of America, it started to make sense. I knew that if I told anyone at the agency about my findings, then I'd end up off the mission . . . or worse."

"So you ditched all contact with the agency and Sallad Musad?" Rain said, remembering what Dalton had told them at the agency.

"Yes. I ditched contact with the agency but I didn't know Dalton would be so relentless without proof that I knew anything. I followed his movements, got the message from Tolley about you looking for me and being placed from the CIA into the army. We knew it was a ploy to get me to contact you. That's when I first suspected Prescott Willow as your handler," Dahlia said with a shrewd glance. She swirled her drink around in her glass and lifted it to her face, pausing for a second before letting the liquid touch her top lip.

"Why didn't you turn Dalton in as soon as you found out?" Rain popped the lid on a soda and poured it into the glass, then added a splash of rum behind it. Tolley sat up and looked at her disbelievingly before taking a sip of his own drink.

"I couldn't. I didn't have all the facts. Just an inkling. I needed a real shipment to go out so I could intercept it with enforcement I could trust. But Dalton started moving in on me sooner than that happened. He called me directly once, which was odd because the agent in charge would normally call. That's when I knew I had to get out."

"So how do we catch them?" Rain asked, almost in a trance by the news. The enemy was even larger than Dalton and more powerful. She downed her drink in three swallows and returned her glass to the table. Her hands were shaking.

"We don't catch them, Rain. Men like this cannot be caught . . . or tried in the court," Dahlia said, resting her hand on Rain's balled-up fists that lay in her lap.

"So we just kill them? Does that make us any better? Aren't we taking the law into our own hands?" Rain uttered into the dim room. She stared at the flicker of the candles with worry filling her.

Tolley sighed heavily. "We are the law. We are the last protection for this country. We don't know who we can trust to pass this information along. If we told anyone what we know, we'd be missing . . . and not lying on the beach on a secluded island type of missing."

"Rain, you have to understand. I know you're scared but we can only trust our team. The people who we know are not bought and paid for by Dalton and Bolen or God knows who else," Dahlia pleaded.

"There has to be another way." Rain shook her head, not wanting to aid in a conversation about killing the defense secretary and the chief of staff for the CIA. It was too much to digest.

"I promise you, if there is another way, I will find it," Tolley said, leaning forward so Rain could see his steely green eyes.

"But right now, we have other matters to discuss. We need the final part of the puzzle to link Dalton to the shipments," Dahlia said with eagerness. "Did you bring the chip?"

A silence stewed between the three as Dahlia glanced back and forth between the two, confusion flooding her face.

"Prescott has a guy who can decrypt the chip for us. We've sent him to get the information," Rain said quickly. She didn't know why she felt shameful sharing the information with her mother.

"You what? I'm sorry, I thought you said you gave the most important chip of our lives to Prescott Willow, the traitor and master manipulator." Dahlia stood swiftly and paced the room.

"Calm down, Dahlia. He's being escorted by Mogli. Shanty flew them. So he won't be escaping with the chip." Tolley said.

Dahlia continued to pace, her hand on her forehead as if she'd suddenly come down with an unknown illness. She swayed left and right as she walked, her black leather pants making a soft whirring sound. Rain felt as if her mother had abandoned her again as she paced and mumbled unintelligibly to herself from one edge of the room to the other. Tolley stood up and pulled her to the corner of the room and whispered to her. Rain's eyes locked with hers and Dahlia looked away with anger. Rain felt a stab in her heart; her breath felt as if it was cut off to her lungs. She'd only wanted to get the information so Dahlia didn't get hurt, couldn't she see that? Rain kneaded her knuckles, bending and folding her fingers until she felt the tension ease in her body.

"Hold on a minute. What happened?" Tolley eased away from Dahlia who looked confused at his untimely retreat. He walked to the center of the room, holding his finger to his ear. His dark eyebrows scrunched together tightly.

"Are you sure?" His barrel chest heaved in his sweater.

"What's wrong, Tolley?" Dahlia put her hand on his back, looking over his shoulder at the profile of his reddening face.

"Dammit!" he said, startling both women with his roar of a yell. He balled and unballed his fists as he stood there looking as if he was searching for someone or something to punch in the room. "That slimy asshole," he spat through a sneer.

Rain found herself standing in front of him, worried about what he had heard in his earpiece from Black. He was standing watch across the street. She worried that Black had seen someone from Dalton's camp enter the club. There was only one exit to the private room but Rain knew they could get out in enough time if they needed to.

Tolley's eyes were red and emblazoned. He nearly shook with anger. "Prescott took the chip. He's disappeared."

Rain heard the wails in the room before she knew it was her own voice. Her body quaked as she crumpled to the floor. Why had she trusted him with their lives?

NINETEEN

KIEV, UKRAINE, 2004

SHANTY HAD LANDED THE single-engine plane only three hours earlier on a small strip outside Kiev, Ukraine. Prescott knew from the moment they'd left the safe house in Moscow that he needed to get the chip out of Mogli's grasp. Fortunately, it wasn't too difficult when he studied the behavior of the two gentlemen. Shanty was a relentless lush, so a bottle of Jack Daniel's and a warm chair had his head bobbing into sleep. Mogli stoked the fire, embers crunching under his poking. He'd always been so straight and methodical, Prescott surmised. He wouldn't turn down a drink with his buddy, Shanty, but he also knew he wouldn't take much for fear of being caught off guard. Red embers flew from the mouth of the fireplace and quickly died into gray ash, floating on the cabin's stale air. The warmth of burning wood filled the house with the delicious smell of mesquite. They'd found a formidable hiding hole, a log cabin nestled in the Carpathian mountainous region near Dnipro River. It was a place that Prescott had told them his contact would meet them. They waited for Prescott's contact to arrive, which he knew would come within the hour.

He'd wanted to save their lives, so he slipped a small amount of benzodiazepines—tranquilizers—into their drinks and shared a glass of Jack Daniel's with the gentlemen as he waited. It took only twenty minutes for the effects to clutch both men into submission. He recalled Mogli trying to stand, in hopes of using his last grip on reality to thrash Prescott. He'd made it halfway to Prescott before falling to the wooden floor in a groaning heap, his legs splayed toward the fire. Prescott placed his half-empty drink on the wooden side table and scooted Mogli's leg from the flames. He didn't want the men to burn to death, just sleep peacefully until he'd gotten away. Shanty lay slumped in the chair, unmoving, an odd smile on his face. Prescott fished the chip from Mogli's trousers and pushed his hair from his face before whispering, "So sorry."

He'd made it down the mountain and near the river in time to see his contact, Mitchem, rowing carefully to the edge.

"Mitchem, good to see you." He hoisted his backpack onto the slender boat and stepped with care into the center as it teetered on the water.

"You, too, my boy," Mitchem said through teeth that looked brown enough to fall out. "Thought you said there were two more."

"No. Just me. Let's get this thing going, shall we?"

Mitchem responded with a nod and a sturdy shove from the shore. Prescott looked at the beautiful nature that surrounded him, felt its peacefulness. He could hear the boat oars lap in the water in rhythmic cadence, smell the fishy scent of the water. The birds flapped overhead and scanned the surface of the water for their meals. Prescott spotted an eagle, a rare sight on any occasion. The sight of something so rare reminded him that his luck was in order. He felt the fear grip him and he almost begged to go back to the cabin, but he couldn't. He saw Rain's face in his mind. Her face battered and bruised. He saw the barrel of the gun pointed at her head, felt the queasiness in his stomach at the thought that things might have gone differently for her. He remembered hugging her after she'd shot the terrorist in the tower. He felt her body heat again, even though the cold was fierce and moist from the river. Lastly, he remembered Rain's kiss on his lips. A kiss that he knew was not fabricated for gain or manipulation. He rubbed his bottom lip and dropped his head. He needed to do this. It was the right thing to do. He could end it all. End all the running and the suffering. He'd save all their lives.

"We're here," Mitchem croaked from the rear of the boat, reminding Prescott of space and time.

Mitchem pushed the boat onto the dirt outside his cabin that looked more like a yard sale than a high-tech genius's lair. Mitchem wasn't an old man, maybe forty-five or so, but he was the smartest tech that Prescott had had the pleasure of working with on a separate mission. He'd been kicked out of the army with a disability check that revealed he'd never work again. Prescott was sure he hadn't seen battle but he guessed the amount of knowledge he had with ten years in army intelligence earned him a handsome paycheck to stay unseen and unnoticed. Mitchem wiped his hands on his dirty overalls before plucking the chip from Prescott's hand. Prescott settled on a sunken couch that smelled of moth balls and potato chips, taking in the numerous gadgets hooked to computers that curved around Mitchem's swivel chair. The place looked more like a warehouse for a big-box manufacturer than a cabin off the river in the middle of nowhere.

Mitchem slid his fingers across the touch-screen monitors quickly and without effort before typing vigorously. Prescott looked around the room again. He saw Mitchem's old photographs of his army buddies. He noticed Mitchem in the center holding an award in his hands, smiling with teeth that looked much whiter than present day. Then he saw a man that looked like Mitchem sitting with a child on his lap, a little girl of about nine years old. She was beaming with pride with her hands clasped over her knees.

"You have a child, Mitchem?" Prescott tossed a glance over his shoulder and saw Mitchem stop typing. A pained look crossed his face.

"No."

Prescott turned back to the picture and noted that the girl looked like him—same hazel eyes.

"How long have you been living here? I didn't know you moved from the States. The old number was an American line."

"I've been here, hmm . . ." He stopped typing briefly, then started again. "Almost ten years. It's safer than America. Can't hide in America, kid."

"Tell me about it," Prescott whispered under his breath.

"I was surprised to get a call from you. What you running from anyway?" Mitchem said without looking up.

"Not what. Who," Prescott stated matter-of-factly as he continued looking through book titles on Mitchem's shelf. "Christopher Dalton is the *who*. Death is the *what*."

Mitchem tsked-tsked and shook his head slowly.

"How long 'til you decrypt it?"

"Not long if you cut the chatter," Mitchem said with a chuckle. "Feel free to take a look around outside if you want. I'll let you know when it's done."

Prescott stood slowly, rubbed his hands over his cropped hair. "No. I think I'll wait in here."

Mitchem stopped typing and breathed out heavily in annoyance. "Willow, I don't want your information. I have way too much stored up here—" he pointed to his temple, "—that I'm already trying to get rid of."

Prescott felt shitty for alluding to the fact that he didn't trust Mitchem with the chip. Mitchem had more secrets than the CIA, FBI, and DEA put together all crammed into that graying head. It was doubtful that the chip would bring him any new information. Prescott decided he needed some air. He found himself on a porch that creaked under his step as he wrapped around the cabin. He looked into the dusty window and saw Mitchem typing away steadily, a look of determination on his face. Prescott wondered how many jobs Mitchem got to do being this far out the loop. By the looks of his house, it seemed he was still working. The fact that he saved his American number after all these years also implied that he was still doing business or keeping communication open for some reason.

The river moved slowly down the bank as Prescott picked up a few rocks nearby and tossed them into the water. He assumed that Rain probably knew by now that he was missing with the chip. *There's a lot riding on this damn chip,* Prescott thought. Prescott found his way back into the cabin after looking through what must have been old technology and unfinished projects that sprawled across the lawn toward the door. Mitchem was still typing but instead of leaning over the keyboard, he was leaned back in his chair with a satisfied look.

"I think I found what you're looking for, Willow. It's some pretty rough shit and I had to dig deep but I think this is it," Mitchem said, spinning the screen around for Prescott to view when he entered the room. The screen looked like layers of documents and jumbles of digital numbers. It would take Prescott months, even years, to fully understand what he was looking at.

"I don't see anything that makes sense." Prescott gave up and looked over to Mitchem.

"I know. I just wanted to make sure you understand how difficult my job is when you call me. Lot of people don't have respect for the work it takes to do this. They just see it takes a few hours and wham-o, they have their answers. Then it's 'thanks, Mitchem' and out the door they go."

Prescott sat down in a swivel chair nearby and scooted close to the screen. "I know what it takes and I'm grateful for your help." He placed a hand on Mitchem's shoulder and nodded. "Go ahead. Explain it to me."

After listening to what Mitchem found on the chip, Prescott grew more nervous about his plight. The plight of his team and of Rain.

"I've been so stupid," Prescott whispered when Mitchem had concluded his lesson in terrorism, espionage, treason, and money laundering.

"Yep. Looks like you got yourself into a pickle," Mitchem said with a sigh.

"I need to get to Dalton. Finish this once and for all." Prescott's words sounded braver than he felt.

"You'll need this as a security blanket." Mitchem pressed an identical chip into his palm. "It's a copy. Maybe you should hide it somewhere safe, just in case."

"Thanks, Mitchem," Prescott said, then caught himself. "I appreciate what you're doing for me. Is there something I can do for you?"

"Thought you'd never ask." Mitchem smiled.

"Anything you want."

"Kill the bastard," Mitchem said with a hard glare.

PRESCOTT HIKED BACK TOWARD the city of Kiev and found a reliable phone in a bar. He placed the call that would end the war Dalton had been waging.

A kind receptionist answered on the first ring. "Greenbreadth International, how may I help you tonight?"

"I need to speak with Christopher Dalton."

"I'm sorry, sir. No one works here by that name."

"Tell him I have the chip," Prescott said, peering over his shoulder at the group of men who just entered the bar.

"Yes, sir. Please hold," the receptionist said mechanically.

Minutes passed and Prescott grew more and more fearful with the silence on the line. Finally, a male voice answered.

"Who is this?" It was not Christopher Dalton.

"I said I want to speak to Christopher Dalton."

"You cannot speak to him. You will speak to me," the man said with a thick accent that Prescott couldn't place.

"Will he be happy to know that you have lost him access to his chip? I will hang up now and disappear," Prescott warned casually.

He could hear the man wrestling with his need to control and the need to save his own hide. His hide won out as Prescott heard a grunt of disdain then seconds later a ringing sound through the receiver.

"This had better be life or death," Christopher Dalton's voice grumbled into the receiver.

"It is, Dalton. I have what you need."

"Prescott Willow. Is that you?" He sounded as if he'd sat up, more alert.

"Yes, sir. I have the chip."

Dalton chuckled heartily into the phone, loud enough to make Prescott pull the phone from his ear. "So you've gotten my chip back, huh? After you had my men killed at the Basin? They were two of my favorites, you know? So talented."

"Cut the pleasantries, Dalton. I want to end this."

"This wouldn't be an attempt to save your little playmate, Rain, now would it? You are a clever boy, Prescott, but you don't have the least bit of bravery. I will trade you Rain for the chip. Is that what you want to hear?"

"I want her safe. Not one finger laid on her . . . ever."

"That's a formidable deal. When will you bring my chip?"

"I want her family safe as well, Dalton. I know how you operate."

"Oh, well, now that's a different story entirely. I would love to give you the family discount but I just can't. Dahlia knows too much, and as much as I love to think she wouldn't find some way to be a patriot and leak what she knows, I know she will. She's like a bitch in heat. The smell of what she knows will bring all the dogs to the yard, and that, my friend, will cause a brutal war between some pretty vicious dogs." Prescott heard the clank of metal on porcelain and surmised that Dalton must've been at dinner when he called. He heard the smack of Dalton's lips as he chewed and swallowed before going on. "And Tolley. Tolley was my best and arguably may still be the best and he, dear Prescott Willow, will not hesitate to kill me when the moment seems fitting. Whether two months, two years, or a decade from now. He's the scariest type of enemy. The kind that will never forgive and forget. So, no, I will not save him. He will be put down on sight. Are we clear?"

"Then there's no deal," Prescott said through clenched teeth. He was tired of hearing his incessant voice and only wanted to return to Rain. Maybe they could make a plan to kill Dalton.

"No deal? Prescott, don't be foolish. You actually think you have a choice, don't you?" Dalton laughed into the phone. Prescott wanted to hang up on him but Dalton continued. "If you look over your shoulder, coming in the front door are a few friends of mine. They won't hurt you unless they have to. I'll see you in an hour." Dalton hung up the phone abruptly as Prescott scanned the room. He'd only returned the receiver to the phone before three burly men in black leather jackets entered the front door. Patrons in the bar saw their guns and quickly paid their tab to leave. Four people escaped from the front door as Prescott sat at the bar and ordered a scotch. The bartender looked at the men at the door as she poured the drink. Prescott scooped up the glass, drained it, and flipped the glass face down on the bar top. He walked over to the men, their muscles twitching beneath their jackets as if aching for a reason to thrash him.

"You must be my ride," Prescott said with a smile.

TWENTY

SAFE HOUSE, RUSSIA

THE RINGING CUT THROUGH the darkness. Tolley picked up his watch and eyed the time with a groan. It was 4:14 a.m. For a moment he thought he was back at his farmhouse with his oversized king four-poster bed and his plush mattress. He sobered quickly as he scanned the room and realized that he was back in the safe house, in a far too bouncy bed next to his daughter, who was shifting from the shrill sound of the world phone. She'd wanted to stay near the phone, she'd told Tolley as he'd lumbered to one of the two bedrooms after the meeting with Dahlia. Tolley knew she just wanted to know when they found Prescott and if he was truly betraying her, but he went along with it and allowed her to sleep in his room.

They'd met with Dahlia earlier that night and had talked every hour on the hour with Shanty or Mogli. They were searching for Prescott but had no idea where his contact was or where he'd run off to. Shanty was watching for his name to pop up on any radars—banks, airports, or rental cars—but he'd told Tolley that they were in the middle of nowhere in a cabin, so he suspected Prescott was on foot or traveling by boat. Therefore, Mogli was tracking him on foot so he felt confident that sooner or later the next call was going to finally reveal Prescott's whereabouts.

"Get it. It could be Prescott." Rain tried not to sound too hopeful, but it didn't work.

Since she'd heard that Prescott was missing, she had a nagging feeling that something bad had happened to him. She couldn't fathom the thought that Prescott would betray her again. His apology had seemed so sincere. She pushed Tolley's shoulder to nudge him toward the phone. Black poked his head in the door as Tolley waved him to come in. Finally Tolley punched the answer button and held the phone to his ear.

"Tolley Wilson? Is that you?" the male voice said into the phone.

"Who's this?" Tolley sat up in the bed and twisted his tank top back to the front of his body.

"I have a message for you," the voice said with an undeniable accent. Tolley thought it sounded Arabic. "Mr. Dalton would like to make a deal with you. He wants your wife delivered to him by sundown."

Tolley looked at the receiver and shook his head. He couldn't believe the audacity of the caller. Did this guy think he was going to willingly give up his wife? Or the chip?

"And if I say no?" Tolley said.

"Then we will kill the boy. We already have the chip and will not hesitate to continue our search for Dahlia."

"So what are you offering me exactly?"

"Freedom."

"From Dalton? Is that what this is?"

"Yes, precisely, Mr. Wilson. Your freedom, your daughter's freedom, and Prescott's life will be contingent upon handing over Dahlia tonight.

Mr. Dalton has been generously allowing you to live even with all the destruction and mayhem you have caused for him. I think the deal is quite formidable under the circumstances. You would be wise to consider it carefully." The man sounded as if he was an old friend of Tolley's and was advising him on an investment scheme, not a life-or-death option. Tolley snorted at the man's vain attempt at being a negotiator.

"There is no deal. I don't know you, never even laid eyes on you, and you think I will trust whatever deal we make over the phone? Dalton can call me if he wants to make a deal." With that, Tolley pushed the end button on the phone and ran his hands through his hair in frustration. Rain had heard everything from sitting so near to him during the conversation, and Black was intuitive enough to figure it out on his own.

Black sat at the end of the bed. "We need to find Prescott's guy. He's the only other person who saw what was on that chip."

"And we need to talk with Dahlia. She knows more than what she told us. Dalton would not be after her for just knowing that the secretary of defense is involved. There must be something else. The chip has to provide some proof of what she knows and that's why Dalton wants her, too." Tolley looked forlorn but Rain could tell he was trying to think of a plan.

"He'll have everything he needs to cover up his lies. He'll wipe the chip, if he hasn't already, and kill Dahlia," Rain added. She felt like with every step something was going wrong. Dalton was always set up to win, two moves ahead.

Tolley was not going to give up Dahlia. Whatever she knew, she needed Tolley's help, and he wouldn't leave her out there alone. She'd been gone too long already.

Black took the world phone from Tolley and punched in Mogli's number. He prayed that Mogli had found a trail. They needed to find the tech who decrypted the chip and they needed him before sundown.

"Mogli. We have news from one of Dalton's cronies. They want to make a deal. Dahlia, for our freedom."

"I hope you politely declined," Mogli said, breathless. He sounded as if he was climbing rugged terrain.

Black stiffened. "Tell me something good. We could use it."

"Found the tech. He was upriver a ways but with all the techie junk outside his home, I figured that was the right place."

"Is he willing to help?"

"Yep. I gave him proper incentive and he wants to help Prescott."

"You didn't hurt him, did you?" Black smiled to himself.

"No. My easiest job ever . . . he wants me to mail his daughter a gift for every holiday for the next five years."

"I don't even want to know."

"Nope, you don't. But you will want to know that I'm having him upload the chip's contents to your IP address right now. Check it out. We're on our way back to you."

Black pushed the end button and was out of the bedroom before Tolley and Rain could ask what was going on. He typed with lightning speed as Rain finally sat down next to him on the couch in the living room and Tolley perched on the edge, squinting at the screen intently.

Within minutes, file folders were layered on the screen. Many files had the Greenbreadth International logo and the origami bird that Rain noticed on her letter. Others had images of missiles and weapons that looked as if they could blow a sizable hole into a country. Rain's eyes scanned the documents until they watered from the blue-and-white flicker of the screen. Along with the files, a host of names trickled down in list form, and it didn't take Rain long to realize that these were names she'd seen in the news. One in particular, General Jeffery Mansfield, made her gasp. She'd been right under his thumb the entire time. *No wonder he'd tried to detain me so quickly.* Rain thought back to the Iraqi base that she and Prescott narrowly escaped from. General Mansfield had been in on the scheme from the beginning. The thought of Prescott made her blanch. She leaned back on the couch to stare at the ceiling. He couldn't have known what was going on. Rain could feel it deep inside her chest that she was making a mistake by turning her back on him.

Tolley's voice broke through her thoughts. "We need to decipher each file, make copies, and start planning our next move. We have over twelve hours to get everything planned if we want to end this."

"What about Prescott?" Rain ventured to ask but could feel Black's and Tolley's eyes peering hard into her.

Black looked up from his screen momentarily. "What about him? He's the one who gave them our only bargaining chip, remember?"

Rain saw his jaw clench in agitation. Stubble had begun to grow on his cheeks and down the front of his neck. When had that happened? Rain wondered. He looked like he should have been walking the streets asking for change in his stretched-out jogging pants and ill-fitting T-shirt.

"We aren't going to try to save Prescott. He's a liability at this point," Tolley added.

"We *are* going to save him. He can explain how this happened. I know he wouldn't do anything to hurt me, hurt *us*. He was sincere. I could feel it," Rain pleaded. She almost didn't believe the words coming from her lips but her heart and mind were racing to save him.

"Rain, this isn't some love story. He's screwed you over twice and I know I taught you to use your instincts," Tolley countered, stabbing his hand through his dark hair angrily.

"You're right. I'm using them now. My gut tells me that Prescott is innocent. You have to believe me. This isn't some puppy-dog love. This is life or death." Rain scooted to the end of the couch. Her brown eyes bore holes into Tolley's, pleading for him to not let Prescott die at Dalton's hands. She only hoped Prescott would do the same for her.

"We don't even know if he's alive, Rain. I wouldn't trust that he is. He crossed Dalton and . . ." Tolley made a point at rolling his sleeves, leaving the thought to linger. He crossed his arms with a look of finality after a few moments.

"He's alive." Rain pounded her fist on the wooden coffee table for emphasis.

"Alright then. If it's possible to get him out then we will. But I'll be honest with you. Dalton is not going to be the only one he needs to look out for. I reckon Shanty and Mogli have a bone to pick with him, too."

Rain nodded. He was right. She'd be saving a sheep from a lion, just to bring him to a den of hyenas. Shanty and Mogli did not seem like the forgiving type, but at least he'd be alive. She'd take her chances on them hurting him but not killing him.

"Tolley, look at these names. I think I understand what the imposter meant about the agency."

Tolley spun on his heels and looked over Black's shoulder at the screen. Rain saw his face turn from inquisitive to fearful within seconds.

"Shit. We just uncovered the biggest terrorist scam in history," Tolley whispered almost inaudibly above Black's constant keystrokes.

"Scam?" Rain asked, scooting closer.

"The CIA fabricated the Iraq war. They've been funneling guns and weapons to small cells in Iraq, Syria, Africa, and even to drug cartels in Mexico. They've been releasing diseases across these countries through vaccines. Ushered right in through nonprofit companies promising to help foreign nations."

"Dirty bastards," Black muttered.

"Shit." Tolley's hand found his mouth.

"There's millions of women and children that get those vaccines. How could they . . . *why* would they?" Rain could feel her stomach quiver. The thought of intentionally killing helpless poor people made her want to throw up but mad enough to raise hell.

"They fabricated the Iraq war. All those soldiers . . ." Black said, blinking away tears that he wouldn't let fall. His cheeks grew cherry red beneath the stubble.

"I can't believe this," Tolley said, dropping his head. "All this for money?"

"No. For power. When people fear sickness and poverty, they turn to whoever can help them out of desperation, even a country they hate," Black said, his glossy eyes finding Tolley from the computer screen.

Silence hung over the trio as they saw the layers of folders and photos of mangled bodies, blistered with pus-filled bubbles all over their bodies, medical reports showing slow, agonizing deaths.

"So what does Mom—I mean, Dahlia—have to do with all this?" Rain asked, trying hard to put the pieces of the puzzle together. She needed to focus on something else or she'd have a nervous breakdown. She was more confused after the reveal than she was before.

"I don't know, baby. I don't know." Tolley shook his head in disbelief. The implications of treason and terrorism from American leaders could crash the government and send the international community into a rage. Rain feared riots would be the least of America's worries.

"We could be looking at the next world war." Black pushed the laptop away, as if its distance could erase what he'd seen and read on the screen. "We can't fuckin' release this to the public. That would be the end of American society as we know it. All our allies would band together to neutralize the threat we are to humanity. Hell, even Americans would turn against our own. America would be the number one worldwide target."

"Let's call Dahlia. We need a plan," Rain said, standing to retrieve the world phone.

Black turned to Tolley. "When the names on this list realize that we have their information, it will be more than Dalton looking for us." His eyes were glassy with emotion and fear.

"You're right, but I have a feeling Dalton doesn't want to be the jackass who leaked the information and have all those names crawling up his ass like ants at a picnic, so he's keeping quiet. He doesn't think we have the information right now and we'll keep it that way. He wouldn't think twice about getting rid of anyone with this information, and Dahlia obviously has something of extreme value or she's seen what we've seen. So we can use that to our advantage."

"So he's going to kill Prescott because he knows too much and now he wants Dahlia," Rain interrupted.

"So we give him Dahlia," Tolley said matter-of-factly.

TWENTY-ONE

GETTING DAHLIA TO SIGN ON TO the plan was easy for Tolley. He'd explained to her that they'd act as if they were turning her in to get close to Dalton. Close enough to turn his lights out for good, Tolley had said. Convincing Mogli that they were going to save Prescott was substantially harder. Luckily Tolley handled the negotiation between Mogli and Shanty and settled on allowing only one flesh wound on Prescott from each of the men. Rain objected vehemently but Tolley told her it was their code. She didn't want to believe him but she had no other recourse. She worried that Mogli or Shanty would kill him or turn on him as soon as he was in their grasps. Tolley explained that it would be the only way he'd be allowed in the group again without taking friendly fire. She struggled with the conversation but ultimately unwound enough to agree. Mogli felt overly satisfied with that outcome but Rain grimaced as he delighted in figuring out what wound would hurt the most and leave a scar. She could sense both men fantasizing about tools, dark dungeons, and torture tactics but she shook the thought away. She needed to save him first. Then she'd worry about Mogli and Shanty's revenge.

Dahlia had sent a message to meet Tolley and Rain at a nearby shelter called Nochelzka on the outskirts of Moscow. They had arrived on time at the dilapidated building. It had green walls, probably considered festive and inviting at one point but was now covered in black grime and littered with empty beer bottles and scraps of paper. Rain used her boot to kick aside a used needle that rolled into a divot near the concrete wall. She looked up and down the street and noted an old woman with a thick, brown scarf drawn low and tied at the nape of her neck walking toward them. Her hunched back looked as if it pained her with each step. A child lumbered from behind her, a young boy with black hair disheveled, as if he'd been in a wind storm, and long, lanky limbs that were accentuated by burlap pants tied with string at his tiny waist. He looked up at the woman with a smirk and she shooed him away with her hands but he stayed glued to her heels.

Rain let her eyes fall to the ground as the woman walked closer. Tolley was glancing in the other direction as the old woman's scent hit Rain hard, jolting her like a nightmare. It was a scent she knew quite well and would never forget. It reminded her of a time when she was much younger. A perfume only reserved for one person in her memory.

The old woman lumbered along the concrete wall to the building and the boy hung back a few feet now, playing with an object on the filthy sidewalk with his beat-up brown shoe. Rain tried to see the woman's face but her head hung low. Only then did she realize the cane under the woman's oversized coat. Or is that a cane? Rain wondered, squinting to see beneath the shadows of the woman's layers.

Tolley was at her side in an instant. "What is the message?"

The old woman's voice was a creaking sound as she hummed to herself as if she hadn't heard Tolley's request. The sound gave Rain chills. Her voice was roughened by age and smoking two packs a day, which was evidenced by her extremely wrinkled face. She coughed as she looked up at Rain and then to Tolley. Her eyes scared Rain more than her voice because they looked like black coal, darker than any eyes she'd seen before. Who was this woman?

Tolley stood still, waiting for the woman to speak. Rain wondered how he'd known the woman was delivering a message when she looked as if she needed a bed in the shelter they were standing in front of.

"She wanted you to know, just in case," the woman croaked slowly.

Rain's eyes grew big. Just when she thought Tolley was wrong about the woman.

"To know what, old woman?" Tolley said in a firm whisper as he looked in both directions. Rain could tell he was not particularly fond of the area or the woman in front of him.

"She wanted me to bring *him*." She pointed to the boy who was now sitting in a crouched position skipping rocks across the pavement into the street. "He is your son."

The sounds on the street—the distant car puttering down the road with its bent muffler, the faint *ping* of the rocks as they landed on the metal sewer grates, the whooshing sound of the old woman's labored breathing—could not hide Tolley's grumble of surprise in his throat.

"Who sent you?" Tolley asked, straightening his back and stepping closer to the woman. She edged against the building, her eyes showing a bit of defiance mixed with fear.

"Your wife, of course. She has given me money to care for him for many years. But today she asked me to bring him here. To you. She is not sure if she is able to continue giving me money. She say his father will care for him now."

Rain could feel the heat rushing into her face; her neck burned. What the hell was Dahlia thinking? How many secrets could one person keep from the people who loved her?

"How old is he?" Tolley forced out. Rain could see that he didn't believe a word the woman said. He hadn't allowed himself to even look at the boy who was now looking intently in their direction, wondering why a man had stepped so close to his caregiver.

"He is eight. Born on the fourth of July and he is a firecracker, as you say in your country. Very smart." The woman let her lips curl into a toothless smile as she looked over her shoulder at the boy and nodded to him. He smiled a toothy grin and continued his hunt for rocks on the pavement.

Tolley groaned and put his hands on his head as he walked away, down the street from where they'd come. Rain watched his back as he bent over, then squatted down on his heels. His hands were rubbing through his hair. Rain knew that was how he calmed himself. He was thinking. Fitting the pieces together of the night he and Dahlia made love in the cut-rate hotel room. The night he'd asked Dahlia to come home and she said she wouldn't come until the job was done. He had thought she'd come back even then as he lay beside her, but looking at the boy, *his son*, he now realized the weight of Dahlia's vow. She was not going to stop until she finished, no matter what. Family would never stop Dahlia.

Tolley stood tall and walked to the boy who was now collecting rocks in his pockets.

"What is your name?"

"Anton Tolley, sir." The boy spoke with a high-pitched Russian accent and smiled as if he'd found pride in his name early on.

Tolley's cheeks reddened. The boy had no idea who he was talking to. A stranger, Tolley realized.

"Come on, son." Tolley led the boy by the hand back to the old woman.

Rain could feel a tinge of jealousy skip through her heart as she watched them hand in hand. She pushed it away. How could her mother keep this boy so close to her but never come to see her? She had been eight when her mother left her as well. Maybe that was her cutoff on children, Rain thought to herself with resentment. Maybe she didn't want to deal with kids after they turned eight years old? Rain looked at the boy again and started to see more features in him that looked like Tolley, reminding her of herself. The long, dark hair, the intense green eyes. She'd had her mother's eyes, brown as toasted chestnuts.

"Where is she?" Tolley said with more force than he wanted to.

"She say she is to finish her job. She never say what work she do." The woman's eyes fell to the boy, who was holding Tolley's hand and playing with the rocks in his pocket with the other.

"She's going to do it on her own," Rain said urgently, turning to Tolley.

He looked wearily at her. "Yes, I'm sure she will. She knows the deal Dalton offered and that we have the information. She wants to keep us safe."

"That was always her plan." Rain finally realized.

"This changes things. *He* changes things," Tolley said, jostling the boy's hand.

"We can still go after her. There has to be time," Rain pleaded in a whisper. She didn't want to startle the woman or her *brother*.

"We have to go," Tolley told the woman. "You can say your good-byes." He put the boy's hand in the old woman's thick palm.

"Anton, you will be good boy, yes?" she said sweetly.

"Of course, *Babushka*. Always," he said, putting his hand to her cheek. "Don't forget to check the oven before bed," he reminded her as if he was years her senior.

Rain could feel herself slipping into an emotional state so she looked toward the graying sky. Away from the heartbreaking and confusing scene in front of her.

"I will. Don't you worry, Anton. You will go with your family now." She kissed her palm and patted his cheek. He nodded easily as she shooed him toward Rain. The boy grabbed Rain's hand without hesitation and waved politely to the old woman who slipped her cane handle from the inner pocket of her coat and began walking slowly down the street, away from the confused and broken family left behind.

It didn't take long for Tolley to get everyone back to the safe house and brief Black on the mind-blowing news that he'd just discovered. Black stood silently watching the boy sitting in the sunken chair across from the couch, dangling his feet back and forth, the toe of his shoe skipping against the shabby carpet.

"So Dahlia has already gone to Dalton?" Black said after he heard everything.

"I'm sure of it. She wouldn't release this secret—" he gestured toward the boy, "—without thinking she wouldn't be coming back to care for him."

"So she thinks dying a martyr will save us? That's her ultimate plan?" Black said, snorting in disbelief. "You and I both know that when Dalton has what he wants—namely her—he's going to clean up the rest of the mess—*us*."

Rain didn't like what she was hearing but she also knew that without Dahlia, Prescott was not going to get released. And if Prescott died, Dahlia would always be on the run. They all would. Believing in a snake like Dalton wasn't a good idea, but Rain was grasping on to any hope that maybe, possibly, Dalton would leave them alone and return both Dahlia and Prescott alive. She felt sweat bead on her neckline as she thought about it. The odds were not in their favor.

"Are you hungry?" Rain asked Anton. She didn't want the young boy to hear all these things about his mother. He looked up, his eyes bright and eager.

"Yes. A little," he said.

His front teeth had grown in large and slightly gapped. He was missing the fourth tooth on the right, which gave him a goofy, lopsided smile.

"Come on. Let's let them talk. I'll make you something in the kitchen," Rain said with more enthusiasm than she actually felt.

She found lunch meat and bread and decided to create a monster sandwich with two layers of meat for the boy. As she layered on the mayonnaise she looked at the skinny kid across the kitchen. "Did you know your mother well? I mean, *our* mother."

She had been curious as to whether Dahlia had actually took the time to raise him. She didn't know why it even mattered now. She'd left them with a child they'd never seen, didn't know, and she'd gone and gotten herself killed. She didn't deserve to be anyone's mother.

"A little. She'd come to bring me gifts and books mostly. She read to me in English a lot. She was pretty." He said it as an afterthought, as if her being pretty made everything a little better. Maybe in his eyes, Rain thought.

"I didn't know her too well, either," Rain said, breathing out. "But at least we get to know each other, right?" She tried to smile.

"Yes. At least we have each other now." He grabbed his half of the sandwich and bit into it. "It's good."

Rain giggled as she chewed. He had smeared mayonnaise on his cheeks from biting the middle of the sandwich. Rain figured he was a nice kid. His *babushka* must have been a good woman, she thought. A vision of the old woman with the raspy voice and scary eyes faded away into the woman who had smiled sweetly and patted the boy's cheek.

Rain peeked out the window and saw the darkness closing in. She'd wanted to hear from Dahlia one more time. Hear her syrupy sweet voice and see her confident smile. It sickened her to think there was nothing she could do.

Tolley rounded the corner to the kitchen and spotted the boy gobbling the last of his sandwich. He stared at the boy, then Rain. He didn't know what to say. How to say what he felt. He was feeling this burning loss in his gut. He tried to bury the aching feeling that Dahlia was not with him anymore. He couldn't reach her. He'd never see her again. He didn't know how to relay the feeling to Rain, to Anton, even.

"Can you make me one of those?" he finally said, forcing a smile. "Looks good."

"It was good, Father," the boy said with a crooked smile.

A silence crept into the kitchen and sat on the air like a weight ready to drop. Tolley was visibly wrestling with a response when finally he said, "I bet it was, son. Your sister makes the best sandwiches in all of Colorado."

The boy looked confused about the mention of Colorado. A place he'd probably never heard of. Rain smiled and grabbed two pieces of bread from the bag. Maybe she had all she'd ever need in these two.

After they finished their sandwiches, Tolley shooed Anton to the shower to prepare for bed. He smiled delightfully when he realized that Tolley was going to let him run his own bath and prepare himself for bed. Rain wondered if he'd always been sheltered by his *babushka* or his mother. Regardless, the boy skipped off toward the bathroom with his head a little higher. Tolley balled up his napkin and leaned against the countertop, his silence spread across his tightly pursed lips while Rain focused on cleaning crumbs from the countertop with her bare hand.

"I don't want to believe she's . . . gone," he said in a pained voice. Rain could hear him trying to speak through the lump in his throat. He had been trying to be strong for them this whole time, she realized. It dawned on her that Tolley probably still loved Dahlia more than anything in the world. He was the only one who really knew who she was. Rain hadn't even thought about how difficult this was for him.

"I don't, either," Rain offered, busying her hands with the few dishes in the sink.

"I'm still trying to figure out why she would do something like this."

"Not telling you about Anton? Your son? Or . . ." She looked over her shoulder briefly.

"No. I fully expect those kinds of secrets from Dahlia. I can't understand why she wouldn't follow through with the plan of all of us working together to bring Dalton down. It was ironclad." He tried to reason with himself more than with Rain. He added, "Maybe she didn't trust me anymore."

"That's silly. I have a feeling you were the only one she trusted. Maybe she had a plan from the very beginning for all of this."

"I don't know what I'm going to do without her, Rain." Tolley's voiced cracked and caused Rain to turn from the sink. She'd never seen her father this hurt and in pain. He was always the pillar of strength. The sensible, rational one. Now, as she looked at him, he was a broken man. A cracked shell. The dented can on the shelf. For the first time, she was seeing her father as a man, not a hero.

"You got us. Me and Anton." Rain stepped toward Tolley but didn't know whether she should hug him or let him continue to be strong. She was as confused as he was. She missed Dahlia, too, but she hardly knew her. It wasn't the same.

"I know . . . but she is . . . *was*, my soul mate, my wife. I would have waited forever for her to come back." Rain could see the wetness building in his eyes, the redness blurring his vision from trying to fight back the tears.

She crossed the kitchen in two steps and embraced him tightly as she whispered, "I'm so sorry." She could smell the salty sweat and shampoo of his hair as she buried her face in his shoulder.

"I'm so sorry." She repeated it until she knew it would sink in.

She felt his body quake in her arms as she struggled to hold tight to his massive form. Her shoulder was wet with tears as he silently released all his emotions. She could tell he needed her. He needed someone who he could trust, and that was her. She would never let him down like Dahlia did. She could feel the anger boiling in her for Dahlia being selfish enough to die without a good-bye or keep her father from his own flesh and blood. She felt the embers of hatred fan into flames as she heard his pained gulps of air between wretched tears. She was starting to feel less mournful for Dahlia and more vindicated. Did she really need Dahlia anyway if all she ever brought them was pain and longing?

TWENTY-TWO

RAIN COULD FEEL THE HEAT in the room like an oven pressing against her chest, drying her throat. She shifted in the bouncy bed, bumping into Anton's back as he lay balled up on the mattress beside her. His body felt warm and comfortable lying next to her. She opened her eyes a slit, looked around the room at the dusty curtains, and remembered that she was in Russia. She was not in Colorado, not on the farm. There were no roosters crowing at dawn, the smell of manure thick in the air, or the constant chattering of the chickens in the coop across the yard. She turned over to look at Anton's small body; his lips smiled faintly. She pulled the cover up to his chin. She wondered how he could sleep so peacefully in a strange place around strange new people. Maybe he had found solace in finding his family. She felt that when she'd met Dahlia for the first time in years, but now that was over. She was gone again. Rain felt a little hope tonight in the kitchen. It felt good to have a family, *feel* like a family. Even without Dahlia—being with her father and the guys, and now Anton—felt like she'd found a place in the world. She cleared her throat softly into the quiet room. She didn't know if the lump in her throat was from all the emotions she had been storing away since her mother was likely dead, or if it was simply the lack of air-conditioning in the stuffy room. She knew the real reason but was trying hard to put Dahlia in the back of her mind where she had always been for the past umpteen years. Rain kicked back the covers and padded to the kitchen for a glass of water.

She'd only taken the glass from the cupboard when she heard a shuffling noise near the front door. She peered out the drawn curtains and her heart quickened as she stared at the pitch-black parking lot. She knew Dalton could go back on his word and send someone to kill them. She slid the butcher knife from its block and padded against the wall down the front entryway. When she made it to the door she pressed her body to the wall even harder, listening intently for any sound.

She saw the knob turn an inch, then back in the other direction. She stopped breathing and watched the knob turn again. Her heart raced at the thought of who was on the other side. She could feel her skin prickle and a cold shiver run down her body. Sweat beaded and tickled her forehead.

The knob jerked twice, making only the faintest of sounds before going still again. She could look through the peephole but she remembered from her training not to stand in front of a door. If they had a gun on the other side, she could end up with a few extra holes if she wasn't careful. She gripped the knife tight in her hand; the smooth handle on cold metal made her feel confident. She moved quickly to look through the peephole then fell back against the wall quietly. There was nothing she could discern from the dark shadows outside the door. No silhouette. No masked man. She breathed in and out, tried to relax her breathing and think. She closed her eyes and listened. Listened for any sound outside the door. She heard a shuffle of footsteps and jerked her head back toward the living room.

Anton was standing there in thin pajama pants that were too long and pooled at his tiny feet. He rubbed at the sleep in his eyes before saying, "Rain?" in a whisper.

Rain put the knife behind her back and placed a finger to her lips to tell the boy to be quiet. She pointed toward the room vigorously, motioning him to go back to bed. Suddenly, a loud *bang* rattled the door. Anton took off in a run toward the room. Rain's head snapped back to the door, knife drawn and shaking.

"Rain, pleeease." She heard the voice, faint but clear.

She looked in the peephole again, scanned the area around the door, and then looked toward the ground. Leaning against the door in a heap was a man. Rain stared harder, trying to see his face. He resembled Prescott. She drew in air as she felt a hand on her shoulder. She whipped around, knife drawn, to see Tolley, Black standing not too far behind with his pistol. Tolley held out his palms until Rain rushed with relief and dropped the knife by her side.

"I think it's Prescott," she whispered quickly. "He looks hurt." Her voice quivered.

"Move back. Let me look." Tolley peered from the peephole and also found the heap on the ground. "Looks clear. Let's get him," he said to Black who had crept up beside him in the narrow hall.

Tolley swept the door open and Black grabbed Prescott under his arms and dragged him into the entryway. Tolley shut the door softly then continued looking out the peephole for any movement.

Rain was happy that Prescott was alive but considering his physical state she wondered if maybe he were better off dead. He was shaking uncontrollably, and beyond the metallic stench of blood and dank smell of feces and urine, Prescott was battered beyond recognition. She remembered what he'd looked like at the Basin and she thought that was the worse he'd ever endured, until now. He lay on the linoleum floor with bloody gashes to his arms and neck, large swollen knots dotting his forehead and eyes. His eyes were leaking fluid and barely open, but Rain saw the busted blood vessels. His clothes, torn and soiled, looked as if he been tossed from the back of a truck.

"We need to get him to the couch. He's not doing well," Black said as he pressed his finger to Prescott's neck, searching for a pulse.

"Rain," Prescott whispered through dry, split lips that could barely move. "Rain."

Rain knelt beside him and pushed her hand into his clenched fist. He held her fiercely and shuddered with tears. "I'm . . . so . . . sorry." He wretched with sobs that sounded more like a dying animal than a man. Rain held back her tears; she didn't want to cry. She wanted to be strong for him.

Black darted for the first-aid kit and Tolley went for a bucket of warm water. They'd be up all night fixing Prescott. Rebuilding the man he was when he walked out that door. Somehow Rain knew that Prescott would never be the same playful man she'd met in the tower in Iraq.

THE NIGHT DRAINED RAIN. She found herself asleep on the floor near the couch that Prescott lay on when the sunlight finally hit her face. She pushed herself up and felt the ache in her shoulder and hip as she rubbed them absentmindedly. She winced as she peered over the edge of the couch at Prescott. He looked worse for wear with caked-on blood still stuck to his neck and ear. He looked still, too still.

"Prescott?" She moved his shoulder softly. He didn't respond. Not even a flutter of his lashes.

"Prescott!" she said with more conviction, jostling him harder, but his body just swayed loosely. His arm fell from his chest limply and hung from the couch. She could feel the desperation in her need to wake him before she realized she was yelling his name repeatedly.

Black came running to the living room first. He was shirtless with black jogging pants.

"What's wrong? What happened?" he demanded.

"He's not waking up!" Rain shouted.

"He's sedated, Rain," Black said, with a sigh. His calm demeanor brought down her hysteria. "He was in too much pain. I needed to sedate him."

Rain slumped back on the floor. She was still trying to bring her heart rate down.

"If you want to help him, you can clean him up some more while he's sedated. I'm sure it's going to hurt like hell," Black said before walking back toward the bedrooms.

Rain steadied her breathing. "Don't ever scare me like that again. You hear me?" she said in his ear.

Cleaning Prescott was a time-consuming project since he was too heavy to lift from the couch. After two hours, Rain had finally managed to lift his upper body enough to slide his musty shirt over his head and guide his head back to the couch pillow. She saw the deep purple U-shaped marks on his ribs. They looked like the toe of a boot. She saw the cuts and scrapes across his chest, the redness in the center of his breastbone as if someone had pounded him there. Rain felt weird looking at his wounds. She thought she'd be sad looking at his injuries but her mind kept going back to how she felt at his betrayal of Mogli and Shanty. She felt bad for him but she also knew justice had been served in a sick way.

She raised his arms and glided the rag across his bruised ribs as softly as she could. She saw his face wince when she rubbed his right side and stopped abruptly, lowering his arm. She wanted to see the slits of his eyes.

She leaned over him, waiting for him to come to.

"I always wanted to wake up next to you . . . but not under these circumstances," he whispered, eyes still closed.

Rain couldn't stop the chuckle from escaping her lips. She dropped her head and put her cheek to his. She was pleased he was awake. Alive. The sunlight shined on his face, and as mangled as it was, she still felt the same jitters she'd felt when they were hiding in the pipe. It seemed so long ago.

"You know you stink?" she said to him.

"Yeah, I traveled a long way to see that face again. Thought I'd have a bath, a meal, and your smile waiting on me." He grunted in pain but a smile followed.

"Not quite what you had in mind, eh?"

"No, not quite."

"Are you hungry? You must not have eaten for days." She eyed his slimmer frame.

"No. I haven't."

"Oatmeal?"

"Sure. But first I have something to tell you." He tried to turn his head toward her but decided against it when the pain rose in his neck.

"What is it?" Rain said, inching closer to him on the carpet.

"Your mother," he said after a pause. "She's dead."

Rain sat in silence. She didn't think the news would affect her since she already knew what would likely happen to Dahlia. But it did matter. It stung when she heard the words. Her hope that it was all a misunderstanding was aborted.

"How do you know?" she questioned, still holding on for some kind of miracle that they'd all return to the farm and raise Anton.

"I saw her when she arrived. I was locked in a cell and I saw them walk her past. I heard them beating her from my cell. She was beaten worse than me, if that's even possible." Prescott swallowed hard. "I heard Dalton order her killed before he walked by and told me that she was the reason I was still alive. I tried to plead for them to kill me instead but they wouldn't listen. I heard a gunshot." His voice quivered.

Rain could feel her skin prickle with hatred for Dalton. She was hearing the story but her body was reacting. Her rage was making her vibrate.

"I don't know if you want to hear this. I'm sorry." Prescott's voice trailed off.

"No. I want to know. I want to know because when I kill Dalton, I want to remember everything you've said as my reason for not hesitating for a second when the time comes."

"Rain, you have to let this go. Her going there has saved us all," he pleaded. "They took me from the cell and dropped me off in the city center. I took two cabs to get here, just in case I was followed. Let's just go back to America. Forget this ever happened."

"I won't ever forget." Rain pushed herself from the couch and walked to the kitchen to breathe. Prescott was stifling her with his fear. She understood why he wouldn't want to go against Dalton after all he'd been through, but she wouldn't let him get away with killing her mother, no matter how much she despised her mother for her lack of family values.

Rain heard the front door open and boots on the linoleum. She splashed cold water on her face from the sink. Shanty's voice was the first she heard.

"Well *goddamn* . . . who dragged in the dead body?"

"He's not dead . . . yet," Mogli said, sucking his teeth.

Rain rounded the corner to see Shanty dressed in overalls and a gray T-shirt that barely hid his swollen belly. His long beard had been braided into a stiff tail that pointed outward instead of down. She kissed him on the cheek. The smell of alcohol lingered as he walked off toward the bathroom.

"Can't travel with this guy. All he wants to do is stay the course. No pee breaks, know what I mean?" Shanty grumbled on his way down the hall.

Mogli shook his head and dropped into the chair across from Prescott who still looked dead in the sunlight. The bruising made his skin look a sick shade of bluish-gray.

"Glad you made it back." Rain stood beside his chair, looking with Mogli at Prescott's still form.

"No thanks to him." Mogli's voice dripped with attitude. Rain patted his shoulder knowingly and pursed her lips.

"He told me Dahlia is dead. Killed by Dalton's men." She sat on the arm of the chair.

Mogli put a hand to her knee. He nodded silently before saying, "You okay?"

She nodded. Weariness etched across her face. His eyes peered into hers and she remembered when she first saw him as a real person after their car accident. His eyes still looked as sad and needy as they did that day. She had the urge to run her hands through his long, wavy hair but stopped when she heard Prescott stir. Mogli removed his hand from her knee, its warmth slowly fading.

"New hairstyle? Looks good on you," Mogli said, fingering the bottom of her jagged blond bob.

She blushed under his appraisal. "Thanks, just needed to do something different."

"Makes you look more mature," he said, smiling with his full lips, showing a flash of white teeth.

"I don't think it's the hair," she said with a smile, pushing her hair from her face.

"Ah yes, the international car chases, espionage, and torture have done all that."

She couldn't help but laugh. This was the first time she'd seen this side of Mogli, and she liked it. He seemed more human than when she'd first met him. Of course he was attractive enough with his square jaw and curious eyes, but he seemed *real* when he laughed. Prescott groaned deep in his throat from the couch. Rain knew he was listening. She hoped her flirting with Mogli ate away at his heart like his deception had done hers.

"I guess I better get him cleaned up so he can help us," Rain said finally, gesturing toward Prescott.

"Help us do what?" Mogli questioned, his brow raising skeptically.

"Kill Dalton."

Mogli tapped his knee with his fingers, contemplating her answer. "You might want to talk to Tolley about that."

Rain stood to retrieve the bucket by the couch. She stopped when she realized what Mogli was insinuating. Did Tolley want to run away like Prescott did?

"For what?" She looked over her shoulder.

Mogli shrugged and stood up from the couch. Rain could sense that he knew something she didn't. Curiosity burned within her. She was getting tired of the endless secrets her parents kept. Rain watched as Mogli walked toward the rear of the apartment and disappeared down the dim hall.

"So you still want to kill Dalton?" Prescott's voice almost made Rain's heart leap from her chest. She was so upset with what Mogli alluded to that she'd forgotten that Prescott was listening to everything.

She spun quickly on him, her anger still front and center. "Of course I do. He killed my mother. He had me tortured. He had *you* tortured *twice*. Why wouldn't I want him killed?"

Prescott sighed as if the world was heavy on his chest. "He released me as he said he would. He will stick to his word. He'll leave us alone." Prescott's hand groped for hers, which were gripping the edge of the couch. She moved it away.

"You're a bigger fool than I thought if you'd trust anything Dalton says," Rain spat at him in annoyance. She wondered when everyone around her had gotten so complacent, as if they hadn't seen what was on the chip.

"The information on the chip is too damaging for us to release. It could destroy America," Prescott said, as if reading her mind. Rain could tell he was getting weaker as he spoke. She grabbed a glass of water still on the coffee table from last night and held his head up as he sipped.

"Thank you." He swallowed breathlessly.

Rain set the glass on the table. "I'm still going after him. We won't be safe until he's dead. Not captured. If we give the chip to the authorities then he'll only go to trial and find some way out of it all. Then we'll still be running," Rain reasoned. "We need to kill him now. Take away his power. The rest of those in cahoots with him will lie low if he dies. They won't know what we have or don't have because I'm pretty sure he hasn't shared with his group that he compromised their involvement. We could turn the chip over after he dies. Take them by surprise." Prescott's eyes looked glassy between the swollen edges of his face, but she could see they still held determination.

"And what do you suppose we do about Anton?" Tolley's voice was firm behind her. She swirled around, heart pounding as if she had plotted to kill her father instead of Dalton. She felt horrible for planning behind his back but Mogli had already let her know that she was outside the loop anyway.

"Anton will be fine. We can hide him with someone while we finish this."

"Good idea. Maybe we will hide him with you and Prescott while *we* finish this." His brow hooded his emerald eyes.

"I'm a part of this, too."

"Rain, you don't understand. All I have left are you two and this team. I can't let anything happen to you guys." Tolley's eyes were watering with the thought. "What happened in the Basin almost killed me, Rain."

Rain dropped her head. She remembered his face when he'd blasted through the doors and saw her bloody and beaten in the chair. She remembered the pain in his eyes and the darkness when he'd asked her to leave. She knew that fighting Dalton was bringing him closer to his darker side, and she didn't want to lose him, either. Not the father she remembered on the farm. Anton deserved to know that Tolley. The Tolley who made breakfast in the morning and carried injured women to safety.

"I want to do this," she said finally.

"Dammit, Rain." Tolley rubbed his hands through his hair but he also knew that she wouldn't be detoured when she made up her mind, much like himself.

"Then it's settled," Prescott said through a groan. "My job on the team will be a babysitter."

Rain and Tolley eyed each other like infamous rivals, each waiting on the other to fold. They knew this was the decision that could mean life or death for either of them. Tolley dipped his chin and walked away. Rain felt as though she'd won a small victory but she feared that she might have lost the war.

TWENTY-THREE

BROOKLYN, NEW YORK

THREE MONTHS SEEMED TO fly by as the team prepared to avenge Dahlia's untimely death. It was clear that Dalton had indeed kept to his word and seemingly left them to their escape, or so he thought. Black had been relentless in tracking Dalton's every move, flying from New York to Pakistan, from Dubai to Tokyo. He always stayed in the shadows. Rain soon realized why he had earned the nickname Black, because he was invisible as most things are in the dark of night. Shanty was dutiful in keeping a constant hack on Dalton's technology, and he took great pleasure in his findings. He tracked Dalton's whereabouts through his many cronies, inserting phishing attempts every few days in the beginning of their plan until two or three of them slipped and allowed him access. Now Shanty resorted to eating Philly cheesesteaks and licking at his knotty fingers as he watched them search porn, book plane tickets, and email their family members from their computers and cell phones.

All valuable intel, Shanty had explained when Rain asked why he was watching porn.

Mogli, on the other hand, took a more serious approach. He had taken to training Prescott in martial arts, which usually amounted to Prescott being sore and bruised for weeks. Rain figured it was his way of slowly and steadily getting his own revenge on Prescott for drugging him and taking off with the chip. Prescott was a willing participant, probably a glutton for punishment to atone for his many betrayals.

Tolley was invigorated since the day Rain decided to go after Dalton instead of run. He'd started training again and was even teaching Anton a few tricks. Anton was like a sponge, soaking up everything Tolley taught him and relishing in small accomplishments like stealing wallets on the train and replacing them before the unsuspecting victim found out. He learned quickly that his cute and innocent demeanor made him an easy host for overly nice couples. Rain didn't like that he'd been learning negative things from his father instead of the good that he'd taught her on the farm. She felt like his childhood was being stripped away each time he came home with his smile beaming like a badge of honor. She also knew that in order for him to survive he needed to be able to take care of himself, so she frequently relented when Tolley bristled at her judgment. Tolley bulked up considerably since Dahlia's death and Anton mirrored his movements like a robot, cinching his belt loosely, wiping his hands on his jeans, and even scratching through his dark hair like Tolley. Rain noticed Tolley was taking his frustration out on the punching bags less and less, but the look in his eyes remained. She knew he was still reeling from the loss of Dahlia, his only real love. But he had decided to put his energy into Anton and he seemed to flourish with his new understudy. She could fight the twitch of jealousy over Anton and his time with Tolley now because she knew she'd always have memories of the farm. Something Anton would never have.

After Dahlia's death and Prescott's slow healing process, they'd flown from Russia to New York, staying at a pad in Brooklyn that Mogli said was safe. They'd nestled themselves like refugees into a gray row house with creaking stairs and wrought-iron banisters that housed a training studio downstairs. Its walls cement blocked and soundproof, the team used the building for heavy training, preparing for the moment when Tolley would call them together to start the plan. No one knew what they were waiting for but they waited without worry.

After a few days in the house, Rain was curious about the old, nearly empty house. During her exploration of its many levels she ran across a turned-down photograph in the attic. It was a framed picture of two older people smiling widely next to a very young and thin Mogli with his hair at the nape of his neck tucked messily under a graduation cap, tassel hanging over his eye. Even in the photo he looked stern and distant during a time most kids would have been beaming. She'd thought maybe the agency had changed him into the quiet, brooding man she now knew. She wondered what he was always thinking about, why he was so distant with everyone when it looked like he'd had a fairly normal family life. Hell, he'd even had both parents at his graduation. Rain felt a tinge of envy as she wiped the dust from the frame. Her mother had missed hers. No call. No letter. She propped the photo up on a wooden crate and left it there. They looked too happy to be face down in an attic, she thought to herself.

With Anton tagging along through Mogli and Prescott's training, Tolley took Rain on the train for more of his own infamous survival training. He'd put her through shooting ranges, physical training, and speed tests, as if she was preparing for the apocalypse. To her it was more brutal than the agency's training, especially coming from her father who she had to please or else she'd be doing repetitions into the night. She wondered if he was training her the same way he was trained when he was going through the agency. She felt the jolt of the train as it passed over the tracks and could hear the steady hum of its wheels careening across the metal underneath. She leaned back in her seat across from Tolley with growing anticipation. The train whizzed by blurs of greens and browns as Rain looked out at the passing terrain.

"Where are we going now?" Rain questioned after the train had stopped three times and Tolley made no move toward the exit.

He didn't answer, just smirked and continued reading the newspaper as if he was on a typical Sunday excursion across town with his daughter. When the conductor finally announced that they'd reached the last stop, Rain saw Tolley gather his pack and she did the same, hoisting the heavy bag over her shoulder, causing her to stumble a bit toward the door. She wasn't sure what he had packed for them but she could tell it was potentially a long stay since Tolley only packed what he needed, never the extras Rain adored like shampoo and lip gloss. They exited the train easily, moving through the passengers who stopped to gather their luggage and chat with their awaiting family members. Rain enjoyed listening to the excited conversations as she followed behind Tolley until they were outside the station. Tolley walked toward the line of buses waiting for passengers. He boarded a bus crammed with people of different smells, looks, and ages. They found two seats unoccupied near the back and she slid near the window as Tolley landed heavily in the seat next to her with a grunt. Rain looked across the aisle at a bald baby straddling its mother, dribbling spit down its chin as it pulled at the mother's hair. The mother whispered, "Be a good little girl," as she pushed a finger into the baby's chubby hand.

The bus route ended in a small town named Blotsville and Tolley took off away from the heart of the town. Rain looked back over her shoulder at the grouping of mom-and-pop stores down the street. She knew she was going to wish she'd stopped for shampoo later.

Tolley trekked into the woods, over hollowed tree trunks and through thick vines of greenery for what seemed like miles. She could feel the sweat trickling down her back, tickling her spine, then smashing into a wet glob along the back of her T-shirt. She'd felt the moisture on her upper lip as she'd struggled to climb leaning trees to get to higher ground. She nearly bumped into Tolley when he abruptly stopped in a clearing. She inched her bag off and let it fall to the grass without asking if they were there. She knew he wasn't going to stop until he found where he wanted to sleep. It wasn't a bad clearing, perfectly hidden from outside the mountain by thick green brush and flat enough to sleep. Tolley groaned and rubbed at his lower back when he threw his pack to the ground and looked off into the distance, listening.

She knew what his expectation was and she immediately started looking for kindling and materials to build a fire for the night. Within an hour, they'd made a pretty decent camp and had started a fire. Not bad, she thought to herself, looking at the sheltering half Tolley had made over his rolled sleeping bag. She also noticed that he hadn't made her one while she'd built the fire.

"Two hours left of daylight. Are we getting takeout?" Rain joked.

"Looks like you better get out there then, huh? Are you taking any orders?" he said with a smirk.

Rain huffed under her breath, "Do I ever?"

She had to make the fire and find the food? This wasn't the way she envisioned having a partner in the wilderness. She stalked off into the woods without a second glance at her father, barely hearing his chuckle over the stomp of her feet through the vegetation. At dark, she returned with a rabbit, smaller than would satisfy both of them, but she still felt proud offering it to her father.

"Little small, don't you think?" He stoked the flame in their makeshift rotisserie then turned the rabbit a half turn to brown on the other side. Rain leaned back on her pack, legs splayed in the dirt and moss. "Good thing it's a meal for one."

He laughed heartily at that. "Not sharing?"

She admired her father, his wide smile that made her feel better about everything, "Depends on if I get shelter for the night." She pointed above her head at the vast openness.

"You're trying to bargain? I could just go kill something myself. And probably quicker."

Rain leaned forward. "Mmm . . . smells good, doesn't it?" She turned toward the dark woods and sighed. "Sure is dark out there tonight but be my guest." She pointed her open palm to the dark nothingness.

Tolley chuckled under his breath. "You drive a hard bargain, Rain Wilson."

He unfolded his legs and dug into his pack for the other sheltering half. He had the shelter built in as much time as it took for Rain to ration out the small, bony body of the rabbit onto two thick cloths as makeshift plates. They sat and ate the grisly meat in silence, the sound of nature buzzing around them as they chewed.

"Why'd you become an agent?" she asked after Tolley had settled back on his rolled-up sleeping bag, rubbing his belly.

He looked at her, then at the fire again. "At first I thought serving my country and keeping it safe from bad guys was important."

"And then?"

"And then I realized that I worked for bad guys, too," he said with a huff. He scratched the bridge of his nose and looked out into the forest.

"That why you left your team?"

"No. I never left the team. I just wasn't going to kill anymore. I'd seen enough meaningless death."

"But you killed bad guys, too. Did that make you feel, I don't know, *different* about it?" Rain slipped her hands into her hoodie. The night air was creeping in on a cool breeze.

"Killing anything can take a toll on you, especially if you value life. When you stop valuing life, that's when you know you're in too deep,"

Tolley said, looking into Rain's searching brown eyes.

"You were losing yourself."

"I was losing myself." He nodded. "Then your mother was pregnant with you and everything changed." Tolley smiled at the thought. "She was so beautiful, you know? Her belly was so swollen. I was scared I'd hurt her if I touched her." He shook his head at the memory.

"Was she happy to have me?" Rain asked with a deep yearning.

"You were everything to her. The difference between me and her is . . . she never lost herself. She had the same goal when she started all the way to her last mission. The greater good. Truth. Transparency," Tolley said, his eyes glassy. He flicked a finger at the corners of his eyes and wiped his face with a dirty hand. Brown dirt smeared down his cheeks and across his neck. "She wanted to expose *all* the bad guys, not just the foreign ones."

Rain could feel the heat from the fire fan against her face as the breeze grew stronger. She wiped her eyes with her sleeve, the smoke causing them to water, and unrolled her sleeping bag. She knew that Dahlia was a good woman. Rain just couldn't forge a bond with a person who was never there for her. The stories helped but she still felt a gaping hole in her heart where her mother should have been.

TWENTY-FOUR

When Rain and Tolley returned from their training a week later, they received the call they'd been waiting on from Black. He'd finally found an opening that would allow them to get close enough to Dalton. He promised it would be Dalton's weakest point after consulting Shanty's surveillance reports.

"It's time," he said to Tolley.

Tolley breathed deeply. He knew that things were going to change after the call. He wasn't sure if it would be for better or worse but he knew it would undoubtedly change for all his team members, especially Rain.

Black revealed that Dalton was scheduled to attend a black-tie charity gala in two weeks. He relayed that he'd stay in the area of the gala's location to prepare their safe houses and transportation. Shanty immediately started working on getting invitations to the event while Mogli started packing the small amount of belongings he liked to travel with. Rain watched everyone move quickly from the living room and separate in the hallway. Prescott stood in the doorway of the living room leaning against the frame. His hair had grown longer over the months and she realized that it was curlier than she expected. Rain saw the look of worry creating lines on his forehead. She'd grown familiar with them over the months since his return.

"You ready?"

Prescott shrugged and crossed his arms. "Ready as I'll ever be, I guess."

"Then why do you look so worried?" Rain said, trying to find a comfortable place for her hands. She settled on shoving them in the back pockets of her jeans. She hadn't said much to Prescott after they'd arrived in New York. She didn't really feel the need to. He'd betrayed her too many times, and even though she still felt a buzz in her gut when he laid eyes on her, recently she'd grown adept at ignoring it.

"I'm worried about you," he said, looking down at his scuffed boots. "Alright, that's a partial lie. I'm worried about *us*."

"You mean us as a couple?" she stressed with a hint of a chuckle. "Why worry about an *us*? You made it clear your feelings about me when you lied to me over and over again. I'm supposed to believe you now and act like nothing ever happened?" She hated sounding so harsh but her venomous tone was far easier than what she'd endured because of his actions.

"Then why bring me all this way, Rain? To torture me?" Prescott stood up straight, as if a board had been placed along his spine, and stared intensely into her eyes. She could see his neck pulsating with his heartbeat or his need to grind his teeth. She wasn't sure which. "You know they would love nothing more than to drop me off in the middle of nowhere. So why torture me like this?"

Rain walked close enough to Prescott to feel his breath warm against her face. She eyed his plump lips as she spoke, remembering the way they felt pressed against hers in a moment of passion. It felt like ages ago now. "Because I want to torture myself apparently." Her eyes traveled to his. "And I don't trust you not to flip on me again. I need to keep you close so

I can watch you."

She bumped his shoulder as she walked toward the hall then turned to look back. "And if you cross us again, torturing you will be the only thing left between us."

Prescott nodded with his brow tense above his penetrating stare. His jawline worked rhythmically and he looked as if he wanted to embrace her and strangle her at the same time. Rain felt like she'd hurt him and for an instant felt guilty but as she walked away from him, she knew she had to stay focused on the mission. She wasn't going to let Prescott Willow make a fool of her again.

RAIN FOUND TOLLEY IN THE basement, sitting across from Mogli at a table with a map splayed across it, its creases standing up on the wooden top. She grabbed a chair, slid it across the cement floor, and took a seat at the table. Behind her, she heard Prescott inch his chair to the table slowly until he also sat across from her, eyes averted. Tolley glanced at Prescott as he saddled next to him, then leaned farther over the map. Seeing both of them so close together, Rain wished things were different. She would have loved to bring Prescott home to her father on the farm. He might've liked the Prescott she knew in Iraq. She pondered whether she even knew the real Prescott.

"Here's the gala location." Mogli pointed at the map and dragged his finger to another point with a blue circle. "This is the safe house." He looked quickly around the table before continuing. "Shanty will be at the safe house covering technical surveillance. We want him far enough away that he's not in the action but close enough to help out if we need to get out of there quickly. The airfield is here." He pointed at a square piece of flat terrain close to the blue circle. "So if we need to ditch one another at any point, meet on the airfield. Otherwise we all meet at the safe house after the mission is complete. Anton and I will be on the street, here and here. He will be placing the tracking beacon on Dalton's vehicle and I will be backup for him and for you two." He looked at Rain and Tolley, his mouth set in a line as he nodded quickly to Tolley.

Tolley leaned across the map, finger sliding against the page. "Rain and I will be attending the event, so we will be entering through the main entrance after Dalton has been spotted entering. We will start the plan from there. It should take us roughly one hour to complete the mission unless something else happens, at which point you'll all be wired to us and will know it as soon as we do."

"And for me?" Prescott said.

Tolley and Mogli looked at each other for a moment. Mogli couldn't hide the disdain in his face at the idea of Prescott helping with a mission so vital.

"Mogli, you've trained me for this," Prescott offered. "Let me help, please."

Mogli dropped his eyes to the floor. He was not the person making the call. Tolley's gaze traveled across the table to Rain and she could sense that he wanted her approval. She felt a sense of responsibility similar to the moment she'd decided to let Prescott take the chip to the decoder. She swallowed a hard lump that had formed in her throat. She shook her head.

"Not this time," Tolley said definitively.

Mogli chimed in quickly, "You will wait at the airfield after dropping off Rain and Tolley at the event. If you receive the word from Shanty to start her up, then that'll be your job."

"So basically you're saying you don't need me?" Prescott's chair made a screeching noise as he exited his seat stiffly, his injuries screaming against his will. "I'm much better than a chauffeur. That's bullshit and you know it." He stalked out of the basement. No one said a word until the sound of his boots faded from the stairs and across the wooden floors on the second level. They heard the front door slam faintly before Mogli said, "Don't worry. You made the right call."

She smiled weakly at him and pushed her cropped blond hair behind her ears. "Yeah. Thanks."

Her voice couldn't hide her anguish at pushing Prescott off the mission. He was right that he had more to offer but she couldn't live with herself if she trusted him again and someone else got hurt. She knew he didn't have anyone or anything right now. Like her, all he had were these guys. But she'd made her decision and she was going with her head instead of her heart this time.

ON THE DAY OF THE GALA, Rain's nerves were pinched tight. She'd sat in her room on the bed, looking at the black high heels and elegant dress strewn across the comforter. As she sat on the edge of the bed, she remembered a time when she'd guffawed about her neighbor Mrs. Billingsley coming over with heels and skirts to see Tolley. Now that she'd slipped into her own understanding of what beauty meant and felt like, she understood why Mrs. Billingsley had done it. She wanted to feel pretty. Like a woman. Something Rain was starting to feel in the strangest way. She recognized that she was doing some of the roughest training and probably looked worse for the wear, but she still liked the way Prescott's eyes appraised her every time she put effort into her hair or makeup. Even Mogli had given her a reason to feel like a woman with his rare smile.

Rain dressed in the black gown that Mogli picked up at a local shop. It was a basic dress that didn't call too much attention to her, but it fit perfectly around her curves, which were now bowing out at the hips and chest. She liked the feel of the soft fabric against her skin as she zipped the dress closed and turned in the mirror to admire herself. Her back was exposed, skin glowing with oils, the dress pooled around her high-heeled feet. She pinned her blond hair up and slid in her blue contact lenses. She wanted to disguise herself so Dalton wouldn't spot her at the event. She wouldn't want to ruin the plan. It was important that she slip in and out of the party unnoticed.

They'd waited months to find a weakness in Dalton's schedule and she didn't want to blow their last chance at finally finishing what they'd started. She glanced at herself in the mirror above her dresser and didn't fully recognize herself. The light hair and eyes against her skin, faded scars covered with makeup—she looked like a girl who had seen too much. She gave one last glimpse at the girl she didn't want to be anymore, lonely and scared, and went to wait downstairs for Tolley. Her belly ached at the uneasiness over the coming night.

Tolley entered the living room in a black tuxedo that fit snugly across his chest and arms, then pulled in at his waist. Rain wondered if Mogli had found his suit as well. She knew that he'd had a quirky personality but his taste in fashion was impeccable, yet another surprise to Rain. Tolley's graying temples made him look even more distinguished, and for the first time Rain realized how much he had aged. At the farm, he always looked young and vibrant, but now she noticed the crow's-feet at the edges of his eyes and the fine lines etched in faint parentheses around his mouth. His eyes still shone like vibrant gems as he caught sight of her.

"You look beautiful," he said, opening his arms to her and pulling her into a hug.

"You aren't half-bad yourself," she smirked.

"Aww, ain't that sweet."

Tolley turned to see Prescott in the doorway, smiling, dressed in all black, a hat curled in his palm.

Rain blushed under his surveillance; she could feel his eyes roaming over her hips before stopping at her face. "You look absolutely stunning, Rain," he said with a redness creeping into his cheeks.

"Alright already. Keep your head in the game," Tolley said with a sigh after catching the kindling fire between the two. "Mogli and Anton have already left."

Prescott's smile faded quickly and he only glanced at her once before turning on his heel and leaving them in the room alone. Tolley heard the front door close behind Prescott and sighed under his breath.

"He can be an emotional wreck but that boy seems to be in love with you."

Rain blushed and slapped her dad's arm playfully. "I thought you said to stay focused." She smiled.

"You know it's okay to forgive people, Rain. You've forgiven me for lying about my past."

"Yes, but your lies didn't get me tortured or my mother killed," Rain said bluntly, searching Tolley's eyes for understanding.

"No. But my lies were what got us in this mess in the first place. Had I told you about my past and your mother's past, you wouldn't have felt the need to find her." Tolley rubbed a finger down Rain's smooth cheek like he'd done since she was a girl.

"Yes, I would have. I needed her as much as she needed me," Rain said, her eyes locked in on Tolley.

He gave a tight-lipped grunt before gripping her warm palm and leading her to the car outside. Prescott was in the driver's seat, the engine purring softly into the early-evening air. Smoke from the exhaust billowed white before disappearing into the air. When Tolley and Rain settled in the backseat of the town car, he took off smoothly in the direction of the gala, his knuckles white against the steering wheel.

They arrived outside the banquet hall within the hour. Rain craned her neck to see the top of the historic building raising in pointed arrows toward the sky like an old cathedral. Flags from every country flew in a steady yet light breeze, making a soft popping noise as they folded and unfolded against themselves in the wind. The line of cars leading to the banquet hall inched slowly up to a red carpet surrounded by men in dark suits, white wires budding from their ears and disappearing down their necklines. Ahead a few cars, Rain watched the well-dressed men and women exit their vehicles and step onto the carpet only to be flanked by the men in dark suits. They pointed miniature flashlights against their lists before penciling the sheet and ushering the couple to the front door. Rain noticed they circled around and walked back to the line of cars, opening the door for the next guests. She breathed a nervous sigh. *This is it*, she thought to herself, leaning back on the soft leather seat.

Tolley pushed his earbud deeper into his ear. "Has Dalton arrived?"

He waited for a moment before Mogli affirmed that he had arrived twenty minutes before. Mogli and Anton had successfully tagged his car once it parked.

"Good," Tolley said into the quiet as he turned to Rain. "Looks like he's here as planned. Ready?"

Rain squeezed his rough hands for reassurance. She held Prescott's gaze in the rearview mirror. He smiled at her and nodded as if to say, *you can do it*. She turned her focus to the dark-suited man who opened the car door and offered his hand to help her onto the carpeted sidewalk. The night breeze swept across her back and gave her a chill. She felt Tolley's warm hand across her flesh within seconds. Even now, he was her protector. She walked steadily up the walkway, her steps soft against the red fabric. Tolley ushered her to the front door and soon they were inside the building. The rush of noise flooded her senses. Clicks from photographers, the smell of sweet pastries, and the punchy mix of perfume merged with the cumulative voices of each hushed tone. Rain took a moment to settle herself and took in the opulent design. Golden tapestries lined the thirty-foot windows that surrounded the space, its view of a grassy promenade peeking through. The wait staff carried golden trays of champagne through throngs of people, their trays hoisted high. Tolley tapped her twice on her back and she already felt lonely as he eased away. She saw him joking and making small talk as he made his way to his mark. She was shocked that he was the same man who didn't even know how to talk to a neighborly woman back at the farm yet he could instantly turn on his charm in a room full of strangers. She was only beginning to peel away his many layers.

It was time to begin.

She headed to the bar to wait until her moment arrived. She waited to spot Christopher Dalton.

At the bar, she could see the entire floor of guests. Men in military uniforms that exposed their rank with shiny gold stars talked closely to men in tuxedos who oozed high society through their ridged postures and buttery-soft hands. She rung her hands in thought. Where was he? Rain scanned the crowd, her eyes falling on the women with their overinflated lips and faces pulled taut as they bumped glasses and tilted their heads back to drink as if their necks wouldn't bend. Her eyes bobbled past Tolley talking with a gentleman in a black tuxedo with badly thinning hair. Her eyes continued to search the crowded ballroom until her breath caught in her chest. She saw the beady eyes staring at Tolley from across the room. His hand was frozen to his companion's shoulder as if he'd only just seen Tolley. Rain turned toward the bar, pressed her ear inconspicuously, and spoke low. "Dalton at your six. He's spotted you." She smiled at the bartender, hoping she didn't look as uneasy as she felt. She knew if Dalton saw Tolley, he'd be looking for the rest of the team at the banquet. He'd either lock them in or have them ushered out.

Her first task was complete so she moved on to the next.

She headed toward the ladies' bathroom down a dim hall with unmarked and pristine taupe carpeting. It was surprisingly empty down the wide hallway. She passed windows overlooking the front of the banquet hall where hordes of people stood on the red carpet awaiting entry. She passed oversized paintings of sailboats on rough waters and enlarged prints of stately women in loose-hanging garments along the way. When she finally spotted the bathroom door and entered quietly, she checked each stall and found that she was alone. Her instructions led her to the third stall. She flushed the toilet with her shoe to provide adequate cover. Quickly she traced her hand along the tile, counting as she moved along. Two across and four up, she repeated to herself, although she knew it by heart. She used her fingernail to break the loosened grout on the tile behind the toilet and it popped off easily to reveal the small handgun stowed inside. The cylindrical silencer rolled in the hole as she pulled it out, stuffed them both into her handbag, and replaced the tile. Her bag felt heavy now but she felt instantly powerful with her new possessions. She didn't have to wait long before getting it to Tolley. With no time to waste, she flushed the toilet again, feeling the sound drown out the rest of her nerves. She exited the bathroom stall, stopping in midstride to find a woman standing in front of the sink closest to the door. Rain hadn't heard her come in. She scanned the woman quickly—the angular facial features that looked too harsh to be considered beautiful, a prominent chin with a deep dimple.

"Beautiful party, no?" Her accent was thick and Russian. She looked in the mirror at Rain, an odd smile on her face as she ran her hands under the water.

Rain could see the tensed muscles of the woman's arms flex as she rubbed her hands together. Suspicion bubbled inside Rain. She walked to the mirror with a shy smile at the woman and smoothed her hair from her face. She didn't want to turn her back on this woman, so she'd wait her out. The woman dried her hands leisurely then smiled wide until Rain could see her silver caps. Rain gripped her handbag tighter, the feel of the weight easing her mind as she looked at herself in the mirror with the woman in her peripheral vision. With lightning-quick speed, the woman was behind her, choking her. Her thick arm locked tight around Rain's throat. Rain's feet lifted from the floor and back down again as she hopped against the woman trying to force her loose. The woman was quicker and stronger than Rain could have anticipated with her brutish size. She felt the heat rising from her chest, her head beginning to pound at her temple from lack of oxygen. In the commotion, Rain heard the faint sound of her handbag falling to the marble floor. She could hear their heels clicking on the hard floor as they wrestled with each other. Rain struggled for enough stability to push off the woman, but the much taller Russian was planted firmly behind her. Rain's feet slid out from under her in the struggle.

Rain found her moment as the woman raised her hands to her head in an attempt to snap Rain's neck. With her elbow raised, Rain pushed upward with a force that stunned the woman, but she was strong and wrestled to get her position back. She could not. Rain bent her over the sinks, her hands around the woman's thick throat in exchange for what she'd done to her. Rain felt the woman's thighs wrap around her waist and squeeze tight enough to make her gasp in pain. She elbowed the tender meat of the woman's inner thigh and heard a slight yelp before her legs released. Rain snatched her from the sinks, slinging her into the handicap stall and into the wall. Rain followed close behind but felt the thud to the side of her head as it connected with the stall door. The woman had kicked it closed and was now opening it again as Rain felt warm wetness at her hairline. The woman wrapped her large hands around Rain's wrists and pulled her into the stall. Rain fought to exit the stall, legs kicking at the woman but not getting any result with each blow that landed. She needed to find her handbag. Rain punched her quickly in the nose; a trickle of blood escaped and streamed to her top lip. Her eyes jolted with psychotic glee as she touched the blood and looked at her fingertips. The woman chuckled as if the hit had only made her stronger, reinvigorating her. She dove at Rain, grabbing her arms and kneeing her in the stomach. Rain felt the breath-stopping pain but she willed it away and rammed the woman into the side of the stall, knocking her head hard with a sickening *thok*. A groan escaped the woman's lips as she fell to the floor. Rain used her high heel to kick the woman in her stomach but she wouldn't stop moving, clawing for Rain's legs and ankles. The woman began crawling under the stall door. Rain gripped her legs before she could escape and pulled her back into the stall, away from her purse lying a few feet away. She used all her power to grind her heel into the woman's neck as she squealed in pain until Rain heard the *crack* of her spine. The woman became limp, her dark hair pooled on the bathroom floor.

Rain heard the door swing open and the sound of women entering the bathroom, chattering coolly with one another. She closed the handicap stall behind her and picked up her purse from the floor. The three women stopped in their tracks at the sight of her and stared in confusion. She glanced sideways at the mirror and saw the slight cut above her eyebrow and at her hairline, cheeks red, and her hair disheveled.

"Honey, you should leave him," a woman with long, black hair and a mole next to her cherry-red lips said. The others hummed in agreement.

Rain answered calmly, "Yes, you're probably right." She fixed her hair and dabbed at the cut before walking toward the three women who hadn't moved an inch from the door.

All three women moved to the side, creating a wide lane as she walked near them. Before she left she said, "The handicap stall is out of order. Someone left a huge pile of shit in there."

She let the door close behind her.

TOLLEY HAD FOUND THE SECRETARY of defense easily enough. He was the gray and balding man who stood ramrod straight and exuded confidence and affluence. Tolley had been able to gain his interest as he passed off as a military weapons manufacturer—at least that's what his business card stated. Before long he'd had the gentleman laughing easily, but after he heard Rain's message about Dalton seeing him, he laid the charm on even thicker.

"I'd really be interested in meeting with you, sir. I'd love to show you some of the new weapons we've been manufacturing and my R & D team will blow your socks off. Well, not literally, of course." Tolley heard the old man laugh loudly again and in the corner of his eye he caught sight of Dalton making his way through the crowd.

"You are one hell of a businessman, Mr. Roskabine. I think we can make that happen." The secretary chuckled as he dug his finger into his jacket pocket and extended a card to Tolley. Tolley turned to see Dalton stop a few feet away, attempting to hide his eyes behind a glass of brown liquor. Tolley smirked as he took the secretary's card between his fingers and planted it in his jacket pocket.

"Ah, I think I see a friend of mine. You don't mind, do you?" Tolley said with a gracious smile. The secretary patted him on the back stiffly and turned toward another group of guests.

Dalton's face was red with anguish as he rounded partygoers to reach Tolley. A quiet jazz ensemble kept the partygoers swaying with their wineglasses as they networked heavily with other rich and powerful guests. Dalton stood three feet from Tolley before stopping, the area opening and shifting around him as people moved from one group to the next. Dalton swirled his nearly empty scotch in his hands.

"What do you think you're doing?" he said slowly, his words careful and clear, barely heard over the chatter and music around him.

Tolley could sense Dalton's frustration as his jaw worked and the ice clinked noisily against his glass in nervous anticipation. He was trying hard not to cause a scene around so many of his potential supporters.

"I'm attending a gala to give to charity. What do you think I'm doing?" Tolley said, his smile large and confident, eyes scanning the crowd for any of Dalton's cronies.

"So why were you talking to the secretary? I didn't think he was lobbying for a charity." Dalton pulled the hem of his tuxedo over his protruding belly. His eyes bore holes into Tolley. Tolley could almost feel the heat radiating off of Dalton.

"Oh, I don't know. Just making friends with people in high places. You know, ironically, he doesn't seem the least bit worried that you've leaked information that he's involved with. I'm sure he'd be very angry to find that out. Maybe even a little *desperate* to make sure whatever despicable shit you guys have done never gets out," Tolley said, eyeing the crowd coolly, his words clipped and tense.

Dalton looked over both shoulders before replying, "What do you want?" he said through thin, tight lips.

"I want you dead. Can you do that for me?" Tolley looked down on him as he inched closer.

"I don't think that'd be a good idea. In fact, as I recall, you need me."

Tolley chortled loud enough for partygoers to look in his direction before turning back to their conversations. "Oh, I seriously doubt that."

"Let's go somewhere and talk in private," Dalton said.

Dalton made his way through the crowd without a glance over his shoulder at Tolley. Tolley shrugged and followed. He stopped as Dalton spoke to the elevator attendant then stepped onto the elevator, alone with Dalton. Tolley fought the urge to grab the goose-like neck of the man next to him and strangle the life out of him as the elevator chimed to the tenth floor. He didn't know why Rain had not met him to give him the gun, but he knew he wouldn't need it to handle Dalton's pudgy frame. It was only a second option anyway. He much preferred the hands-on method, especially for swine like Dalton.

Dalton walked out of the elevator, his shoes clicking on the marble floors only slowing when he reached a meeting space that was dark inside. He flicked the switch and the room lit with a dimness that brightened over several seconds. Tolley surveyed the space—the long mahogany table, fifteen chairs around it, a projector screen at the far wall, and in the corner, a banquet table with empty glassware on top. Dalton turned on his heels and faced Tolley. Before Tolley knew it, he had punched Dalton in the face and watched with satisfaction as he bent over with a cry. Tolley closed the door behind him silently. "You must have a death wish to invite me up here alone."

"Goddammit, did you have to hit me so hard? I think you broke my nose," Dalton whined through his hands.

Tolley grabbed his jacket and stood him up. Dalton tilted his head back and pinched the bridge of his nose.

"Wait a minute! Wait!" Dalton pushed his palms out to Tolley and stepped back. Red blood pooled around his nostrils and he dabbed it with the handkerchief from his breast pocket.

"Why should I wait? I can think of ten reasons to end you right here and right now," Tolley said through gritted teeth. "But honestly, I only need one." His adrenaline was racing and the sound of Dalton in pain awakened the beast in him.

"You don't want to hurt me. It's actually quite simple," Dalton said breathlessly. "Everything you do to me will happen to a loved one of yours. You wouldn't want them to hurt someone you love, now would you?"

Tolley clenched his jaw. *What is he talking about?* He pinched his earbud quickly and said, "Sound off."

In minutes, each member of his team said their name. He waited for Rain's voice. His chest started to heave in anticipation. He looked over at Dalton who was still dabbing at the corner of his nose, red spots dotting the white silk fabric.

"What have you . . ." Tolley started, then he heard Rain, breathless, state her name. He breathed in deeply and dropped his head in silent thanks. Dalton rolled a chair out and sat, legs crossed, facing Tolley. His nose had stopped dripping.

"Sorry to tell you but you have no one I love. Which means you understand what has to happen now." Tolley took off his black tuxedo jacket and laid it over the back of a chair. He started to unbutton his crisp white shirt when Dalton said, "On the contrary, Tolley. I *still* have someone you love."

Tolley stopped pushing the buttons through the holes and stood there, staring at Dalton's beady eyes dancing with the delight that he'd beaten Tolley.

"What are you talking about?"

"I have your wife. I have Dahlia," Dalton said without hesitation.

"Dahlia's dead." Tolley tripped over the word but Dalton just chuckled in response.

"Oh boy, you thought I really killed her, huh?" Dalton slapped his forehead sarcastically. "I knew Prescott would run back to your daughter and tell her everything. Glad to see he came through for me yet again." Dalton reached in his pocket and set his phone on the table. "Prescott couldn't stay away from Rain. Foolish boy thought he loved her. Couldn't just do his damn job." Dalton caught himself getting angry and breathed heavily. "I didn't kill Dahlia because I knew that I would never get rid of you if I did. I needed to know what Dahlia knows and now that I do, she's of no use to me anymore. No use to me other than as a bargaining chip with you, of course."

"What?" Tolley's shock was evident. He couldn't move, his fingers glued to his shirt button.

"I knew that you needed to believe Dahlia was dead because I needed to see if you would try to do something stupid. Something like what's happening right now—you thinking you can kill me in a room full of people who saw both of us, and get away with it. I have security on the elevators waiting for me and if I don't return, well, you get the gist of it. No need for me to walk you through all the things that will happen to you because, well, you already know." Dalton shrugged his shoulders and leaned farther back in the chair, his foot bouncing easily.

"Dahlia's alive," Tolley muttered in confusion.

"Yes. She is. She's relatively well under the circumstances."

"So what do you want?"

"I want this to be put to bed ... finally."

"And how do you suppose we do that?" Tolley questioned, sliding his coat back on.

"Well, you can come get her, but under the condition that you and your team never set foot in America again and release every copy you have of the chip. I think we can let bygones be bygones, don't you?" Dalton cocked his head to the side like a child asking for dessert.

"Yes," Tolley said, still trying to swallow the shock that jolted his body. Dahlia was alive. He'd kept her alive for all these months because he knew Tolley was coming after him. He couldn't believe it even though he wanted to. "I need to see proof of life."

"Of course. I wouldn't have it any other way."

Dalton reached to the center of the table and pushed a button on the remote control. The screen at the far wall jumped to life and a blue screen buzzed quietly. Dalton pressed a code on his phone which connected it to the screen. Tolley felt his knees go weak as he saw Dahlia in white pajamas curled in the fetal position on a gray metal bed. The room was small and dark, a prison-like cell with a metal toilet in the corner and matching sink without a mirror. Her dark hair fanned across her pillow as she lay. He waited for her to move, to stir, and when she did, Tolley gasped. His hand inadvertently rose to his mouth and he fought back the urge to kill Dalton for keeping her locked away and using her against him. He couldn't imagine what she'd endured while being detained and drained of information. She'd been alive all the time, waiting for him to come rescue her, save her. And he hadn't.

"So I can take her as long as we leave today and never return?" Tolley repeated the terms as he understood them.

"Most importantly, you release to me any copies and discontinue any plans associated with the information on the chip." Dalton gave a sinister smile. "Just look at it as another early retirement."

"And if I refuse?" Tolley asked, still staring at Dahlia on the screen, her face revealing bruises.

"If you refuse then I make your life a living hell and the people I work for will make your life a living hell, too. I'm sure you saw the names involved. You can only imagine the reach, both domestic and foreign, associated with this group. I wouldn't want you to *really* lose your family one day over something that doesn't concern you at all. I'm throwing you a bone here, Tolley. The same bone I thought I buried twenty years ago when your team was taken off the case. I was trying to save you both even then but Dahlia wouldn't let it go. I hope you can talk her into it now. She seems to be ready to hear a resolution."

Tolley remembered being taken off the case twenty years ago. Dalton had been the control team lead back then, full of pomp and bravado with no real field experience. He'd had hair then but still wore glasses that made him look older. Dalton had cautioned them to let the case go months before he formally suspended it, citing lack of evidence and waste of funds.

And that's when Dahlia and Tolley left the agency to start over on the farm, have a family. But Dahlia could never stop searching into it. She was engulfed by the mystery and vowed to find out who and what was hiding behind the Sallad Musad front. They'd been close then, even finding out that an American was behind the infrastructure. He wasn't scared when they left the case behind—he was refreshed to retire and start a family— but now that he understood the full scope of the heinous group Dalton was involved with, he knew they were only alive because Dalton had not told the others about the breach, probably to save his own life. Tolley knew in that instant that he would never be out from under Dalton's grasp but he still had no choice.

"I'll take the deal. Lead me to her."

TWENTY-FIVE

R AIN EXITED THE TOWERING structure, padded down the steps quickly, and tried to walk as swiftly as she could without arousing suspicion. She headed to the line of cars still waiting curbside with her head hung low. A valet attendant asked if she needed his help as she reached the landing but she shook her head and continued down the sidewalk away from the banquet hall and the body they'd soon find in the bathroom. She hoped Tolley had finished his task and would be right behind her. She prayed Dalton was dead and it was all over. She had undoubtedly messed up the schedule and now Tolley was on borrowed time. As soon as the body was found, they'd be searching everyone going in and out. She was sure the women in the bathroom would point her out. She shook away the thought as she rounded the corner and crossed swiftly through traffic, her handbag clutched tightly to her chest.

She saw the lights flash twice on the white van parked a quarter mile down the block, and picked up pace. The neighboring homes were dark or dim, the occupants settling in for the night, unbothered by the lights and celebration only blocks away. She felt winded when she arrived at the van but didn't know if it was the length of the walk or her adrenaline leading way to guilt. The van's rear doors popped open with a metallic sound and she grabbed the handle and swung in without looking over her shoulder. She didn't care if anyone had seen her. She just wanted to be back to safety. Wanted to know where her father was. The last she'd heard from him was after she'd left the bathroom and he'd demanded they check in. She figured he'd been looking for her since she missed the exchange.

Anton's slim face peered around the edge of the passenger seat with a smile that made her almost forget that she'd just killed someone.

"You made it. And you're early," Anton said, glancing at the glowing digital numbers on the dash. Yes, she was early, but not because she'd worked efficiently. She might have ruined everything. She knew she should tell Mogli about what happened but he stayed glued to the tablet in his lap watching miniature screens shift from tracking Dalton's car to various cameras around the perimeter of the banquet hall.

"Have you heard anything yet?" Rain said, sidling up to her duffel bag and pulling out the change of clothes and boots, feigning nonchalance.

Mogli answered without turning in her direction. "Yes. Prescott made it to the airfield. Shanty is at the safe house still monitoring every guard associated with Dalton and he's been trying to tap in to their cell phone speakers to hear if we can get a lead on where they are heading next. He's still monitoring their emails and Internet but not much action since they're on the job tonight. Tolley is still inside. Did you get him the gun?"

The silence was unnerving. Rain couldn't force herself to answer but knew she needed to do something before Tolley was captured or worse. Mogli spun in his seat, his eyes like darts as he waited for an answer.

"No," Rain said quietly enough that she didn't know if she'd really said it aloud.

Anton turned in his seat now. His smile had faded and somehow in his young mind he realized that Rain had screwed up. She prayed he didn't understand the potential consequences of her mistake, but Mogli's face made it evident.

"I'm going in after him. It's been radio silence since he confronted Dalton," Mogli said, putting the tablet in Anton's lap. "Can you monitor it for me, buddy?"

Anton nodded with an intensity that said he wouldn't let Mogli down. Mogli patted his dark hair and opened the door.

"You won't get in. Not now, anyway," Rain offered as she swiped the hair that stuck to her cut with a wince. "I was attacked in the bathroom when I was retrieving the gun."

Mogli stopped moving and closed the door. "By who?"

"Some woman. A very large, Russian woman."

"And is she . . . ?"

Rain nodded. Mogli looked to Anton, who had enthusiastically started on his mission of watching the tablet closely.

"Dad!" Anton said, pointing his tiny finger at the screen. Mogli and Rain leaned over the seat to see the grainy image of Tolley trailing behind Dalton and his guards. He didn't look like he was in distress; in fact, he looked focused.

"What the hell is he doing?" Mogli said under his breath.

"Where are they taking my dad?" Anton's voice cracked. The sight of Tolley welled emotions in his small body that his brain was fighting hard to make sense of. He felt like Rain had as she saw him get into the back of the black sedan with Dalton and the car pull off toward the street.

"I don't know where they're taking him but we aren't going to lose him," Mogli said, turning the key in the ignition and swiveling out of their parking space. Rain held on to the edges of the van as it rumbled along the streets and over dips in the road, causing the bags and cases in the back to shift violently. She took the time to change her clothes quickly as Mogli talked to the team over the earpiece. She needed to be prepared for wherever they were taking her father because she wasn't going to lose him, too. She couldn't.

She wrestled on her boots last and stuffed the dress and heels back into the black bag, zipping it closed. She took the handgun from her purse, screwed on the tiny silencer, and put it in the back of her jeans.

"He must've lost his earpiece." Rain took a knee between the passenger and driver seats, adjusting her T-shirt. Anton still held the tablet which showed a blue blip that moved over the map grid. It was Dalton's car.

"He would never lose it. They had him destroy it once they realized we were on the other end. They probably think we are blind right now," Mogli said, maneuvering through the streets. He kept a block between the car and the van. "And that's a good thing."

They maintained the element of surprise. Dalton thought he had the upper hand now that Tolley was alone. Rain felt her hatred for Dalton flare up inside her with a fierceness she didn't think she could contain. Dalton had taken everything from her. The farm. Her mother. Life as she knew it. Her *innocence*. And now her father was in his grasp.

"Look in the back. I brought you something," Mogli said as he entered the highway at a steady speed. "Tolley thought you probably missed it."

Rain turned to the rear of the van and saw a few duffel bags near the doors and a black case in the corner. She cocked her head. Was that what she thought it was? It had been months since she'd seen it.

She slid to the case on her butt, felt the heaviness as she hoisted it to her lap and clicked the locks open. She lifted the lid to find the black SR-25 that her father had bought her after she'd made the lucky shot at the shooting range in Colorado. He'd kept it for her until she'd finished Langley training as a graduation gift. She smiled as she ran her hand over the cool, matte steel. While most girls who graduated from college got a new car, she'd received one of the most powerful and deadly rifles she'd ever shot. It was sentimental to her. She would never forget that shot at the range and her dad's face when she passed him the binoculars. It was the pride in his eyes that stuck with her. She'd never made that shot again since that day so the weapon had a memory locked in the case with it. She wasn't sure how he managed to get the rifle here, in New York, but she was happy he did.

They seemed to drive behind Dalton for hours and Mogli started to worry about the gas in the van, whether they'd make it the long haul. Then he turned on the route toward the District of Columbia and Mogli radioed it in that everyone should meet at a downtown pub he rattled off. Rain wondered how he knew so many places everywhere they went. Was he just prepared or had he been there before? Mogli was a mystery to her and she could never truly grasp who he was.

"Have you ever lived in DC?" Rain was sitting on her case between the seats, following the blue blip on the tablet. Anton had dozed off an hour ago, his chin tucked to his chest in slumber.

"Lived around there," he said, staring out the front glass, watching the road. His hair had been stuffed into a low ponytail and his eyes were alert but his body looked tired.

Rain tried another angle. "I saw your graduation picture. It was in the attic. I just assumed you went to school around there since you knew that pub." It was a stretch but it was the only thing she'd found out about him.

"I trained for the agency in Virginia. So we spent a lot of nights in DC trying to unwind." His lips rose into a slight smile as he reminisced. "I have a few ties to the area."

"I'm sure your training was a lot better than mine. I was a pariah to the men I trained with. They couldn't understand how an eighteen-year-old girl could get there. So they shut me out." Rain remembered their not-so-secret meetings without her, the looks, the chiding during group activities.

"Well, look at you now. A certified badass," Mogli said with a chuckle. Rain wanted to be one but she'd failed more times than she succeeded these days. One mistake after the next.

"No. I'm just a girl trying to get her life back. Screwing it up all the while. Nothing too special about that."

"Rain, you're special." Mogli's voice was convincing enough to make her cheeks redden as he stole a glance at her. She turned away to watch Anton sleeping peacefully before chancing a look in his direction.

"It doesn't feel like it. I barely know any of you guys even though you put your lives on the line for me." Without thinking, she asked, "Am I going to end up like you and the rest of the crew? Never having a family, risking my life for random people who will never know my name? It just seems so sad. So lonely."

"It is," Mogli said after a long pause.

He turned the van off the highway as they reached downtown DC. The monuments shined in the dark like historical pillars of hope. Rain watched as they crossed the bridge; the water looked black and calm as they continued on past the Jefferson Memorial. Mogli knew exactly where he was going as he maneuvered through the potholed streets until he parked next to an old pub called Marty's.

"They'll be here in about an hour or so. Let's go in." He shook Anton awake. Anton's eyes glazed over until they settled on them both and then he peered over the edge of the window at the street, realizing they'd stopped.

"But what about my dad? We need to stay on their trail," Rain demanded.

"We are." He lifted the tablet and waved it in her face.

"What if we lose them?" Rain sounded more scared than she wanted to and Anton looked back and forth between the two, fully awake now.

"We won't, Rain. Trust me." Mogli stared at her in the dark van. She could still make out his face in the glow from the streetlight. His eyes tried to reassure her but she still didn't like the thought of not actively moving toward Dalton and her father. She needed to *do* something. She wasn't going to hang out in a bar when her father was with Dalton, possibly captured. Mogli was still waiting for her to comply. She second-guessed it. He wouldn't hurt her like Prescott, would he?

The bar was definitely not a place to meet in silence. Rain entered through the heavy wooden door, an Irish flag painted crudely on the center below the stained-glass windows, and followed closely behind Mogli with Anton's hand buried deep in hers. The sound of the bar hit her long before the smell of cigarette smoke, stale chips, and lemon-scented cleanser. Her eyes danced across the men sitting around small wooden tables. Beer glasses covered the tabletop as more glasses were poured by waitresses with black shirts and green plaid pleated skirts. She saw a redhead glance in their direction and smile hugely at Mogli. She nodded her head toward the rear of the bar before tending to her clients. Mogli started in the direction the woman pointed as patrons noticed he was there and patted him on the back as he walked by. He was gracious as he shook their hands but still moved swiftly toward the door at the rear of the bar. Music droned beneath the sound of laughter and chatter. The feeling was infectious and Rain felt bad for momentarily getting caught in its lightheartedness. She needed to find her father and being here was not going to get them any closer. Her patience was thinning with Mogli but she nudged Anton along behind him, her curiosity piqued just enough to continue. Anton's head swiveled in delight at the lights and sounds. The merriment. Rain realized he hadn't seen anything other than the old house in New York and had likely been housebound in Russia as well. This was essentially his first look at human beings together in sheer joviality and drunkenness.

Mogli opened the door behind the bar and nodded at the bartender, a woman with raven hair to her chin and large, dark eyes that looked confused rather than delighted like everyone else. Rain saw the look in her eye as Mogli walked past. She was the least happy person to see them since they'd walked into the bar.

She shuffled in the door and realized they were directly in an office space with a large round table, map of the city on the wall with red and blue pegs all over the District of Columbia and even in places farther out in Virginia and Maryland. It reminded Rain of the map that they'd used in Russia; they didn't have pegs but the color scheme looked the same. There were papers and files stacked in the corner of the room, as if someone was moving out of the office but hadn't made up their mind to actually go yet. A mahogany desk, which looked too nice for the space, sat in the farthest corner of the room with a colorful glass lamp and laptop open in front of an oversized burgundy leather chair. Rain moved Anton toward the matching burgundy leather couch beneath a number of framed photographs as Mogli sat behind the laptop and hooked up the tablet.

"The rest of the team should be here soon," Mogli said without looking up from the laptop screen.

Rain nodded and, realizing he couldn't see it, she murmured her response as she walked around the room exploring. The map fascinated her as she looked at each peg. Blue pegs were lining the Potomac at various points; red pegs were inside the city center.

"Is this your bar?" Rain asked, knowing it must be another layer to the mysterious man. He'd known everyone and came into this office as if he'd been there yesterday.

Mogli hesitated. "Yes. Well, not right now."

Rain turned away from the map and walked over to the edge of the desk. Mogli was typing quickly but she knew he had more to say, so she waited.

"I was running the place until I came on to help Tolley. To help you. It's actually my father's place and he passed it down to me when I got out of the service. But as you know, I've been gone."

Rain felt her heart skip a beat. She was ruining so many lives. Her decision to go after her mother had led to so many people getting hurt. She didn't know how to atone for her stupidity and selfishness, so she just said, "Oh."

Mogli looked up from the laptop and saw the pained look on her face. He hadn't wanted to hurt her feelings but the truth was sometimes complicated.

"It's not your fault we're doing this. You may have started it but we chose to stay, chose to finish this after seeing what was on the chip. It was the same thing your mother saw and couldn't turn her back on," Mogli said in a hushed tone, his hand reaching for hers.

She let him take it. Felt the warmth of his skin, the dryness rubbing against hers as he rubbed her bruised knuckles gently. She didn't want to meet his eyes or she was sure she'd fall apart. He'd left a successful business and a normal life to get thrust into a worldwide quagmire, a fugazi as they called it in the military. A fugazi she'd kicked off because she wanted to see her mom again. Now she'd gotten her mother killed, her father captured, Mogli ripped from his seemingly normal life, and Anton . . . she didn't want to think of all the things Anton had lost and would never be able to know about. She needed to find Tolley. Rain pulled her hand away from Mogli as a quiet knock filled the room. Seconds later the dark-haired girl from behind the bar poked her head through the cracked door. She still looked as confused as she had when they'd walked into the bar.

"Ben?" she said clearly before stepping through the door and clicking it shut behind her.

Rain looked over her shoulder at Mogli, unsure of who the woman was looking for. Mogli looked back down at the screen with his jaw clenched tight. Rain felt odd sitting between the two, so she sidled over to sit by Anton on the couch. He'd found a string from the side table and was working diligently at tying it into a knot, oblivious to the visitor. Rain lowered her head to watch Anton's efforts in a weak attempt to give space to the woman and Mogli.

"Yes, Brit, what do you need?" Mogli said, not hiding the impatience in his voice.

"Um, did you get my letter?" Rain looked up to assess the woman who had clearly been personally tied to Mogli. She was wringing her hands behind her back like a child awaiting a scolding. Her breasts were large for her petite frame but her face was thin and bony, almost birdlike. .

Mogli leaned back in his seat after several seconds. "Do you really want to do this now?" His hands clenched both sides of the armchair as if he'd spring up at any second to pounce on her.

"I don't want to do anything right now except say what I said in my letter. I'm *sorry*, okay?" She glanced at Rain who tried to drop her head back down to Anton's knot. It wasn't in time; she could feel Brit's eyes on her.

"Yeah. I read your apology. Many times over the last couple months. You plan on giving the ring back?"

Rain's eyes darted to Mogli's face then to the woman, Brit. Her eyes trailed down to the hand behind her back and she caught sight of a small diamond solitaire on her finger.

Brit shifted from one foot to the next uncomfortably before answering, "I don't want to give it back. I still want to marry you."

Mogli's laugh startled Rain as it filled the room. It sounded foul, not like the laugh she longed to hear. Anton looked up from his knot. His eyes rolled over the woman then to Mogli who had quieted to a chuckle now, his hands wiping at his eyes as if she'd told him the best joke he'd heard in a while.

"You can't be serious," he forced out between chuckles. "Brit, it was over the second you slept with someone else." His face turned cold. "I really don't have time for this."

"Well, can we talk about it later? When you come back for good?" Brit's voice took on a whine that made the hair stand on Rain's arm. It was painful for her to watch but this was the most information she'd gathered about Mogli and, frankly, it was entertaining.

"No, Brit. There's nothing to talk about. Please leave," Mogli said, switching back and forth between the laptop and the tablet. His hair fell into his face as if to shield him from her pleading gaze.

Rain saw the woman deflate in front of her, shoulders sagged and face somber, as she exited the room.

Rain let a few seconds pass. "So your name is Ben, huh?"

"Yes. That's my real name. Benjamin Sanders," Mogli answered, his finger sweeping across the tablet.

"Well that's as normal as it gets," Rain said in attempt to lighten the mood. It didn't work.

"So your next question will be how I got the name Mogli, right? Well, when I was in the service, I was able to live in jungle conditions with ease for months on end. The team started calling me Mogli like the boy from *Jungle Book*. It stuck, and now I prefer it," he said with an edge of impatience.

"Are you alright, Mogli?" Rain offered, slightly hurt by his tone with her. "I'm sorry about your fiancée and what happened."

Mogli breathed out heavily. "Sorry. I don't mean to take it out on you. Let's just get back to work, okay? The guys should be here any minute."

She nodded silently. She'd like it if someone else was in the room with them. All of sudden it seemed too small for the three of them.

TWENTY-SIX

WASHINGTON, DISTRICT OF COLUMBIA

B LACK ARRIVED FIRST. His shaved head, prickly with blond hair, was tucked beneath a black beanie that covered the back of his head. He donned a light leather coat with a high collar to his jawline and dark denim. His blue eyes looked intense as if ready to charge as he breezed through the door and moved quickly behind the desk with Mogli. He patted Mogli's shoulder as he observed the tablet then the laptop screen. It blinked with a blue haze across Mogli's chiseled face. That was the extent of Black's welcome even though they hadn't seen him in months while he'd tracked Dalton in the field. Rain felt a little slighted by that but realized her feelings were the last thing he cared about. Tolley was priority number one right now.

Rain left Anton to his knot conundrum and moved to the desk to analyze the screen that jumped with data and maps. She saw the blue blip on the screen showing her father's whereabouts, but it didn't look like it was moving anymore.

Black broke the silence moments later. "I had Shanty fly into Stafford Airport. He'll prepare the plane for our departure. He sent Prescott here after they landed. I take it he's arrived by now." He pointed at the screen. "Looks like we found where Tolley and Dalton stopped. I was following their movements on my end. I think we're ready to get . . ." Black looked around the office, finally noting Prescott's absence.

"Where's . . ." Black started.

"Don't know. Don't care," Mogli said under his breath, turning in his chair to lay annoyed eyes on Black and Rain who were huddled behind him.

Mogli noticed earlier that Prescott hadn't arrived from Stafford, Virginia, only a forty-minute drive to the bar. Shanty had landed the plane nearly two hours ago. He'd been in contact with Shanty but could not get a word back from Prescott since he'd left the airport; even his tracking beacon was not showing up on the screen. He'd been checking for Prescott the first hour and realized that he was chasing a wild dog that no one wanted to return back home anyway. So he focused his efforts on locating all the cameras around the building that Tolley was in. The only thing that nagged Mogli was that Prescott had taken one of the tablets and could track all of them, including the tracker on Dalton's vehicle. He hadn't anticipated that Prescott would bail on Tolley, on *him*. Not after he'd worked so closely with him at his house. He knew the kid was screwed up about something in his past but Mogli hoped whatever it was didn't cause Prescott to go without them. It would not only blow their mission but get himself killed. Mogli was getting tired of his forced heroism, which almost always landed someone else hurt. First time it was Rain. Last time it was Dahlia. This time it could be Tolley. The kid was definitely aching for a bullet, Mogli thought to himself.

Mogli went over the plan twice with Black, Shanty, and Rain before he felt sure that everyone knew their parts. It was going to be a long night but he was confident that they would get Tolley back from Dalton. He just couldn't figure out why Tolley had gone with him in the first place. He must've had something Tolley wanted badly but Mogli couldn't think of what it could be. Whatever it was, it had Tolley walking into the lion's den without his team.

THE LION'S DEN WAS A glass-enclosed building in the heart of the city. Rain could feel the strong breeze wrap around her exposed neck like a chilled hand, causing her to pull up her hoodie over her blond hair. She carried her case across the roof of the building directly across from where her father was being held. She was slightly lower on the roof than the other building and felt like she was in a fishbowl, exposed. The crisp night air smelled of fresh dirt and barbecue smoke that billowed from the roof of a restaurant three buildings down. She licked her lips in anticipation. Her mind was flooded with thoughts that shook her focus. Was her father hurt? Why did he go with them so *willingly?* He hadn't looked harmed when they saw him on the camera in the van. She pushed the nagging thoughts to the back of her mind as she reached the edge of the roof and peered over the precipice. The street was dark and quiet, dimly lit by amber lights dotting the sidewalks. There was a clothing boutique at the base of the building next door to the glass monstrosity across the street. Rain let her eyes linger on the mannequins in the front, remembering how she felt putting on her gown before the party tonight. She'd dreamed of a day she'd get to be so beautiful that she'd be the center of attention. As luck would have it, the night had only ended in her breaking the neck of a Russian in a bathroom stall and bouncing around in the back of a dingy work van for hours. She sighed at the thought. Her eyes spotted the origami bird symbol etched into the glass entrance of the building. The same bird her mother used on the wax stamp and the symbol from Shanty's online research.

Her eyes scanned each lit window, citing the cubicles on one floor. A bank on the next floor. Then, only one floor down from where she stood, she saw a man, dressed in black, a gun holstered around his midsection, looking out the window down at the street. Rain ducked quickly, unsure of whether he'd seen her. Her breath quickened as she stayed below the edge of the concrete half wall and clicked open the latches on her black box, the case that Tolley had been holding for her. She hadn't wanted to use it again. She felt as if putting the rifle together and propping it against her body would make her kill again with too much ease. That was what scared her. She feared how easy it was for her to pull the trigger and take a man's life. That moment had changed her. Just as Tolley had warned it would. She bit her lip in frustration as she realized once again that she should have listened to her father that day and never searched for Dahlia.

But now she was flipping open the lid, eyeing the black matte steel of the rifle, and feeling a familiar rush. The same rush she'd felt on the farm before a hunt. The anticipation, the doubt, and the power raced through her again. She wanted to save her father but she didn't want to kill again and wasn't sure if it was even in her to shoot a man. She knew she could make the shot but she didn't know if she could live with herself afterward. Granted, she'd defended herself against the Russian, but that was purely self-preservation, not *hunting* a human being as they were doing to Dalton. She knew she'd do whatever it took to save her father. He was all she had left. But would she be able to actually kill Dalton if she had the chance?

She looked at her watch, pressed the perimeter of it as the blue light lit the screen. It was time to get prepared. The night was starting and she needed to be ready to do her part.

She handled the rifle with an affection similar to an old woman greeting her long-lost love—with care and admiration. Familiarity tingled in her fingertips as she felt the coolness of the metal, heard the metallic click of each piece locking into place, and steadied her finished product on its sturdy, retractable tripod. Everything was in place as she peered over the precipice and down at the window from which she'd seen the man staring. The floor was alight with activity. She settled her binocular lenses over her eyes and scanned the floor. She saw three men in black, bristling and muscled, standing with their backs to the window. A desk was in the center of the room, black and sleek with an open laptop on the center of the desktop. Rain saw the modern decor, the black leather chairs that looked stiff and uncomfortable. The rug, a swirl of greens and blues, covered the white tile floors. Rain focused her rifle on the desk, unsure of whether that was where Tolley or Dalton would be but guessing she'd better have her sights ready, just in case.

Black was supposed to be making his way up the rear stairwell, blocking any possible escape. Mogli had found blueprints on the building and had outlined everyone's movements to converge on the floor. Without Prescott, they were down a shooter to cover the back of the building. So Black had taken a good guess on which office would be Dalton's. Of course, choosing the largest space with the best view wasn't really a difficult guess, Rain surmised. But she was grateful his decision was panning out as she didn't want to walk back down the twelve flights of stairs in an abandoned building just to reset herself one block over.

Mogli was on the ground, in the van with Anton, one street over. He'd be running the communication and watching their movements, ready at a moment's notice to step in. Shanty was readying the plane, getting flight plans signed off and deciding the next hiding location should the plan not go as expected. Rain believed that if they failed, her father would be dead. She'd made it clear to Black and Mogli that she wouldn't get on that plane until Dalton was dead if he hurt her father. She knew the others felt the same but didn't want to think it. Didn't want to show their inner fear about potentially losing Tolley like they'd lost Dahlia.

Rain was so lost in her thoughts that she didn't notice the movement in the building across from her, see the men grab Tolley by his arms—which were handcuffed behind his back—and usher him into the office space. She snapped out of her lamentation to see her father prodded into the room, his face stony and emotionless. The man holding his biceps pushed him into the center of the large office, his moving lips letting Rain know he was speaking to her father. Tolley had a scowl on his face as if he wanted to tackle the guy and pummel him with a barrage of punches. She pushed the bud in her ear quickly. "I have eyes on my father. He's in the office now. Can we get audio?"

Her heart was racing. She wanted to hear his voice, hug him again, and tell him she'd made a big mistake. She heard Mogli's voice cut through the silence, clear, as if he was standing next to her on the dark roof. "No audio, too high up. What are you seeing?"

"He's in the center of the room. Wait. I think that's . . ." She squinted in the scope to see the trousers of a man. Her angle would not let her see his face. She remembered Dalton had on a black tuxedo and shiny black shoes. She guessed it must be him just outside her field of vision.

"What is it, Rain?"

"I think Dalton's in the room, too. I don't have a good angle. I can't see his face." She was speaking quickly, her mouth moving on autopilot. She wanted to see Dalton so badly. Get him in her sight line. She'd feel better if she knew she could protect her father.

"Can you move to a better angle?" Mogli asked.

"No, I'm too high up." She looked down the length of the building then back through the scope. There was nowhere for her to go.

"Guess we just have to wait for him to move." That was Black's voice, barely a whisper.

"Black, what's your status?" Mogli commanded after hearing the voice.

"I'm in the north stairwell. Taken out three guys. I have their radio. Sounds like they're preparing to bring someone here. Not sure who but it can't be good," Black said, his voice even and low.

Within minutes, Rain saw headlights as a van pulled in front of the boutique and parked. The lights went out immediately. It looked odd on the street, Rain thought, but then realized that the van looked like it had a ladder attaching to a power line. She saw Mogli exit the vehicle and climb the ladder, a hat pulled low over his eyes. She looked back in the scope on her rifle and scanned the room in her field of vision but couldn't see the legs anymore. Her father still stood in the center of the green swirling rug, shoulders relaxed, head straight forward. Where was Dalton?

She watched carefully. Waited for something to change. Felt her giddiness edging in on her, wanting to make a move, do something to help her father as she observed him. He seemed calm. Why was he so damn calm right now? Confusion gave way to fear. She knew her father, and if he was captured by Dalton, it was because he wanted to be ... but why?

Her answer came through the door minutes later escorted by two men. The breath caught in her throat, suffocating her with disbelief. The woman walked into the room, reached out her arms, and gripped her father in an embrace. It looked like her tearful mother. She saw the dark hair, not as long as it was when she'd seen her in Russia, saw her skinny body draped in browning white linen pajamas. Her arms wrapped around Tolley's neck as he bent to welcome her embrace. Tolley, arms still cuffed behind him, moved his face against hers as a dog would nuzzle its owner. She pushed his dark hair away from his face and kissed him on the lips. Within seconds two men grabbed her arms again and forced her, fighting, toward a man who stepped into Rain's view. Dalton still donned his tuxedo, still looked like a weasel with his tiny nose and upturned lips. The men pushed Dahlia in his direction and she stood ramrod straight when she was close enough to touch him. Rain zoomed in, saw her mother speak venomously to Dalton before spitting a glob of mucus into his face. Dalton's eyes blazed with anger as he grabbed his handkerchief and wiped it across his glistening face with force.

Rain couldn't gain her composure. Everything was happening too fast. Her hands shook against the rifle. She had no power to stop it. She was seeing her dead mother, alive and defiant. Rain tried to calm her erratic breaths but couldn't seem to be quiet. A moan escaped her lips that sounded like a wounded animal.

"Rain, what's going on up there?" Mogli interrupted her meltdown just in time; she was feeling queasy.

"It's . . . its Dahlia. Mom. She's alive," Rain muttered through the lump in her throat.

Black responded first. "Say again. I thought you said you saw Dahlia." His voice still monotonously low.

"She's alive. I am looking at her right now. I have eyes on Dalton," Rain responded. "And he's just gotten a face full of spit from her."

Rain couldn't hear the responses but she knew that they were either laughing or cheering for Dahlia. She could only imagine what Dalton had put her mother through for months. Rain pulled her face from the rifle, struck by the realization that her mother had been waiting for them the whole time. Waiting for them to come get her. While she'd been camping, training, planning, they'd left Dahlia behind. Figured she was dead because of . . . Prescott Willow. Her belly flamed with anger, felt it rush from her chest to her head until she growled into the wind. Prescott had found a way to detour them again. He'd been on Dalton's team from the very beginning and even though her gut had told her he was on their side, he'd proven otherwise again. Not surprisingly, he had found a way to come up missing when his lie was being exposed. She seethed with the thought that she'd ever liked him enough to fool herself into thinking about a future with him. She'd toyed with the thought of loving him, bringing him back to the farm with her, being a family. That was all gone now. She never wanted to see him again.

"Rain? I said do you have a shot?" Mogli repeated into the earpiece.

Rain snapped out of her anger and looked through the sight again. Dalton had Dahlia around the neck, a pistol pointed to her head. He was yelling at Tolley now, face red. Tolley was begging him, his body limp and pleading. Dahlia was talking to Tolley. Her face was bruised but strangely beautiful as she seemed to be soothing Tolley. *She's telling him it's okay*, Rain realized. She needed to take a shot, save them both.

"Black, Tolley is in the center of the room. There's five Joes, two along the window to the right of the door. Armed. Two beside Dalton and he's got a gun to Dahlia's temple right now. There's one behind Tolley. I need your help."

"I got you. I'm en route now. I'm on your count."

Mogli chimed in, "I'm getting in the van. I'll be ready for you out front. There's a car pulling into the parking garage, looks like backup. You better move before the party gets bigger."

Rain tried to breathe, attempted to settle her emotions so she could do what she was meant to do. Everything that had happened to them happened for a reason, she believed as she looked at the debacle in front of her. Her mother leaving the farm would save millions of people when they found the chip and would soon release it. Her father teaching her to shoot at the farm prepared her for this very moment. Her bravado in working with Dalton to save her mother helped them find Anton. Now her father's decision had helped the team get to Dahlia. *He must've known all along that we'd track him and lead us to her*, she thought. Knowing that she had made the right decision calmed her. She raised the rifle until it lined up directly with Dalton, although he kept wavering and Dahlia was often in her sights, too. It wasn't a clear shot but it was all she had.

She made the countdown to Black, "Three, two . . ."

On the count of one, Black burst into the door, shooting the two men at the window first then placing a bullet in the leg of the man standing behind Tolley. He crumpled to the ground with a flurry of screams. Rain kept her scope on Dalton as his two sidekicks crouched behind the desk and fired at Black who had already crept back out of the room, outside the door. Dalton ducked low behind Dahlia, using her as a human shield. Tolley was on his knees, head bowed, avoiding the spray of bullets. Dahlia kicked at Dalton—a mule kick—but he held her arm firmly, gun pressed to her head. Time slowed as Rain saw the distinct movement of Dalton tensing his arm, the tension leading to his hand with the pistol. The pistol pointed at Dahlia's head. Rain envisioned where the chain reaction would stop and it left her mother in a bloody heap. Rain felt the nanoseconds pass as her own finger bit down on the trigger. Rain watched Dalton's lips curl into a smile as he discerned in that moment that he'd finally see Dahlia dead and Tolley not soon after. The two quick bursts from Rain's rifle entered the glass of the building, causing a spiderweb-like break, then traveled to Dahlia's shoulder where a red dot blossomed on her white top. Rain saw her arms flail backward as she pushed into Dalton who stumbled behind her. Dalton landed haphazardly on the white tile floor before kicking Dahlia off of him as if he was swimming underwater. Tolley crawled toward Dahlia who was prone on the floor, the red dot becoming more prominent. Rain swiveled her rifle toward Dalton who took off in a run toward the rear of the office, holding his shoulder; a slash of red soaked through his fingers. Within seconds he'd dashed out of sight.

"Dalton is escaping from a back door!" Rain blurted.

Mogli's voice sounded winded as he answered, "I'm on it. On my way to the van now. He's probably getting a car."

Black was preoccupied with the last two men in the office who were still stuck behind the desk as Tolley and Dahlia were on the front side, seeking shelter from the gunshots with an overturned chair. Dahlia was still lying down but Rain could see movement as Tolley talked to her, his head just above hers on the floor. Then he looked at her. Rain caught her father's eye as he scanned the rooftop through the shattered glass and found her. He nodded knowingly with hope in his eyes and she felt a surge in her body. She didn't have a clean shot on the men behind the desk but she'd do the best she could to provide cover. She shot the rifle at the closest man to the window, her bullet landing in his ankle which was exposed to her. It shredded like pulled pork. Rain could only imagine the sound he made. Tolley moved clumsily to stand up without the use of his hands, and Dahlia pushed herself off the ground with her arm cupped to her chest like an injured bird.

"Mom and Dad are up and moving, Black. I'm providing cover."

Rain shot a couple more rounds directly adjacent to the desk. The tile popped and kicked white dust into the air with each shot. Both men stayed huddled behind the desk, out of sight, limbs included. She knew one of them was in agony and probably wouldn't be an active threat unless he didn't care if he bled out. Dahlia turned away from Tolley, who was shuffling to the door, and instead limped to the edge of the desk near the blood spatter. She picked up the pistol that Dalton must have dropped and walked to the edge of the desk. Her face was contorted into a grimace as she raised the weapon. She fired two rounds into the men behind the desk, her face a mask of exhaustion and pure determination as Rain saw the quick bursts in a flash of light through her scope. Dahlia kept the gun in her good hand as she limped over to Tolley. They left the office and joined Black in the hall. Rain could see that they were headed for the stairwell and a rush of relief flooded her. They were safe. For now.

She knew it wasn't over. Not until they'd found Dalton.

Rain dismantled her rifle in the time it took for them to get down the stairs and into the van. Within minutes she burst from the side alley at a run, throwing her case into the van and sliding the side door shut as it shot off down the darkened street. Dahlia was in the rear of the van with Tolley who was now uncuffed and holding her against his chest as the van jerked and swayed.

"Did you have to shoot me?" Dahlia croaked, her eyes blurry, lids heavy. "I thought your dad said you were a better shot than him."

"Did I say that?" Tolley said, looking down at Dahlia and smiling for the first time in a long time. Rain couldn't contain her emotions anymore. She crawled across the van on her knees and hugged her father and mother until tears wet her cheeks. The scent of her father calmed her, a mix of sweat and Old Spice. Her mother—a new smell, foreign yet welcomed—made her melt into their bodies. She could barely contain her excitement and relief that they'd managed to save them both.

"I should be the one crying," her mother said. "You shot me." Her face was pale and her breathing measured. She brushed Rain's cheek softly with a smile.

"Yeah, sorry about that," Rain whispered. Even injured, her beauty shone through. A pang of memory rooted her in place. The night her mother kissed her good-bye for the last time replayed in her mind. This time instead of confusion, Rain felt a sense of pride.

Tolley kissed Dahlia on the top of her head as she nursed her arm, keeping it sturdy with a dingy ripped shirt made into a sling. Dahlia's lips rose at the corners into a brief and fleeting grin. "You're everything I could have hoped for in a daughter."

Rain's chest swelled with pride. Her mother's words erased all feelings of ineptitude and doubt. Rain watched her father holding her mother. Dahlia seemed content to have blood soaking through her shirt, sticking to her skin, and pain coursing through her body as long as Tolley was holding her. The van lurched around a corner and Rain struggled to hold on. Tolley bumped into the side and tried to prevent Dahlia from jostling too much.

"Easy, Mogli. We only have nine lives," Tolley said.

Mogli intensely watched the tracker that Anton was holding for him from the passenger seat. Rain moved toward the front and kissed Anton on his head, glad that she'd found him. Grateful that he was more than she'd ever wanted in a brother. He looked up with a smile that was too bright considering the night's events. He was a tough kid, Rain thought to herself as she watched the blue blip on the screen move through the city at a high rate of speed.

"Either we are very lucky," Mogli said to Rain, "or Dalton's incredibly stupid to use the same vehicle as earlier. Either way, we aren't going to lose him. We're close."

Rain believed him when he said it because of the intensity in his voice. He wasn't going to let Dalton slip through his fingers. She was sure Mogli was still reeling at the thought that Dahlia was now in the van with them, not dead as they'd all been led to believe. It'd been a miracle none of them could have imagined.

The van stayed slightly above the speed limit until it turned into congested traffic on Pennsylvania Avenue. Police and security would be heightened on the road so near to the White House. Mogli slowed the van, ensuring they wouldn't get pulled over downtown. It would waste precious minutes and potentially lose the target.

"Rain, did you shoot Mum?" Anton said in a whisper. His large eyes, starry and innocent, awaited her answer.

"I shot the bad guy *through* Mom," Rain corrected, trying to keep her gaze on the road ahead. She didn't want to face his judgment. She already felt bad enough.

Anton's little lips formed the shape of an O as he bobbed his head in understanding. Rain rustled the hair on his head, dark like her father's. She wondered whether Anton would be scarred for life seeing his mother bleeding in the back of a van. A mother he barely knew but one who had been shot by his sister. Would he resent her? Fear her? She shook away the thought. They were a family now. Soon, when they returned back to some semblance of normal life, she'd show him the farm and her hunting grounds. Teach him to milk the cows and mend the fences. She'd show him something he'd never experienced: a real family, a normal life.

Rain felt pride well again in her chest. She had her family with her but now it was time for her to end this. She looked at the screen again and couldn't make out where the car was heading. It looked to be zigzagging around the city in no particular direction. Where was Christopher Dalton going?

TWENTY-SEVEN

PRESCOTT WILLOW

THERE WAS ONE THING THAT Prescott Willow hated: being lied to. He knew that being at the airfield with Shanty was busywork that only served the purpose of him being far from the action so he wouldn't ruin anything. He also understood that they wanted him far from the action because he'd lost their trust. It burned him up to know that he'd sacrificed his relationship with Rain. She'd never trust him again after all the things he'd done. She didn't want to understand that he had made those sacrifices for her, to keep her safe. It just all went to shit. Hell in a handbasket, they'd said when he was a soldier. He had to regain their trust even though he'd been playing it their way ever since Christopher Dalton had released him. The nagging feeling that he'd gotten Dahlia killed was etched in his mind. Had she come to save him that night? She hadn't even looked his way when she was thrown into her cell before the screaming and painful sobs began. It was a closeness he never wanted to have with Rain's mom. An image forever tattooed in his memory.

When Shanty told him to board the plane and they were going to Washington, DC, but wouldn't tell him why, Prescott knew that he needed to break away. Do his own thing without the pressure of Mogli on his back. Without the secrets and side glances that made him seem less than a common criminal. He'd still stay connected to the team through their tracking beacons but he was no longer along for the ride. So when the plane landed and Shanty rattled off the details of the meeting point, Prescott made up his mind to find his own path. He didn't know where yet but anyplace without judgment seemed the most appealing to him.

Now, riding down I-95, passing Woodbridge, coasting to the speed limit, Prescott relished the feeling of freedom. He could just keep driving. No one would look for him. He had no family. His only family was the team and they'd made it pretty clear he was no longer welcome at the table. So why not keep driving? He pondered the idea of losing himself in New York's hustle and bustle. Taking on a real job, maybe a desk job that required a suit and tie. He laughed loudly into the cabin of the black town car, amused at his ability to trick himself into thinking he could live a normal life. It was a nice thought, he surmised, but knew it would never come to pass. He wasn't the type to have a family, live in a house with a white fence and midsized dog in the perfect neighborhood. He remembered Rain speaking of her home in Colorado and wished he'd known a place like that growing up. He was stuck with a solitary existence from the time his mother dropped him off on his grandfather's doorstep, and maybe a little before that as well. But he hadn't known it as hard. He'd just *adapted*. That's what Christopher Dalton saw in him. The ability to adapt, learn people, and get them to trust him. Prescott scrubbed his fingertips under the scruff of beard that threatened to drive him crazy. He hadn't shaved in weeks and was sprouting rough patches along his jaws. A blue blinking on the upturned tablet caught his eye. He glanced at it quickly. The blue blip was moving. But wasn't that Tolley? It was in sync with the red dot that indicated Christopher Dalton's tagged car. What the hell? Prescott tapped on the screen to zoom into the map. He noted where they stopped.

"Oh shit." Prescott felt his stomach drop. Tolley was in trouble. He realized why they'd left New York so quickly now. Something was very wrong. Tolley and Dalton would not be together, not unless . . .

Prescott pushed the gas pedal to the floor and felt the black car nearly stall before shooting off. He swerved through traffic hoping to hell he made it in time.

PRESCOTT WAS TRACKING EVERYONE'S movement when he pulled into a parking lot on M Street and put the car in Park. He noticed Tolley was in the same vicinity as the tracking device on the vehicle he'd ridden in to the location. Black was also in the same building and it made Prescott's hair stand on his arm. They were trying to get Tolley out and it was happening now. He rubbed a hand down his face. Quickly he swiped across the tablet and located Rain across the street and knew that she was probably in sniper position on the roof. He smirked, a mix of pride and relief flooding his veins. She was safe. He found Mogli's yellow blip one block over from where he was parked on M Street but saw his tracker moving slowly to the same street as the building. What was going on?

He knew he didn't have time to waste. He ignited the engine and made a right turn onto M Street heading for the parking garage where Dalton's car tracker was leading him. He figured from their placement on the tablet that they had all the exits covered. All but one.

The garage was not covered—a perfect escape route, Prescott thought to himself. Even though he wanted to run away, go to a place where no one could look at him like a liability, he couldn't abandon the team when there was something going wrong with Tolley. He'd grown fond of Tolley, even with his grunted replies and untrusting glances. He respected him, secretly wanted to end up like him one day. A great leader but an equally great father to a woman he couldn't stop thinking about since she'd kissed him. Leaving Rain was the hardest part of disappearing. One that he hated to admit since she'd been as clear as a punch in the head that she wanted nothing to do with him. He'd already ruined his chances. But he couldn't quite stop memories of her from flooding every other thought in his mind, sufficiently pushing any thought of leaving her to the back of his priority list. The only thing he could do now was keep her safe and try his best to prove that he was worthy of her.

He tapped his fingers on the steering wheel to the tune of Elton John's "Madman across the Water" which had come on the radio just as he was pulling into the parking garage to Dalton's building. He spotted the white van down the street before the turn, saw Mogli squinting in the front seat at his black vehicle. Prescott was pretty sure he wouldn't be able to see into the dark-tinted windows as he turned. He didn't stop as he drove down the ramp and into the depths of the garage. The attendant was missing from the booth at the bottom of the ramp, the gate left up and the door to the tiny white booth left open.

"Not good," Prescott whispered into the empty car, wheeling it near the elevators and seeing two men standing at the base of the elevators with their hands clasped across their chests. One man, black and oversized, reminded him of Tony. He remembered how Tony looked when they'd shot him at the Basin, and shivered. Some memories needed to stay tucked away. He heard the screech of his tires like wet hands rubbing against plastic as he circled through the support beams and backed his vehicle in front of the elevators. The two men eyed his vehicle as he looked in the rearview mirrors at them. He checked his Glock and heard the metallic click of his full clip sliding back into place. He carefully screwed the silencer onto its end, hearing the metal grate against itself until it wouldn't move any further. He rested it against the door as he saw the black guard nod to his compatriot and start the short walk to the driver-side window. Prescott felt a buzz in his chest; his fingers tingled like they used to in Baghdad before he fired his weapon. His adrenaline told him it would happen again and he tensed with giddy pleasure. He got the chance quickly as the guard eased alongside his vehicle and tapped the glass with the butt of his pistol.

Prescott pushed the window down before leaning his head carefully through with a grin.

"I was told to wait for the boss here. I think there's something going on up there," Prescott said in his most authoritative yet charismatic tone.

"He didn't tell us anyone was coming." The man's voice was deep and husky. He spoke slowly as if unsure to even speak to him.

"Ah shit, not this again. This happened at the gala tonight, too. I heard him go off on the last crew. You know how he gets. He doesn't want to be questioned and definitely hates feeling like he has to answer to a couple pissants like us, right?" Prescott added quickly. "It was sad what he did to the last guys, though. A fucking bloody mess. I hated to watch it. In this very same car, actually. That's why I just sit and wait. I drive. I go home. You know how it is."

His ploy was working as the man's brows relaxed and he started to stand upright, less tense. He still had the gun trained on Prescott's head. His professional side was warring with his human side. Finally he motioned to the other guard at the elevator, a yellow-haired fellow with acne, even though he looked to be over forty. He walked over promptly and stood next to his partner before asking, "What's going on?" in a tone that did little to hide his agitation for having to walk ten feet.

"He's waiting for the boss. You sure you didn't get the call? Before I call it in, I don't want to end up with a boot up my ass for a mistake." The black guard spoke with more force now. Clearly he was the one in charge and didn't like who he was stuck waiting in the parking garage with.

"Nah. I didn't get no call about it. Hey, why you get here so late anyway?" the blond man said, leaning down to get a closer glimpse of Prescott.

Prescott glanced at the guard who was preparing to talk into the radio attached to his shoulder. In an instant time slowed down for Prescott; he saw everything in slow motion as if it happened in the span of a breath.

He raised the Glock an inch, aimed straight for the yellow hairs on the guard's chin, and pulled the trigger. A mist of blood settled on the air, reminding him of running through an amusement park water mist on a hot day to escape the heat. The sticky warmth of it laced Prescott's face as he leveled the gun at the tall guard after the body had disappeared from view. He fired rapidly, the bullet catching the guard in the arm as he ducked away. Unfortunately, Prescott had parked in the open space of the parking garage, so there was nowhere to run or hide. Not that Prescott would let him run as he shot the back of his calf. A burst of red spilled onto the concrete beneath him as the man stumbled to one knee, his other leg working hard to reach a pillar that seemed within reach. The last sight he had was the pillar as Prescott emptied a bullet into the back of his head from the driver's-side window.

Prescott scanned his surroundings, made sure the sounds of a quick death hadn't traveled too far. Or at least far enough to raise suspicion. He fingered the glove compartment until the black box sprang open like a miniature suitcase to reveal his napkins. He grabbed a few from the box, wiped his face in the mirror, and then sponged off the small traces of bloody fingerprints on the interior door. After he was satisfied with the cleanliness of his space, he pushed open the door to find it had heavy resistance. He poked his head out the window to find that the blond guard had fallen against the door.

"Well I'll be damned. Now that's what I call dedication," he said to no one in particular as he pushed the door open with a swift hand and foot combination. The body sagged against the ground, the man's hand splaying out and dropping his weapon with a skidding sound on the concrete. Prescott picked up the gun, a stainless-steel AutoMag, and turned it over in his hands. It would be a nice addition to his collection, he thought to himself, throwing it into the passenger seat before dragging the body behind the pillar. Next he slid the larger guard by his armpits behind the same pillar. He looked around under the fluorescent lights and noticed the blood pooling in various spots leading up to his car. He looked up, located the source of his problem, and shot the fluorescent lights illuminating the area outside the elevator. The dimness made the blood look like dark oil spills. He hoped that it would work if it needed to. He thumbed the tablet on the seat next to the gun, switched the beacons, and leaned his head back on the seat. Now he was ready. He only needed to wait.

PRESCOTT HAD STARTED SINGING along to the electric hum of "Welcome to the Jungle" by Guns n' Roses when he saw the elevator door slide open and a bloody, running Christopher Dalton hightail it to his awaiting black vehicle. His face was flush as he half stumbled, half lunged into the back door of the car, fiddling with the handle for longer than an average person would. Prescott was sure that Dalton wouldn't think twice about taking the quickest escape route, regardless of the nagging intuition that screamed that something wasn't right. He hadn't looked twice at the empty corridor outside the elevator, his eyes alighting on the brake lights of the town car. He didn't notice the bloodstains near the car or red streaks across the painted white lines of nearby parking spaces. Dalton noticed only the steam from the tailpipe like a ghost in the dark parking lot. It seemed the safest place for him in his mind. He hadn't known how terribly wrong he was as he settled into the backseat, his weight on the leather making it screech like a siren into the cabin. Prescott could hear his labored breathing. *He probably took the stairs*, Prescott thought with a grin. *It would do him some good to shed a few pounds from his waist.*

Prescott locked the car door and sped away from the darkness. He turned up the ramp, past the empty ticket booth, and out onto the slick Washington, DC, streets. Prescott saw the dancing neon blues and reds bounce across Christopher Dalton's pasty face as they passed the capital's storefronts. He'd been sweating—it soaked the neck of his white shirt and made it opaque against his skin. Sprouts of hair escaped from beneath his shirt, next to the red stain that almost reached it from his shoulder. He was nursing his wound, pulling his black jacket off the gaping hole in his flesh with a grimace.

"Take me to the airfield," he said without looking up from his wound. His voice was shaky from the adrenaline coursing through his veins. Prescott turned the vehicle in response to his request. Dalton looked out the window with a quick glance between breaking open his buttons and sticking his balled-up jacket inside his shirt to apply pressure on the slowly bleeding wound.

"You need to turn right on Fourteenth Street," Dalton croaked from the backseat, his voice confirming that he was coming down from a super adrenaline rush. It was leaving his speech tired and sluggish.

Prescott continued past 14th Street, his mind on where in the world he was going. He was deep in thought when Dalton tapped his shoulder roughly snapping him from a trance.

"Hey. Did you hear me back there?" he said with an edge to his voice as he sunk back into the seat with a huff. "Just take the next left."

"I heard you loud and clear, Dalton. But the last place you're going is the airfield. We have a lot of time to make up." Prescott's eyes met Dalton's.

Dalton tried to hide his surprise and maybe his fear but Prescott had been taught well by the brooding Mogli on how to read emotions. He studied Dalton's stony face for a hint but there was only a smug twitch of his lips.

"What do you think you're doing, Prescott Willow?" His name slipped like soap through wet hands from Dalton's lips. He'd grown lucid under the realization that he was still in danger but his body was working against him, forcing him to weaken.

"I'm ending this. For all of us," Prescott retorted.

Dalton breathed out heavily, his voice nothing more than a whisper. "You still think this starts and ends with me." He shook his head as if watching a small child failing to grasp an easy mathematical equation. In this case, one plus one didn't quite equal two. It was complicated.

"What did you do to Tolley?" Prescott forced out. He jerked the wheel down a side street until he could see the place he wanted to go four blocks ahead, rising like a beacon in the night.

"Tolley is alive and well, albeit through no choice of mine."

"So why was he there? Did he shoot you?" Prescott questioned.

"No. That was your little puppy, I think." He groaned at the pain in his arm as he let his head fall back on the seat. "So I take it you don't want to drive me to safety and keep your immunity deal."

"I'm done making deals with devil," Prescott said, coasting to a stop.

"They'll come after you when I'm gone. You know that, right? Military prison is nothing like private prisons. Are you sure you wouldn't mind staying out with your little puppy just a while longer?"

"She's not a puppy, you sick fuck. Call her that again and you'll be counting your teeth on your fingers." Prescott's voice raised an octave. Dalton could talk about him, strip his immunity deal, but Rain was off limits.

Prescott looked across the sidewalk dividing the parking space from the beautiful white boats, bobbing up and down like a hundred seesaws along the pier. He smelled the salt air even in the vehicle. It had the strange scent of moss, something green and earthy clinging to it like an afterthought. The night cast shadows along the boats. Only a few lampposts spread amber light in wide circles against the concrete. The blackness was dense everywhere else. Outside the car was quiet but inside Prescott could hear the wheezing from the backseat and he wondered if Dalton was asthmatic or injured worse than he looked.

He turned off the ignition and looked across the seat at the AutoMag before slipping it into the back of his jeans. He turned to stare at Dalton and the pitiful sight that messed his backseat with blood and sweat. Dalton's blood slowed from the gushing wound but his face looked worse, sweat glazed and even more drained of color. His hair—what was left of it—was haphazardly combed to one side, the part now crooked.

Prescott pulled the switch to open the large trunk and they heard the telltale *blunk* before feeling the car lift slightly. Prescott clicked the unlock button and exited the car. Dalton watched him through the window. Prescott could tell his mind was still working. He hadn't given up yet. He pulled open Dalton's door and dragged him out, standing him unsteadily on his feet.

"How can I change this?" Dalton said incredulously, looking out at the black water and feeling a sense of urgency when Prescott's face showed no remorse in return.

"You can tell me why. Why all this? Why Dahlia?" Prescott shook Dalton's shoulder and he whimpered with pain.

"Okay, okay! Please." Dalton bent low but tried to keep his feet under him. Prescott still gripped the flesh around his wound with his thumb. The throbbing electric pain almost rendered him unconscious. His vision was going and his head was pounding. He wondered if this was what it felt like to bleed to death. Dalton wasn't going to give up yet.

"On your knees." Prescott shoved Dalton into the grass and he fell harder than he wanted to. His face was nearly to the ground by the time he realized and protected his head with his forearm.

Prescott walked to the rear of the car as Dalton heard the sound of metal clinking against itself and plastic bags shifting from one area to the next. *Can I get up and run?* He thought to himself, swinging his head to look in both directions. There was only one sidewalk and it was as long as the pier—no place to hide unless he was going to swim his way out of this mess. In his condition, he'd drown before he even kicked away from the dock. He felt the hope seeping out of him. He'd followed Prescott's story in the military, knew that he was a man of many talents, but had attitude and stubborn perseverance that was a gift and a curse. He knew Prescott would not spare him. His loyalty to Rain had developed early in Iraq. He feared Prescott would get too attached to the fiery brunette and abandon his own self-interests. As he had predicted, it came to pass. He just hadn't predicted that Tolley wouldn't go away after Dahlia turned herself in. There was no way to harbor her alive without Tolley coming yet no way to kill her and not send Tolley crashing down on him. He gambled that if Tolley thought she was dead, he'd save their children and stay away long enough for his team to get information from her. He was only partially right on that account. Tolley had stayed away for months but he was not gone for good. He'd thought he'd had a good fail-safe plan of revealing Dahlia when Tolley came knocking on his door with a death order, but things had gone awry. Tolley's team had somehow overpowered his, even when they knew they would be coming. *How did that happen?* Dalton thought to himself, squeezing the jacket closer to his shoulder and wincing.

Prescott was carrying two silver handcuffs that had metal chains attached. He carried a black satchel with him, small and scuffed by what Dalton could imagine was simply aged leather. He laid the bag on the ground in front of Dalton, unzipped it slowly and painstakingly as if prolonging the inevitable was of great satisfaction for him.

"I never told you about how I got into the CIA. I was a young, smart wannabe field agent when I waltzed into an interview and told them I was going to be the director one day. No one believed me but they liked my confidence." A dry chuckle escaped Dalton's chapped lips. "After going to training and realizing that I wasn't the best shot or even the toughest, for that matter, I found what I was really good at. I'm good with people. Same as you. I saw a lot of me in you. In your story." Prescott grimaced at the thought but Dalton continued. "I worked with Tolley and his team. Dahlia was the lead back then before they got married. She was smart. She had intuition like a cat. Could just sense things. We said she had the mind of a criminal back then. I was lucky enough to get them on my team and solve a lot of cases that got me recognition. With recognition in the CIA comes money and power. I had mayors, governors, and senators all wanting a favor for a favor. So I ended up with more secrets than I could keep track of." Dalton coughed until spittle landed in the grass beside him. His blurry eyes looked up. "I made some bad decisions along the way but I tried my best to save that damn family. Took them off the cases that were dirty. Cases that would get them killed. I was the only one who cared about them, stopped the others from taking too much of an interest in the dream team set on righting all America's wrongs one white-collar terrorist at a time."

"So why did you hire Dahlia back? Why not just send her back home?" Prescott was intrigued that Dalton was sharing his personal life with him. He remembered that men did strange things when staring through the lens of death.

"Greed. After Tolley and the team left for those eight years, I hadn't had a good break since. People were starting to notice. So I couldn't turn her away when she came back with all the hope and determination in her eyes." He shook his head. "I didn't put her on this case. She secretly reopened it without my knowledge and when I found out, she was already off the grid."

"So why get Rain involved? She had a good life before this. You ruined that."

"I didn't want her involved. I needed Tolley to help me find Dahlia. She stepped in his place when he wouldn't cooperate. She was just a girl. I didn't expect her to last. Especially not in Baghdad."

"So you wanted to kill her in order to get Tolley to find Dahlia or for Dahlia to come home?" Prescott's voice was dripping with disbelief at how evil Dalton really was.

Dalton shrugged guiltily at the question. He had indeed hoped she would have either walked away or at least given him a funeral at which to find Dahlia weeping. Instead she defied expectation and became an excellent soldier and sniper like her father once was. He hadn't bet on that and it had come back to shoot him in the shoulder.

As if reading his mind, Prescott said, "Guess you didn't expect her to bring the house down over your head? One girl could do what you couldn't do. She got the team back together to find Dahlia after all. And you killed her mother. Took away the one thing she wanted in her life."

Dalton sat up, his eyes boring holes into Prescott's angry face. "Dahlia is alive, Prescott."

Prescott couldn't hide his surprise. He paced back and forth, moving to keep his brain from jumping out of his skull. "What do you mean *alive*? Don't lie to me!" Spit flew as he thrust the gun under Dalton's chin.

"Dahlia is with Tolley. They shot me during their exit. I was giving her back to Rain," Dalton pleaded, his face changing from weary to hopeful after sharing the news. "That was my deal with Tolley."

Prescott didn't know what to believe. Was he going against Tolley's wishes? Had they shot him in anger or to escape? Was he supposed to be killing Dalton? His mind raced with the news that floored him. He couldn't believe Dahlia was alive but that would explain why Tolley was with Dalton willingly.

"You don't have to do this. You can drive away. I'll keep up my end of the deal as I told Tolley I would. You won't ever see me again," Dalton implored, his hand gesturing down the sidewalk as if suggesting he'd just walk away quietly.

Prescott looked into Dalton's eyes, which reminded him of his grandfather's. Never trusting. Never letting anyone in. Always critical. Prescott unlocked the handcuffs and wrapped them around Dalton's wrists. Dalton believed his tactics would work, Prescott thought. Not this time. He deserved everything that was coming to him, including the swift and long overdue death that Prescott was preparing.

He tightened the handcuffs until the skin pinched and Dalton gave out a guttural yelp. He used the other set of handcuffs on his ankles, the chains hanging between as if he was already on death row for his crimes. Prescott knew that Dalton was not the worst of the traitors involved with what was on the chip but he felt patriotic as he grabbed the chains and ushered Dalton toward the pier.

"Please don't do this." Dalton cringed as they neared the water. Prescott jerked him along roughly by the chain each time he resisted.

"Shut up!" Prescott yanked the chain and Dalton let out a hollow moan like wild prey captured by a lion. "I'm doing the American people a big favor tonight. Since you've had my military service stripped from me, I feel the need to give back in a big way. First I'll start with you. And then I'm going after the rest of Greenbreadth International."

"You'll never win. They're too powerful." Dalton gasped as he was now along the edge of the dock, the dark and glassy water lapping against the wood below in constant rhythm.

"I once thought you were too powerful. Yet here we are," Prescott said before opening the satchel on his shoulder to reveal a thirty-pound kettlebell.

"You'll never stop them. All the big corporations and politicians will bury you before you even get to the *real* scary men, the cartels and Mafias. America was built on these people. They own everything. Killing me will not change a thing. I read your file about what happened to you. You shooting up all those people. The night terrors. If you do this, you will never sleep again. It will haunt you forever."

Prescott saw lights in the distance bounce over the dark facade of the boats then rest on them for a brief second before blackness welcomed them again. He glanced over his shoulder, spotted a white van in the distance, heard doors slamming. He wasn't going to be detoured from his plan. He quickly threaded the chains through the kettlebell and hooked it around Dalton's handcuff chain.

"I can promise you, Christopher Dalton, I will sleep like a baby when you are no longer on this earth." He nudged Dalton ever so softly toward the black water that seemed to beg for him. Dalton teetered on the edge of the dock, wrestling with his footing, fighting against his body's urge to fall. Prescott threw the kettlebell into the water and it disappeared with a splash under the moss- and debris-laden surface. Prescott looked into the fearful stare of Christopher Dalton as he was pulled off balance by the weighted kettlebell and pulled into the black water. The stubborn pride in Dalton would not allow him to scream as he pulled in vain at the chain, trying his best to stop the weight that was pulling him farther down. Water now passed his nose. His eyes grew into two huge, dark buttons as he was fully submerged.

Prescott felt the hand on his shoulder before he tore his eyes away from the top of Dalton's head as it sunk below the surface. He smelled the familiar scent, his face scrunching away tears as he turned to face the woman he'd been longing for. Rain stood there, her hands buried in her jacket pockets, watching the water bubble where Dalton had been. He fought back the urge to embrace her slim frame.

He tried to brush the blond hair away from her eyes but she jerked away, her eyes intense.

"Don't." Her dark eyes grew glassy with unspent tears. Relief and hope poured from her tensed brows. He didn't care whether she still wanted him or trusted him. He could spend a lifetime reminding her that he was hers. Proving that he only made his decisions to protect her and her family.

"Thank you for finishing this," Rain said matter-of-factly, stepping closer to the edge of the pier.

"We aren't finished yet," Prescott retorted, standing beside her.

Rain's chin bobbed up and down. "I know."

Prescott rubbed his hands through his hair. "I feel like I've been the one screwing up everything from the very beginning."

"We all had our fair share of screw-ups. I won't let you fall on the sword for all of this," she said, her brown eyes searching his face.

"I'm sorry, Rain." He had told her too many times but he'd meant every word each time.

"No need to be. Dalton's gone. That's a step in the right direction."

Prescott stepped closer to her. "Is there any chance you can forgive me?"

Rain looked at the ground, her face a hardened edge from hours of worry. "It'll take time, Prescott. I can't promise you anything."

Prescott nodded. "We've been through so much together. I don't want to let you go just yet."

"You don't have a choice," Rain mumbled to him. She backed away without her eyes meeting his, then turned her back on him.

"One down, thirty-two more to go," Prescott stated over Rain's shoulder. She turned her head slightly and nodded in silent agreement. He watched her steps fall in the grass as she returned to the van wishing things had gone differently for the hundredth time in the past year.

Mogli's voice rang out in the stillness. "Always the proverbial hero or fuck-up, depending on how you look at it."

Prescott hadn't seen him near the water's edge until just then. He tried to smirk but found it difficult to pull his lips into anything other than a tight line.

Mogli walked over and placed a hand to his shoulder. "Come on, we have to go. We don't want to be seen out here when the body washes up."

Prescott whispered, "I don't think it's going to wash up anytime soon."

"Good job," he said as he tried to turn Prescott toward the van but was met with resistance.

"I'm not going with you guys." Prescott's voice seemed too firm. He looked at the van with Black standing outside it then back at the black town car he'd driven.

"Where will you go?" Mogli asked as Prescott walked to the car, slammed the trunk closed, and sidled to the driver's side.

"Somewhere safe," he said easily, sitting inside. Their eyes met briefly and Prescott could sense that Mogli didn't want him to go even after all the turmoil they'd been through. Mogli hit the hood twice and said, "You know how to find me" before he turned on his heels to head back to the van. Prescott started the engine, looked around the cabin of the vehicle half expecting to see Dalton in the rearview again, and turned on the radio. The Eagles came on; "I Can't Tell You Why" wafted through the speakers and Prescott shook his head at the irony. He wheeled the car away from the pier and drove slowly past the van. He spotted Rain in the open rear door, sitting next to Anton who had nuzzled close to her. She looked beautiful and Prescott wished he could have made her as happy as he wanted to. Her eyes were sad as she watched him drive by but he didn't see in them the desire for him to stay. He gave her a small smile until her image faded from view and he was back on the side streets of DC heading back to the old Victorian house.

Prescott Willow was resigned to the idea that things would be different now. They were far from over. He didn't know if the team would be ready for a mission as big as the one he would one day propose but he'd try to convince them in time, after things had settled. He was a soldier through and through and would never walk away from an injustice against America. He dreamed that in time he'd get Rain to see who he really was, not the culmination of his mistakes. He reveled at the fact that Rain was just like him, only a girl soldier, with the heart of a warrior. He knew he'd see her again in due time.

OTHER BOOKS BY T.R. HORNE

Thank you, Reader. You're always there for me when I need an eye or ear. Because you have been so gracious, I'll share the title of my current and future work including an upcoming suspense trilogy . . .

Contemporary Romantic Suspense
Breaking Mobius Available NOW

Dystopian Suspense Trilogy
The Unmasked Nation: The Upper Guild (Book One) Available Late 2017
The Unmasked Nation: Schizm Division (Book Two) Available 2018
The Unmasked Nation: Junta (Book Three) Available 2019

First Published Book of Poetry
Bottomless Available Mid-2016

Flash Fiction (eBook only)
Crazy Dirty Love (Second Edition) Available 2017

ACKNOWLEDGEMENTS

A great amount of love goes to my publisher, Yoshima Books. I want to thank my copyeditor, Michael Mandarano, for giving me good feedback and having tireless eyes. Thank my cover designer, Humberto Glaffo. He operates under the pseudonym WATCH THIS! He did an exceptional job on the cover and the Special Edition cover (soon to come). I also want to thank my interior designer, Pink Ink Designs. Special thanks to my beta reader, Christy Howell for being angry at the alternate ending and adamant in my needing to change it. I think it's much better now from your thorough feedback.

I also want to thank my friends and family who have listened to me tirelessly talk about this novel. Thanks to my son and husband for putting up with the zillion things I do on the daily basis. A special thanks to my fans who have picked up this novel after reading my debut novel, Breaking Mobius and have waited over a year for this one. It's very different from the first novel but I appreciate you accepting my need to explore all types of genres and I hope I made it interesting for you in the end. I have a special treat for readers that love my brand of suspense. My new dystopian trilogy, The Unmasked Nation, will completely blow you away! I can't wait for you to read what is happening in my head. And thanks to my brother, Terrance Horne II, I have a movie reel playing every time I write.

To my fans, please share this story with others by talking about it, sharing it and reviewing it. Make sure to #GirlSoldier so I can see your posts. It's a story of love, loss and determination that I believe is entertaining yet has a deeper meaning. Here's something to post about . . . would you have gone as far as Rain knowing what you know now?